THE CO............ ..
THE SHADOW

In Lands Overseas

VOLUME I

Alessandro Spina was the nom de plume of Basili Shafik Khouzam. Born into a family of Syrian Maronites in Benghazi in 1927, Khouzam was educated in Italian schools and attended university in Milan. Returning to Libya in 1954 to help manage his father's textile factory, Khouzam remained in the country until 1979, when the factory was nationalized by Gaddafi, at which point he retired to his country estate in Franciacorta, where he died in 2013. The Confines of the Shadow (Morcelliana) was awarded the Bagutta Prize, Italy's highest literary accolade, in 2007.

André Naffis-Sahely's poetry was most recently featured in *New Poetries VI* (Carcanet, 2015) and *The Best British Poetry 2014*. His translations from the French and the Italian include Balzac's *The Physiology of the Employee* and Émile Zola's *Money*. He has also translated several works by North African authors among whom Rashid Boudjedra, Abdellatif Laâbi, Mohamed Nedali and Tahar Ben Jelloun. His translation of Abdellatif Laâbi's *Selected Poems* was selected for a Writers in Translation award by English PEN in 2015.

ALESSANDRO SPINA

THE CONFINES OF
THE SHADOW

In Lands Overseas

VOLUME I

Translated, edited and introduced by
André Naffis-Sahely

DARF PUBLISHERS
LONDON

Published by Darf Publishers 2015
Darf Publishers LTD, 277 West End Lane, London, NW6 1QS

First published in Italy as *I confini dell'ombra* © Morcelliana, Brescia 2006

English Translation Copyright © André Naffis-Sahely

The moral right of the author has been asserted

Translated by André Naffis-Sahely
Cover by Luke Pajak
Cover Image by Morné Visagie

www.darfpublishers.co.uk

Twitter: @darfpublishers
ISBN 9781850772781
eBook ISBN 9781850772804

Printed and bound in Turkey

Typeset by Palimpsest Book Production Limited, Falkirk, Stirlingshire

Contents

Introduction 1

Author's Note 15

The Young Maronite 19

The Marriage of Omar 223

The Nocturnal Visitor 331

Translator's Note 367

Glossary 369

Introduction

Although variously described by the literary press as the 'Italian Joseph Conrad' and 'a twentieth-century Balzac,' Alessandro Spina's books had almost entirely fallen out of print by the early 1990s, leading one critic to refer to him as a 'ghostly presence' in modern Italian literature. Three months after Spina's death in July 2013, his editor Ilario Bertoletti published a memoir describing his first encounter with the notoriously reclusive writer: 'It was June 1993. The bell rang in the late afternoon. Moments later, a colleague entered my office: "A gentleman dropped by. He looked like an Arab prince, tall and handsome. He left a history of the Maronites for you."' Bertoletti made inquiries and discovered Spina had quietly published a number of novels and short stories from the early 1960s to the late 1980s, which together constituted one of modern European fiction's most ambitious epics: a sequence that charted the history of Libya from 1911, when Italy invaded the sleepy Ottoman province of Trablusgarb, all the way through to 1964, when the independent Kingdom of Libya under Idris I discovered it was sitting on one of the world's largest reserves of petroleum and natural gas. Although Spina had retained his title as one of the 'lions of the literary world,' his books were almost impossible to find, and few seemed to realise the extent of his project's scope. Determined to correct the situation, Bertoletti spent several years persuading Spina to allow him to reissue his books, and in 2006, Bertoletti's imprint, Morcelliana, assembled Spina's seven novels and four short story collections into a 1,280-page omnibus edition entitled *I confini dell'ombra: In terra d'oltremare* (*The Confines of the Shadow: In Lands Overseas*).

The following year, *The Confines of the Shadow* was awarded the Premio Bagutta, Italy's highest literary accolade. It was an impressive achievement, especially for an author who'd insisted on publishing limited editions of his books with tiny presses. However, the Bagutta nod caused only a few ripples: a single radio interview, a handful of glowing reviews and a conference in Spina's honour (which he didn't attend). Without a recognisable persona to market – the back flap doesn't even feature an author photograph – the book receded into obscurity, and although Spina remains little known even in Italy, where he spent the last thirty years of his life, *The Confines of the Shadow* belongs alongside panoptic masterpieces like *Buddenbrooks*, *The Man Without Qualities* and *The Cairo Trilogy*. Spina died two weeks before I concluded an agreement with Ghassan Fergiani of Darf Press to translate the entirety of *The Confines of the Shadow*. Denied the privilege of meeting him, I was faced with a conundrum: the translation of such a monumental opus in the immediate wake of Spina's death meant that any introduction I produced would have to deal with his life, of which I knew next to nothing, save that 'Alessandro Spina' was a nom de plume adopted in 1955 when Alberto Moravia published his first story, 'L'ufficiale' (The Officer), in Nuovi Argomenti. Sporting an English reticence and safely ensconced behind his pseudonym, Spina had spent half a century eluding the limelight, refusing invitations to make public appearances or give interviews. Consequently, I real-ised that any clues to his life story would have to be culled from the work itself. I therefore retreated to the books, sleuthing through *The Confines of the Shadow* and a 300-page *Diary* that Spina kept while composing his epic. And thanks to quasi-involuntary slips on Spina's part, I slowly began to assemble a narrative.[1]

Alessandro Spina, né Basili Shafik Khouzam, was born in Benghazi on October 8, 1927, into a family of Maronites from Aleppo. His father, a wealthy textile magnate, had left his native Syria at seventeen to make his fortune and arrived in Benghazi, the capital of Cyrenaica – then a quiet city of 20,000 Turks and Arabs ringed by Bedouin encampments – a few weeks after Italy and the Ottoman Empire signed the Treaty of Ouchy. Ratified in October 1912, the treaty brought 360 years of Turkish rule and thirteen months of war to a close, and formalised Italy's possession of Tripolitania and Cyrenaica. A latecomer to the scramble for Africa, acquiring Eritrea and Somalia in the late 1880s, barely a couple of decades after they had been cobbled together out of squabbling fiefdoms, Italy had long sought to lay its hands on the *quarta sponda*, or fourth shore. After all, the Libyan coast – the last remaining African territory of the

---

1 All quotes from Alessandro Spina, *Diario di lavoro. Alle origini de 'I confini dell'ombra'* (Morcelliana, 2010), translated by André Naffis-Sahely.

Ottoman Empire, which, as Baron Eversley put it, had grown used to having provinces 'torn from it periodically, like leaves from an artichoke' – lay only three hundred miles south of Sicily. With trouble brewing in the Balkans, and sensing that the 'sick man of Europe' was on his knees, the Italians seized their chance. Knowing they would merely have to contend with a crippled navy and a handful of ill-equipped battalions, they delivered an ultimatum in September 1911, their soldiers disembarked in October, and by November the Italian tricolour could be seen flying from every major city on the Libyan littoral.

Nevertheless, what was expected to be an easy conquest instead turned into a twenty-year insurgency that was quelled only when the Fascists took power in Rome and Mussolini, in a quest to solve Italy's emigration problem, dispatched one of his most ruthless generals, the hated Rodolfo Graziani (1882–1955), to bring the *quarta sponda* to heel and 'make room' for colonists. Genocide ensued: a third of Libya's population was killed; tens of thousands were interned in concentration camps; a 300-kilometre barbed-wire fence was erected on the Egyptian border to block rebels from receiving supplies and reinforcements; and the leader of the resistance, a venerable Koranic teacher named Omar Mukhtar (1858–1931), was hunted down and summarily hanged – a chilling story that is elegantly depicted in *Lion of the Desert* (1981), in which Oliver Reed and Anthony Quinn play Graziani and Mukhtar, respectively, and which was banned from Italian screens for several years. These events – one of the bloodiest chapters in modern North African history – were also witnessed first-hand by the intrepid Danish traveller Knud Holmboe (1902–1931), whose *The Burning Desert* will be reissued next year in a new translation and who was murdered by Italian intelligence officers upon publication of his best-selling book. In 1939, when Spina was twelve, Italy officially annexed Libya, by which time Italian settlers constituted 13 per cent of the population and over a third of the inhabitants of Tripoli and Benghazi, the epicentres of Italian power. At the outbreak of World War II, Spina's father dispatched his son to Italy, where he would remain until 1954. Initially leading a peripatetic existence that saw him alternate between Busto Arsizio and the spa town of Salsomaggiore, Spina – accompanied by his mother – eventually settled in Milan. There, he became a devotee of opera: as luck would have it, the hotel where they lodged, the Marino on Piazza della Scala, was directly opposite the Teatro.

While in Milan, Spina – by then fluent in Arabic, English, French and Italian – studied under Mario Marcazzan; penned a thesis on Moravia; and began drafting his first stories, lush tapestries of history, fiction and autobiography that featured a cosmopolitan array of characters: Italian officers, Senussi rebels, Ottoman bureaucrats, chirpy grande dames, Maltese fishermen, aristocrats, servants and slaves. Spina nevertheless described each caste with the same finesse, empathy and intimacy, partly thanks to his immaculate fusion of Eastern narrative quaintness and the passion for encapsulating an entire way of life that informs much nineteenth-century European fiction, thereby distinguishing sentiment from sentimentality. There is perhaps no better example of this balancing act than 'Il forte di Régima' (The Fort at Régima), an early story set in the mid-1930s, in which an Italian officer, one Captain Valentini, is ordered south of Benghazi to take command of a garrison stationed in an old Ottoman fortress that 'recalled the castles built in Greece by knights who had joined the Fourth Crusade.' Valentini is glad to leave the city and its tiresome peacetime parades behind, but as he's driven to his new posting, his mind is suddenly flooded with the names of famous crusaders who had 'conquered Constantinople, made and unmade emperors, carved the vast empire into fiefs, and run to and fro vainly fighting to ensure the survival of a system, which owing to its lack of roots in the country, was never destined to survive.' Employing only several hundred words, Spina slices across seven hundred years, showing the inanity of the concept of conquest as well as the existential vacuum it inevitably leaves in its wake: 'As he weltered about in his armoured vehicle, it seemed cruel for the captain to be forced to undergo the same rigmarole after so many centuries had passed.' Our technological genius may be growing, Spina implies, but so is our historical ignorance. It is no coincidence that Spina collected these sketches under the title *Officers' Tales*. His men-at-arms perfectly typify his concept of the 'shadow': their minds are haunted by the maddening darkness of the colonial enterprise, which still overshadows our own supposedly post-colonial times. More than a metaphor intertwined throughout his novels, Spina's shadow can be interpreted as an allegory of how the Italian presence in Libya was both visible by dint of its brutality and yet incorporeal because it sought only to rule, never to integrate. Ultimately, the shadow is also life itself: amorphous and mysterious, because history has seen us repeatedly fail to envision what lies beyond what we can see, past the horizon of our ephemeral lives and experiences.

At the end of World War II, Italy relinquished its claim to Libya, which was then administered by the British until 1951, when the country became independent under King Idris I. In August 1953, Spina –now twenty-six, and with the ink still fresh on his degree – returned to Benghazi to help run his ageing father's factory. Although typically working twelve-hour days, he somehow found time to write, and would lock himself in his father's office, whose windows looked out onto the fourteenth-century *fondouk* (caravanserai). Throughout his life, Spina firmly believed that he'd acquired his discipline not despite being an industrialist but because of it, in the same way that Tolstoy refused to leave Yasnaya Polyana so as to stay among his people, and the chief source of his inspiration. In his spare time, Spina would pick up the copy of Proust's *Le Temps Retrouvé* that he always kept by his side, or send letters to friends, which often featured pearls encapsulating the transformations that his country was traversing. In a letter dated 26 July 1963, to Cristina Campo (the pen name of Vittoria Guerrini), he wrote:

> A young scion of the royal family – 'of the highest pedigree,' as Hofmannsthal might have said – the grandson of the old King who'd been deposed by the current monarch, has died in a car accident. Having come to convey his condolences, one of the King's cousins also suffered a crash on his way home to his desert encampment, an accident that took the lives of his mother, wife and son (he remains in intensive care at the hospital). I went to convey my own condolences. The Prince is very handsome, around sixty years old. He's extremely tall, his skin's a milky white and he sports

a little aristocratic goatee. Eventually, the talk turned to the accident. The old man (his medieval view of the world still unmarred) remarked: 'Are automobiles meant as vehicles for this world or the next?'

During the first decade of Libyan independence, Spina completed his first collection of stories; published *Tempo e Corruzione* (*Time and Decay*), a novel based on his days in Milan; and worked on a translation of *Storia della città di Rame* (*The City of Brass*), a tale excerpted from *The Thousand and One Nights*. However, it was only in 1964 that he truly hit his stride and began writing the first volumes of *The Confines of the Shadow*. From 1964 to 1975, arguably his most productive decade, Spina produced *Il giovane maronita* (*The Young Maronite*), *Le nozze di Omar* (*Omar's Wedding*), *Il visitatore notturno* (*The Nocturnal Visitor*) and *Ingresso a Babele* (*Entry Into Babylon*), which while occasionally featuring diverse locales such as Milan, Paris and Cairo, are chiefly set in Benghazi. *The Young Maronite*, the first act of the Cyrenaican saga, begins in November 1912. The new Italian conquistadors have barricaded themselves inside Benghazi and nervously look on as the Libyans muster their strength in the desert and begin their gallant guerilla war against the usurpers. Meanwhile Émile Chébas, a savvy young merchant from Aleppo, arrives in town with a meagre cargo. Émile nonetheless lands on his feet, thanks to a chance encounter with Hajji Semereth Effendi, one of the city's wealthiest men and a former Ottoman grandee, who takes Émile under his wing and helps set him up, even lending him one of his servants, Abdelkarim. Although Émile is technically the book's protagonist, it isn't until later that he emerges from Semereth's shadow. Spina's portrait of Semereth is immediately ensnaring:

In Istanbul, the Hajji had occupied several public positions that prophesied a stellar career, but after a plot had been uncovered, the shadow of conspiracy had settled on him and triggered his fall. He had then withdrawn to that obscure provincial backwater and been quickly forgotten. Regardless of whether he had in fact been guilty or the victim of calumny, he was out of the game. Salvation had come at the cost of silence and renunciation. [. . .] He was very tall, and his face was frightening. A gunpowder charge had exploded close to him during a military campaign and he had been left disfigured. His hair had been reduced to a few tow-coloured clumps. A foul smell emanated from the wrinkles on his skull. He exuded an air of seriousness and authority that made anyone who talked to him instantly bashful and hesitant. It was like a spell that separated him from everyone else, but he was a victim of it, rather than its conscious master, as others tended to assume.

The first section deals with Semereth's unrequited love for Zulfa, the youngest of his four wives, who later betrays him with Ferdinando, an orphan raised in his household. Unbeknownst to Semereth, his family tragedy is being quietly observed by two Italian officers who, adrift in a violently hostile land – and having arrived assuming they would be welcomed as liberators – grasp hold of what they can to try to make sense of their new surroundings. Of all the book's characters, it is once again the officers who attempt a systemic understanding of the alien world around them, but perhaps unsurprisingly, the results are never positive. Here is Captain Romanino's take on Italy's

African venture during a soirée in Milan, where he is on leave:

> Just as a language is only useful in the area in which it is spoken, and is pointless outside of it, so it goes with Europe's liberal moral values, which don't extend anywhere south of the Mediterranean. As soon as one reaches the other coastline, one is ordered to do the exact opposite prescribed by God's commandments: kill, steal, blaspheme ... Once the Turkish garrison was defeated and a few key locations on the coast were occupied, we found a vast, obscure country stretching out before us, into which we were afraid to venture. Thus, we cloistered ourselves in the cities while waiting for daylight. Instead, the night is getting deeper, darker, deadlier and teeming with demons.

Although the initial instalments of *The Confines of the Shadow* attracted some notice in the mid-1970s, with several of them, including *The Young Maronite*, making the shortlists for the highly prestigious Strega and Campiello prizes, Spina's existence in Libya became increasingly tenuous, especially once his father's factory was nationalised in 1978. The years following Qaddafi's coup had seen the despot eliminating foreign influences in Libya, a process he began in 1970 with the expulsion of thousands of Jewish and Italian colonists. Thus, at age fifty, Spina witnessed the Italo-Arab-Ottoman universe he'd been born into vanish completely. One can't help but wonder how Spina kept track of all those momentous changes: the street he lived on in Benghazi had been known as Shara' el-Garbi ('Street of the West') during the Turkish era, had been renamed

Corso Sicilia by the Italians, and finally re-baptised Shara'
Omar Mukhtar in the 1950s. While being caught in the
maelstrom of these metamorphoses didn't impair his work,
it certainly impacted its publication. Although Spina had
penned *The Nocturnal Visitor* over the course of a few months
in early 1972, he delayed its publication until 1979 to avoid
scrutiny during the turbulent early years of Qaddafi's rule,
when dissidents – including a number of Spina's friends
– were routinely rounded up and imprisoned. Between his
novels, Spina had also composed *The Fall of the Monarchy*,
a history in the style of Tocqueville that analyses the events
leading up to Qaddafi's coup, which, per Spina's wishes,
will only appear posthumously. Circulated in samizdat
among a select group of acquaintances, the book attracted
the attention of the security services, and when Spina left
Libya for good in 1980, he was forced to smuggle the
manuscript out in the French consul's briefcase. Safely
removed from the reach of Qaddafi's men, Spina sojourned
in Paris and finally retired to a seventeenth-century villa
in Padergnone, in the heart of Lombard wine country. He
consecrated his *buen retiro* to completing *The Confines of the
Shadow* – as well as various volumes of essays, the penul-
timate of which, *L'ospitalità intellettuale* (*Intellectual Hospitality*),
a title inspired by Louis Massignon's dictum that 'one
shouldn't annex the other, but rather become his guest,'
featured essays on Synesius of Cyrene, al-Ghazali, Fontaine,
Flaubert, Thomas Mann and Lawrence of Arabia. Published
only eighteen months prior to his death, it displayed an
intellect that was arguably at the peak of its powers.

Like Joseph Roth, another inveterate chronicler of a crum-
bled empire, Spina had from a young age set himself to

resurrecting his lost world on paper, thus ensuring its survival in our collective consciousness. While historical novels habitually focus on the rise and fall of specific castes, very few of them – Roth's *The Radetzky March*, published in 1932, being a notable example – ever capture the confused excitement that makes the very earth those characters tread tremble with unregulated passions. As Chateaubriand put it: 'In a society which is dissolving and reforming, the struggle of two geniuses, the clash between past and future, and the mixture of old customs and new, form a transitory amalgam which does not leave a moment for boredom.' It is exactly these fleeting junctures in time and custom that infuse Spina's sophisticated prose with such an unbridled sense of adventure. Besides being the 'right' person for such a job, Spina also found himself in the right place at the right time: a Christian Arab born at the apogee of colonial power, who then combined his Western education with his intimate knowledge of Libyan and Middle Eastern traditions and history to produce the only multi-generational epic about the European experience in North Africa. Yet despite winning such diverse admirers as Claudio Magris (his closest confrère), Giorgio Bassani and Roberto Calasso, Spina occasionally professed surprise at the utter indifference prompted by his work, or rather his subject. Toward the end of his *Diary*, he recalls a run-in with the poet Vittorio Sereni at a theatrical premiere in the early 1980s, and being introduced to Sereni's wife as follows: 'Darling, this is Alessandro Spina, who is trying to make Italians feel guilty about their colonial crimes, all to no avail of course.' Not that he hadn't been warned: when Spina had sought Moravia's advice about his project in 1960, Moravia had counselled him against it, saying that no one in Italy would be interested due to their sheer ignorance of the country's colonial past. Twenty-first-century readers might do well to heed Solzhenitsyn's warning that 'a people which no longer remembers has lost its history and its soul.'

This essay was originally published by *The Nation* as 'Spina's Shadow' in their August 18–25, 2014 edition.

Author's Note

This sequence of novels and short stories takes as its subject the Italian experience in Cyrenaica. *The Young Maronite* (1971) discusses the 1911 war prompted by Giolitti, *The Marriage of Omar* (1973) narrates the ensuing truce and the attempt by the two peoples to strike a compromise before the rise of Fascism. *The Nocturnal Visitor* (1979) chronicles the end of the twenty-year Libyan resistance; *Officers' Tales* (1967) focuses on the triumph of colonialism – albeit this having been achieved when the end of Italian hegemony was already in sight and the Second World War appeared inevitable – and *The Psychological Comedy* (1992), which ends with Italy's retreat from Libya and the fleeing of settlers. *Entry into Babylon* (1976) concentrates on Libyan independence in 1951, *Cairo Nights* (1986) illustrates the early years of the Sanussi Monarchy and the looming spectre of Pan-Arab nationalism, while *The Shore of the Lesser Life* (1997) examines the profound social and political changes that occurred when large oil and gas deposits were discovered in the mid 1960s. Each text can be read independently or as part of the sequence. Either mode of reading will produce different – but equally legitimate – impressions.[2]

2 The dates indicate the original publication dates of each of the novels.

THE CONFINES OF THE SHADOW

In Lands Overseas

I

The Colonial Conquest

The Young Maronite
The Marriage of Omar
The Nocturnal Visitor

II

The Colonial Era

Officers' Tales
New Officers' Tales
Colonial Tales
New Colonial Tales

III

Independence

The Psychological Comedy
Entry into Babylon
Cairo Nights
The Shore of the Lesser Life

1912

THE YOUNG
MARONITE

BOOK I

CHAPTER 1

November 1912

I

The young Maronite had lied. Only a quarter of the cargo belonged to him, and the rest was owned by Rabagian the Armenian, his business partner. He was only entitled to half the profits, once the shipping costs from Alexandria to the Cyrenaican coast had been deducted. Hajji Semereth eyed the young man closely: he suspected he was lying, but instead of decreasing, his benevolence towards him grew. That Christian owned very little, perhaps even nothing, yet he was so sure of himself that he wasn't afraid of lying. Lies were promissory notes he would eventually settle on time. He pretended to take the young man's words at face value. Cowardly obeisance to reality is the rot that eats away at the mediocre. That young man was ambitious, and lying was simply a form of risk-taking. Hajji Semereth decided to take him under his wing.

He asked to be shown the merchandise, and despite noticing its inferior quality he praised it, because he knew he would be able to sell it. The war had paralysed commerce and depleted all stockpiles. Hajji Semereth said he was prepared to purchase part of the cargo, but he wanted a discount. Trade at the market was slow that day and that first deal might expedite the sale of the rest. Hajji Semereth paid in cash.

The young Maronite accepted Hajji Semereth's offer, thinking that Hajji Semereth might prove useful to him in that city where he'd only just landed: the young Maronite was looking for a patron, and Hajji Semereth seemed kindly disposed to him.

'We have ourselves a deal,' the merchant said, 'I'll take a quarter of the stock.'

The young Maronite looked at him. He trustingly put his hand into Hajji Semereth's enormous palm and said, 'Deal.'

Hajji Semereth invited the young man up to the stern deck to have some tea. The young man didn't seem impatient; it looked as though he trusted that giant faith had been put in his path.

'I've brought so much stuff with me!' Hajji Semereth exclaimed, as he climbed the rope ladder to the deck ahead of the boy, 'Cloths, copper, medicine, sugar, oil, tea.'

Then the giant who towered above Émile leaned his hand on the latter's shoulder and cheerfully added: 'And a new friend!'

II

Hajji Semereth told Émile where he could find a warehouse for his goods not far from the market, and sent a boy to accompany him. They had come ashore that morning. The young man thanked his new friend and promised to meet him later that afternoon. Hajji Semereth told him he could keep the servant with him until that evening.

Émile looked for an inn, but the small town didn't seem to offer anything suitable. He regretted not having taken up the merchant's offer to lodge with him, but he didn't want to be in the man's debt. There was something larger than life about that man, not only his height but his corpulence. His intentions were generous, but Émile's desires didn't correspond with those intentions. Hajji Semereth's heavy cloak, which hung down to his feet, made him look even more imposing.

The young man decided to sleep in the warehouse he had rented. It was spacious enough, and dry. A window on the roof lined with thick, strong bars allowed a little air to waft in.

The servant that Hajji Semereth had given him proved most useful. He procured Émile a bed and some pitchers of water. He also helped him open two cases, whose contents he checked: perhaps his first customers might show up as soon as tomorrow. He was itching to be put to the test.

The boy was well acquainted with the market. The Maronite listened to his chatter and translated his words into prices: that servant was as valuable as a spy. They worked solidly for the next four hours.

While he was arranging the merchandise, Abdelkarim learned about the goods and seemed to be etching everything the foreign merchant was saying into his memory, as though he were his employee. This was an effort that bore no correlation to the humble assignment Hajji Semereth had entrusted him with, which was to help his young friend for the day. The Maronite was surprised by this, and grew wary. First, on the deck of the ship that had brought him to that African port, the giant in the dark cloak had bestowed his patronage on him, and now the giant's tiny servant seemed utterly devoted to him. Too many favours can be deliberately misleading.

Exhausted, Émile stretched out on the bed. Abdelkarim immediately stopped working and cosied up by the latter's feet, as though that was exactly what he'd been waiting for. Without being asked, he told the young Maronite all about Hajji Semereth's sombre past.

CHAPTER 2

I

Colonel Romanino walked down the corridor. Once he'd reached the far end, he stopped and turned around. The corridor was more than four metres wide and extremely long: it looked like a road. All the doors that looked onto it were black. Standing behind the only window, the Colonel's face was enshrouded in darkness.

'Who were the owners of this villa? It's difficult to think of heirs, it already belongs to the creditors. It's a wreck, even though there's hardly a brick out of place.'

Signora Ferrara left the group and headed over to the Colonel.

'My dear Colonel, you're so unworldly. Heirs are far more persevering than creditors and blindly tear everything apart – they're driven by a sort of passion. Creditors, on the other hand, are only interested in turning a profit.'

'You're wrong: the villa had clearly fallen into ruin before that. Did you notice how the halls down there were decorated? They're in keeping with styles that only went out of fashion a few years ago. The villa has all the hallmarks of wealth's violent vulgarity. The same hand that erected this edifice also caused its destruction. The owners left their creditors nothing but a carcass. Death has delicate hands, and handles objects reverently.'

'What a clever reply! My dear Colonel . . . While the motherland enjoys her gilded age as though it had robbed Africa of its light, here you are making up dangerous stories. You remind me of those suicidal men who stake their lives . . . on a game of roulette. Might the ingenuity with which you weave spiders' webs of intrigue and craft arabesques out of logic be a way to conceal your criticisms of the times we live in, of our patriotic and aesthetic excitement? After all, isn't criticism the mask that betrayal usually wears?'

'But I still haven't understood who wants to buy the villa,' Signora Passa said.

'A captain, a friend of Romanino's. He went missing in Africa, who knows where. Maybe nostalgia has led him here and made him want a villa in our beloved Lombardo-Veneto. At the same time our government is opening up new horizons for us in Africa, and Italy is taking its first steps as a 'great power,' the captain wants to buy a villa here: he risks his life in our colonies, but my place – he says – is here, and this is where I must return if I wish to survive. Gross insubordination! If our own officers forsake the colony they've given their lives for, this presages a rift that won't lead to anything good.'

'The Colonel is right,' Miss Cella said. While Signora Ferrara continued talking to the Colonel, Miss Cella detached herself from the group, and having walked down the corridor attentively, as though following someone's tracks, was now standing at its far end.

'There's only one card left to play in this game. The

present owners are merely custodians who wish to rid themselves of it as soon as possible. The villa's a hot potato.'

'Come in.'

Standing still in front of a door, the Colonel was inviting
his friends to enter.

A gargantuan wardrobe took up the entirety of the
scene. They had evidently tried to drag it out of the house,
but the plan had failed. How had they got it inside in the
first place? Miss Cella gave the wardrobe a conceited knock.
Strictly utilitarian, Signora Passa opened its doors and then
shut them; Engineer Restivo palpated the back of the
wardrobe, unbothered by the layer of dust that glued itself
to his palm. Nevertheless, nobody seemed capable of
discerning the secret of how to dismantle it. The wardrobe
had grown in that house as though it had sprouted out of
the earth like a tree.

'The villa's frontispiece is in the Louis Philippe style.
It reminds me of how Franz Liszt once described a ball:
*only down there can one truly understand how that dance can
contain such pride, tenderness and allure . . .*'

'It's this new addition that doesn't quite fit,' Colonel
Romanino said, 'as though they'd been bitten by the frenzy
of bloating everything out of proportion, for the lack of
anything better to do. The bourgeoisie made it to the end
of the Risorgimento panting and heaving. Now it has no
benevolent objectives, and so it has made one up. We don't
need the colony: it's yet another symptom of that same
frenzy for bloating everything out of proportion for the
lack of anything better to do. We've lost all sense of scale,
just like the builders who worked on the villa after the
Louis Philippe frontispiece, which you praised all too rightly.

'Are you done? Romanino, your confession is quite

touching. These vulgar, hollow walls have a hypnotic power to them. I too made a connection between our motherland's destiny and the parable of this villa, and I also thought it was a sinister omen. When you said that the same hands which built this house were responsible for tearing it down, I too thought about who governs us and how patriotism seems to have taken a wrong turn. The obsession with 'making it big' that infected the bankrupted owners of this house seems identical to the one ruling this country. But is it right to let ourselves get frightened by omens such as these, which are only illusions, the relics of our superstitions? The younger generations have their needs, and we have granted them this colonial war in the same way that one might overlook an amorous escapade, so as to avoid anything worse. After all, don't we tolerate those infamous bordellos right here in our country to keep society – which is set on being so morally demanding – in equilibrium? Well then, going to war in Africa is like turning an entire continent into a bordello and offering her up to our young men, so they may vent the entire spectrum of their human, heroic, sadistic and aesthetic emotions.'

II

(AT THE THEATRE CLUB. SOME MEMBERS ARE IN FANCY DRESS; OTHERS ARE IN CONVENTIONAL EVENING ATTIRE, A PECULIAR CHOICE CONSIDERING IT'S MARDI GRAS)

FERRARA: I'm keen to meet that captain who went missing in Africa and entrusted us with finding him a villa here, and to carry out God knows what sort of inspection.

It makes me think of the day when I'll have to hand over the keys to *his* house: to a man whose past is so similar to ours, but who has been to mysterious places where he's made new acquaintances or been dramatically deprived of certainties so familiar to us.

PASSA: I can't understand how prattling on like this can give you any pleasure.

FERRARA: Not prattling, but formalities − so as to send Romanino back to Africa with a lighter heart. The memory of the day we set foot on the Libyan coasts fills him with dread, but he feels like a stranger here, as though in that long descent to that Underworld he too, like Captain Martello, had been subjected to unbearable apparitions that now make his sweet Lombardy as incoherent and random as a nightmare. In other words, he sees things that neither you nor I can see, he dreams of a reality that torments him.

ROMANINO: You're afraid − or you're pretending to be afraid − of individual logic and experience. But our last hopes rest precisely on the individual. This is the moment to love Salvation more than the Motherland, to think of ourselves as Christians before Romans, as we once did.

PASSA: But what did you see down there? The Africa I know from the newspapers seems so picturesque.

ROMANINO: So long as journalists and vested interests exist, the truth will always remain on the other side of the sea. Truth is a domesticated animal, it can't survive outside a safe enclosure. The Expeditionary Force had the misfortune to come face to face with a people who took advantage of our arrival to live their defining hour: they were able to discover exactly who they were by encountering a completely different worldview to their own. But the other's truth imperils our own, which thought of itself as universal and tasked with the duty of establishing a new world order, meaning, *thus*, that it must sweep away everything in sight.

FERRARA: (SARCASTICALLY) Do you mean to say – perish the thought! – that journalists are deceiving us when they glorify our officers' heroism and their civilising mission even though most officers are illiterate? That the government is lying when it says that 'fertile horizons' are being opened up in Africa? That even priests misled us when they sprinkled our warships with holy water before they left our ports – and that even our secular luminaries and humanitarian organisations lied to us when they said the natives in those lands were good-natured souls who were just waiting for our gunships to leave Naples and free them?

(*CHANGING HER TONE*)

I shuddered when I read an account by a French journalist that a certain Rémond published in *Illustration* about some skirmish or other at the gates of Benghazi, where a young lieutenant was killed. When one of the *others* saw the lieutenant's beautiful face in the dust, he leapt off his horse and bent to kiss it. A highly disquieting and inconvenient gesture. How can anyone make sense of that war? I'm still reeling from that item of news – which our own newspapers wisely censored – and yet you speak to me of that mysterious captain's worries, who wants to pursue a re-examination of those events to rescue what truths he can out of that past, as though anything other than chaos could come of it. The Civil Code is crystal clear on the issue of inheritance: it explicitly forbids any estate to be broken up where said division would dishonour said estate. That also applies to the past: both we (and the people we don't like) are the heirs of a single, indivisible past.

In a subsequent dispatch, Rémond reported an even ghastlier detail. A lady from Bergamo (meaning someone wearing a mask) recognised that the precious body of the soldier lying face down in the dust while the exalted enemy stood next to him was that of her only son, and had written to Rémond, not to ask him to keep quiet, but to write even more about that dead soldier. How confused someone's mind must be to watch that scene without feeling repulsed, to insert that into the sequence of memories that constitute her son's existence, to accept it as a definitive seal on his life.

May God grant peace to that young lieutenant who left this world with an enemy's kiss on his lips instead of a viaticum . . .

ROMANINO: Do you wish to know when an officer's resolve cracks?

FERRARA: It makes me apprehensive.

ROMANINO: If the officer stops thinking of the enemy as automaton and instead considers him as guileful. It's laughable to accord those things such abstract concepts as rights, responsibilities, consciences and souls . . . it's an entertaining game, *like hunting* – and massacres are taken lightly. But if said officer is rash enough to think of those two peoples as living under the same sky and under the same law, lights and shadows begin to assume such a mysterious shape that he'll start questioning himself while absorbed in the act of killing the enemy; he'll start to tremble and his anxiety will lead him down any number of paths. If that happens, the connection between the troops and their commanders will be severed. In times of war, isolation is fatal: enemies become supernatural knights, one's own comrades become demons, comfort and morale vanish and an officer's heart can rarely weather the ordeal. A hero can become a saint; but if he doesn't, guilt will crush him and the warrior will begin to fear that he's no better than a common murderer. Cruelty and suicide become the easiest way out of this dilemma. Just as a language is only useful in the area in which it is spoken, and is pointless outside of it, so it goes with Europe's liberal moral values, which don't extend anywhere south of the Mediterranean. As soon as one reaches the other coastline, one is ordered to do the exact opposite prescribed by God's commandments: kill, steal, blaspheme . . . Once the Turkish garrison was defeated and a few key locations on the coast were occupied, we found a vast, obscure country stretching out before us, into which we were afraid to venture. Thus, we cloistered ourselves in the cities while waiting for daylight. Instead, the night is getting deeper, darker, deadlier and teeming with demons.

CELLA: (WHO HAS IN THE MEANTIME JOINED THE GROUP AND IS LOOKING SOMBRE) We don't have the slightest intention of wasting our soldiers' lives.

ROMANINO: The Arab patriots' courage is admirable. They're as nimble as acrobats.

CELLA: Courage devoid of consciousness is pointless. Besides, we have no intention of competing with *those* people, but instead with other European nations. The latter will be more impressed by our efficiency than by our courage.

ROMANINO: Yes, our preparations for the war were so judicious that we didn't know who our enemy was. We thought we'd only have to fight an inadequate Turkish garrison and instead found ourselves faced with an entire nation who'd taken up arms against us. Our nationalism is very recent, being forged in the ideals and wars of the Risorgimento. But with this miserable venture, we've gone back to square one. What now? We return here only to trip over the various newspapers, all the lies, and the public euphoria for the colonial enterprise, for this new Risorgimento, and we can only feel tired, bored, or as Captain Martello drily put it, 'estranged.'

(A YOUNG MAN APPEARS IN THE DOOR THAT LEADS TO THE STAIRWAY. HE IS WEARING A ROMAN TOGA AND THERE IS A LAUREL WREATH ON HIS HEAD. HE STOPS ON THE THRESHOLD, AND THE MUSIC CEASES)

ROMANINO: Time is tired and it's vomiting history.

FERRARA: Time is just drunk, that's all. By tomorrow, this confused dream won't have left a trace. Must we give this woebegone tradition any real significance? It has no political subtext, is in no way connected to the Tripoli enterprise and Giolitti certainly didn't make it up. The handsome young Roman by the door with the laurel wreath doesn't threaten our awkward foundations. Everywhere you look, you can't help but see the omens of a tragedy hanging over our heads like a Damoclean sword, of which the Libyan enterprise is but the prologue.

(SHE PLACES HER HAND ON THE COLONEL'S AND IN A HALF-FEELING, HALF-IRONIC TONE)

Tell me, does the *Mal d'Afrique* really ache so bad?
(MUSIC)

Chapter 3

Hajji Semereth's House

I

Hajji Semereth was a reticent man. He had spent his entire life under an unmerciful light, but the essence of what he said, as well as the opinions he formulated, were always ambiguous. They characterised him in a misleading fashion, as did the sophisticated clothes he wore, his gait and his slow, heavy movements, which were those of a man wading through water with difficulty.

In Istanbul, the Hajji had occupied several public positions that prophesied a stellar career, but after a plot had been uncovered, the shadow of conspiracy had settled on him and triggered his fall. He had then withdrawn to that obscure provincial backwater and been quickly forgotten. Regardless of whether he had in fact been guilty or the victim of calumny, he was out of the game. Salvation had come at the cost of silence and renunciation.

He led a comfortable, quiet life, playing the role of a merchant to fill the void of his days, now that the arena in which he could move had been so drastically reduced and could barely contain him. People said his heart nursed a longing for the life of the public official he'd led in the capital, but no one else in that small African port city seemed less interested in titles and positions.

The doors to his house were always open. It was amongst Benghazi's most beautiful, but only silence grew within its walls. Hajji Semereth's presence in that house accentuated the sense of encumbrance and isolation. He received guests with all due honours, but never warmly. His relationships with people were bland, insignificant, unsolicited and a pointless waste of his time. He was very tall, and his face was frightening. A gunpowder charge had exploded close to him during a military campaign and he had been left disfigured. His hair had been reduced to a few tow-coloured clumps. A foul smell emanated from the wrinkles on his skull. He exuded an air of seriousness and authority that made anyone who talked to him instantly bashful and hesitant. It was like a spell that separated him from everyone else, but he was a victim of it, rather than its conscious master, as others tended to assume.

He had four wives and a great many servants.

Zulfa, the youngest wife, was twelve years old and the daughter of a poor gardener. When word of her beauty had reached the Hajji's ears, he had asked for her hand in marriage. The gardener, ignoring the girl's sobs, had consented: Semereth Effendi's wealth would dry all those tears. The advantageous match had been sealed with a contract.

The wedding was celebrated in the most splendid pomp that provincial backwater could possibly offer. That night, when Zulfa saw the tow-haired giant who would call her his wife, she grew so frightened that she fainted before uttering a single word. Hajji Semereth was mesmerised: he caressed the little girl, and although he guessed he was the one who had made her faint, he didn't become at all angry, but instead looked touchingly at her, with awe: he had never seen such light in anyone else. It was as though there were three people in the bridal chamber, one of them a shadow that didn't seem to want to leave.

Zulfa threw herself desperately at his feet, begged him to forgive her and send her back to her parents and her home – how could she ever be his wife? The girl was so afraid that her words fused into a whimpering song, or an unchanging dance that endlessly repeated the same movements. That repetition was agonising. It was as though she'd got lost in an unknown country, armed with a language known only to her. At best, she could have tried to soothe her heart by singing to it, but the gracious melody would've been unable to save her.

Hajji Semereth took hold of Zulfa's arm and helped her to her feet. He didn't speak to her about his rights. In fact, he didn't speak at all: he knew she wouldn't have understood him and would have just grown more frightened. Zulfa continued imploring him, but the gargantuan idol stayed silent. Hajji Semereth's hand scooped her up like a spoon. That gesture was tender, but the idol seemed either powerless, or subject to a higher authority. Endowing it with miraculous virtues, Zulfa kissed the Hajji's blessed hand.

Semereth Effendi let her implore him until her voice went hoarse, and she'd cried herself dry. Finally, more tired than scared, Zulfa let herself go, sinking into his arms as though she were drowning.

Hajji Semereth had then tried to exercise his husbandly rights, but tormented his wife in vain: their bodies were so disproportionate that the marriage couldn't be consummated. Wrath had taken hold of that fragile creature: Zulfa had begged, cried and threatened to end her life, to the point that in the end she'd reclaimed her liberty.

Semereth Effendi's body took up nearly the entirety of the room. Zulfa vainly tried to distance herself from him, but as in a nightmare, the monster loomed over her as though he were chasing her. However, Hajji Semereth hadn't moved at all.

Zulfa then crouched in a corner. She was so tiny that the giant might not have found her. Silence, thick as water, seeped into the room. If there had been no other way to separate herself from him, she'd have accepted to die without a word. Once the Hajji had also had enough, he decided to speak. He told his wife not to be afraid of him, that she would be his favourite, and that as soon as she'd learned to treat her husband with the deference he was due, he would divorce all his other wives so as to be hers alone. To conclude, he told her he would wait for nature to take its course until her body could allow the marriage to be consummated, whether it took a year, or two, or even ten.

He nevertheless begged her to pretend to the other women – her mother and their relatives – that the marriage had indeed been consummated. He wanted her to hide her sadness, as he would do, and didn't want her to show anyone how afraid she was of him. Perhaps with time their union would be blessed by nature. As far as Hajji Semereth was concerned, he would patiently try to earn such a blessing.

II

Time became the indifferent arbiter of that wedding which nature refused to bless. The days went by indistinguishably, a clock veiled by an invisible hand. Semereth Effendi returned to his routine, hoping it might bring them together. Although he found his other wives insufferable, he often sought out Zulfa's company.

Their souls were as equally mismatched as their bodies. Hajji Semereth would speak to her of his business, of his former life in Istanbul, which he hungrily sought news of when in the company of others, but the shadow cast by these subjects made the man who projected it appear even more frightening to Zulfa.

Rejected, Hajji Semereth tried to dispel this shadow by adapting his interests to Zulfa's in an attempt to enter her inner sanctum: he asked after the women who came to visit her and the topics they talked about, as though trying to force her to express her emotions. Sometimes he would tell her a funny story, or feed her bits of the gossip that made the rounds of the market about the private lives of the city's most illustrious men. Zulfa felt her privacy was being intruded on.

It was as if they were two beasts locked in separate cages and condemned to look at each other without ever drawing nearer: their proximity made irrelevant by the insurmountable distance – and the distance between them poisoned by their proximity. Hajji Semereth would bring the bland, broken dialogue to an end with an impatient jerk.

Zulfa had learned to keep quiet and conceal her rebellious heart; it was the only deference she paid to her husband's pride and social status. When other women came to visit her, she didn't show how unhappy she was, nor how impatient or disillusioned. She even avoided crying and confiding in her mother and sisters. Hajji Semereth was fully aware of his young wife's dignity, and attempted to show his appreciation by showering her with gifts. Zulfa had either consented to Hajji Semereth's request on their unconsummated wedding night, or else feared his wrath lest she should disobey him. Regardless, she didn't inflict any indiscretions on him.

Henceforth, Hajji Semereth never returned home empty-handed. Zulfa would timidly accept his gifts: they were prayers she didn't know how to answer.

Hajji Semereth would experience the same humiliation he'd suffered on his wedding night when nature had rejected him. As soon as he returned home, he would shut the gates and refuse to receive any visitors. He would cloister himself in his *majlis* without speaking to anyone or doing anything with his time. His other wives vainly tried to fill that void.

Those women became malicious: they hated Zulfa, who was the Hajji's favourite, and made overt and excessive displays of kindness in an effort to gain the Hajji's recognition but, safe in the knowledge that Zulfa would never summon the courage to denounce them, they pestered her with perfidious questions.

Whenever Zulfa heard Hajji Semereth shut the gates with that melancholy, deafening clang, she would run and hide in her room, listening out for that monster's steps in the silence, on the off chance he would go out into the courtyard or onto the balcony. Whenever the Hajji entered her room, Zulfa would freeze and the Hajji would feel every vein in her body tremble while she perched on her chair like a critter shivering in the cold. More often than not, Hajji Semereth wouldn't even enter the room, but would merely block the doorway with his bulk.

The spell of distance had been cast on them.

III

The Italian fleet under the command of Admiral Aubry had anchored before Benghazi. If the city didn't surrender, it would be subjected to indiscriminate shelling.

The council of the city's notables would have to decide whether to give in to the ultimatum or reject it. Hajji Semereth was sitting among them. He observed himself, having been exiled to that isolated province, sitting on a council that could casually decide whether or not the city would resist, without being able to change the fatal course of events. Italy had been planning that campaign for years, while the Turkish government's reaction had been sluggish at best. Pride, which the ultimatum had injured, and rights, were both useless. In fact, the council was powerless to do anything other than ratify the verdict.

Having been torn away from his house and his shops, Hajji Semereth wasn't able to focus on the fiery speeches being made; neither did he believe he belonged to a political and military force that was powerful enough to counter the aggression of another. Admiral Aubry had granted his victims a deferment to find out whether they intended to welcome him with suspicion or joy. The meeting was irritating Hajji Semereth: everything had been predetermined and the characters moved around like ghosts, like a dream that would vanish the following morning. He paid scant attention to the speeches the others were making, and only said that since the majority were leaning towards resisting the invaders, he would cast his vote in favour of that. It was useless to try to convince the others that their refusal didn't matter, because they already knew that. It was only a means to soften the harsh blow that reality had dealt

them. Why rub salt in the wound? Those who so passionately refused to resist, would tomorrow become devoted
friends of the Italians.

The city was shelled. A bomb struck the Franciscan
mission where the Christians had sought shelter, killing six
Maltese men. The mission was only a few steps from Hajji
Semereth's house.

★

Benghazi's Turkish garrison had mostly evaded capture, and
after beating a hasty retreat its soldiers had been forced to
retrace their steps by the firm determination of the Sanussi
Brotherhood and the tribes from the hinterlands to oppose
the enemy's infiltration: the resisters' camp had been set up
just twelve miles away from the city and it was swelling to
a prodigious size.

The enthusiasm that reigned in the Benina camp was
a sound that eluded Hajji Semereth. It had nothing to do
with his age, but was due to an even stricter impediment.
It was as though he were still bound by the oath he'd sworn
never to meddle in politics again after he went into exile,
and which he'd abided by during his time in that province.
In the upheaval the country was experiencing, he could
have finally found a destiny befitting his high ambitions,
all without breaking a rule or carrying the heavy burden
of guilt which fell squarely on others. Instead, his heart
stayed cold. He was only interested in what dwelled in the
realm of rules, because all transgressions were doomed to
be short-lived. Without the heavy burden of guilt, even the
wide expanses beyond the confines of rules became empty
and insignificant. His business affairs, to which he devoted

himself in order to fill his days, were going well, but it was an ironic and humiliating blessing imparted by destiny.

The city belonged to the assembly of notables which had voted to reject the Italian fleet's ultimatum, thereby only delaying the course of events by a single day. The two warring parties, the Italian government and the Sanussi Brotherhood, didn't hold it in much esteem. The outcome of the war would be decided outside the city's walls, in the immense country that opened up before the aggressors' eyes like a great abyss, and into which nobody dared set foot.

Hajji Semereth had been asked to spearhead a peace initiative or a compromise, and join the city's other illustrious citizens, who had already embarked on this project; the city could mediate between the invaders' strength and the uncompromising hinterlands. Some wanted the Hajji to help the invaders, others instead suggested they were emissaries from the other side, bearing mysterious messages so that the Hajji would stop dithering and flee the city. Hajji Semereth had told one of these guests that if he joined the other side, he would only weaken it, that he was unlucky, and that his passions had come to nothing. These sophistries bored him, but there was no other way to avoid declaring for one or the other.

The oppressors had also heard about this merchant. On one occasion the Hajji had been summoned and questioned, but he had been able to restrict the interview with so many punctilious formalities that anything he said amounted to empty expressions. Aside from finding conversation difficult, Hajji Semereth also knew how to stop others from talking. He was living in a different dimension to Benghazi's other residents, and his detachment from them was thereby accentuated. The other notables thought the merchant's obliviousness to the city's tumult – as though he didn't even live there, but somewhere else – was almost insulting.

Tiring of this situation, Hajji Semereth decided to leave for Egypt, as though he were only interested in exploiting that tragic situation to further his business interests and increase his profit margins.

The Hajji had wanted to take Ferdinando – a boy who was very dear to him, and who it was said was the son of a Christian – along on the journey, but the latter had fallen ill just prior to the scheduled departure. The Hajji had entrusted him to the care of old Abubaker, expressly instructing his other wives to look after his favourite, words that seemed, to those finely tuned ears, as bitter as threats. He entrusted the running of his household to the Venetian, a repudiated woman he'd brought with him from Istanbul.

IV

Hajji Semereth's departure sent his household into a sort of hibernation. The wives became more indolent and alleviated their boredom by bickering amongst each other.

Lethargy and disorder seeped into the house in the wake of the master's departure, spreading like a puddle of oil; but the vague tension Zulfa's presence amongst the other wives generated didn't elude the Venetian woman's attentive ear. The slumber that had settled over the house wasn't tranquil and carefree – instead, it was populated by confused images that guided its steps.

The Venetian woman was shrewd, and while she was prey to the winds of the other wives' moods, she in turn controlled them. The wives often threatened to throw her out on the street, and this was the worst sort of fate someone her age could suffer, since she had no attachments whatsoever in the world. However, she knew exactly how irreplaceable she was, constituting the only link to the outside world those women had, as they weren't allowed out of the house. Thus the wives were in her thrall, and tried to ingratiate themselves with gifts, which the repudiated Venetian coveted. Because society denied her the chance to lavish her affections on people, she lavished them on objects instead.

Abubaker was the only one who wasn't afraid of her. He'd lived in that house since the days of the Hajji's father. When everything appeared ready to fall apart and collapse, his mere presence acted as a bulwark. He had defended Semereth and his wealth from the greed of his relatives and his rivals' interests, and now he was protecting it from the Hajji himself, forcing Semereth to respect the equilibrium of the house.

The wives hated this stern, intractable man who spent the whole day loafing, but kept them under lock and key like a jailer, without according them any more importance than the other objects in the house entrusted to his care. Abubaker hated the Venetian woman for usurping his position: she was the one who was allowed to spend money and render accounts to the master, whereas he was only charged with looking after the house. He always ensured every intrigue led back to her and didn't hesitate when it came to beating her.

V

Ferdinando, the boy the master was fond of, had been committed to the Venetian woman's care after becoming ill, since she was both a physician and a necromancer. The Venetian woman nursed him so conscientiously that he was soon cured. Hajji Semereth had left orders that the boy should be sent to one of the Hajji's villas outside the city as soon as he recovered. But while the Venetian woman had been washing and perfuming him, she'd hatched a plot that would require his presence in the house. Instead of handing him over to Abubaker, who'd have then transported the boy out of the city on a boat – as the walls were well guarded and traffic in and out of the city forbidden – she instead sent Ferdinando back to bed, saying she'd got confused and that the boy would need to be looked after some more.

One evening, while the Venetian woman was as usual absorbed in narrating stories she'd heard during the day to the housebound women, making them laugh with salacious anecdotes set, as always, in that distant Istanbul none of them had ever set foot in and which they were thus ready to believe the most extraordinary things about, she suddenly starting speaking of Ferdinando. The wives had never seen him, since he was forbidden to enter the part of the house where they lived. The Venetian woman began describing the boy's beauty down to the boldest details, adding that Ferdinando was such a tender morsel that she too would have been tempted if her advanced years hadn't snuffed out all traces of desire.

The women grew curious. The most insignificant detail that reached their ears excited them beyond all measure. They now wanted to see that paragon of beauty with their own eyes and by dint of giggles, sweet-talk and all sorts of promises, they tried to persuade the procuress to slip Ferdinando into their rooms even just once. The Venetian woman knew how to assess the risks involved, and the possible profits; her hesitation in granting their request was not because the risks were excessive, but because she wanted to raise her profit margins. She swore to the women she would keep their secret, but expected gifts commensurate to the task in return.

All that remained was to trick Abubaker. Having grown impatient of the boy's protracted illness, and distrusting the Venetian's reports, the surly old man was on the alert.

One day, a messenger from the authorities came to ask after Hajji Semereth, even though the latter had been granted permission to leave the city; Abubaker then had to leave the house to go and clear up the misunderstanding. A moment later, Ferdinando – who'd been washed, perfumed and dressed in a blue waistcoat and white breeches – was ushered into the ladies' quarters. He was sixteen years old.

A chorus of exclamations greeted his arrival, just like when the Venetian woman ended her stories with an unexpected twist. Accustomed to seeing a gigantic monster in their rooms, the ladies felt marvellously happy at seeing the boy's face. They said how unlucky they'd been that fate hadn't sent them a husband like Ferdinando, as they caressed him tenderly.

But the Venetian woman and the wives had noticed both Zulfa's shocked silence and Ferdinando's obvious confusion at seeing that beautiful creature he couldn't stop staring at. The Venetian woman then tore Ferdinando away from his adoring crowd and sent him off to bed again, where Abubaker later found him when he decided to check, on his return, that the boy hadn't disappeared. The procuress said that Abubaker wanted to throw ashes on every pretty object or creature that he saw: youth and beauty offended his eyes.

A few days went by, and the women often spoke of

Ferdinando to the Venetian woman. The boy's appearance in their rooms had dispelled the monotony of their lives. They said that women, being subjected to a man's full discretion, always had unlucky destinies, but that a woman blessed with so delicate a husband as Ferdinando would be lucky indeed. They wanted to know a little more about his background and those Christian parents people attributed to him. However, the Venetian woman didn't know any more than they did, and all her conjecture was taken with a pinch of salt.

Zulfa pretended not to listen to their chatter, but the others nevertheless knew she'd heard them. One day, when Zulfa wasn't in their presence, the wives and the Venetian huddled tightly together, as though scared that Abubaker's guards were hiding inside the walls so as to eavesdrop. Each of the women revealed the web of intrigue they'd weaved, which turned out to be identical. As Zulfa had shown such great embarrassment – and there being, of course, no doubt whatsoever as to Ferdinando's own embarrassment – the ladies decided to act as a screen behind which the couple could secretly meet.

The Venetian woman was tasked with taking each of the two youngsters aside and helping them disclose the object of their affections to one another. It was imperative to make them conscious of the void that had opened up before them, of the precipice they were approaching with each step, and simultaneously sprinkling the beatific balm of the revelation of their true feelings for one another. Owing to their tender years and inexperience, it was highly unlikely they would bear the strain of a double discovery. At which point, they would need to guide their steps lest they forget to trick Abubaker in the blinding heat of the moment.

Ferdinando unwittingly endorsed the Venetian woman's plan by feigning a continued illness so as to remain in Benghazi. The procuress finally made him understand that she knew his secret and the real reason for him not wanting to leave, throwing the boy's heart into bewilderment. But, she also added quickly in an irritated tone, as though that wretched feeling was sure to lead them all to catastrophe, that it was too late to pretend otherwise, that he had compromised himself with Zulfa and that he'd have to follow the Venetian's strict orders if he didn't want her to denounce him to Abubaker, and thus abandon him to his fate.

The Venetian woman's threats prevented the boy from articulating his thoughts, but the blackmail was laced with flattery and seduction. The Venetian would talk about Zulfa and Ferdinando would eagerly listen, lacking both the strength to repel her chatter – especially given that the Venetian was his sole link to Zulfa, who was otherwise remote and unreachable (Semereth's house was partitioned by interdicts as powerful as spells) – and the courage to freely confess his love, thereby experiencing the relief such a confession would bring him. Despite hesitating to let his imagination carry him off, the necessary steps he would need to take already seemed easier, thanks to the Venetian woman having plotted them out in her mind.

While the boy experienced the delights and torments of love for the first time, and while he easily played the role of the invalid, the Venetian busied herself with delicately persuading Zulfa. Feigning perplexity and fear, she said that the boy had changed, and that he no longer wanted to go to the countryside as the master had ordered. She worried that Abubaker would discover the boy's subterfuge and accuse her of having colluded with him. She then ran off to Ferdinando to tell him that Zulfa had been unsettled by her disclosure and might have guessed his secret. But she didn't add anything about Zulfa's feelings, and didn't explain whether Zulfa was tenderly disposed to the idea, or instead regretted having consented to see Ferdinando.

Returning to Zulfa, the Venetian woman would question her, start to sob and say that she was the most wretched of women, since she was always accountable for everything while simultaneously being kept in the dark. Zulfa would look at her, but she didn't have the courage to reply, even though she could guess the reason behind the boy's reticence. So the two would linger in silence, until the Venetian woman would grow bored and go off to update the other wives on how their conspiracy was progressing, but not before having asked Zulfa for either a gift or a loan, which request the young girl would oblige. The Venetian woman also extracted the same from the other wives: it was better to have them all pay her on the spot, without waiting to settle it all at the end, at which point the women might capriciously renege on their promises.

As for Ferdinando, the Venetian woman told him she was now certain that Zulfa loved him, but that he should also remember that he couldn't entertain any hopes in that regard, that Abubaker was watching them closely and that she would rather have her tongue cut out than risk falling into the old man's trap, as Abubaker would undoubtedly exact retribution without even waiting for Semereth Effendi's return. Besides, in those days death was running amok in the streets of Benghazi and people disappeared at night as though they'd been abducted by demons. She said she would flee at the slightest suspicion, and would ask the city's new authorities to take her in, forswearing the new faith she'd embraced out of convenience and thus freeing herself from that accursed house forever and boarding a ship bound for her homeland, from which her adverse fate had torn her away.

Ferdinando believed everything the Venetian told him, adopting her as his guide along a path on which he'd never thought he'd venture; on the contrary, he found himself so overwhelmed that he became genuinely ill once again. The Venetian woman was the architect of the maze where he'd been allowed to roam.

The Venetian was triumphant: it was so obvious that the boy hadn't healed, that the suspicious Abubaker would be forced to lower his guard – which was exactly what happened. The old man didn't suspect there was a plot involving Zulfa. It was the boy's idleness that truly irked him, as Ferdinando continued to lie in his bunk instead of obeying the master's orders. But once his calloused hand touched the boy's feverish forehead he was finally persuaded to lay his suspicions aside, and he cursed the Venetian for being a charlatan and failing to cure him.

The procuress was growing impatient. Time was running short and the plot was far from its climax. The other wives had begun to make rash suggestions that seemed like veiled threats.

The Venetian entered Zulfa's room and revealed that Ferdinando was in love with her, reproaching her for it as though it were her fault. Zulfa threw herself at the Venetian's feet, imploring her – in the name of God! – not to betray her. She admitted she loved Ferdinando, but promised she'd never see him again.

The Venetian bolted out of the room to apprise the other wives of this latest development, who then commanded her not to hesitate any further. They would all keep an eye on Abubaker, and at the first available opportunity would usher Ferdinando into the ill-starred youths' bridal chamber.

The Venetian woman rushed back into Zulfa's room and said it was all over, that Ferdinando was being consumed by an inner fire and was ready to die at her door, but had steadfastly refused to be leave her behind. Abubaker was preparing to take the boy out of Benghazi by boat that night. The Venetian said they only had a single day left, and that while she wouldn't help Zulfa meet Ferdinando, as she'd never consent to betraying her master like that, she would however help Zulfa flee. She cursed fate for having forced her into servility, and complained of how everyone defrauded her of her rightful dues. Zulfa comforted her, even while sobbing, swearing she would be forever grateful, and begging the Venetian to speak to Ferdinando and convince him to leave and take Zulfa's pledge of love along with him. Carrying the little necklace Zulfa had worn on the one night the two had seen each other, the Venetian woman hurried out and went into Ferdinando's room.

Once she'd entered the room she found the old man keeping guard. She pretended to tuck in Ferdinando's sheets more tightly, and while doing so let the necklace slip down by the boy's side. Every vein in Ferdinando's body began to tremble. It was as though he was overflowing with blood: his delicately rosy complexion was replaced by bright red flames. Furious, Abubaker sprang to his feet and said the Venetian woman was casting an evil spell on Ferdinando and that he, being a wizard with a multitude of *jinn* at his service, would break the hex. The old man formulated his counter-spell, as though wanting to make her disappear, but instead the Venetian ran out of the room and into the courtyard, shouting that she couldn't care less about the stern guardian's hex as even the jinn were fed up with him and were actually devoted to youth and beauty, or rather everything the old man detested.

Abubaker curtly retorted that he didn't want to bother with that woman, who was clearly possessed by the devil, and that one day she would disappear just as suddenly as she'd been found as an orphan, and be irrevocably consigned to the damnation which had always been her destiny; and so as not to hear her voice any more, he left.

In a flash, Ferdinando was pushed out of his bunk and led to Zulfa's room.

There, the two youngsters became acquainted with all the pleasures of love.

Chapter 4

I

The previous events took place before Hajji Semereth's journey to Egypt. Having disembarked the ship that had brought him back to Cyrenaica along with the young Maronite, from whom he'd purchased some merchandise and to whom he'd assigned a young apprentice, Hajji Semereth reached his abode. The hour of departure and the hour of arrival were nothing but two different moments in time from which exactly the same reality emerged. As soon as the Hajj entered his home the servants rushed to kiss his hand. Having met his master at the docks, Abubaker was now sternly supervising the ceremony. Any effort to detach himself from the little in life that actually interested him, like his master's presence and the latter's immobile steadfastness, was proving bothersome.

The Venetian was the first woman to come towards Hajji Semereth, as though she'd closely watched the other women so as to be the first to greet him. The Hajji observed her drained features. Now that the Hajji had returned, the mere act of him looking at her would translate into recognition: life was resuming its habitual, circular course, which had a way of making time stand still. The servants were pleased the master had returned because it would free them from his wives' excessive high-handedness, as well as from Abubaker and that shrewd Venetian. For his part, the Hajji was fully aware they were welcoming him as one does a judge. These pointless storms that raged in his house were like birdsong and the barking of dogs, the domestic soundtrack of a part of his reality: one of the few constants in the inexhaustible variety of life. Throughout his absence harmony appeared to have reigned over his bickering wives. Yet as they were both astute and disingenuous, perhaps they were merely feigning such serenity, but so long as they carried on in this manner, it didn't really matter much.

Zulfa was the last to appear; she was so dwarfed by the other women that Semereth didn't see her until her silken hands gripped his fingers. It was as though he were standing atop a mountain looking at someone in the valley below. He would have liked to hurl himself off the precipice and land at her feet, but he would only have frightened her. She'd have just run away, like a vision one chases in a dream. Zulfa immediately withdrew and Semereth followed her every step, straining his eyes as though he were watching a bird in mid-flight. Abubaker begged God to bestow his blessing on the house.

Ferdinando only appeared much later. He kissed the master's hand. Hajj Semereth told Abubaker that he'd often seen the young man's face in his dreams – as Ferdinando had been in poor health when he'd left, he'd worried about losing him. Abubaker gruffly replied that Ferdinando had refused to go to the countryside as the Hajji had commanded in collusion with the Venetian woman. The Hajji listened without interrupting him once. Ferdinando didn't dare lift his gaze. For the second time, he had the impression of spotting a silhouette, off in the distance, of someone walking in the cool shade. But it wasn't a painful feeling, like when Zulfa stood in front of him and yet seemed out of reach; on the contrary, he was soothed by the sight of that silhouette. The Hajji placed his hand on the boy's head. 'I forgive you,' he said, placidly.

After lunch, the Hajji paid his favourite wife a visit. Ashamed of what she'd done, and fearing the consequences, Zulfa both welcomed and abhorred the monster's entry into her room. Hajji Semereth noticed that the way they communicated had changed, and the happy omens led him to draw nearer to her. Zulfa could no longer bear the grief and repugnance the Hajji inspired in her, and plagued by guilt, begged him to save her and send her back to her parents, or, should he not wish to grant her request, to kill her himself, meaning she would thus pay for her youthful foolishness with her life.

Hajji Semereth left Zulfa's room as though he were sleepwalking. He tormented himself over his gigantic stature, as though it were an irremediable injustice, like old age, or death.

II

The reception hall was swarming with people. Hajji Semereth's friends, who had come, as custom dictated, to celebrate his journey's happy conclusion, were sitting on a row of chairs lined up against the dark walls.

The hearts and minds of that little coastal town were at

odds. The desire to take up the hinterland's cause against the colonial aggressors conflicted with their interests and traditions, which were inclined towards patience and compromise.

The peace treaty between Italy and the Ottoman Empire concluded at Ouchy hadn't resolved anything. It stipulated that the Ottomans withdraw all their troops, ratified the Italian occupation, but granted the natives the right to recognise the Sultan's authority as Caliph. The invaders didn't know the meaning of these words and didn't understand that the Caliph was both a spiritual and temporal leader. Thus, from a legal standpoint, sovereignty was split between the Italians and the Ottomans. Not because both parties had agreed to it, but because of a basic misunderstanding.

Anwar Bey, the Ottoman government's representative in that province, had gone to the oasis of Jaghbub to take his leave from Ahmed Sharif as-Sanussi, the head of the Sanussi Brotherhood leading the resistance. The Brotherhood had refused to recognise the Treaty of Ouchy. With that trip, the Ottoman representative handed the keys to the country over to Sayyid Ahmed. Henceforth, the Sanussi Brotherhood began to refer to itself as a government. The disintegration of Ottoman authority, which the Brotherhood inherited, meant that Benghazi's influence also began to wane, since it was solidly in the hands of the invaders, whereas that of the tribes of the boundless inviolate hinterland grew accordingly.

Hajji Semereth found it difficult to follow these conversations, which bored him. The guests were tangles of endlessly unravelling conversations. The Italian government insisted on pretending that the road to the Seraglio Point lay open to them, and that Istanbul was ripe for the taking. The Sublime Porte refused to do anything for that province, and some there may well have hoped a European power would rescue it from its abandon and neglect. But it distrusted Italy's intentions. After all, it was the seat of the Papacy, and it would try to colonise the region with its own citizens; furthermore, the lamentable conditions of Italy's southern regions didn't presage anything good. In addition, while a truly great nation only needs to make a show of strength, a second-rate power is forced to actually employ it. The game was far from over: the Treaty of Ouchy didn't hold much weight on the coast of Africa.

Always one for following his own path, Hajji Semereth observed the young Maronite sitting in front of him and talking with the others in a hushed tone. If accomplished with wisdom and caution, adopting an ambiguous stance towards both camps could prove to be that young man's springboard to fortune: he was a Christian, like the invaders, and yet spoke Arabic like the Libyans. Both factions would consider him one of their own. Would he experience this duality as a mark of his unassailable foreignness, or use it as a talisman, a source of strength? How different that young, well-proportioned young merchant was to him: he wouldn't lust after the impossible, but rather tailor his ambitions according to what reality could offer. His interactions with nature and society were both understated and coherent, and his desires were the product of the times he lived in, and not in opposition to them. Therefore, if the young Maronite remained in the city, he would undoubtedly rise to the higher echelons of Benghazi's notables.

Hajji Semereth stood up, pointed to Émile and said: 'You must convince my young friend to stay with us. Let this be his country, his city.'

It seemed as though the Hajji had chosen his heir, but

this didn't inspire any jealousy. Purely by picking a successor, the Hajji had finally found the inner peace that had long been denied him.

A chorus of good wishes rose from the assembled guests.

III

Zulfa's betrayal had become public knowledge. Only Abubaker, whom everyone feared, didn't know anything. The wives had disclosed the tryst in order to accuse Zulfa and prevent the Hajji from finding a way out of the situation through silence and forgiveness.

The Hajji's maternal uncle, an old bachelor, undertook the thankless task of informing the Hajji of what everyone else in the city already knew. He also made a peremptory request: that the Hajji either repudiate that wretch, or kill her. As for Ferdinando, he could either murder the boy himself or commission someone else to do it, that is unless he wanted one of his servants to become an actual rival.

Hajji Semereth treated his uncle courteously, honoured him with all the compliments dictated by custom, but sent him away without an answer, although hinting that one would soon follow. He nevertheless recommended the uncle exercise the same self-restraint everyone else in the city had shown and keep Abubaker in the dark, in recognition of the latter's flighty mood. The Hajji's uncle found this request rather irksome – what was the Hajji thinking? Did he fear Abubaker because he would take justice into his own hands? Zulfa's tryst had brought shame on the entire family, not just the Hajji, and in accordance with tradition, every male relative had the right to redeem the family's honour. If the

Hajji's sleeve was caught in a snag, someone else's hand would carry out the deed, with or without his consent.

Hajji Semereth replied that he'd listened closely, and that although he didn't want to offend anyone's feelings, he would act however his honour demanded. 'But there isn't enough room for both honour and emotions in this situation!' his uncle retorted, growing exasperated. He had taken on the role of ambassador out of his own volition, not only because he knew his nephew's ears would better bear the burden of the malevolent truth if it came from his lips, but because he was the only one of his relatives who wanted to leave the final decision in the Hajji's hands, rather than dictate the necessary course of action. What would he tell the others now? 'What should I say? That you're dithering over retribution? Should someone else be entrusted with the role of executioner? Why are you hesitating? Are you still in love with that hussy? Can you really tolerate sheltering your wife's lover under your roof? Or are you protecting him?'

The Hajji listed to the crescendo of questions without forming a reply. When the old man stood up, the Hajji placidly ushered him to the main gate.

IV

Abdelkarim loves Ferdinando – the young Maronite thought as he lay stretched out on the bed, as Abdelkarim had told him all he knew about the affair – *and he would joyfully welcome forgiveness and a compromise. But he simultaneously fears forgiveness as a sacrilege that might unleash a host of terrible consequences: there would be less to fear from Ferdinando's death than from his absolution. The world would become drearier and gloomier, but at least it wouldn't be turned upside down.*

The sky out of the window on the roof was an unchanging blue, like a painting.

To understand Hajji Semereth, Émile had to postulate a different reality to the one the Hajji had once belonged to, the paradise from which he'd been chased. Istanbul and the failed conspiracy followed the same old patterns and thus seemed made up; still, they were necessary components in forming a full understanding of the man. *Maybe it wasn't a failed conspiracy, but a different mistake.*

It hardly matters: there was a rule, and there was a transgression, which precipitated the fall. It's useless to get so worked up trying to discover which rule was broken, especially since Semereth seems to contradict them all — his gigantic stature is unequivocal proof of that. Ferdinando and Zulfa are a double sacrifice the people are demanding to appease a God so vulgarly offended by the barbarians from the North. Now that the government and the streets obey different rules, he must defend the integrity of his household and his family.

Would Semereth Effendi forgive the lovers? No man had ever done so, but maybe various secret variables had entered the Hajji's equation. A guarded man, who spent many years in a faraway place and only partially belonged to the city, seeming to dwell in another place altogether. But how could he spare the lovers his family's revenge? It's a well known fact that an insult inflicted on an individual is an insult to the whole clan. The latter had only waited until Hajji Semereth's return out of deference. They could have meted out justice in his absence. Hajji Semereth was hesitating. His prying servants hadn't detected the slightest trace of wrath on his face. Would he give in? Had he already given in? Can someone who is alive remain as absent as the dead? And what was holding him back: love and compassion? Or was it weariness and indifference? How could he tolerate such a grave offence?

Oppressed by various invisible threads in the Hajji's house that impeded his movements, Abdelkarim was pleased with his new master, who was young and impatient. The young Maronite hadn't come to that coastal town as an exile like the Hajji, but so as to play his hand, like the Hajji had done in Istanbul. With the arrival of the young Maronite that world had levelled its decline, and consequently the young man had left the realm of shadows and stepped into the kingdom of light, where he dwelled in its inexhaustible fount.

The Maronite knew that Ferdinando had cried when Abdelkarim had entered his service. He had embraced him convulsively, as though they'd been parting forever. Disdained, Abubaker had denounced Ferdinando's tears to Semereth Effendi, leaving the latter in a sombre mood for the rest of the day. That courteous man was tormented by how his shadow snuffed out all life before it.

The market was shut on Sundays. During the interminably long hours when no one went out, the Maronite would labour away in his imagination in the hope of speeding up the course of events, as though he were plotting to take over the entire city. Abdelkarim followed his new master's trajectory. He too was mulling over secret thoughts while curled up in a corner. But something set him apart from the Maronite during those lazy hours. Mimicking his master didn't satisfy him: he wanted to complete him, not imitate him, to become the missing link in a perfect circle that would then encompass them both. But on Sundays, the master was a loop of his own.

Therefore, crouched in his corner, Abdelkarim set to constructing a little parallel loop of his own.

V

The deferment Hajji Semereth had tacitly asked for helped placate his wounded pride and wear it down until it no longer posed any threat. His unrequited love needed to resign itself to reality for his deluded hopes to stop oppressing his aching heart. Just as he had let Zulfa cry herself dry on their ill-starred wedding night, he patiently waited until the well of his own tears was depleted. He let his agony consume itself with steely determination: he simply had to bide his time and consider all the likely scenarios, to avoid acting impulsively.

He could crush the two youngsters like insects; the law was on his side, and custom craved retribution – even the public was impatient to see this happen. Zulfa and Ferdinando's fates were wholly in his hands. The injured party could act as judge and executioner.

Semereth Effendi's opinion was that the judge had his own faults to atone for. He could only make amends under one condition: that he, as the injured party, should defend the accused. Only then could he be granted absolution and pass sentence on the matter impartially.

In a display of deference, he decided to head to his uncle's house, regardless of how humiliating it would be. Late in the morning, he dispatched a messenger to announce his arrival. Thanks to this messenger, the news of Hajji Semereth's embassy spread through the house before the Hajji had even accomplished his mission. The servants focused their eyes on the master's face, which remained impassive. But his lips, like those of the dead, seemed to suggest a smile. The house was enshrouded in silence, as though people saw it as a place for hiding, not living.

Torn between a desire to second his nephew and his relatives' impatience, the Hajji's uncle was anxious. If the Hajji had sent a messenger, it meant he undoubtedly wished to show his respect for the family, whom he would personally visit to deliver his answer. But what would he say? Respect didn't equate to acquiescence, and the Hajji's painstaking decorum seemed to herald a refusal. The Hajji's relatives were already exasperated by the injured party's unexpected hesitation, and various theories had been put forward to explain it. The Hajji's uncle had been forced to weigh all these arguments in order to stay the clan's hand and preserve Semereth Effendi's right to defend his own honour: yet didn't tradition make allowances for men who renounced the right to defend their honour, delegating said responsibility to any family member to punish the perpetrators, in fact even going so far as to include the Hajji – who was either too impotent or too complicit in the affair to act – in the same category as those who'd grieved him?

The uncle welcomed the Hajji in private.

Semereth Effendi was handsomely attired and prolonged the customary greetings longer than he needed to. The strain in Semereth's soul manifested itself in an accentuation of formalities. Life exhausted itself in rituals during those difficult moments.

The uncle suspected that the Hajji was solely concerned with keeping him at arm's length so as to avoid him spying on him or questioning him. Nevertheless, he couldn't hold out for long. He suddenly blurted out the question that had lingered on his lips from the start. What had the Hajji decided?

The old bachelor's eyes were bewildered: Semereth's words didn't presage anything good. Instead of accusing the lovers, he accused himself. He spoke slowly, but effortlessly. The uncle felt as though he were playing the role of a notary who'd been called on to certify a contract that had already been signed. His bony hand jerked with a horrified shudder.

Hajji Semereth had given his speech a rhetorical spin, signalling that his decision was final, as if he were reading a text out loud rather than arguing a case or exculpating himself. Why, he asked, had he married that girl who was so much younger than him, who'd cried when she'd seen him, implored him to repudiate her, whose nature was so incongruous with his own that they hadn't even consummated the marriage? Why had he clung to her? The Hajji's mistake, while not excusing what had happened, had been fatal. The marriage, which nature hadn't blessed, had thus been annulled by nature itself. Zulfa had grieved him, but she, being little more than a child, had also been harshly grieved. Her father shouldn't have consented to that match. Neither should the Hajji have insisted on keeping her in his house when the situation proved so impossible. What should he have expected from a twelve year old? Time had been called on to arbitrate their marriage, but nature had forced it to submit to its will and betrayed all expectations. Zulfa had tried to fulfil her conjugal duties. Tradition had put her in an unfair situation and now the same tradition, and its laws, were accusing her without even first listening to her justifications. The bride had remained a virgin for two years. As the injured party, Semereth Effendi took full responsibility for this. It was an atonement he was glad to make as it proved he too was guilty. He had therefore decided, since after all he had taken the role of judge upon himself, to return the following verdict: he would repudiate Zulfa.

His uncle had been on the verge of interrupting him several times throughout his speech. But as both the offended party and the judge, Hajji Semereth had only allowed his uncle to play the role of court stenographer. Regardless, the Hajji's uncle chose to overlook the slight, and said the verdict was acceptable. The strain these events had caused were clearly legible on his face. The Hajji's clemency towards his wife was undeserved, but repudiating her was an adequate solution. The uncle turned his thoughts to the restless accusers in the family, those fanatical vigilantes. He seemed solely concerned with avoiding a conflict between Semereth and the family. Zulfa's fate was of no consequence. So long as she disappeared, it didn't matter whether she was repudiated or murdered.

Semereth Effendi listened attentively. He even appeared interested in the proverbs his uncle peppered his thoughts with, as well as in his gelid scrutiny of life, and the hopes and honesty that endowed his words with a deeper resonance.

It was now time to discuss the *rival*, the boy the Hajji had raised under his roof. Semereth began by saying he couldn't possibly expect to trust the young man as he'd done in the past. Ferdinando wasn't a boy any more. Hadn't the Hajji considered that by taking the boy into his home and raising him, he had in fact signed a contract and fulfilled his end of the bargain, thus turning the rest of Ferdinando's life into a mortgage that could never be repaid? Ferdinando's origins were enshrouded in mystery; it was said he was the son of Christians. Couldn't the upheaval caused by the arrival of Christian soldiers – who perhaps were even his fellow countrymen – into Benghazi, prompt the restless boy to leave the home he'd been raised in? He could thus escape his boyhood and prison in a single stroke. Wasn't it up to Semereth to foresee all that and keep a hold of him, as though he could preserve his youth? Wasn't it his responsibility to emancipate Ferdinando, just as one does slaves?

The old bachelor had grown impatient. His bony hand now seemed to be scratching away, as though gripped by the same spasm that makes a man's limbs twitch when close to death. He interrupted him, curtly. He said he knew how painful such a decision must be, but he wanted justice, not excuses, and the sooner the better. If someone else acted in his place before he could, the Hajji's name would henceforth be smeared by the indelible stain of suspicion that he'd either hesitated or had refused outright. As for the rest, namely the feelings of the people involved, these were negligible and he had no desire to meddle. They had to find a compromise between the demands dictated by justice and the feelings, and surprising hesitations, of the injured party. Whatever collateral damage justice caused was of secondary concern. If weighing scales are a symbol of justice, this means the accused also has a right to weigh in, as he might have had his reasons and also been the victim of an injustice. But nothing else mattered apart from discovering which way the scales ultimately leaned.

The uncle was trying to spare Semereth the pain of additional confessions. This was why he had interrupted him, so as to expedite a conclusion.

Hajji Semereth listened closely, told his uncle he was right, but picked up the thread of his discourse exactly where he'd left off. However, noticing that his uncle was growing irritable, he tried to be concise. He said that the offence (the Hajji being the offender) shouldn't be overlooked, but instead punished. He was prepared to forgive both parties, so long as his own mistakes could be forgiven, which could only come about through generosity and mercy.

The uncle, by now choleric, interrupted him, arguing that he couldn't possibly expect that servant to be forgiven in any way whatsoever.

'Zulfa isn't my wife,' the Hajji retorted. 'We were divorced that very night when the marriage couldn't be consummated.' That this wasn't ratified through legal formalities was an error that fell squarely on him alone. Once Zulfa was divorced, she could choose whichever man she liked, so why not Ferdinando?

The uncle could only muster the strength to object that Ferdinando wasn't a Muslim.

'This is why,' Hajji Semereth concluded as he rose to his feet, 'my renunciation and forgiveness will translate into a good act: I'll ask Ferdinando to embrace our faith. Once this condition is met, I will repudiate Zulfa and recognise her as his lawful wife.'

Chapter 5

Saverio Delle Stelle

I

CAPTAIN MARTELLO: There you have it General, that's the end of Semereth's story. After paying his venerable uncle that visit, he returned home and called for Ferdinando. You can imagine what low spirits that boy must've been in: he knew he'd been condemned to die. However, he must have feared Semereth's wrath more than death, since he didn't disobey the summons and went into the reception room instead. The master – the injured party, the judge and the executioner all in one, namely Semereth – was seated at the back of the room, as though on a throne. 'I forgive you,' Semereth said, 'I'm going to repudiate Zulfa and recognise her as your lawful wife. But on one condition: that you forsake your faith and become a Muslim.' Who was he talking to? The master's presence had paralysed the boy, who couldn't even conceive of a future. That wretched merchant can never get a conversation going: despotic or kind, guilty or innocent, he always winds up talking into a void. He sacrificed it all for all those tender little creatures of his, but what did he get out of it? Either they're too far away, or if he manages to reach them his presence crushes them. It seems he had an equally pathetic conversation with that old man, Abubaker. He was the only one who was still in the dark, and Semereth decided to let him linger there: he merely told him he'd decided to repudiate his latest wife and give her away to his servant Ferdinando, who would forswear his faith in return. The old man replied that if this was the master's decision, then it must be a good one, and that Allah would reward him for initiating an unbeliever into the true faith.

GENERAL DELLE STELLE: And so the conspiracy ultimately led to an annulment! It certainly won't make a good impression that this Christian slave abjured his faith just as we were flinging open the prison gates. But hey! Young men always make mistakes when a pretty girl is involved, like incurring a debt with a family friend, or in this case, with God.

MARTELLO: I followed the whole affair from its very beginning, intrigued by the haughty answer that Venetian woman had given Colonel Romanino when he asked her if she'd come and work for us: 'I'm not looking for a master.' I was present at the time, and I wanted to interrogate her. Her idea of us is rather offensive – she considers us barbarians. The idea of leaving Semereth's big house to serve a soldier seemed risible to her. I retorted that Romanino is an officer in the army of His Majesty Victor Emmanuel III, but she sarcastically replied that very little of that majesty filtered down to Romanino, that these fairy-tale origins vouched for by official seals and stamps were just a bunch of papers that had no weight in the world of human relations. I feel like I'm going berserk every time I speak to someone who lives here. That Venetian humiliated a fellow

soldier, and a high ranking one, at that. Nevertheless, it
proved quite difficult to disentangle my wrath from my
concern. The ties that bind people in that house are indis-
cernible, they're often contradictory, and they have indecipherable roots: like Semereth's link to the Venetian woman,
who I believe was either the wife or daughter of one of
his victims, or better yet, of one of the Turks' victims. When
the questioning was over, I ordered her to send Ferdinando
to me as I wanted to interrogate him too. When he showed
up, I explained that I wanted him to come and work for
us. The boy really is very handsome: the Venetian woman's
praises don't do him justice, in fact quite the opposite.
Ferdinando was dumbstruck and tried to run away. Once
apprehended and forced to talk, he finally confessed that
he'd worried we wanted to enslave him, and he only calmed
down once we'd reassured him of our integrity and sworn
an oath to that effect. Although we had a different impression, Ferdinando doesn't consider himself a servant in that
house: he obeys Hajji Semereth, in fact since he's an orphan
he belongs to him, but that doesn't mean – at least as far
as he's concerned – that he's a servant. In other words, my
proposal turned into a total blunder. The boy didn't have
the Venetian woman's vivaciousness, or her flair for blarney.
Thus, once the misunderstanding was cleared up, I let him
go. But some time later, I used a pretext to head over to
Semereth's house before his trip to Egypt. I was courteously
received, spoke of my conversation with the Venetian and
Ferdinando to avoid being found out and make him suspicious, but I could only see the master's unappealing face,
and not Zulfa's, the one I'd so ardently longed to see. After
drinking a cup of fragrant tea, I got up, and before taking
my leave mentioned that I was curious to see the rest of

the house, since theirs are laid out so differently to ours. As the rituals of receiving a guest dictate strictly formulaic answers, Semereth immediately replied 'My home is your home,' meaning I was free to see it. I already knew that the women's quarters – where each wife has a room with two windows and a door facing onto the inner courtyard – were off limits. But as I was walking through a corridor, I thought I saw such a little face glued to one of the windows that it could only have belonged to that beautiful wife of his. Using some pretext or other, I backtracked a few steps. It was dusk, and when I finally managed to get a glimpse through that window, I saw the face I'd spotted a moment earlier. But it wasn't Zulfa. It was Ferdinando, who scampered off the minute he recognised me. Perhaps he'd feared I'd come to see his master to buy him! I had been one of the first to hear of Zulfa and Ferdinando's tryst, having learned of it from the Maltese man who works as an interpreter for us, and who knows all the stories that make the rounds of the citadel. The story had piqued my desire to lay eyes on that beautiful face. But how to go about it? I'd chanced upon Ferdinando in the shop of a Maronite while he was speaking to a boy who'd once been in Semereth's service and who now works for the Maronite merchant. I entered the shop without being seen by Ferdinando and once I'd asked Chébas a few questions about his business, and to show me his merchandise, I stopped to greet Ferdinando, who'd seen me by then, but was too terrified to run away. The young Maronite offered me a cup of tea with mint leaves and peanuts at the bottom. Their tea ceremony is really quite intriguing, it's just like the bathing ritual at the pagan temples two thousand years ago: the refreshments are really besides the point, it's all about getting to know one another. It's as though my interlocutor were a high priest, and merely talking to him allowed me to consult the local gods.

DELLE STELLE: Your devotion is unassailable, my dear Captain. Which is why I'm rather perplexed by what you've been saying. What are you looking for? We've come to Africa to carve out a colony for the motherland and to lay down rules and regulations, not to put these people to the test. An officer is a man who identifies with an Order and who devotes his life to guarantee its longevity. I often wonder what our African campaign truly means to you. Did you see it as a means to realise a personal need to escape the society in which you were raised and educated? The cruel irony of course being that you were instead asked to impose those very laws and customs on a reluctant country? Or is this some miraculous change that occurred the moment you set foot here? In other words, did you leave Italy convinced you'd be a paladin of truth and justice and yet your certainties were shaken when you saw how the locals were so unwilling to accept you? Or maybe this has nothing to do with these recalcitrant locals and you're genuinely enthusiastic about African society and its laws and customs? Or should one come up with a different hypothesis, and posit that on seeing such primitivity and poverty, you were moved to side with those humiliated, downtrodden natives in an outburst of passion – a secret that bourgeois Western Europe has forgotten? I don't want to pester you with questions about the life you led before you came here. Regardless of whether it was mediocre or fulfilling, that doesn't change the meaning of the experience. Were you ever this interested in anything that happened back home? It seems to me that your feverishness is on the rise, and it's my duty to try to restrain you before eventually having to punish you. Naturally, this has nothing to do with the story itself, which I found interesting, but rather with your conduct. For instance, why did you go to the market? Frankly, I can't quite understand why an officer would go there. Semereth as the baritone, Ferdinando as the tenor, Zulfa as the soprano, the maternal uncle as the bass and the Venetian woman as the contralto . . . Louis Philippe had a passion for Turquerie, and it was all the rage in the eighteenth century. Giuseppe Verdi might have made one hell of an opera out of it, replete with choruses and ballets. Semereth is exactly like Verdi's unlucky heroes: one of those beasts whose tenderness – like Philip II coming between Carlos and Elisabeth in *Don Carlos*, or like the Count di Luna in *The Troubadour* – tends to have deadly outcomes.

II

MARTELLO: We chatted for a long time while those two boys sat on the bench and stared speechlessly at us. I wonder why they were so curious? Ferdinando was very bashful. As for the other one, who I learned is called Abdelkarim, he's an average sort of chap. Which is exactly why Ferdinando stood out so prominently, even though they were dressed more or less alike, but obviously *incognito*. Claiming I didn't know where the goldsmiths' market was situated, even though it's a stone's throw from here, I asked my gracious host if I could take Ferdinando with me. And so it was I went for a stroll with the boy, who was enormously embarrassed. I steered the conversation to this exact topic and tried to question him on his origins, of which he knows nothing. Then I asked him why he didn't go back to his country, whether it was Italy or Portugal; after all, we'd offered to give him the freedom that he surely must have longed for. I told him he'd have the chance to grow up safely and serenely – and perhaps one day, if he happened to show the disposition for it and he were His Majesty's subject, he could embrace a military career. This conversation had a result diametrically opposed to the one we'd had a couple of months earlier when I'd offered him a position as a servant at our headquarters. He kept screwing up his face to look at me, and asked me questions of his own, as though afraid I was trying to trick him. He took my hand in his and begged me not to deceive him, to swear that what I'd said was true. Was it true? I told him that I didn't know, but that it certainly wasn't impossible. My young friend seemed even more distressed. I already knew about his tryst with Zulfa. The dilemma that was plaguing his soul was the following: abandoning his master's wife, whom he had a boundless love for, and escaping to become an officer in the Italian army – or remaining in his master's employ so as to share a life of beatitude and martyrdom with the latter's wife.

DELLE STELLE: Melodramas have been preoccupied with exactly these sorts of dilemmas for as long as anyone can remember. Do you remember those lines from *Dido Abandoned*?

> *Se resto sul lido*   *If I linger ashore*
> *Se sciolgo le vele*   *If I loosen my sails*
> *Infido, crudele*   *I hear someone call*
> *Mi sento chiamare.*   *Me cruel and false.*

E intanto confuso	*Meanwhile I'm dazed*
Nel dubbio funesto	*Amidst sorrowful doubt*
Non parto, non resto	*I won't leave, I won't stay*
Ma provo il martire	*But suffer just as much*
Che avrei nel partire	*As I would if I left*
Che avrei nel restar.	*As I would if I stayed.*

Lyric opera is the only art form I ever had any aptitude for: the only discipline that escaped becoming an academic discipline and eschewed the miserable righteousness of our times. The routine of reality kills art. I don't know if my taste for melodrama led me to a military career, or if army life led me to melodrama as an equivalent substitute. Eighteenth-century operas excelled at resolving private conflicts with military violence. (HIS NARRATIVE CUTS OFF HERE, OBVIOUSLY TO MAKE WAY FOR FERNANDO'S ARIA).

MARTELLO: I was expecting him to ask if I could arrange for his escape; in other words, if it would really be possible to present this retrieved subject to His Majesty the King, along with his incredibly young and beautiful lover, of course.

DELLE STELLE: But of course! It's like in *The Magic Flute* when the King turns into Sarastro.

MARTELLO: Would he ask me to swear another oath? This time, Ferdinando didn't grab my hand, but instead walked silently beside me as he let his hopes slowly evaporate. When we'd neared Semereth's house, he stopped: his eyes were bright and alert. Without sharing his enthusiasm, I understood he'd opted for martyrdom and beatitude. I held out my hand to say goodbye. He seized it, and in the blink of an eye brought it to his lips and planted a kiss on

it as local custom dictated. By adhering to the local traditions, he showed me he'd renounced my offer of protection,
released me from my oath to remain beside his beloved.
Thus, someone from that house had refused my offer a
second time. Perhaps you were right all along, General: our
baritone is cursed and doomed to be rejected. I only hope
I didn't cause that boy any more bad luck, or rather, using
your words, that I was nothing more than an innocuous
beast. Verdi always infused his baritones' arias with an oppres-
sive melancholy. Think of *Il balen del suo sorriso*. General, as
our librettist, if you would kindly write me an aria, please
place it at that moment, when I was alone in the middle
of the street, standing amidst curious and ignorant passers-by,
just a moment after Ferdinando kissed my hand and disappeared, refusing to make his escape to go back to Semereth's
house, where his lover lived with her husband, the master,
the monster.

DELLE STELLE: I would prefer a *concertato*: you out on
the street and the other characters situated in various parts
of the house. I would even give the Venetian a line – after
all, we did say she was the contralto. Curtains! Curtains!

MARTELLO: The curtains certainly fell. How could I
possibly re-establish a connection with Semereth's house after
being turned down twice? Once, during one of Semereth's
absences, I'd sent for Abubaker, the old custodian. But the
old man's world is so alien from ours that I failed to get
anything out of him. My attempts to poke a little fun at
Semereth were met with such obvious disdain that I got
confused and immediately stopped talking. To cut a long
story short, I let him go without having drawn anything
useful out of him. One day, while I was strolling through
the market, I found myself face to face with the young

Maronite, who invited me into his shop and dispatched his servant to fetch a second cup of tea. I gladly accepted. If Ferdinando had been in his shop, this meant the young Maronite knew Semereth Effendi, or had at least heard of him. The Maronite is young, intelligent and industrious, he runs around Benghazi – where he showed up a couple of months ago – with enviable self-confidence. I can't tell what thoughts he might conceal, but he seems utterly indifferent to the political situation and avoids speaking out either for or against either side. Every time I tried to steer the conversation to make him compromise himself, he would deflect my questions by saying that he'd wound up in Benghazi purely by chance, and was only interested in commerce. But despite having subtly tried to force him to do so, he refused to disapprove of what the rebels were doing. He seemed courteous, obliging and well disposed towards a compromise, but only within the confines of dignity. I believe he thinks taking a stance against the rebels would be dishonourable. But what do we care whether he approves or not? Is that what I was looking for? I was far more interested in another detail: that the young Maronite had met Semereth Effendi on the ship from Alexandria. I asked him a number of questions about Semereth: the man has a keen eye, is never indiscreet, but is definitely sagacious. I understood that he knew the whole story, and that I'd found the key to unravelling this puzzle.

III

Abdelkarim hurtled through the market to be the first to deliver the unbelievable news to the young Maronite:

Ferdinando had been murdered. The sheer unlikeliness of the incident had momentarily cushioned the blow and muted the soul's emotions. The tears that would flow in the wake of his friend's death would come much later.

'*Mais quoi! La vie içi est à un très grand bon marché!*' was a saying that had been attributed to Anwar Bey, the leader of the Libyan partisans stationed in Derna.

Ferdinando had been stabbed by a dagger belonging to the eldest son of that uncle who'd so affectionately tried to help Semereth Effendi through the ordeal that destiny had subjected him to; and it hadn't taken place in a dimly lit alley far from prying eyes, but in public. In fact, when Ferdinando was about to be circumcised, thus making him a Muslim, and surrounded by curious onlookers, they'd discovered he was already circumcised. Hajji Semereth's cousin had been blinded by rage, and unsheathing a dagger had exclaimed: 'This man isn't a Christian, but some sort of apostate or Jew. How can we condone such a profanation of our customs?' and before anyone could intervene, the cousin had stuck his blade through Ferdinando's heart.

MARTELLO: Goodbye Ferdinando! I wasn't able to save you! We flung open the gates of those prisons far too late for you! Escape meant too great a sacrifice and at that price, life itself would lose all meaning and become merely a lie! I'd assumed he was becoming a man, and that the metamorphosis would see him freed from bondage, but there was more to it than that, far more! His metamorphosis was leading him to his very death! Besides, how can anyone imagine that delicate young man leading a real life? His mysterious origins had made him an object of curiosity, but he seemed to wander this earth like a lost soul! As though he'd fled from another kingdom and been brought here, to another climate, with different laws, where he'd have only grown more sorrowful and died. He must have either escaped or been kidnapped. Did Semereth really have no clue as to his background? Or had he lied about that? Whom had he kidnapped the boy from? Now that we can be certain he wasn't a Christian, but most likely either a Muslim or a Jew, the mystery of his origins deepens and thickens.

DELLE STELLE: Your soliloquy right in the middle of the story left me a little perplexed. Tell me, my dear Captain, did you compose this passage on the spot, or did you recite it at the market? It's as though someone from the audience had leapt onto the stage to challenge the brother or lover in the final scene of *Lucia di Lammermoor*! Need I remind you there's an even thicker wall separating us from the natives than between the audience and the stage? You're forcing me to take a heavy-handed approach: an officer who drinks tea with merchants and jumps up on stage to weep over a pretty character's death can't help but perplex me – in fact, it perplexes me greatly. These are tears that should be dried while in the darkness of the theatre, not flaunted at the market.

MARTELLO: And I'm telling you that this wall is inviolable, I want to leave this country tomorrow. We're living a lie in an artificial reality, ripped from our native soil and transplanted into cramped pots. Ever since we blustered our way in here, my most precious hours were spent in the Venetian woman's company, or in Ferdinando's, or in Semereth Effendi's house. Semereth welcomed me courteously, but made no effort to steer the conversation in a more intimate direction. When about to leave, he told me, 'You have honoured us with your visit,' but didn't ask me to return. Whereas I would've returned that very evening, if invited. Sure, you may say I would only have gone there so as to spy on Zulfa or Ferdinando, but in fact I would have done so even just to glimpse once more Semereth's scarred face: I'd sit and watch that face all day, as though he were the supreme deity of Benghazi and his face concealed the secrets to this city. Semereth's face was disfigured by a gunpowder charge, just like the prince who was transformed into a monster by an evil spell. Semereth came into the picture wearing a golden mask that only half concealed his disfigurement . . . Why are you smiling? Even the asymmetry between him and anyone or anything he comes into contact with is a magic spell! My sword is useless except for breaking into that house where I'm not wanted, forcing the Venetian woman who refused to work for us to wait on me, forcing Ferdinando, Semereth's valet, to enter my service (at least I would've protected the boy!) and usurping Semereth's place, wearing his cloak and appropriating his child bride. I have no interest in *mimicking* either the young Maronite who moves so freely about town or that giant; instead I want to take their place, to *supplant* them. When I visited Semereth's house, I had the impression I'd entered a dissociative state: I was Semereth. As for the officer in me, he was just an unhappy genius waiting to be freed. Semereth is a giant captivated by all that is ephemeral or fragile, which he could easily crush with one hand. Worshipping one's own slave is the most horrible of traps. Seducing what he already owned − it's the very essence of hope and the painful prison that encages all powerful men. I can't help recalling Philip II, loved not by his inept and emotionally incontinent son, nor his young bride, nor the loyal but cryptic Marquis of Posa. Opera is the complete repository of all human nadirs. Once, when I was in Spain, I saw a dance involving a strong, seasoned man and a frail, diaphanous woman: the more passionate he became, the more robotic or puppet-like the woman seemed. She never once looked him in the eye, and her gaze was immobile, just like a robot's. I was convinced they were a couple, but he was unable to get her to love him. To dance is to run around in a fixed circle where distance remains constant for the length of the spell.

DELLE STELLE: Is the story of Semereth and his wife a metaphor for our role as the unloved conquerors in this splendid African province? Still, the desire to be loved, to seduce – if I am to employ your librettist's language – is a poison that *you* have succumbed to. This has nothing to do with *us*. After all, being loved by people we already control is superfluous. We are powerful men who stare into the mirror of glory, lingering as motionless as portraits, almost immortal. We're not lovers chasing shadows on the road to perdition – the shadow being the dream of bending another's will to our own by offering them the gift of our hearts, freedom, and strength, which would in turn guarantee their safety. Seducing what we already own, as you put it – that's the role allocated to Philip II, who dreams of himself and walks off the grand, brightly-lit stage of history and onto the frantic, illusory one of opera. My dear Captain, at times you seem as though you were a lyrical character drafted into the army, someone unfathomable and intangible, like the Marquis of Posa in fact, an invention arbitrarily inserted into Philip II's life by Schiller and Verdi. Your quest constantly grows more obvious and impatient. It would be both amusing and cruel to send you back to Italy – and thus immure you *alive*, given that it's nothing more than a prison to you now – while you're actually running in the opposite direction. But I want to indulge you, and I'm willing to wait. In fact, I want to see your hopes wither away and see you use your sword in a fight where it's not needed. If you employ your blade to chase your dreams, you'll fall into a trap. I'll give you an example: Semereth Effendi purchased Zulfa and she can therefore burst out of that house with sword in hand, but neither you nor that beast will ever be able to exact anything other than terror from her. The more you try to shorten the gap between you and the object of your desires, the further you'll distance yourself from it. Semereth's fate is to be stuck in an interminable monologue, which he uselessly tries to expand into a dialogue. The disproportion between that juggernaut's body and Zulfa's puny frame clearly suggests their lives are running on different tracks destined never to cross. Similarly, you too are mismatched, but in a different way: you can drink as many cups of fragrant tea in Semereth's house as you like, but your foreignness is painfully obvious. Good intentions are like a Baedeker Guide and you're the eager tourist traipsing through the museum: but life in that house unfolds in an alien dimension – and Semereth Effendi, whose disfigured face transfixes you so, is as indifferent to you as if you were just another painting. Establishing a dialogue with a painting would be just as impossible as consummating his marriage with that little girl . . . Ferdinando's death sends a very specific warning. Did our cumbersome presence here, which put the city in a particular situation, give that whole affair a special prominence? Was the act of following their barbaric customs to the letter intended to embody the country's refusal not only to submit to our occupation, but to accept any changes to their laws and traditions? If that's the case, and the weight of our presence precipitated the tragedy, then we are responsible for Ferdinando's death. But there's more: we too accorded the affair a distinct significance since we tried (or rather, you tried) to break through that wall and burst into the story as a human being without remaining trapped in that circle of fear, like demons or gods. By murdering Ferdinando, the city voiced its refusal. To put it bluntly, Captain, you were tossed out of Semereth's house just as the giant failed to make love to his child bride, and your attempt to turn a monologue into a dialogue met only with failure. Ferdinando's pierced heart proves this failure. Indeed, the natives spilled his blood for the explicit purpose of demonstrating how they are protected behind an invisible wall. Only now (and don't forget that I am one of the Supreme Guarantors of the Social Order here) that the divide between audience and stage has been re-established, conforming to the colonial situation we're in, can I allow you to proceed with your story. Actually, on second thoughts I'd like to ask you a question (perhaps prompted by guilt): Was I wrong not to summon the boy and take an interest in the matter?

MARTELLO: You'd have simply shared my fate: a mixture of admiration and tears.

DELLE STELLE: I would have acted more prudently. I wouldn't confuse myself into thinking I was one of those people. I would have been happy to intervene like the gods of yesteryear: saving the hero or the favoured offspring only to then climb back up to Olympus immediately after – whereas you . . . you seem as though . . . you're trying to escape Olympus altogether! Couldn't I summon Zulfa to headquarters right now?

MARTELLO: It's too late! Even more inflamed after

Ferdinando's death, Semereth convinced the judge to question Zulfa. He arranged it all in a hurry as he'd worried that, unbeknownst to him, a blood relative of his might decide to kill her next. He said that Zulfa was still his wife and that he wouldn't tolerate anyone meddling in the affair: a warning that also extended to his family. Semereth had hoped Zulfa would be forgotten once he'd repudiated her and sent her back to her parents, even relying on the judge, who having been appeased by the act of repudiation would then help placate any hotheaded relatives. After Ferdinando's death, these barbarians started thinking this compromise was inadequate. Being a brave and introverted man, Semereth Effendi would have travelled as far as Istanbul, to the very gates of the Sublime Porte if need be, simply to prolong the lives of those two for a few more hours, or even humiliated himself by asking you for help, General. He was convinced that the judge would do everything in his power if only he had the girl right in front of him. When the old judge saw that the sinner's face was so small it would fit in the palm of his hand, he was dumbstruck. But the onlookers didn't seem all that keen on the judge's procrastination. Were there agitators present in the room? Where had they come from? If Semereth carried on being so indulgent, he might well risk being killed too. He noticed they were complaining about Zulfa's repudiation merely so as to strike at him without overtly causing offence. Those stooges considered Zulfa a hussy because she'd cheated on her husband with a slave. They humiliated her by uncovering her face in public. Once unveiled, Zulfa was so ashamed she fainted. It had nothing to do with remorse, but although those stooges wouldn't suspect such a thing, Zulfa's modesty had survived her sin. It was around this time that one of the stooges – the judge – decided he would act like a real man. Overwhelmed by Zulfa's beauty, he did all he could to save her. All it amounted to was one pointless postponement after the other – and Semereth knew that. Only that which cannot be delayed truly matters in the end. There was something rather pathetic about this man trying to save two flies from drowning. I really do think he would be willing to travel all the way to the Golden Horn to beseech the Sublime Porte to defer her demise by a single hour, or even go knocking on the Quirinale's doors to kiss the King's feet, so long as His Majesty were capable of stopping all the clocks in the world. Even Semereth – you see? – tried to break through this wall and failed. General, I hope you'll spare me narrating the rest of this abominable story. I'll merely add that, in keeping with the customary way of punishing adulterers, Zulfa was eventually drowned.

DELLE STELLE: The fifth act is always the most turbulent. Tell me about the others who died and let's speak of the matter no longer.

MARTELLO: I don't know who told Semereth about the part his wives and the Venetian played in the affair. The story goes that Abubaker killed the wives, either acting on his master's orders or on his own initiative.

DELLE STELLE: Cut to the chase, Captain. The death toll has risen to five.

MARTELLO: The Venetian hurled herself at her master's feet and begged for forgiveness. It seems she'd had the opportunity to escape, as she'd been in the courtyard when Abubaker went into the women's quarters to slay the wives. Instead, she submitted herself to Semereth's judgement. An odd move for such a shrewd woman, and certainly voluntary. Her master's cave was the extent of her universe. Just as she refused to come and work for us, she disdained bolting out of the door to save herself. People say that Semereth crushed her head under his foot.

DELLE STELLE: Death is meted out quickly in tragedies – after all, it was his palace! But can't we do anything about all this? Despite the botched circumcision, Ferdinando was still technically a Christian, and the Venetian woman was repudiated. Why don't we arrest Semereth and the old man?

MARTELLO: They both disappeared last night. Semereth miraculously re-established his connection to the real world: he's gone to the rebels' camp. As for me, I've been granted the right to avenge those youths that were so dear to my heart. I hope God sees fit for Semereth and I to meet face to face one day.

DELLE STELLE: A duel? If Semereth finds out that an officer wants to avenge the two lovers – who were also dear to him – then he'll let himself be killed. As we've had an active part in shaping his destiny, let's deny him death's restorative balm and swing open the gates of nothingness for him.

BOOK II

CHAPTER 1

I

Abdelkarim always woke up before his master. Émile Chébas's arrival at the market was invariably announced by Abdelkarim's zigzagging gait as he sniffed around for customers. If there was no work to be done, he would perch himself on one of the colossal shelves that nearly protruded right out of the shop and into the street. The shop front was devoid of windows and thus wholly exposed to the comings and going of the narrow, covered street. Abdelkarim would observe the passers-by and keep vigilant even when he looked distracted, or appeared to be dozing. People had got used to the sight of him perched on his shelf: his clients would provoke him, and his debtors would try to camouflage themselves by melding into the crowds. Abdelkarim would address the debtors by name and greet them with much deference, in order to warn his master that these deadbeats had come into firing range.

Depending on the case, the young Maronite would pretend not to hear his servant, or loudly greet his debtors too, in a way that made it seem as though he were pulling on their ears. If verbal warnings produced no results, Émile would get up and call the person in question over, or order the boy to fetch him. Abdelkarim would then jump off the shelf and overtake his prey in the blink of an eye, inviting him to retrace his steps because the master wanted to speak to him. In order to ensure he wouldn't slip away, he would take him by the hand and kindly drag him along, as though guiding a blind man through the crowds.

Abdelkarim wouldn't usually intervene while his master – who would sometimes limit himself to offering his prisoner a cup of coffee and then sipping it in studied silence – was speaking, but when the unlucky debtor took his leave, Abdelkarim would shower him with ceremonious greetings to let him know he'd overheard everything. The debtor would then mutter curses under his breath, or else grumble in a tone that left no doubt as to his mood. But these were like innocuous pebbles that always fell back down to earth without striking the young servant.

Abdelkarim knew how to tell real customers apart from unwelcome guests, and he would scrutinise the intentions of the passers-by in the way one rummages through someone's pockets, inviting customers who seemed unsure into the shop, hovering in the background so as to assist them when ordered to, or else barring the path to those visitors who were unwelcome by adopting an authoritarian tone and informing them that the master was too busy to receive them, and that they should come back some other time. Sitting at the back of the shop, Émile Chébas would hear everything without ever lifting his gaze from his ledgers. Abdelkarim's voice was like a sixth sense that kept him informed about everything happening in the market. His voice filtered the chaotic flux of people as though he were an autonomous body connected to his master by sound waves.

Abdelkarim's ears were always pricked up, and his memory was as sharp as his eyesight. His mind was like an enormous blackboard where he'd scrawled the price of every item in the store: a landscape of numbers that could be consulted by his master or the customers. He remembered everything clearly, and the information could be flipped through as easily as one does with a book.

His assiduity never varied in intensity, regardless of whether his master was negotiating a business deal or had got dragged into a conversation that drew on typical themes in the Oriental repertory: the inexorable decline of the Ottoman Empire, the intrigues of Western powers, the questionable role colonialism had played in history, the inevitable reawakening of the Arabs, the virtues of their literary tradition and the sophistication of their rituals. And if the tapestry of his master's memory ever unravelled, Abdelkarim knew how to rethread it. Émile Chébas's memory thus benefited from an external warehouse which he could draw from at will when he needed to. Every ledger he kept had been memorised by his servant.

Émile would occasionally become exasperated when he thought Abdelkarim knew too much about him or might even replace him – Abdelkarim's subtle mimicking skills sometimes made him seem like Émile's doppelgänger, at which point the master would send him off using any old pretext. The boy's devotion cancelled their duality, the shadow was attached to the man who projected it, and grew more obvious the more Émile theatrically tried to shake it off.

But Émile was so used to the boy's presence – or at

least to his voice, his ears being utterly synchronised to that external receptor – that whenever he sent him off on some errand, or kicked him out on some pretext, the shop seemed empty. If Émile kept his gaze fixed on his ledgers, the comings and going of people in the market became as opaque and indecipherable as the nocturnal ebb and flow of the sea. If he put his papers aside and tried to observe people himself, all the usual unwelcome visitors would seize the advantage, slip into the shop and cost him a great deal of time. He would welcome Abdelkarim back with a muffled reproach that was only really an expression of the relief he experienced at being freed by the servant's return. Abdelkarim would then perch himself at his usual post and from the top of his mast, would steer the shop back to its normal course and return it to calmer waters. Everything would become clearer and livelier, and the chaos would be transformed to order once again.

One day, the young Maronite noticed Abdelkarim was not himself. He seemed lethargic, and wasn't paying much attention to anything he heard or saw, while his memory, which had never known uncertainty, was now like a net caught on a snag. Émile questioned him, but the boy was either incapable of furnishing an explanation, or unwilling to do so. Irritated by what he perceived as reticence, Émile reproached him harshly and for the first time had the impression that his words had fallen on deaf ears instead of being appropriately filed in the servant's repository. The boy's hostility annoyed Émile like a speck in his eye or a thorn in his thumb. He began to suspect Abdelkarim had received a better offer from a rival merchant. His wrath was such that the boy slipped off his perch and began rearranging the piles of fabrics, turning his back to his master while doing so. Annoyed over all the time he'd wasted, the young Maronite returned to his ledgers.

Abdelkarim sat down and buried his chin in his chest. The Maronite had announced his brother's forthcoming arrival to a friend and Abdelkarim was tormenting himself in the vain effort to picture life in the shop *with a third person*. There was the master, and Abdelkarim complemented him. This intruder would make Abdelkarim's presence superfluous.

The Maronite was churning numbers in his head. Even Abdelkarim put in a little effort when it came to numbers: he was trying to picture the transition from two to three, but failed each time he tried to make that leap – there simply was no third place. Meanwhile, the market was starting to empty out, and as for the master, who was poring over his figures, who knew where his thoughts were? Abdelkarim continued his solitary game awhile, then his head sank even lower.

The master woke him up a half hour later, benevolently placing his hand on Abdelkarim's head.

II

Armand was nineteen, six years his brother's junior. He had studied with the Salesian monks, but had left without a diploma.

Émile welcomed him with a contrived warmth, as though his younger brother's arrival had cast a shadow on his life. Armand was very loquacious, and attracted people's attention whenever he spoke. He behaved as though he knew everything, even the answers to the questions he asked.

He formulated these questions to draw attention to his needs. The modesty of his arrival expressed itself very ceremonially. Armand put several questions to Abdelkarim, who didn't answer any of them, being enveloped in his master's silence. Speaking loudly, Armand said he thought the boy was rather simple. 'Couldn't you find anyone better?' he asked.

Once they'd left the docks they climbed into a carriage. The two brothers sat on the back seats, while the front ones were taken up by Armand's baggage. Abdelkarim sat next to the coachman.

Abdelkarim knew his master was irked by all that chatter. But the siblings were so captivating that they made life seem doubly real.

As soon as they'd arrived home the brothers locked themselves in a room; a long conversation ensued, which Abdelkarim only overheard snippets of. He understood that the master was reproaching his brother over some matter, perhaps how he'd interrupted his studies, the displeasure he'd caused his family, and the wastrel lifestyle to which he'd abandoned himself. *Promissory notes*, a term that had often been repeated, eloquently summed up the situation. The rest had been left to the eavesdropper's imagination.

This was the first time Abdelkarim realised Semereth Effendi's friend also had a past of his own, even though he hadn't appeared to when he'd arrived at the docks that day. The morsels of news the master had sent home to his family over the past couple of years were rather obvious. But thanks to the snatches of sound emerging from the room, the master's family was beginning to assume a vivid appearance. It was difficult to picture the passenger who'd left the latest ship to dock in town in a happy context. Armand had been forced to leave one of the Orient's oldest cities for an extremely shabby provincial town against his will. It was a punishment.

'Haven't you ever made any mistakes?' Armand asked animatedly.

Whenever he reacted to his brother's recriminations, their voices grew louder. They sounded like stressed blades on the verge of snapping.

'You seem to think that having a lot of money makes you the only one with a sense of honour!'

Abdelkarim knew that his master was absolutely right. If asked to choose a side, he wouldn't hesitate. But the truths the master spoke were contradicted by the other's presence. Armand had no use for the things that were sacred in life – family, one's good name, industriousness – that his brother kept mentioning. All that talk of respectability his brother was raining down on him was irksome, and he refused to keep quiet. Abdelkarim had the vague intuition that over the course of one's destiny, the truth tends to shatter into thousands of shards, and Armand's presence allowed him to understand the concept of multiplicity – and that it was legitimate. Abdelkarim nevertheless found the experience fabulous and engaging: he remained perched behind his master, as immovable as a reef, but for the first time realising that the sea, which had hitherto seemed so uniform to him, was actually the sum of endless routes.

Émile left the room in such a fury which Abdelkarim, who lingered in a corner of the courtyard, had never seen before. Émile commanded Abdelkarim and Armand to follow him, and then left the house.

As soon as the master had slammed the door, Abdelkarim entered the room Armand was in. He was like an arrow shot out of a bow: his master's will personified. Abdelkarim explained that the master had ordered them to go to the shop, but he lost his thread in mid speech. Armand's indifference was disorientating.

Armand began unpacking objects from his luggage and demonstrating their use to Abdelkarim, boasting of the variety of colours and the refined craftsmanship. Although Abdelkarim was illiterate, he even showed him some books. Bewildered, Abdelkarim praised everything he was shown, praising the new arrival even more since the latter's enthusiasm for both himself and his objects was a novelty that swept Abdelkarim in its forceful current. Abdelkarim's relationship with Émile was very different: Abdelkarim was simply a medium who relayed words between the master and his customers, depending on the former's needs. Their work was the axle that connected them in the same way momentum exerts torque on the wheels of a carriage. For the first time, Abdelkarim had a palpable sense of an elsewhere – like Semereth Effendi's Istanbul – which he'd so often heard described. Armand was like a magician conjuring remote, magnificent worlds; his knowledge wasn't confined to the cramped field of experience, but instead stretched over endless plains.

Armand began getting ready to leave. The master only needed a moment to do so, but Armand seemed to be taking forever, changing out of one outfit and into another. In the end, Abdelkarim could no longer contain his curiosity. Having spent the past half hour inside the room, Armand had finally exasperated Abdelkarim, who was waiting outside in the corridor. But when Armand emerged, Abdelkarim was astonished. He was completely different from the young Maronite or Hajji Semereth: he was as smooth as a feather, carefree and strikingly handsome.

Once out of the house, Abdelkarim felt a sort of pride at being seen with such an extraordinary master. This pride explained why when Armand refused to duck down a tiny lane that was as a shortcut to the market, thus avoiding an unnecessarily long route, Abdelkarim for the first time chose to disobey one of his master's orders and could barely conceal his glee: he was delighted to wander the streets with that magnificent creature. Abdelkarim's world had suddenly grown more complex and layered.

Armand was repeatedly asking questions about the elegant, distracted Italian officers they kept seeing on their way. Abdelkarim knew very little about them as the master didn't mix in those circles.

By the time they arrived at the shop, Abdelkarim was in a heightened state of fervour. But the master's sombre face made him conceal those emotions as though he were hiding some ill-gotten loot. He leapt onto his usual perch at the shop's entrance.

At that moment a few merchants entered, having come to congratulate the Maronite on his brother's arrival from the East. The master's sombre face cheered up, and he introduced his brother to his friends without the slightest trace of embarrassment, inviting them all to sit down. The conversation that ensued passed without incident.

It was only in the evening, while they were sitting at dinner, that the master suddenly interrupted Armand as he was talking about a cousin's wedding – and poking fun at the couple, their parents, their guests, the rite and the priest – and said 'Anyway, the past has been forgotten, and we forgive you. After all, you're young and you can find your way back to the straight path. Everything depends on you. My position here is fairly good, and looks set to improve.

If you show goodwill in your work, one day you'll become a partner. If you walk the straight path you'll receive all the respect you're due – and I'll be the first to show it to you; otherwise, I'll be the first to punish you. So consider yourself welcome in my house, so long as you abide by these conditions.'

Armand abruptly stood up and retreated to his room, locking himself in.

Abdelkarim continued to serve the master. He was as afraid, as though he were guilty. But when the master retired to his chamber an hour later, Abdelkarim knocked on Armand's door and brought him his meal.

III

When Abdelkarim entered the shop – carrying two spotlessly clean cups of coffee on a brass tray – and heard the master speaking in a grave tone, he immediately surmised who was being discussed. A wealthy merchant Émile would sometimes visit in the evenings had come to intercede on Armand's behalf: a sign relations between the brothers had worsened.

Armand had gone into an independent orbit.

As Abdelkarim had been raised in Hajji Semereth's house, where the Hajji's will or desires were all that mattered and the intrigues of the others who lived there only existed by the grace of whatever space the master's will conceded, Armand's open challenge towards the master had made a striking impression on Abdelkarim: it thrilled, frightened and tormented him.

Armand's presence hadn't altered Abdelkarim's relationship

with his master, even though whenever Armand was in the shop there were now three of them. The master was embittered, deluded, and often irritated: Abdelkarim would let him vent all his wrath on him and patiently absorb it. However, the fact that his relationship with the master remained unchanged didn't prevent him from following Armand's progress. The captivating man who'd appeared in town and now worked in the shop didn't complement the master, but rather dared to show his indifference to the latter's rules and orders: Armand was following his own plans, and brazenly carried them out in full view. The master's wrath was useless, since his principles hadn't made any impression on his brother. Armand knew how to talk back, and any dispute eventually ended in agitated voices, slammed doors and ultimatums that sounded more threatening than they actually were.

The wealthy merchant was listening to the Maronite's words in a benevolently cheerful way, limiting his interruptions to encouragement, and tender interjections like 'I know, I know, you're right. But are you keeping in mind he's your brother? That's a bond you can never deny or disown, it's enduring and irrevocable. You must start from that realisation and see what you can do.'

The merchant, who was well built, in his fifties and had long grey whiskers, was wearing the traditional whitish robe made out of coarse wool over his usual merchant's outfit – which consisted of a white untucked shirt over breeches, topped by a thin waistcoat – as though he wanted to give his presence the impersonal weight of ancient values.

Abdelkarim was sitting by the sales desk, at a respectful distance, but still within earshot. The master wasn't even aware he was there, and besides, the boy was as secretive as a wall. What the master was saying about Armand both bothered and thrilled him, to the point that he could barely contain his excitement. It was certainly true that Armand always arrived late at the shop, and sometimes not at all; that all the business he brought was inappropriate, that he sold goods on credit to insolvent merchants, that he underestimated difficulties, and yet didn't know how to confront them when they came to pass. He always took the initiative, but could never see matters through to their end, and spent his time chasing chimeras.

What truly bothered Émile, however, wasn't how useless Armand was: he knew that he could look after the business entirely on his own. On the contrary, he hated it if anyone ascribed any successes to his brother's presence. 'You don't want a partner, you want a servant!' Armand had shouted at him the other day in front of strangers.

'What should one say about his friendship with Italian officers? They are our co-religionists, to be sure, but our way of life, traditions and language are entirely different.'

Émile Chébas's narrative build-up had been meticulously planned. The guest didn't seem to be in a hurry: he had come to invoke Émile's generosity, not his powers of logical reasoning, which instead counselled caution.

Abdelkarim was waiting for a climax like the one that had happened in Hajji Semereth's house, precipitating his tragic end. Was the wealthy merchant playing the same part the Hajji's uncle had when he'd gone to denounce the adulterers? Émile didn't have any sins to expiate. Life for him was a brightly lit path, absent of any shadows. But lightning could strike from another direction, and Abdelkarim was keeping his eyes peeled.

'Is it possible to ignore the duty that an officer has been called here to accomplish?' Émile asked. 'Armand plays cards with him, they gossip about women, about theatre, and they drink together, amusing themselves with jokes. But the officer is on leave from the battlefield, and that is where he must return. If I don't overlook the reason he's here, and still seek out his company, it must mean I am sympathetic to the aims that brought the officer here. Is this the way for a Maronite to behave? I don't want to look too deeply into the anxieties some of those officers feel, while the rest have mistaken life in Africa for a holiday – a dangerous holiday. This only eggs on Armand's adventurous spirit, and this recent development has nothing to do with the merchant's trade or our family's traditions. When young men from oriental communities first encounter western society they quickly adopt its vices, but rarely go beyond that. Once outside of his family circle, the provincial is a marked man. He can only save himself by coming to terms with how provincial he is, by neither playing up to it, nor being ashamed of it, just like nobody should be embarrassed by the language they speak. This is not to refute the concept of cultural exchange, but to say that imitation is only a masquerade of that cultural exchange: because one party immediately declares himself the loser from the outset.'

Abdelkarim didn't understand much of what was being said. Émile Chébas was talking about a reality whose outline eluded him: nonetheless, he listened attentively.

'Colonialism humiliates and offends, and whenever it shows a more benevolent face, it corrupts. As Christians and foreigners we are treated kindly, and they've offered us a chance to assimilate. But we must keep our guards up. Could Armand ever become 'a good Italian'? It would make me happy if he became a good Maronite merchant, like his father and grandfather before him. As you know, we consider receiving a guest but not inviting them to a cup of coffee as an affront, even when either party is in such a hurry that doing the opposite might seem wiser; at which point I must sacrifice my own interests for the sake of custom. In turn, I expect said guest to be ready to make the same sacrifice, as a show of respect to my home and business. It matters little to me that such considerations have fallen into desuetude in more advanced civilisations, where people live in a permanent state of haste. I would consider someone's refusal an affront, and this, amongst other factors, would inevitably colour how I chose my friends. On the other hand, Armand doesn't care about any of this. This does not mean that our customs are superior to others, simply that they are the foundations upon which our code of conduct has been built; it is the narrative of our history, the language with which people have expressed themselves, reached an understanding, or even how they respect and come to love one another. Whereas I find myself disgusted by the Italian officers' disdain for anything that contrasts with their education, and by their incapacity to either comprehend or accept other ways of life, to recognise the existence of a different order to the one they were raised in, which they assume is the ultimate paradigm of truth. Italy's efforts to set up military bases here to replace the Ottoman Empire is alien to my interests and passions. But when such efforts are compounded by a stubborn desire to extricate the locals from the spiritual flow of their way of life and transport them into a different world, my conscience completely rebels against these Italians, and refuses to have anything to do with them.'

Émile Chébas continued at length, and the merchant who'd come to intercede on Armand's behalf listened patiently. He then pleaded with Émile to be more compassionate towards his brother by flattering both Émile's intelligence and his generosity.

Having extracted a promise that Émile would forgive Armand and let go of the past, as well as an agreement to guide the latter more kindly, the merchant stood up to take his leave.

He then suddenly drew near to Émile and employing a distant, threatening tone, added: 'Criticise your own faults and weaknesses with the same vigour you apply to Armand's. One must measure oneself against perfection, not other people's mistakes.'

IV

When the work on the first floor of the house the Chébas brothers lived in was completed Armand vainly tried to convince his brother to let it out, so as to turn the three rooms on the upper floor into a salon and two new bedrooms and thereby avoid sleeping downstairs, where it was damp and dark. Armand tried to persuade Émile to abandon the ground floor for the one above, but Émile displayed no interest whatsoever in the proposal. Armand said he was embarrassed to invite his Italian friends to the house because he could only receive them in his bedroom. Émile contemptuously replied that he couldn't see the point of those get-togethers in the first place.

According to local custom, men who wanted a little company in the evenings should go to cafés, instead of closeting themselves in their rooms like women, and during the day, anyone who wanted to see Armand could find him in the shop. Émile didn't even believe in those traditions, having been used to seeing friends come in and out of his father's house in the evenings – but Armand's presence had instilled in Émile an enmity against life, and he had wound up confusing a merchant's life for that of a hermit.

Émile already regretted the two years he'd spent in Benghazi, before his brother's shadow had come to darken his path. He was annoyed by his own frosty aphorisms, as though he were choking on his own Sibylline fumes, but his urgency to set himself apart from that moody, superficial young man answered such a deep-seated need that he was sacrificing a part of himself in the process. When, as periodically happened, one of them would get fed up with the other and uncork his resentments, Armand would tell Émile that not only was his brother discouraging and annoying him, but that he was also doing it to himself. Prone to tears, Armand would then begin to sob, cursing how fate had put him in the hands of a man who hated everything that was precious and delicate in the world: youth, beauty, happiness, serenity and love. That he would rather leave and take up whatever profession came his way, repudiating the family's venerated mercantile tradition, rather than continue to live under such persecution in that godforsaken city at the edge of the world. Armand would tell tall tales about extraordinary offers that had come his way and, growing more excited and emphatic with each passing moment, would mark the bottom of his downward spiral by screaming that he was free, young and healthy, invoking the heavens to arbitrate their dispute.

The next day, at the shop, Émile would call his brother over and condescendingly inform him that since he'd heard he was unhappy and wanted to leave Benghazi, he should feel free to do so, that Émile had brought him over simply to help him through his infantile lack of direction and put him back on a straight, traditional path. Caught unawares so early in the morning, Armand would fail to summon the convictions he'd voiced the night before. All that delirious gibberish seemed so unreal and nonsensical when mouthed by his brother's implacable voice in the light of day. Émile would then dismiss Armand with an annoyed wave of his hand, complaining that he'd already wasted enough time on him for the day.

CHAPTER 2

Olghina

I

An Italian physician and his wife, one of the first women to arrive in that distant colony, soon moved into the first floor of the Chébas house. The woman was from Trieste, and she was shapely and blonde.

Olghina had got bored with that little border town where her husband exercised his profession, and she had cheerfully welcomed the decision to leave for the colony. 'It's like I've taken on a lover,' she'd confessed to her friends with a hint of ironic malice. It was as though Africa wasn't a place, or indeed a continent, but a character. She assembled a formidable vanity case, 'mercilessly depleting' her savings, as she put it.

Nevertheless, as soon as she'd disembarked in that African port city, she realised her blunder. This wasn't a pleasure trip: she'd been deported. She had arrived in a place without history, and that was the way it would remain, as though the whole country were a prison cell. Like the heroine in a fable, she'd fallen victim to an evil genie. What mysterious law had she broken? Hadn't an overseas voyage been synonymous with a sentence in a penal colony, for centuries? The ghost of Manon Lescaut seemed to have been waiting for her. Her anxious mind vacillated between a vague feeling of guilt and a weepy rebelliousness against a punishment she hadn't deserved. Where was the Prince Charming who would awaken her from her slumber, and how much longer would she have to wait for him? Through her vain fantasies, which made her weary and yet yielded no benefits, she recognised she was now like a prisoner. She refused to unpack. She spent seven days secluded in her hotel, refusing to set foot outside.

Until, on the eighth day, they arrived at the Chébas house.

Armand went to meet them, and from the moment he'd introduced himself, he no longer wanted to be parted from them.

He paid for the carriage, despite Doctor Pietra's protestations, who was irked by how that young man seemed to be trying to take them under his protection. Armand accompanied them up the stairs, and entered the apartment with them – all the while speaking without pause, furnishing them with all sorts of information, even asking a number of questions to which there was neither rhyme nor reason, but which instead scattered confusedly through the room like a swarm of flies. Quick and nimble as a harlequin, Armand leapt up and down the stairs, providing the newcomers with whatever they might need, craving their attention.

At first, Doctor Pietra tried to shoo him away, then, growing annoyed, he let him carry on.

Olghina was far friendlier. Those seven days she'd spent in the hotel had been so melancholy that this lively little creature distracted her and made her feel less lonely. Thus she listened to that handsome young man, and occasionally rewarded him with a peal of laughter, whose shrill notes enlivened the scene. Everything Armand said was vapid, but her husband's severity was like a slab of bare rock. The surgical, leaden atmosphere of the hospital seemed to follow him everywhere.

They heard the door downstairs swing open. 'That's my brother,' Armand explained, disappearing. He breathlessly announced the newcomers' arrival to Émile, who didn't even answer him. His clothes were dusty, he was tired, and his brother's senseless excitement was bothering him. He hadn't seen Armand at the office all afternoon. Who were these wretches he'd taken up with now?

Armand announced that Doctor Pietra and his wife would come down in an hour for coffee. He immediately started running around the house in order to make it a little more orderly. The amount of clutter Émile had left lying around was immeasurable. Armand cursed his fate. Why should he live with that surly man who always sucked all the fun out of life with that authoritarian and scornful manner of his? It was like having an immovable crate right in the middle of the house.

Armand vented all his disappointment on Abdelkarim, who'd arrived late. Where had he been? Why wasn't he helping him? Why should he assume duties that really belonged to a servant? Abdelkarim looked at him in amazement, wondering what was making Armand so chirpy, nervous and aggressive; but being mild-mannered, Abdelkarim began scurrying around the house in ill-concealed excitement.

Émile shut himself in his bedroom. He already regretted not renting out the first floor of the house, since it would have at least spared him the bother of having those strangers above him. He prepared to welcome them coolly, thus making them understand that although they were neighbours, they had nothing in common and wouldn't need to socialise, except during the return visit Émile would pay them, all strictly out of courtesy of course. In fact, in order to deprive the visit of any intimacy, Émile dressed impeccably. He would need to ensure a chilly atmosphere, so as to snuff out all familiarity, making the occasion immune to any sort of congeniality.

Shortly thereafter, he reappeared. His dusty tunic had given way to a refined gentleman's attire. Armand and Abdelkarim were momentarily perplexed. Émile looked like a high functionary who'd chosen to dramatically allow the crowds a glimpse of his impenetrable countenance. Armand expressed his approval, but didn't manage to extract even a grimace from his brother's marble countenance. He started cursing his fate once again.

Abdelkarim had never seen his master look so cold and distant. He didn't even look like a merchant any more, but rather like one of those robotic officers who strolled through the town. An unbridgeable distance lay between them, and he suddenly experienced an intense feeling of despair, as though his master had left for good. What were they waiting for? Whom were they expecting?

By that time the house had been tidied, and Armand locked himself in the bathroom to change. Intimidated, Abdelkarim fled into the courtyard. Depending on the time of day, or the season, the courtyard and the basement were Abdelkarim's favourite resting places.

Once outside, he heard the sound of shuffling feet and muffled voices from upstairs. Then he saw a bright, smiling face look out onto the courtyard.

When the doctor and his wife came downstairs at eight o'clock, Armand rushed to open the door and he rolled out one greeting after the other, unfurling them like carpets, as though he were a merchant welcoming customers into his shop. Olghina laughed. Her voice was crystal clear, hearty and harmonious; Doctor Pietra, on the other hand, muttered something or other, as though he were taking his leave.

When Émile stood up to greet his guests, he was unable to suppress his surprise and confusion. The mere appearance of that young, beautiful woman seemed to justify all that coldness. He bowed his head ceremonially, while the woman's voice came to rest on his head like a crown. He shook the husband's hand and appreciated his stern expression, which was so unlike the holidaying look that most Italian military officers wore when out in town.

II

OLGHINA: My first impression of this town was horrible. How the houses are painted a blinding white, how the dust lies thick on the trees like ash, the mayhem, the neglect, and the fruitless attempts to clean this up; the new military government, their hurried emergency measures. While I was riding in the carriage to the hotel, I felt a mysterious hand wrap itself around my heart. I couldn't understand the reality in front of my eyes. The further the carriage ventured down those dusty streets, the more frightened I grew.

PIETRA: Are these people really such barbarians? Regardless, we clearly need to think of them as such in order to reassure ourselves. Barbarism is a crime and civilisation is always right, these are what our rights amount to. In other words, we don't want victims, we want criminals. Civilisation always amounts to bloody retribution.

OLGHINA: Had I visited this little town during a long voyage, I might have found it rather pretty. I might have been happier to look at it from an outsider's perspective, and what I saw would have been far more foreign and incomprehensible, indeed, intensely more satisfying. Instead, the spectacle in front of my eyes isn't like that presented to an audience watching a tragedy at the theatre, where the horrors disappear once the curtains come down! No, this is the place where I must live. Everything that might have seemed compelling from behind the safety of the fourth wall instead seems haunting. Now we've been thrown amidst the actors and must share their fate! Pirates once used to capture their prisoners at sea, but now our Royal Government has taken their place; one world replaces another, and a pirate's victim is now called a colonist.

ARMAND: It was horrible for me too, I had come expecting a very different life. Culture means nothing here. Does anyone here know who Anatole France is? It's like being an actor who's prepared for one play and then cruelly gets cast in another. Imagine if, instead of walking into Rosina's room, Count Almaviva were to stumble into the clutches of Ernani's bandits, what would he do then? The same mistake has made my own footing uncertain. I know all of Almaviva's moves, but they are useless here where all I do is grow bored while the audience boos me.

PIETRA: What I'm still unsure about is whether I'm more astonished by the differences between us or our similarities. They *are* different, and this puts our values and beliefs into doubt. But then they are also similar, and this jeopardises our notions of superiority. We're even in a hurry to destroy this civilisation because we're so afraid that its mere existence threatens the worthiness of our own.

OLGHINA: The government wants to build a new town. This does little to cheer me up. The new city scares me as much as these labyrinthine alleys.

ÉMILE: We must be patient. It's a city we will be building with our own hands. The effort required will give our presence here a sense of purpose, and one day the city will have a shape familiar to us. We must however be brave enough not to look over our shoulders, or ponder the different roads we might have taken. It's important that this new city isn't built on the smouldering ashes of the old city, but should instead be its auxiliary, a transplant: even if uneasy, unnatural, unwanted.

OLGHINA: Nostalgia is gnawing away at me, Mr Chébas. Not that I miss one city or the other, but I'm nostalgic for reality itself, as though this city had the illusory confines of a dreamscape or a memory. When the carriage was taking me to the hotel, my eyes examined everything both greedily and hatefully. The shops I was seeing would be the shops I would visit every day. The alleys I crossed would the ones I would walk, where the sound of my footsteps would echo like an alien bell. These people I couldn't understand would be the ones I would eventually meet. The idea that there were so many Italians in uniform was of little comfort. And all those prisoners, and the sick. I have every respect for my husband's profession, but I never wanted the hospital to replace the city, or even to assume the proportions of it! I wasn't on my way through the city, no, this was where I'd arrived, as though I'd reached my final destination.

PIETRA: Italy's obsession with catching up with Europe's great powers is impeding its culture from recognising the legitimacy of other civilisations. We employ reason merely as an instrument in our attempt to imitate a superior model. We disdain civilisations to the south of us; in fact, it's as if they embodied exactly what we wanted to escape. We're a backward country that always keeps its eyes on the other European capitals: Vienna, Paris or London. If Venice had led the Italian unification effort, things might have turned out otherwise, but instead it was led by Piedmont, a lowly vassal of France, and we are the victims of those provincial beginnings. Italian culture seems to atrophy part of our organs. It's no use trying to educate oneself, or to read books written elsewhere; whatever we do, a congenital mediocrity clings to us like a bad smell.

OLGHINA: I'd brought news with me. But a few days after I arrived, having refused to poke my nose outside the hotel, I started to read, and all of a sudden those snippets of news seemed so remote: they're useless instruments here, nothing but rags and ashes.

ARMAND: You're wrong! We haven't been condemned to live here forever! I don't think I have wasted my time getting ready for Paris instead of this stupid little town, which is nothing but a raft adrift on the African sand ocean. Don't tell me we should cut our legs off so as to be on the same level as everyone else! Provincialism be damned, Italian culture gets it right, and Vienna, Paris and London *are* the capitals worth looking at. There's no real civilisation elsewhere. By coming here, we've been distanced from our desires, but all it means is that we've taken a wrong turn, and thus the journey will be longer than we first thought. We've slid backwards! And here is the solution: to forget we're living in a colony, to refuse to change, and to preserve our own ways of life. Then, one day, when the door swings open and we are able to flee, the years spent here will roll off our backs, as though the cloak that kept us hidden suddenly fell off our shoulders, without us ever having changed.

PIETRA: We want to divest these people of their civilisation, which we don't even know anything about, so as to dress them up in a new one. But this changes the very essence of our presence here!

OLGHINA: Or maybe we're not even interested in that, perhaps we want to leave them naked, so we can hunt them down and wipe them out, making room for the new city – which will be our gilded cage.

ARMAND: All this talk of civilisation is rather exaggerated! The sooner they jettison what little of it there is, the sooner they can start on the right track.

ÉMILE: Armand forgets we are Christians. He doesn't even know he's blaspheming because he's confused Paris with the City of God, and the actresses of Parisian theatres for the angels and saints of the latter. Which would be very funny were it not that the people in power think along the same lines as he does. Destroying what we don't understand is a path that leads only to hell.

Olghina would occasionally glance into the courtyard through the corridor door, left ajar. Despite the darkness, growing thicker with each passing moment, she would ferret out Abdelkarim's eyes, which were transfixed on her in spellbound admiration.

She would then break out in loud peals of laughter, which fell on the boy's awestruck face like a fresh sprinkle of water.

III

Abdelkarim crossed the market carrying the secret in his head like a foreign body, like a bullet inside a soldier's body, or an arrow shot from a bow. He cleared people from his path without even looking at them, as though he were running out of time or reaching the end of his strength.

The master had always been the one to order him about, dispatching him left and right, often to carry out difficult tasks. When Abdelkarim would return and relay the results of his mission to the Maronite, he would realise that he was bridging the gulf between them simply by talking, as though the master were absorbing him or swallowing him up, like when he vanished into the sea during the summer. These too were baths, and Abdelkarim always emerged from them feeling blessed.

However, this time the master hadn't ordered Abdelkarim to visit someone in his stead, or sent him on an errand, or given him any message to deliver. A scoundrel, one of those swindlers who ran a stall in the little alleys behind the covered market, a loan shark the master had never even offered a cup of coffee to and whose shop Émile had never honoured with his presence, had grabbed Abdelkarim by the arm, dragged him into his shop and whispered horrible secrets into his ear so that Abdelkarim would deliver them to his master.

When Abdelkarim stepped over the threshold of the shop he immediately lost all heart, as though his strength had failed him, or he felt guilty, or even unable to fulfil his mission. He watched the master's beautiful head as it pored over the books, and he wanted to run away to avoid disturbing that serenity, as though it were in his power to conceal that horrible secret, like an object he could easily discard or bury somewhere distant so the sight of it would never desecrate the master's honest eyes.

The shadow of Semereth Effendi brushed past him. Even that powerful man had tripped on a secret reluctantly revealed by his uncle. Abdelkarim wondered whether he shouldn't tell the loan shark to break the news to Émile himself. But the master would find the presence of strangers intolerable. Abdelkarim then understood he really was the right person to place that grim, appalling gift in his master's hands.

Would the Maronite's destiny follow the same path as Semereth Effendi's? Would he avenge himself in such a cursory manner as the Hajji had done? Abdelkarim had fled Semereth's house just in time – it had since become like the boatman's ferry; in fact, he'd been rescued from it by Semereth himself. However, he would never be able to flee the Maronite's boat: if the master's hour had come, instead of fleeing, Abdelkarim would curl up at his feet just like he'd done in the early days of their acquaintance, when they'd lived at the back of the warehouse in that room with a single window on the roof.

Seeing a merchant walk into the shop was enough to stir Abdelkarim from his reverie. He instantly grabbed the merchant's sleeve and dragged him back outside, heedless of the merchant's astonishment, who was used to the master greeting him cordially while that guttersnipe of a servant usually employed much solicitude. The master himself, having lifted his gaze from his books, displayed no less amazement, but the forcefulness of Abdelkarim's gesture had taken him by surprise. The pair were momentarily swallowed by the crowd and then Abdelkarim re-emerged, at which point, although it wasn't closing time yet, and the master hadn't ordered him to do so, Abdelkarim noisily slammed the metal shutters, then bolted one shut and partially closed the other. Émile Chébas followed all these movements and asked himself whether the boy hadn't lost his mind. He'd never seen him so upset.

'Now what?' he asked, smilingly, once they were alone.

Unable to control himself any longer, Abdelkarim hurried over to his master, and while nearly sitting on his lap, and with his soul in a state of turmoil, he spilled the horrible secret he'd been entrusted with. Armand had run up debts with the worst loan shark in town, for an undisclosed and yet considerable sum, since this loan shark apparently thought he could twist Armand around his little finger. Abdelkarim had been told: 'If it pleases your revered master, he is welcome to pay me a visit and I will be glad to reach a compromise, but it has to happen either today or tomorrow, otherwise Armand belongs to me.' The loan shark had also said that the borrowed money had been spent on pleasures. Armand had ruined himself over a woman, and the woman, that bastard had added, was none other than Doctor Pietra's wife, Olghina.

Émile Chébas grabbed Abdelkarim by the arms and rose to his feet, lifting him up as though he wanted to hurl him to the floor and smash him. Instead, he sat him on the desk and ordered: 'Repeat what you just said!'

Despite being afraid – in fact, beside himself with fear – Abdelkarim couldn't help drawing near to Émile to speak, because he didn't want anyone else to overhear them, thus adding insult to injury, and so he softly whispered his words as though he were a ghost. The loan shark had pulled on his arm and dragged him into the shop, where he had revealed that Armand now belonged to him, that he'd bought him, and that he would only consider selling him back either today or tomorrow. He'd repeated the phrase 'today or tomorrow' many times; he'd then explained that if Abdelkarim's revered master wanted to purchase his brother back, he should hurry and bring money with him, lots of money, and that if he did so, he could have him back. 'What should I do with this?' Abdelkarim had explained quite a few times. 'Armand is worth a lot because your master wants him, and that's why I bought him, whereas others wouldn't have paid a cent for him.' The loan shark also said that the jewels had wound up decorating the beautiful Olghina's bosom. 'Your master can either bring them back to me, with interest, or else pay for them, thus owning a right to that beautiful bosom.' That's what he'd said.

The Maronite stood up and grabbed the boy once more. Abdelkarim was certain that he would be the first victim in this new tragedy, Semereth's tragedy having now come to an end. He thus entrusted his soul to God. However, he found himself back on the ground, all safe and sound, and saw that the master suddenly seemed self-assured once again.

'Go,' he said, 'and tell him I'll come tomorrow.' Then he walked to the back of the vast warehouse, right at the back of which lay his neatly ordered office, and gazed into a mirror. He dusted his tunic.

He would begin his visits by calling on Olghina.

IV

OLGHINA: It's all over. Because of Émile? I don't think so. He didn't tell me anything I didn't already know. Considering how mild-mannered he is, and his weakness for the fairer sex, he didn't even talk much. I didn't defend you, and perhaps this is what reined him in. Relinquishing the gifts I was given, which I returned once I discovered their dishonourable origins, was the price I paid not to be trampled by his speechifying. And I paid on the spot. Perhaps he was prepared to pay a reasonable price to see me cry, or see me fight tooth and nail to hang on to those jewels. If the first scenario had come to pass, he would have let me keep everything; while in the second, he would have pressed charges.

ARMAND: You'd be willing to give everything back, including me, so long as it meant you still got to play the belle of the ball. Our love was contingent on Émile's obliviousness. You wouldn't have had the courage to be caught on the wrong side of the matter in front of him: he's blackmailing you.

OLGHINA: You're wrong. What I'm wavering about is whether I really want to be yours, not whether I have the courage to do so. Émile's notions of respectability don't faze me. If you take his arguments apart, their gist is rather simple . . . He limits himself to dealing out sound advice: *don't spend money that doesn't belong to you; keep to your working hours and stay away from indolence, which is the Devil incarnate; be wary of your customers, but be prompt when the occasion demands it; be patient with debtors, especially because it's in your interest to do so, but base your patience on hard numbers, not sentiments; confide in your ledgers as you would with the law; exercise prudence with friendships, don't rush things, and remain reasonable; friendship is a pact of mutual assistance regulated by protective measures. Don't imitate others' manners, simply respect their customs. Discretion is as valuable as frugality. Always aid the weak, but only within your means. The goals one must strive for are commercial success, public esteem, a reputation as a generous man.* According to these tenets, one's personal values are a private matter. Which is to say mistakes only happen when they're made public, that mistakes don't really exist so long as they're kept secret, and that one must shield oneself against their financial consequences by ensuring others don't feel resentful – you didn't observe any of these rules. *Conduct yourself with dignity when dealing with powerful people: respect who's in charge, and keep your distance. Powerful people don't respect the rules, and thus an intimate relationship with them is always dangerous, because they'll use their influence to bestow favours on you, and sooner or later, they'll use that same power to plot your downfall.*

ARMAND: Why don't we talk about me instead of Émile? Now that's he got those damn presents back, will he still be able to intervene?

OLGHINA: He has no need to . . . not at this point, anyway. Émile's intuition is infallible, and he's already understood everything. He was right to take those gifts away, but he exaggerated their value. As for their trade value, since perhaps he considered selling them, I gave him quite a moderate estimate, in fact one that was wholly inapplicable. This is what disappointed him and made him rein in his speechifying.

ARMAND: Now you're the one who's prolonging his presence here with us. I know I was wrong to leave him an opening – and he didn't hesitate in exploiting it so he could sneak in his poisonous wisdom.

OLGHINA: I had a curious impression, which is the following: compared to Émile's respectability, all your somersaulting boils down to very little. You refuse his rules, but what do you offer in their stead? You speak to me of Paris, but you've never been able to get there. Cursing one's rotten fate isn't a mark of seriousness, it doesn't interest me at all, it's *demeaning* behaviour for a man! Why are you so determined to use European standards? I'll tell you this: in Italy, your qualities would be considered rather common. Your confused protestations are shared by many there, and

I have no sympathy for them. Perhaps you have ideas about a more evolved kind of man, and in comparison to you, Émile might seem rather limited and fastidious. But it's overwhelmingly clear that you can't avoid talking about him. Your brother humiliates you by reclaiming the gifts you gave to a woman, and the only reaction you're capable of is to declare your loyalty to that woman and ask her to keep loving you. I'm well aware you'd be willing to row with Émile: but you'd never be able to do without him.

ARMAND: So it's all fallen apart because of unpaid gifts. What a fragile castle we erected! So paying for those gifts out of love and risk counts for nothing then? You are like a loan shark!

OLGHINA: Your love! You're always generous with that, that's for sure. I would be far more impressed, for instance, with a show of willpower.

ARMAND: You're scolding me for not being like Émile.

OLGHINA: It's still to be determined whether you don't actually want to be like him. Émile keeps you under his thumb, and that's what inspires such resentment in you. But your rebelliousness only amounts to lip service. Your idle boasting grows apace with your incapacity to accomplish anything properly; the more you feel like you're sliding back, the more you rage against Émile and pretend to be more than you are.

ARMAND: All success means to you and Émile is to make money.

OLGHINA: It's not Émile's money that I admire, it's his industriousness, even if it's wholly devoted to making money. Doing so, he displays intelligence, patience, attention to detail, and willpower – it's the stuff he's made of, his character, his personality. But you refuse that industriousness, linger in ambiguity and adopt second-rate role paragons. Seeing as he's far more complex than he appears at first, his industriousness has great range. He's able to move in several directions, and even though he's not particularly erudite, by virtue of his intelligence and considerable experience, and aided furthermore by additional extraordinary faculties like intuition, he commands a prepossessing appearance and a gift for eloquence that is most remarkable.

ARMAND: I'm even forced to watch him triumph – and to hear these words out of your mouth, too! Your monologue is tantamount to crowning him the victor.

OLGHINA: I don't need you to explain Émile's defects, because I'm able to see them myself, and besides, Émile doesn't exactly conceal them. His nature allows him to calmly accept his limitations and the rules that go with them. Whereas you hide behind a smokescreen of chatter in order to pretend you're someone you're not. Whoever has allowed themselves to get mixed up in all of this seems to notice – and with increasing impatience – only one thing: the opportunity to escape. This incident over the little jewels you gave away as presents but didn't pay for was just the occasion I was waiting for. Thanks to Émile, I've been able to extricate myself from a sentimental scrape. At the same time that I returned those jewels, I was also relinquishing his brother.

ARMAND: You're just tired, that's all!

OLGHINA: If, in order to better understand the situation, you have to search for clues on the emotional palette, then yes, I *am* tired. In the initial fire of our rapport, being certain we belonged to a different world, we kicked this little colonial town aside. We imitated a Parisian couple, or repeated the encounter between the White Lady and the

Oriental Prince: we dabbled in provincial pastimes. We disdained bourgeois values. But is the devil that drives you really of a higher calibre? I appreciate drive and intelligence in a man. Opposing Émile's rational, harmonious world with nothing but emotional confusion seems a tad trifling to me. A man should be intelligent, tolerant *und erotisch.*

ARMAND: Just tell me you like money and book-keeping and let's get it over with.

OLGHINA: Émile isn't doing himself any favours subjecting himself to such a strain in order to keep away from you. His marble man to your straw man is highly respectable, even if a little funereal. I think he's more alive than first meets the eye. For all the paragons you hold and all the outcomes you seek, do you really have culture? Perhaps you do, but how mediocre it is! Instead, Émile tries to keep his ledgers in meticulous order – and succeeds.

ARMAND:You failed to notice that Émile wasn't being sincere. He's after my inheritance, but I'll never allow it.

OLGHINA: Your judgements don't really take any of us into account: even the threats that you make are promises you'll never keep.

ARMAND: Émile didn't give the jewels back to the loan shark. He bought them. He can't even fathom how one can be indifferent to objects, thereby rendering their exchange value absolutely worthless.

V

Émile decided to open a branch of his business in Tocra, a little port ninety kilometres to the east of Benghazi that was becoming increasingly important as a market place for the hinterland. He dispatched Armand to run it, and he welcomed his brother's decision with wordy but ineffectual wrath, sincere in its desperation and full of self-pity. Paris now seemed even further away, and his destiny was leading him in the opposite direction. He accused Émile of wanting to get rid of him: he was sending him to that dangerous outpost, secretly hoping he'd never see him again. Émile replied that since this was the decision he had come to, and that it was in the best interests of the business, that was the way it had to be. Thus, he told Armand to stop speaking like a drunk.

Armand left, slightly taken aback by the regret he felt at leaving that wretched little city to which he'd been confined.

One evening Olghina and Doctor Pietra went downstairs, having been invited by Émile. Armand's room had been transformed into a salon – proof that his estrangement was destined to last.

Olghina had dressed with care. She made her own dresses. As soon as she'd entered the flat, Abdelkarim fled into the courtyard, marvel etched on his face. 'Look at me, Abdelkarim!' Olghina exclaimed as she stepped outside, her black dress engulfing the narrow patio.

Chapter 3

I

The rebel camp at Benina was destroyed on 13 April. The doors to the hinterland had been thrown open, and the army flooded through them. Tolmeta had been besieged by sea, which had resulted in a victorious landing. The other cities of the ancient Pentapolis – Cyrene, Apollonia and Tocra – had also fallen. Even the south had surrendered, and Ajdabiya was in the hands of the invaders. But what did owning these places amount to? The Italians' real strongholds were nothing but warships adrift on a vast, unfaithful sea. They could sail in any direction, but the darkness would descend on them thicker than ever once they had cut through it.

After the door at Benina had been opened, the country's roads were nominally free. Death, theft and violence ran along them in all directions. But commerce was an adventurous knight, impervious to intimidation. He too ran along those roads, the highways of death, stalked by thieves and on intimate terms with violence. Freight would cross the mountains and deserts like ships on a sea infested with pirates and battered by storms.

From his office, Émile held the reins tightly in his hands. His bookkeeping remained accurate and he routinely updated it. One could gaze at the business landscape through the ledger's pages as though from a privileged vantage point. Émile found the order in which reality was laid out, having been meticulously transformed into numbers, was soothing. He was the one who handled Semereth Effendi's money now. It had conferred him a place of pride amongst the city's merchants. But Émile's silent partners always received conscientious accounts. Hajji Semereth was barely able to understand the figures Émile quoted him. When those sheets of paper found their way to the depths of the deserted wildernesses where the Hajji now lived, the urban language of commerce was painfully impenetrable. The Hajji admired the papers as though they were paintings: mysterious scribbling where a knowledgeable man had imprisoned reality.

The Maronite handed Abdelkarim an envelope and a map, directing him to a small town in the interior where he would meet Abubaker: it would be the old man's duty to accompany him to Hajji Semereth. This was the first time he had employed Abdelkarim in this manner. Up until then, Abubaker had been the one to negotiate those web-like roads: travel bans didn't apply to that old man, who was as secretive as a stone, and could crumble or hold steady as the occasion demanded.

Abdelkarim had always been afraid of Abubaker. But the fear that Hajji Semereth inspired was different, deeper, and instead of rebelling against that, his willpower fastened itself firmly to him, like a shadowy accomplice. If Abdelkarim had escaped the shipwreck of the Hajji's household, it was because the Hajji had entrusted him to the young Maronite, the same person he'd handed over his wealth to. Abdelkarim had never forgotten the moment when, having been torn from a world in which he'd thought the story of his life would be written, he found himself locked in the bright orbit of a new man: the Maronite had come from the sea and his nature had retained some of that fluidity.

The thought of appearing in front of that giant again was making Abdelkarim highly anxious. No matter how hard he tried, he couldn't chase away the shadow that lingered between them like a ghost. Ferdinando was the one casting the shadow, and everything perished once swallowed by the Hajji's silence. Abdelkarim wanted to throw himself at the giant's feet and hug his beloved Ferdinando's shadow: but it always flitted away, and the giant's feet were made of stone.

In the silence of the desert plains, Abdelkarim felt nostalgic for his master's presence, a man who was afflicted by an unruly brother, but was still very disciplined himself, and who adopted a conciliatory attitude towards life. Abdelkarim already wanted to start on his return journey, and once past the difficult night that trip necessitated, and steering his daydreaming in the opposite direction, he tried to picture himself entering the shop and seeing the satisfaction on his master's face, and the kindness he would show him.

In the meantime he continued walking through the boundless plain, Semereth's form growing frighteningly before his eyes. The long road to the uplands belonged to him. The further he walked, the more detached Abdelkarim felt from everything else. The giant had become synonymous with that vast country: King, kingdom and road had fused into one.

In order to guarantee his safe passage, he had been given the Maronite's papers; he would have to rely on his shrewdness to outsmart the Italian army, but the Maronite's papers would help him overcome those invisible gates and their ferocious guardians. Although he was familiar with that country and he knew its master, something had changed inside him: he no longer belonged to the giant, to that tragic, powerful lord of darkness – instead he was now owned by a merchant, a young man who confidently steered his ship through the boundless sea.

To reassure himself, Abdelkarim patted the Maronite's papers hidden inside his wide white belt.

Until he'd accomplished his mission and delivered his message, Abdelkarim would only encounter obstacles he knew how to avoid: the nets that the occupying army had laid out all over the country, through which the natives of the feudal countryside walked as though they were an open door. And once Semereth Effendi had handed him a reply, Abdelkarim would start on the same journey, just in the opposite direction, once more armed with a talisman. He was the hand that relayed notes back and forth between the two friends, and so long as he was in their service, he would be as safe as a jinn.

Abdulkarim found Abubaker in the town he'd been directed to, deep in the verdant uplands of Barca. The old man immediately took possession of the papers and Abdelkarim feared he would be left there awaiting a reply, or even sent back empty-handed. But it was an unfounded worry. Sure enough, he followed Abubaker to the location where they would find Semereth Effendi. The journey took two days, during which time Abubaker didn't ask him a single question.

They camped in the middle of a wood. Abdelkarim only noticed Semereth Effendi's arrival a moment before he appeared in front of him. He stood up abruptly, but having drawn near to kiss his hand, he froze, intimidated. Semereth Effendi approached until he stood in front of him, and then stopped. He wasn't looking at him, but something was clearly bothering him, and stopped him from proceeding further.

Semereth Effendi saw a wall before him, and for a moment that giant felt as though he had once more taken a wrong turn. Even so, he was only faced with Abdelkarim's shadow, which was as thin as a sheet. Semereth Effendi remained motionless. It was only when the frightened Abdelkarim took a step back, and his shadow flitted away and cleared the path, that the Hajji continued on his way, without even turning to greet him or acknowledge that he'd registered his presence. He had no intention of stepping over that shadow, whose shape recalled Ferdinando.

Abubaker later came to tell him he'd been summoned by the Hajji.

Abdelkarim entered the dimly lamp-lit tent. Semereth Effendi gave him a friendly smile. The young man grasped his enormous hand and kissed it. He then kept his eyes on the floor while standing in front of the Hajji, who was seated on a straw mat.

Semereth Effendi asked him about Émile Chébas, whether he was in good health, if he'd had any difficulties with the Italian authorities, if he still felt at ease in Benghazi, and then invoked the heavens to bless him and praised him highly. He told Abdelkarim that he was very pleased to have found him such a good master. Having said that, he motioned him to come closer. Smiling, he asked him if he was happy with his new master, but Abdelkarim didn't dare answer.

Hajji Semereth spoke for a moment longer, then

stopped. The tent swelled with shadows and the Hajji waved his hand, as though shooing them away. Order only returned to the tent after a long silence, at which point the Hajji held out a sheet of paper to Abdelkarim, who likewise held out his hand and made the paper disappear in the blink of an eye. He then took hold of the Hajji's hand again and kissed it. Observing the boy's head, Semereth Effendi was astonished by how small it was.

He plunged a hand into his pocket, produced a coin, and held it out to Abdelkarim. The boy took it and shamefully put it away.

Abdelkarim saw Hajji Semereth was no longer concerned with him. He had seen Semereth Effendi engrossed in his own thoughts many times before. He turned and scampered off.

It wasn't until he reached Benghazi three days later that Abdelkarim stopped living in fear that the Hajji – who, having regretted his generosity, had come to lead him, as he'd done with Zulfa and Ferdinando, through the labyrinthine streets towards death – was right behind him.

Chapter 4

I

Abdelkarim was very surprised to find the shop closed at that time of day, when the whole market was still lively, but didn't want to ask around and draw attention to the fact he'd been absent from the city. What had happened to the master?

He reached the house, where he hoped to find the master, but nobody answered the door. He knocked at the neighbours' house; he would jump off their balcony and into the master's.

But as he was climbing down a rope into the courtyard, passing in front of Olghina's windows, he stumbled upon a scene, and was most certainly – although he nearly let go of the rope to drop down – seen himself. The master was lying in bed with the beautiful Olghina.

As soon as he'd reached the ground, he scurried off into the corridor, but was already trapped. Not long afterwards he heard someone knocking at the door, but he didn't dare answer. He went to hide in the courtyard.

Having come downstairs, it was the Maronite who

opened the door, and he left with the newcomer: a merchant whose voice Abdelkarim had immediately recognised. But the master shut the door again, and took care to lock it.

Abdelkarim had warily dodged many dangers up in the mountains: now he was sorry he hadn't fallen victim to one of them. It would be better to die purposelessly than for an actual reason. The fact he'd been an involuntary spectator was irrelevant: he wouldn't be punished because he had tried to spy on them, but purely because he'd seen. His secretiveness wouldn't mitigate the offence he had caused his master. Promises and oaths would be useless. Like Semereth Effendi, the master would be both victim and judge. But there was no hope that the aggrieved party would pretend to be guilty out of pity.

Why had the Venetian woman encouraged the affair between Zulfa and Ferdinando? The other wives had never aroused her jealousy. When the child bride had been enthroned as the favourite of the house, the Venetian woman had bided her time and created the opportunity to lure her down the path to Semereth Effendi's dark wrath, or better yet, into the doomed prison of justice. She was a cunning woman and knew she'd have to pay the price. The child bride would drag an extensive retinue of victims with her into death, which Semereth would sacrifice to placate his wounded naïvety. The Venetian woman hadn't fled the house on the day of reckoning, but had instead sought refuge in the room where Semereth Effendi dwelled alone, and that was where she had met her end.

In turn, Abdelkarim could flee into the limitless country before the master returned. The rope was still dangling from the terrace in the courtyard, meaning he could extricate himself from Émile's wrath. But he wanted to stay. He'd vaguely suspected a liaison between the master and the beautiful neighbour, but would never have dared spy on them. However, seeing them lying entwined hadn't been a coincidence. That vision had appeared before his eyes, as though magically conjured to exclude that option. His gaze had torn them apart.

When he had been told of Armand's arrival, Abdelkarim had feared the presence of a third person would separate him from his master. Instead, it was Olghina who turned out to be that third person, and not the vain, blameworthy boy. The scene Abdelkarim had stumbled on while sliding down that rope couldn't mean anything else. His gaze, like an evil spell being cast, had the same impact on that affair as the intrigue which coloured Semereth Effendi's parable. So long as Abdelkarim was alive, the master would be imprisoned by the sight of Abdelkarim holding on to the memory of him intertwined with the beautiful Olghina. Thus, if the master's pity removed the threat of death, it would be on the condition that he remain a prisoner of his servant's memory: as unacceptable to him as it was for the Hajji to relinquish his wife to Ferdinando. The order of things always prevailed on compassion, and the kind master would have to sacrifice the witness. The beautiful Olghina would inevitably make that request, since Abdelkarim's gaze had desecrated her white nakedness.

The Maronite returned home an hour later. The wrath caused by the sudden apparition in the window had vanished, as when the sky seems to presage a storm, but then calms down and becomes sunny again. Émile had thought about beating Abdelkarim and chasing him out of the house: the image of the master's life which he'd stolen couldn't be considered a debt, but instead had to be transmuted into a crime, and punished accordingly.

But being forced to leave with the merchant – whom he had not wanted to receive in the house where he felt so ill at ease – had allowed enough time to pass for leniency to gain the upper hand, and once he'd opened the door on his return, he realised he'd come back from a different direction. It was a tangle of thoughts, images and desires, which had now split into two opposing armies under the flags of wrath on one side, and leniency on the other.

Abdelkarim had sought refuge at the far end of the courtyard. The Maronite seemed to be guided by desires that had been kept concealed during his usual daily walk. The boy's sudden appearance in the window had derailed the natural order of things, and the old rules now seemed obsolete. The boy was helpless. Having gone into his room, the merchant called him in and asked him to hand over the document the Hajji had given him. It had been folded twice. The Maronite read it. He then asked Abdelkarim a few questions about his trip, which the boy was barely able to answer. These were only delays.

At that moment, there was nobody who could spy on that scene, no window which someone might carelessly pass by. The isolation bound them tightly together, like two threads in a piece of string.

BOOK III

CHAPTER 1

I

Mikhail Chébas woke up early. He was a man who always showed off his industriousness. Few could claim to be less inclined to hypocrisy and deceit, but he always exaggerated everything, and was incapable of looking on a situation with indifference and detachment. His eye was always an inch away from reality, blowing everything monstrously out of proportion. His ideas were simple, so his efforts remained stifled. There was a constant imbalance between his modest goals and the exertions he employed to achieve them. His goodwill, scrupulousness and devotion – to family and business, which were one and the same as far as he was concerned and also used up all the time one had 'down there' – were so extreme that they even made his nephew Émile Chébas, the demanding head of the company, feel ill at ease. As for strangers, they found Mikhail's tendency to exaggerate everything highly annoying.

Why should Émile look elsewhere – in other words outside the family circle and the interests of the business – to find friendship and patronage? Mikhail wondered whether Émile wanted to run away as much as he wanted to grow, as though legacies and traditions were an impediment, and as if man could possibly break through the limited confines of his destiny.

Mikhail was baffled by his nephew's indifference to the religion of the people he dealt with: not only with regards to his customers – protecting, in turn, his business – but also with others, the people he met at cafés, or entertained in his house, or paid visits to. He was also baffled by how effortlessly Émile could strike up a rapport with the Italian officers. He didn't simply treat them with respect because they represented the local authorities, he welcomed them cordially, even sought them out. Were these relationships as important to him as his family ties? Did they serve a purpose, or was he simply mistaking them for customers? How could anyone manage affairs that weren't strictly useful or dictated by necessity, and what rules were these affairs subject to?

Mikhail had opened a branch of the business in El-Hania, the little port city in the east that seemed to be growing in importance. The tribes from the interior of the country would favour that market over Benghazi. Mikhail had helped build the spacious warehouse in the clearing where the authorities had decided the new market would be erected, making the doors and windows with his own hands. The warehouse, which had two entrances, faced true north, towards the sea.

Mikhail was always the first to show up for work and he inevitably welcomed his helpers with reproaches for being late, dismissing them with more reproaches for the little they'd done or because they'd left work early, whereas he would have gone on longer. These anti-ceremonies were the bookends to the working day, gloomy prayers that extended a veil of melancholy over the branch of the business he'd been entrusted with. He was never satisfied with anything they did, because all that was good could only concern either his family or the business. He always took part in whatever job needed to be done, even the humblest, but never addressed his subordinates with a kind word, and he could never abide hearing them gossip. It was as though he were the watchman of a tiny penal colony. He ate frugal meals, was highly reserved and stingy even with himself, exhibiting a certain hatred towards commodities, even though his business relied on them.

The letters he wrote to his nephew always began with interminable declarations of fondness, cosseting him like a child: *My dearest, beloved nephew, I kiss your eyes . . .* He always asked Émile if he'd received news from distant relatives, and begged him not to withhold any information. He would appear to lose his patience when Émile told him that no mishaps had happened, and was plagued by doubts that tragedies had in fact occurred, but that nobody wanted to tell him. He would complain about feeling lonely because he was so far removed from his beloved nephew, and then give brief, incomplete accounts of how the business was going, complaining about customers and employees: one lot were parasites, while the others were freeloaders, all of them damned swindlers. He never specified the current quotes for goods, or market trends, or the safety of shipping routes, or expressed an opinion on the political climate and its fatal consequences for trade. The only injections of feeling into his droning soliloquy came at its opening and then at its conclusion; once he reached that end point he would once again affirm his affection for his nephew and beg him to write longer letters, since his was the only voice that broke though that gloomy silence, the only ray of light that pierced the darkness, the only warmth that put his lonely heart at ease.

Losing his patience, Émile would reply, hurrying through the typical pleasantries employed at the time, and would ask his uncle to send him more detailed reports. When said reply finally arrived, Mikhail's words were always imbued with drama, as though something sacred were on the verge of breaking. He would say that he'd dedicated his entire day to work, invoking God to testify to his scrupulousness; he would swear oaths on the lives of his three distant daughters, saying destiny might prevent him from ever seeing them again, that what he was saying was true, and that he – meaning Émile – was more dear to him than those daughters, and that he was more like a beloved brother. Did these requests for financial details mean Émile didn't trust him? Everything was in danger: the family, the business. Then, suddenly growing sparing with words, he would conclude on a note of bitter resentment, saying that if Émile wanted to replace him, he should do so immediately, since Mikhail had the business's best interests at heart – but that if so, he wanted to be told clearly.

When he received this sort of letter, Émile would read it, holding it at an oblique angle, and then shake his head as he folded the sheet and filed it in the folder pertaining to the branch's business, resigning himself to drafting a reply on purely laudatory lines, filled with affectionate statements. He would then try to guess the sales trajectory via the spyhole afforded him by the numbers of returns. He decided that he would pay the branch a visit at the end of November. He sent news to his uncle of his forthcoming arrival, trying to specify the exact date, despite the fact that communication lines were unsafe and one should expect any sort of surprise along the way. On the appointed day he saddled his horse and, followed by Abdelkarim, a guide and a convoy of ten camels, he headed into the interior of the country for the first time.

II

'But dear uncle, it wasn't such a bad trip,' Émile muttered, already irritated. Mikhail's welcome had been suffocating. 'We left Benghazi five days ago and we only arrived today – just like I'd warned you.'

'You don't understand the dangers you have just exposed yourself to. The trip could have ended very differently.'

'Let us offer our grateful prayers to God and exalt him, then speak about it no more. In a war like this, merchants must be as brave as soldiers: otherwise they'll grow poor and vanish. You'll not catch me either hypnotised or held to ransom by thoughts of danger, let alone see me holed up in the house, waiting for the clouds to clear.'

'Truth be told, I don't stay holed up at home either,' his uncle replied bitterly.

'Did I insinuate that? You just don't seem to take into account that I too might run some risks.'

'The family couldn't cope without you. It has pinned its hopes on your ever since you were a boy, and it has waited patiently all along. I hate this village you sent me to. But because it was in the company's interests, I came here without protests and shall stay as long as you need me to. I think I'm also on a mission to represent the business in the most ungrateful of places and thus spare you the task.

I couldn't bear to see you exposed to all these dangers: but have I become useless? Feel free to tell me! You must always remember what the family expects from you, and thus the duties you have towards it, which are proportional to the patience it's had and the hopes it has placed in you.'

'Your confidence in me is like a noose around my neck. You repeatedly tell me that I am essential to the family, that these days the family only stays afloat because of me and the work that I do. It's like you're robbing me of my individual destiny, that I owe my presence on Earth to the role that has been assigned to me in this group, to which I must subordinate all my choices, and that all the paths I've taken must necessarily lead to where the family's interests are best served. In fact, I have the impression they're trying to erect specific confines around my destiny.'

'Don't mock our family bonds in my presence. The paths you must travel don't need much imagination or ideas: they've already been plotted out, by the family's interests and emotions on the one hand, and by religion, which is all-pervasive, on the other. You must work within these schemes, and employ all the intelligence, willpower, strength and constancy that you can muster. You must fulfil a destiny that has already been plotted out for you, and which also belonged to our ancestors. There is room for personal values and individuality along that path, so long as you reach its end. Nobody expects anything original from you, aside from achieving the goals your qualities have led us to believe you can attain. If you choose another path, no matter where it leads you, the family will think of you as lost to them. You can only play out this parable by marrying well. Indeed, the family *demands* it. Remaining a bachelor past a certain age just isn't appropriate. Am I boring you? Are we too limited when compared to your intelligence and experience? Despite this being the first time we've seen each other in nine months, you're already growing intolerant. The prospect of spending an evening with me seems to disappoint you, as though your trip here had been so much more alluring.'

'I only want to chat with the other merchants: this is the liveliest market in the province, the only truly free one in the uplands. I'm interested in the swaying of prices, not the swaying of girls' bodies. You force me to say unpleasant things, but one cannot manage a business in such an adventurous setting if one doesn't keep informed about market trends on a daily basis. Or am I wrong?'

'If you need information about the market, I can give it to you myself, there's no need for you to turn to strangers, who have a thousand reasons to try and trick you.'

'But I kept asking you for your opinion . . . '

'And didn't I give it to you?'

'You certainly doled it out. You wrote more about the family than the market. Besides, I have the right to see things with my own eyes and hear them with my own ears. What would be the point of coming here if all I did was listen to what you'd already told me in your letters?'

'So you mean to say I'm useless. If the owner doesn't take any interest in the person who's been running his branch for nine months, it means that this person is unfit for the job. I'd already understood the situation from the tone of your letters.'

'But even if we belong to the same family and work for the same business, it doesn't mean we're a single organism, we're still two distinct people, each one endowed with a brain, eyes and ears. I can't stay shut inside a room with my eyes closed, while you stay by the window and tell me what's happening in the street. You can't seek to replace my senses, I need – and have a right – to look out of the window myself. And if there's two pairs of eyes instead of one at the window, it doesn't necessarily mean it's a monster.'

'But it's pointless to have two pairs of eyes.'

'What's the point of discussing this further? Dear Uncle, you need to get used to seeing me talk to other people, you need to put up with my curiosity for the rest of the world, and you need to acknowledge my refusal to keep to the confines of the role that the family has allotted me, in other words, you must accept my right to an individual destiny and thus that I have objectives that lie outside the family remit – even if this amounts to a waste of time.'

'Outside the family remit – this means you're forsaking your origins.'

'I wouldn't dream of it. I have the greatest respect for our customs, our language, and our religion, in fact for our entire way of being in the world, and I love our family deeply. But Uncle, our family and the Maronite community aren't an island unto themselves. As a community, as a family, as individuals, we'll always need to come into contact with others, even occasionally to clash with them.'

'Nobody's forbidding you from being in contact with the outside world. We're not as stupid as you think. But as a member of a group, the door of your house shall be open only to those who belong to that group or the wider community. Whoever has another religion or belongs to another group should never set foot in your house.'

'So this means you should be my only source of information on market trends, and if anyone else gives me some information it will be useless?'

'That you feel spending an evening with me would be

a waste of time has nothing to do with your wanting information about the market – what you're really seeking is human contact outside the family.'

'But Uncle, is that a sin?'

'We've always considered this a worrying and negative indicator. What value do you think you'll extract from forming bonds with outsiders? You'll only find traps.'

'Uncle, maybe you haven't realised that I'm twenty-six years old. Everything you said may have been valid ten years ago; these are the teachings families instil in their young ones. They're like a wall we erect between boys and the outside world in order to protect them until they've grown up, like when a farmer ties a plant to a stick of wood to keep it straight until it's strong enough to stand alone. But when that boy becomes a man, one should let him go, like when those plants are allowed to stand on their own; they follow their own patterns of development while still being a part of the community, in the case of man – or part of a species, in the case of plant.'

'Family *is* the community, and it protects its laws and values. Don't make the mistake of thinking – or believing, or pretending – that you can move freely about in this foreign land as though it belonged to you or your people, or of thinking you can overcome their different religion and customs. They are confines that one should respect. To do otherwise would mean opposing the way of the world. Why are you smiling now? Not respecting your elders is to break one of our community's rules.'

'Rest assured, it's a rule that can be found in many other communities, and I honour it. If I'm smiling it's because I was thinking about the strange role I've been playing in the family: what you've been telling me is more or less what I've been telling that good-for-nothing Armand, and now here you are saying the same to me, as though you held the same opinion of me that I do of him. So I'm playing both roles at the same time. I play the tutor with Armand, and the unruly boy with you. The principles I believe in when I speak to Armand seem exaggerated when I speak to you. The teachings espoused by families and communities are to keep adventurous youths like Armand from taking the wrong path. That's when those rules become clear and incontrovertible. This may be presumptuous, Uncle, but I don't think I really deserve your admonishments!'

'You don't deserve them because of what you do, you know all too well that you're on the right path. You deserve them because of your pride. Those rules are there to keep you heading in the right direction, and perhaps circumscribe your ambitions. As for Armand, I don't want to hear you talking about your brother like that. It's as if your only goal were to distinguish yourself from him and make your disdain of him known to all. If you seek the company of strangers, like Muslim merchants or Italian officers, it means there are other dangers lurking in your head that are far worse than the fusillades of the Italians or the rebels, and far worse than Armand's mistakes and escapades. Your intentions are what worry me.'

'Thus, when I learn the current price of rice, I should just get up and leave, completely disregarding the customs of civilised life?'

'Isn't that what I do?'

'And if I couldn't abide by these rules? What if my curiosity proved too great?'

'If I'd lost all hope, I would've already got up and left, going back to what you call a 'group,' which you were the first to leave – then followed by me – with the intention of going back to help raise its social status. If that were the case, I would go back alone and announce that Émile had been lost in a shipwreck. You didn't come all the way here with the sole purpose of adding to the family's riches – you simply fled the family's principles and its time-hallowed traditions. You only wanted to free yourself, to go off on a soul-searching adventure that is fatally destined to contradict our values and religion. If this is the case, then I don't even want to know what your intentions are because I could never abide by them, and I'll never be your accomplice.'

'Don't you think you're exaggerating, Uncle? As they say, I have a good head on my shoulders.'

'But our family knows only one way to *keep* a good head on one's shoulders.'

'Tomorrow, at first light, even our thoughts will have grown clearer. We'll have plenty of work to do, and maybe we'll even find ease and happiness in the decisions we make and the conversations we have.'

'Our family is our centre of gravity, and if you choose to ignore that, every move you make will be a blunder.'

'Uncle, I'm afraid you're a little deluded. Perhaps you see me going down new paths that are different, adventurous and completely different to the ones you'd foreseen. But that doesn't mean I can't still be a good son to our family, nor that I can't still be a good Christian.'

III

The next day, the young Maronite woke up early, but Mikhail was ready and waiting for him already. Mikhail gently scolded him for waking up so early: 'There was no need for that.' Émile didn't pay him any heed. He picked up the branch's ledgers and began studying them. He wanted to know more about each customer before going to meet them. He didn't need to make notes, and was able to memorise everything simply by scanning his eyes across it.

His uncle felt ill at ease, and was unable to conceal his irritation and embarrassment. His nephew had opened up the ledgers without asking him; in fact, he seemed to have forgotten Mikhail was even in the room, and wasn't sharing his thoughts and reactions with him. 'Is something wrong?' he asked in that bitter tone his nephew found particularly bothersome. But Émile was adrift in a sea of numbers and was so distant – or at least pretended to be – that he didn't answer. He was adding, subtracting, multiplying and dividing at an extraordinary speed, and even though he was standing right behind him, Mikhail was unable to fathom what sums he was working on. The sheer multitude of numbers was being worked out so rapidly that the Maronite eventually slowed down and lingered over three or four sums, whose origins Mikhail was at a loss to explain. 'So?' he asked with a hint of trepidation in his voice. His nephew was black-mailing him with the science of accounting.

'As far as I'm concerned,' Émile said as he stood, slipping the sheet into his pocket, 'being excessively prudent is a mistake, it won't pay off. We must extend more credit to established merchants. Then we can double sales without running more risks. Whereas, from what I can tell, we're treating all customers in the same way – stingily. The credit we're giving them is piddly. So long as this is the case, we won't achieve much.'

'You want to throw your money away.'

Refusing to answer, Émile left, with Mikhail in tow. But instead of heading into this or that shop, he contented himself with giving the market a look and then headed straight for the sea. Mikhail would point out a customer's shop and remind Émile of its name, but he seemed distracted and didn't reply. His uncle couldn't help asking: 'Why are you avoiding them now, when you were so impatient to see them yesterday? Have you come all this way just to breathe a little air and look at the sea?'

'The location is magical, those naked hills so close to the beach, the little port, the sea, a beautiful blue sky: it's a simple, temperate landscape and the little fort over there looks like an ancient building, a relic of a forgotten civilisation.'

'I can't stand it when you make fun of me. You should remember that even though you're the owner, I'm still your uncle.'

'And so, as the owner,' Émile retorted, 'I'm telling you that for the time being, all I need to do is show myself, and that I don't intend to rush into anyone's shop, nor make any inspections or solicit orders: the merchandise can wait. People will come to me. We'll drink the ritual cup of coffee, chat about this or that, and then in the end even talk a little business.'

'Do we have to keep strolling for much longer? You're just indulging your own vanity. Oh, Émile! You can't content yourself with simply making money, having your family love you and God's merciful forgiveness. No, instead you chase what's frivolous: the admiration of others. The prestige you seek might initially advance the business's interests, but then it will inevitably sink into ruin when those interests become secondary to your social standing. The difference between you and those Italian officers who have come here in search of glory is getting smaller and smaller – one day you too will wind up in a uniform: you'll become a soldier of the devil's army.'

'As far as you're concerned, a good man is someone who locks himself up in a storage room in the dark, while anyone who wants to go for a stroll in the fresh air must have lost his path. In any case, cheer up, the stroll is over. I want to see how the little port functions. I'm convinced the political situation will soon deteriorate, the hinterland will become ungovernable and this little market's importance will continue to grow, meaning we'll have to ship goods to it via sea, just as though it were an island.'

'If it becomes isolated, there won't be any need for that.'

'You're wrong. The merchandise will be exposed to too many risks if you try to cross the interior, where the locals are fighting against the conquerors' advances. But any goods sold here will be easily transported in and out, even if they have to pass through barbed wire. Cut off from the rest of the country, and in open revolt, the rebels in the interior will have to replenish their supplies somewhere.'

IV

The customers wanted news from Benghazi. The Maronite cautiously answered their questions. He knew there was a flourishing mob of informers.

But Émile wasn't embarrassed at all. He was uniquely gifted in making every conversation both vague and banal, to the point that he could easily confuse any police informer. Having sensed a trap, Émile would skilfully evade it and, like an experienced juggler, would bring the question of European powers into play, talking about the contrasts between them and the glories of the Islamic golden age, and using stories and characters from ancient fables to play on the dichotomies of life: glories and farces, violence and tenderness, the familiar and the barbaric, tolerance and fraud – all of which lent themselves to various interpretations and were easily inter-changeable. Like a spectator at a theatre, the police informer would find himself imprisoned in a labyrinth. Émile would simplify everything as though telling a children's story and yet simultaneously paint a wide panorama. Although he wasn't a learned man, he had a gift for conciliating disparate elements: he would take ancient facts and refashion them into a breezy story. His mere presence allowed the distance between the past and the present to fade before his dazzled audience's very eyes. Like a priest, he would forge a connection between the past and the occult. Although his sermons were brief, their ramifications were all-embracing – like when water flows smoothly along a rugged slope.

Mikhail was proud of his nephew's talents, mistaking his hackneyed stories for sophisticated erudition. Indeed, anything that came rolling off his nephew's silver tongue seemed new and extraordinary, even if Mikhail had heard it all before. Nevertheless, he completely failed to spot the links between Émile's soliloquies and his interests. The owner of the business was extremely demanding, but then wasted whole hours telling vague tales, as though he were a street preacher or a wandering storyteller. Mikhail was green with jealousy.

'Perhaps we could devote a little time to business?' he asked, without even realising that the words had slipped out of his mouth.

Émile broke into a liberating laugh, mocked his uncle's cupidity in front of the customers, and said he was compelled to heed his uncle's commands, briefly asking the crowd about how the market was doing and showing them the merchandise he'd brought. He then extended credit to various merchants, although hesitantly, and people began to flock in. Sitting at his desk, Émile would note down sum after sum, while Mikhail and Abdelkarim looked after the merchants – consigning Alexander the Great, paganism, the Great Wall of China, some quotes from a well-known classic, the marvellous, unstoppable progress of science, and other topics back to the museum of history they had briefly been pulled out of by that talented man, to the sheer delight of the assembled crowd.

An old man who'd greeted the Maronite particularly warmly – and whose visit he couldn't understand, as he hadn't shown any interest in the merchandise but had nonetheless praised it far too extravagantly – was the last to stay behind. He then greeted the Maronite again, employing various ceremonial formulas, invoking the blessings of Heaven to rain down on his head. Finally, he revealed he was Abdelkarim's maternal uncle, a fact seemingly confirmed by Abdelkarim's sudden escape from the shop. The Maronite replied courteously, despite the effort it cost him. The man had a request in mind, and it would almost certainly involve money.

Instead, when Abdelkarim's uncle finally revealed the purpose behind his visit, he said he'd wanted to take advantage of the fact Abdelkarim had travelled there with his master to give the young man, who was now sixteen years old, a wife. The marriage contract would be signed that very day and the young bride led to her lawful husband that Thursday.

The Maronite appeared astonished and mumbled a confused speech. While on other occasions stories from the museum of history had proved useful in extricating himself from undue hassle, both this and any other stalling tactic now seemed impractical. His theatre of operations had been dramatically reduced. Realising the man hadn't come to ask for his opinion, Émile immediately cut his speech short and said all was going well. The man renewed his invitation that Émile take part in the marriage ceremony, when the contract would be signed. The Maronite begged the uncle to forgive him: he had just arrived, and was forced to attend to his business.

Then, unexpectedly, just as his guest had stood up, Émile announced he would gladly attend the party given by the groom's friends on the wedding night: 'I want to acquaint myself with your traditions,' he said.

V

Entering the crumbling room where the friends had gathered to celebrate the groom, the Maronite's expert eye was struck by the carpet the party was taking place on. Although it was worn and dirty, one could still spot the shadow of an intricate design: articulate shapes in dialogue with one another.

The young men were embarrassed by the Maronite's presence. Émile talked with the people next to him without trying to imitate anyone. He knew that once a foreign guest found himself in the midst of an archaic culture, he all too easily succumbed to a puerile desire to jettison his long years of education and ape the manners and customs that once belonged to his ancestors, but which had been forgotten since time immemorial – while more vulgar guests would instead try to show off how different they were. Émile soon realised that all eyes were fixed upon him, and he perceived how foreign he was to the scene, but he neither tried to emphasise that nor conceal it. A melancholy shadow swept through his soul: *privilege always entails exclusion*, he thought. Taking part in an old, compelling world is always accompanied by a loss.

Abdelkarim was wearing the new clothes Émile had given him as a present. His breeches were cut of blue cloth, and were tight at the ankles, but wide from the hips down, like a skirt. The white shirt was untucked and the purple waistcoat was decorated with intricate embroidery.

The Maronite understood he weighed on the groom like a dark cloud.

Abdelkarim was exhibiting a sort of duplicity: on the one hand, he was Émile's servant, and was even wearing the clothes his master had given him, yet on the other he belonged to a society alien to Émile. For the first time, Abdelkarim had been pulled away from the business and his master and reappeared in a context wholly his own. That parrot he'd kept locked in a cage had now flown away, leaving Émile stranded in a wood.

Stranded? He asked himself in bemused irony. *Let's not exaggerate!*

Why talk about punishment? Perhaps because Abdelkarim's community was like an earthly paradise? Émile wouldn't have put up with the company of those peasants for more than a night anyway. What did his presence there mean? The distance created by his being there, and by his awareness of his foreignness, was obvious enough. Did the significance of the ceremony lie in that tension? A spectre entered the scene. It was Semereth Effendi, accompanied by the retinue of victims who had fallen in his wake, and

the unbridgeable distances he'd tried to cross. The youthful-
ness and self-assurance Émile nursed in his spirit like a gift,
and which made him so different from Hajji Semereth,
vanished in an instant. He was traversing a dark hour in his
destiny. Just as when the Hajji had found his frightened wife
in the bridal chamber and filled the room with his futile
presence, Émile was now vainly trying to extend a hand
and catch that colourful parrot as it fluttered above his head.

They're taking Abdelkarim away from me! But that wasn't
even true. Abdelkarim would remain in his service. The
young Maronite was impatient. He would gladly have moved
the hands on the clock and made the days roll by so as to
find himself back in Benghazi in his shop, restored to being
the master of a caged parrot. Nevertheless, once he was back
there, he would no longer notice Abdelkarim's presence
anyway.

The only musical instrument the guests had was a
tambourine. A young man was engrossed in playing it,
snuggled up in the corner next to Abdelkarim.

There were moments in the Maronite's life when everything he'd ever accomplished or owned flashed before his
eyes. There were also other moments when the knowledge
of what he no longer was, or what he wouldn't be able to
accomplish, or would never – or not any more – be able
to be, what he was losing, or had owned and then lost,
began to take on a painful clarity. His conciliatory attitude,
which gave him a tranquil outlook on life, also concealed
a hope that the contradictions inside him could linger
undisturbed instead of being allowed to stifle him, meaning
he could thus live out his life without ever needing to
reconcile them. Émile's reservedness wasn't based on fear
or denial, nor was it even a choice – quite the contrary, it

was forged by his efforts to keep part of his life in a shadowy zone, an area where numerous, and contradicting, possibilities could co-exist.

Could Uncle Mikhail be right? he asked himself in ironic solemnity. *Am I too ambitious?* There was nothing Émile had ever been shown which he would allow himself to be excluded from. *Is that true?* In the midst of that gathering, Émile seemed to have decided to gain some clarity on the matter. Only Armand's presence had been able to limit his ambitions, as he identified with everything Armand disdained. But this was exactly the sort of reductive thinking Émile loathed – just as much as Mikhail's narrow-mindedness. Émile felt rancour towards Armand, as though the latter were asking him to make some sort of sacrifice. *What should I give him?*

At that exact moment, the night's festivities reached a turning point. One after the other, the young men stood up and began dancing like bears. Although their movements were perfectly natural, they also looked clumsy. 'Mister,' the young man playing the tambourine asked, 'what do people dance to in your country?'

That gesture took Émile by surprise: it felt like a trap. But instead of being apprehensive, Émile was grateful. Suddenly, he'd reached a fork in the road. Did the boy's gesture make up for the long wait? *We only ever meet the demons we summon*, he told himself calmly. He took hold of the tambourine and began beating the rhythm of a *dabke*, a popular dance from the mountains of Lebanon. The tambourine player drew closer, made him repeat the movements a number of times, then tried to imitate them. He failed, tried again, then found the right rhythm and kept repeating it. Satisfied, he stood up and retreated to his corner: 'And now dance!' he commanded.

The young Maronite stood up. He was neither bothered nor worried. *Desire*, he thought, *is the most powerful of demons*. His life was flowing in a different direction. The guests were observing him. Would that wealthy merchant really start dancing? Abdelkarim had shrunk to the size of an insect. The more the Maronite grew in that environment, the smaller his servant became. They were like communicating vessels linked by an immutable whole. An invisible substance percolated from one to the other. The groom felt his master's presence as an unbreakable bond.

The Maronite was standing on the threadbare and intricately decorated carpet. He had it removed from the floor, like someone who asks for the blackboard to be wiped clean. Would he overcome his foreignness with a dance? Would he, a merchant, imitate the peasants' dance? The floor was cleared. Foreignness and integration: two rail tracks that led to nowhere. The young Maronite struck the floor with his heel. His feet had begun to move, unimpeded by his thoughts. As a matter of fact, his thoughts actually guided his feet, which sped off like fiery horses dragging their coach and coachman behind them. The guests cheered up: the hostile weight of the Maronite's presence had been exorcised.

The young Maronite covered an enormous distance as he danced. Struggling to stay self-aware, he asked himself, *Where am I?* But the levees had broken and he was being swept away by a violent force. *Broken?* he asked himself irritatedly. His spirit was in a state of extreme volatility. If he was being led by desire, then what was the nature of this desire? Or was he instead in the thrall of a sudden and aggressive desperation? Whom, or what, was he fighting against? Or was this just escapism? Desire and desperation, fighting and escaping – those were the demons that plagued him. But giving in had made him feel euphoric. *Dancing is not about running from one place to another*, he thought in a self-mocking way, *it's a means of expression, a fantastic voyage.*

Abdelkarim felt as though he were carrying the master on his back. That exasperated and nervous way he beat the floor with his foot was like a whip. They were galloping in the dark. Abdelkarim experienced a sort of terror, as though the devil were riding him. But he wasn't the only one who was afraid: the fear had been created by their secret complicity.

The merchant was swift-footed. He was tall, strong and wealthy – but lost in the midst of all the effort it took to express himself in his movements, or using the writing traced by his steps to follow mysterious clues. Abdelkarim tried to understand what his master was saying. Why was he thumping and shuffling so noisily when his feet were barely touching the floor? The silent knowingness of his feet as they hung suspended a few centimetres off the ground was clearly trying to formulate a message. Dancing wasn't limited to a test of one's strength and agility, but was a language unto itself. Abdelkarim wasn't oblivious to its tone – it spoke of violence, and the way the master constantly changed his moves betrayed benevolence and impatience. Indeed, Abdelkarim could detect his master's character from his movements. Relationships are desire and memory. The improvised dance repeated all they'd lived through together, like the opposite of a journey, a tension between what once had been and what was to come.

Abdelkarim had taken refuge in silence and inertia; occasionally the Maronite would stop dancing and look at him, as though wanting to pull him out of that state, or Abdelkarim would lose patience with himself and leap out of it, beating his feet on the floor like a whip, imbuing the strokes with the violence of his reply – unspeakable questions and pledges. Abdelkarim feared his master's wrath, and tried to predict what Émile might want to do next. He concentrated, redirecting his gaze from his feet so as to meet his master's gaze. Was he disappointed? The Maronite began beating the floor with his heels more violently, first one, then the other. Then he leapt into the air and struck the floor with both heels. His dancing was feverish.

Abdelkarim's uncle had signed the marriage contract alongside the bride's father. Having reached the end of that restless, ceremonial dance, the young Maronite also extended a contract towards him. Frightened out of his wits, Abdelkarim jumped to his feet.

At that moment the Maronite suddenly stopped, like when the gears of a machine come to a grinding halt. 'This is the *dabke*, a dance from my country,' he said, laughing. Abdelkarim took a step back. The young Maronite thanked his hosts, waved goodbye to the assembled guests, and left.

CHAPTER 2

The Fort

I

CAPTAIN MARTELLO: You know exactly why you were summoned here. Yesterday, the rebels attacked the market and yours was the only shop that wasn't looted. Did they simply forget? The market is shaped like a square: your shop is at the northernmost end of the western side. It's also the most important shop there, and is housed under what I must say are rather pompous archways. Keeping in mind your presence here, and that you arrived barely a week ago with ten heavily loaded camels in tow, your shop had the wealthiest booty on offer. Instead, the rebels weren't even curious enough to kick down its door to see what was inside. Perhaps you didn't even wake up while all this was going on. The rebels didn't harass you, and our authorities have given you the necessary permits to pass through our checkpoints. You even participated in your servant's wedding; despite the fact people here guard their homes and customs jealously, you were invited. Fortune seems to smile too brightly on you, especially in contradictory ways. It's as though each of the parties involved saw different people in you. Now you'll have to answer my questions, to which the authorities demand answers. Should you refuse, or prove too evasive, then I'll be forced to arrest you and have you sent back to Benghazi under armed guard.

ÉMILE: If the shops in the market had been hit by lightning during a storm instead of being attacked with bullets, I would be just as unable to answer your questions: there isn't always an answer for everything that happens.

MARTELLO: An ingenious reply, but I'm not sure I should relay it to the High Command because it might make a bad impression, since it could seem that you're making fun of the authorities' suspicions. Although it's difficult to know the plans fate has in store for us, it's not that difficult to understand the rebels' politics, which clearly seem to favour you. Why?

ÉMILE: The rebels might well consider their own countrymen who trade in areas controlled by you as traitors. But I'm a foreigner, and as such, I cannot possibly betray them – you can only betray a world you belong to, not one where you're merely a guest.

MARTELLO: They didn't want to punish the merchants. They wanted to make a show of strength: it was an act of propaganda. The rebels buy their supplies from the same merchants as the people who are loyal to us do – and they need them just as much as they do. There are even some Italian officers who are intolerant of the heroic tenacity of commerce, surviving amidst so many calamities. They find such obstinate vitality both irksome and disquieting. Some authoritarian maniacs even consider it unholy. Thus, the rebels wanted to remind everyone the resistance is going to continue. They even wanted to influence the course of the interminable peace negotiations, which have been broken off and started up again a thousand times by now. But the purpose of our interview is not to discuss the reasons that might have driven the rebels to attack. I had you summoned here because my report to my superiors will have to explain why your warehouse was spared in the attack, and address the inevitable suspicions it caused.

ÉMILE: Perhaps I'm just as surprised and curious as you or your superiors. I don't know what the rebels' plans are. What's different about me is that I am understandably pleased that my shop was spared from looting. The market was quite a sorry sight today. Other merchants, who also happen to be my customers, won't be able to get back on their feet. Thus, I was also indirectly affected by the attack.

MARTELLO: Why indirectly?

ÉMILE: My uncle has a reputation as a good, honest man and is respected by everyone. Perhaps the rebels wanted to emphasise this, and reward his good conduct.

MARTELLO: Your uncle has nothing to do with this business. Nobody gives a fig for him. He's not that important and hardly very clever, but as you say, probably good and honest. Perhaps the rebels don't even know who he is. I stopped by the shop several times during my daily rounds of the market: he's never there! Instead, I think that the rebels, using the apt expression you employed, wanted to reward the *owner* of the shop. Well, Mr Chébas, why did they want to reward you? Please enlighten me as to the nature of your relationship with Semereth Effendi.

ÉMILE: Three years ago I travelled with him from Alexandria to Benghazi. While we were still at sea, he expressed an interest in the goods I'd brought with me. He then kindly introduced me to other merchants in Benghazi. Captain, I'm assuming you're aware of the tragedy that struck his family?

MARTELLO: Ferdinando, the Venetian woman, Zulfa . . . yes, I'm well aware of that tragedy. But I'm also aware that Semereth abandoned his remote, fairy-tale niche and became the leader of a rebel band. I would like all the details on your commercial dealings with Semereth since his escape.

ÉMILE: Everyone knows Semereth's uncle has been managing his estate, which seems fairly normal to me.

MARTELLO: You wouldn't have specified that, thereby compromising Semereth's uncle, unless you knew the latter had died in the meanwhile. I'm well informed. Carry on.

ÉMILE: At the time of his escape, Semereth and I had been involved in a number of business deals, which I was then forced to liquidate. Tying up those loose ends was probably what gave rise to all that chatter about me and Hajji Semereth having gone into business together.

MARTELLO: Mr Chébas, your business has expanded rapidly. You're capable, intelligent, full of drive, and people say you run the tightest ship in the city. But you would never have been able to get to this point as quickly as you have without Semereth Effendi's help. The authorities have always known this. In the midst of a civil war, ascertaining the provenance of one's capital might seem excessive and pointless. The possible seizure of such assets based on suspicions rather than proof would also have damaging political repercussions. We've kept the knowledge of Semereth's fortune to ourselves, and are pretending not to notice. The decree issued on 15 July 1912 allows us to confiscate what goods we see fit. The rice, sugar, tea and cloth you sell are used by both the rebels and those loyal to us. It would be very difficult for us to split your customers into categories, since the government's efforts to tell them apart from one another have been fruitless thus far. Cyrenaica is no longer the front line of the conflict, and commerce is following its own course. It's a third army that pursues its own agenda regardless of the warring parties involved. Do you think there aren't any Italian officers who would have set the entire market on fire with the same fury as the rebels?

ÉMILE: Captain, in that case do you think my shop would have been spared? If you had led such an attack, would you have caused me harm? I'm not trying to defend myself by asking that question, I'm simply curious, just like you are.

MARTELLO: I came to see you twice when that tragic affair involving Semereth Effendi was happening. I certainly wasn't there in any official capacity on those occasions, and besides, the authorities didn't even know who you were at the time. You ask me if I would have spared your shop. Why not? It would of course have depended on whether I had the time to spare it some thought, and give the appropriate order in the midst of all that mayhem.

ÉMILE: Why would you have spared me? Perhaps if we knew the answer, we might better understand the rebels' intentions. It might even be that they spared me for the same reason you might have done — or if their reasons are different, knowing yours would still be enlightening.

MARTELLO: There, you've trapped me! I like the way you talk, Mr Chébas. You wisely calculate the risks involved in all your moves. I would have stopped my men in front of your shop — as I would have stopped what happened to Ferdinando, the handsome boy I once met at your shop. Although I didn't have any luck, I did try to do something for him. If he'd appeared through the whirlwind of that attack, his hand would've stayed mine and your shop would be safe.

ÉMILE: It's all clear now. But how could I have guessed? Instead of being part of a wider plan, couldn't the fact my shop was spared be due, so to speak, to a preternatural dialogue like the one that took place between you and Ferdinando?

MARTELLO: Did you leave the shop while the looting was happening?

ÉMILE: Of course not.

MARTELLO: Who led the attack? People said there was a very tall knight, a giant who was running riot everywhere. Shadows make people bigger than they are. Fear exaggerates. But I can't understand why the people's collective imagination conjured the same spectre: the giant figure of a knight, as though a statue had suddenly sprung to life. I think imagination had nothing to do with it; the giant was there. It was Semereth Effendi. Why don't you speak? Didn't you suspect he might have been behind it? Mr Chébas, it would mean a lot to me if you could confirm or dispel that suspicion, and in return I would promise to do all I can to dispel the suspicions against you.

ÉMILE: I never left the shop during the looting and as I don't know who led the attack, I can't say anything at all. I'm sorry to disappoint you.

MARTELLO: If you do know the truth and are keeping it from me, you've lost an opportunity to benefit from my help. For the sake of argument, let's assume that it was Semereth Effendi. If that's the case, then everything becomes explicable: Semereth simply spared the shop that belonged to someone who is either his friend or his business associate.

ÉMILE: So the fact I survived means I'm guilty? No one forgets who their real friends are despite the faction they've chosen or the ideals that inspire them.

MARTELLO: That's not necessarily true. At least as far as feelings go – whereas I have my doubts when it comes to money, which always confuses the situation. But withholding information is a crime, and I am a representative of the law, which expressly punishes reluctant witnesses.

ÉMILE: Perhaps there is a secret at the heart of the matter: but why must one always translate everything into political terms? Someone decided to spare my shop. I don't know who it was, nor do I know why they favoured me above others. Maybe it's someone unknown to me, maybe it was simply fate and maybe it was Semereth Effendi – or maybe it was divine providence. Even you, Captain, might fail to find the real reason. But the fact that there wasn't a political reason should give you all the certainty you need. Life is dictated by a number of factors that always remain indeterminable and obscure.

MARTELLO: And who would furnish me with such guarantees? The accused? The situation appears to refuse any explanation that doesn't have a political dimension, especially considering you're stringing together facts that don't belong together: it's the rules of the game. I've been here for three years, and my aims are to pierce through the secrets of this country and the people that live in it: to observe, to understand. Semereth's tragedy gave me the inclination to do so. I say *inclination* to emphasise that it wasn't strictly a choice. At the time, I tried to intervene in order to save Ferdinando's life, but I achieved nothing. I envied that giant, and everything he owned. I offered him my friendship, and even offered to visit him. He welcomed me courteously, gave me a tour of his house, but didn't pay me a return visit or invite me back. When Colonel Romanino and I asked the Venetian to come and work for us, she said she'd never swap her master for another. This was when the troops had just disembarked. This repudiated woman dared to prefer a simple merchant to those officers in shining uniforms who'd just landed on these beaches like gods. People say the Venetian was a witch. I can certainly vouch for the fact I've been haunted by a demon ever since: I want to take the giant's place. It's as though the people and objects Semereth owned were like hieroglyphs concealing a secret human language – I'm trying to decode this script with a scholar's obstinacy and a lover's passion. I know that you danced at Abdelkarim's wedding last week. Why are you getting so nervous? Our informers' eyes see everything. Do you know what my first reaction was? To *sing*! Yes, go ahead and laugh, our most deep-seated impulses share the same root as laughter. If I'd known about the wedding and that you'd be attending, I'd have mounted my horse, left the fort, and entered the room where you were assembled. To either offer you my presence, or to destroy it all, just like Semereth's house! Everything that denies our presence here must be destroyed, and the Expeditionary Force will act with the same determination as my willpower commands. Does this horrify you? But my destiny is following the same patterns as your friend Semereth Effendi. I'm also unloved and my presence here – the captain locked up in his fort – horrifies the people. Once again, the balance is skewed! Time cast the spell of distance between Semereth and Zulfa: but everything that actually matters is completely out of the ordinary, and distances add up to nothing but constraints. I frequented various merchants' homes and businesses, was on familiar terms with servants, read the Qur'an, as well as all the other texts Italy's lethargic culture bothered to translate from Arabic, read the memoirs of ancient travellers, and even kept an Arabic grammar book by my bed while I slept in a tent. But all I did was display the worst I could find in me and the civilisation to which I belong, as though I could only find salvation by reciting my sins. All my efforts were proved as vain as any desire. All they do is feed one's impatience, they do nothing to shorten the distance between oneself and everything that matters, not even by a single step. It seems Semereth Effendi gave his young bride a new gift every day: our willpower and strength are the violent gifts with which we officers are pointlessly trying to seduce the naïve lives of this country's inhabitants. Semereth's destiny reached its climax in his vain efforts to turn his monologue into a dialogue with the people he loved the most: Zulfa and Ferdinando. Yet all he managed to do was keep them locked up in his house, and they betrayed him by falling in love. Thus thwarted, and a prisoner of himself, he then watched them being murdered in front of his very eyes. But a dramatic change of scene took place in Semereth's parable, which saw him flee from Benghazi to join the rebels' ranks. What test does life have in store for me? The attack on the market utilised the element of surprise, and occurred at night. The natives are all against us, they know every escape route in and out of the camp: if I'd left the fort with my soldiers, we wouldn't have made it back. Of course, we could have easily resisted a siege at the fort: but they didn't attack us. They passed right by us, keeping at a distance that made shooting pointless, scampering here and there to show us that *they* are the masters of this place, then loaded their goods onto a few camels, sent them on their way, and finally vanished at dawn. Then the suffocating desert winds picked up. I watched them charge excitedly into the winds and vanish into the sandstorm. It recalled that famous passage in Herodotus where he narrates how the men of this country would transform into sword-wielding sandstorms. Semereth has vanished. I carry his death like a debt. One day, he won't find the wind in front of him, but a knight, at which point we'll duel. You can go, Mr Chébas: I wasn't trying to turn you into an informer or to punish you in that monster's stead. I simply thought you could understand my reasons for wanting to verify the identity of the person who led the assault on the market. Semereth's presence here was a provocation – and I left him unchallenged on the field. As a soldier, that is a stain on my honour.

BOOK IV

CHAPTER 1

I

'Captain Martello, the Risorgimento belongs to our past and it therefore influences us: how can you say it serves no purpose?' exclaimed Signora Betti, setting down the champagne goblet in her hand. They were toasting the New Year in General Saverio Delle Stelle's house.

'Anything valuable in our past and education,' the captain curtly retorted, 'has little to do with the Risorgimento.'

'Patriotism is blackmail,' Doctor Amilcare grumbled. The part he played in that conversation was to demystify: he was like a reef that stood in the way of reality's efforts to ready itself for the tragic outcome that lay in sight.

'Perhaps the old world had become corrupted and outlived its usefulness,' the captain said, 'but the new one was stillborn and so it never even reached adulthood.'

'Whoever hasn't lived and suffered through certain things, or wasn't educated in the cult of certain memories, will be unable to understand them, and maybe not even able to put them to any use, either.'

Signora Betti boldly scanned the room. Was there a

chance the captain's unfamiliarity had had a magical effect on the scene and could explain the inexplicable – or, considering the monotony of obviousness – could introduce the inexplicable into it? She feared Captain Martello as though she were staring into the abyss of the unknown.

The captain acquiesced and furnished them with a story:

'We once owned a spinning mill in the Lombardo-Veneto that went to ruin precisely because my grandfather took part in the uprisings during the Risorgimento.'

'And?' Signora Betti exclaimed.

'It's a very moving story, truly moving,' Doctor Amilcare said reassuringly, as though wanting to encourage Captain Martello.

'My grandfather's fiery letters from the time are pathetic, and about as moving as a romance novel. But how can one organise life on the frail yarns spun by novels?'

'Our past is rather wretched, especially our recent past. Perhaps this is what makes our present so melancholy,' General Delle Stelle said. 'I agree with you, Captain; the Risorgimento was just a bunch of fanfare, we can hear it pass us by with such pleasure because it's so bright and optimistic, but it doesn't even shake the dust off things.'

'Men are so bizarre,' Signora Betti commented, turning to face Signora Delle Stelle, who was seated at the other end of the table: defining something is a triumph, even if a fleeting one, over reality's ambiguity.

'The only thing that matters to a man is his outlook on life. As for the men who led the Risorgimento,' Captain Martello said, 'their outlook was stubbornly mediocre, and a banal oversimplification. The heirs of the Risorgimento turned that oversimplification, which was quite possibly dictated by circumstance, into a sacred book. Thus, the neoclassical era was the last time our history was adumbrated by the shadow of greatness.'

'What about Manzoni?' Signora Betti asked, alarmed.

'*The Betrothed* is nothing but a bunch of ghosts dancing around insignificant stories told by two peasants. It entirely liquidates our past. After Manzoni, mediocrity stopped being the black hole that all dying stars gravitated towards, and instead became a wan beacon in the miserable prison the world has become. Renzo stops being "the geometrical locus of the destinies of others" and becomes the country's destiny, or rather the yardstick we should measure it by.'

'This is a farce,' Signora Betti exclaimed as she stood, 'nothing but a game, and one that doesn't even amuse me!'

'Life in this country is being snuffed out because there's no more theatre!' Captain Martello exclaimed, surging out of his chair so tempestuously that the shocked Signora Betti immediately sat back down. 'Our problems today are identical to Renzo's: for instance, how to marry off our dear peasant girl despite the high-handedness of the powerful. We only search for perfection in mediocrity.'

'On the contrary, our life is full of theatre, so long as one isn't prejudiced against it,' Signora Betti snapped back.

'The intrigue is there, but the characters are missing. The end result of mediocrity and vulgarity – intrigues are always vulgar. Only the right characters can redeem it.'

'I don't understand what you're trying to say,' Signora Betti said defiantly.

'We're unable to go *anywhere* any more – all we manage to do is run away!' Captain Martello thundered.

II

Having begun amidst such clamour in 1911, by the time the celebrations marking the golden jubilee of Italian reunification were over, the colonial venture had become a fetid wound.

Whether acting on his own initiative or heeding the will of others, Semereth Effendi was captured during a night raid by the rebels on a garrison not far from the gates of Benghazi. Once his case was put before a military tribunal he was immediately condemned to hang, with the execution set to occur in the market square, so as to send a strong message. Émile Chébas, who usually took painstaking care not to let his impulses get the best of him, became prey to an outright − and youthful − burst of wrath when he received the news. The peace treaty between Italy and the Ottoman Empire would be duly signed, the Libyan people were on the brink of exhaustion, and the Italian government, which had entered the Great War against the Central Powers, wanted to recover from the humiliation of that colonial business. Semereth Effendi's death penalty exasperated everyone involved and was a sin that would have to be atoned for sooner or later, he thought. Émile noisily slammed the shutters of his shop and went to the High Command. The general in charge of the square treated that energetic young man with both kindness and respect, which Émile wanted to put to the test so as to negotiate for the prisoner's release. He would be prepared to vouchsafe for either Semereth Effendi's unconditional surrender or for his exile; in other words, he wanted to ask that the prisoner be released from the gallows and into his custody. By the time Saverio Delle Stelle received him in his spacious, high-windowed office, Émile had once again assumed control of his emotions. He spoke calmly, explained the dangers the military tribunal's decision would engender, how this would be nothing but a setback, then talked about peace and mercy, offering the general the most exacting guarantees, and even going so far as to flatter him.

When he heard the news of Semereth Effendi's sudden attack on a garrison while a truce was being negotiated, Captain Martello's first reaction was envy. It was resoundingly clear there would be no tomorrow for either the captain or Semereth Effendi. Semereth had done nothing to block the peace talks; on the contrary, he might even have organised the attack because he'd convinced himself the talks were close to being concluded. But what goal could he possibly have entertained, considering he'd seemed so afraid of watching those events pass him by? Ever since he'd been disgraced in Istanbul, that giant had been unable to see anything ahead of him; time no longer flowed towards a finishing line, but instead originated from a point of no return. Then Zulfa, that little critter, had happened: and for a short while, time had resumed its regular course, and Semereth Effendi had waited for it to free him and his child bride from the spell of disproportion. But he'd wound up being his beloved girl's butcher instead. Locking her up in her room, he had sacrificed her to death. But aboard the boatman's ferry, Zulfa had met that handsome servant, so that both could learn the joys of love before they met their inevitable end. Semereth had then fled to join the rebels. Now that the end of the peace was in sight, would he have to run away again? The giant was afraid of the light at the end of the tunnel! Thus, he had traitorously attacked the garrison near Benghazi to ensure his death.

But a hand had intervened, and made him a prisoner instead. Death wouldn't come to him gloriously on a battlefield, but would be meted out by a bureaucratic military tribunal; or perhaps Semereth Effendi had moved the tribunal to pity during the proceedings, meaning they would reward him with a death the Italian military had maliciously denied him. Having reached the terminus of the dead-end road he'd travelled in parallel with that filthy colonial war, Semereth had forced events to comply with his destiny and bring him closer to death, if not on the battlefield, then atop a dusty gallows in the middle of the market square. *But what about me?* Captain Martello's wrath was growing. Without waiting to be announced, he entered the general's office, where the merchant was pleading Semereth's case, and speaking frankly and passionately, Martello tried to seduce the magnanimity of the King's representative.

Émile Chébas hadn't expected Captain Martello's arrival, and failed to conceal his irritation. The captain noticed it and wanted to pre-empt him: 'I believe Mr Chébas has come here for the same reasons that led me to do so. There are now two of us interceding for Semereth Effendi to be pardoned.'

The young Maronite was convinced the captain would complicate everything, injecting even more confusion into his soul about Semereth Effendi's destiny, thereby compromising any chance to have the execution stayed.

'The problem is simple,' he said, turning to face the general, 'Semereth's actions must be weighed in their appropriate context. The two sides are negotiating a truce. That attack was an attempt to show that the rebels aren't on their last legs, and is thus an endeavour to force a more favourable treaty, since such a thing requires both sides to compromise.'

'Indeed. It was an effort to secure a better price for the truce. It's a political act.'

'Has Semereth confessed?'

'He hasn't confessed to anything,' the general said, 'he was as indifferent as a statue throughout the entire trial, as though he were an actor who'd forgotten his part. Everyone got vainly excited, talking, threatening, explaining and laughing all around him. Semereth couldn't hear them: it was as though he belonged to a different dimension. Which was an unforgivable offence, as it put our authority in doubt.'

'The moment the Italian government decided to enter into negotiations with the Libyans,' the Maronite said, 'it granted their insurgency a little legitimacy. A man arrested while armed is no longer a rebel and should be treated like a prisoner of war. Excellency! Save him from hanging: keep him a prisoner, hand him over to us, exile him from this country, or deport him to Italy – do whatever you like so long as you spare his life.'

'I believe it's too late for that,' the general replied, feeling refreshed by the sea breeze coming in through the windows. Above his head was a photo of Victor Emmanuel III in full military regalia.

'I've come to ask for even less than that,' Captain Martello cut in. 'Postpone the execution. Allow me and Mr Chébas to see him. Perhaps we would come back with some information that could convince you to retry his case.'

'That old fool refuses to speak to anyone.'

'It's of little consequence. I only need twenty-four hours. Once, I visited him in his house and he welcomed me rather reluctantly. Now I'll pay him a second visit, this time in the pitch dark of the prison, and perhaps he'll react differently.'

'It's pointless to delay his execution by twenty-four

hours,' the Maronite said. 'If you don't want to stay his execution, then delay it. Keep him imprisoned while waiting to execute him. When the truce is concluded, the order to pardon him will inevitably arrive.'

'That's fine by me, let's keep him in prison, at our disposal!'

'But that's not fine by *me*,' the general said, smiling, 'I don't think I can grant him more than twenty-four hours. All I need to secure this delay is some bureaucratic pretext or other, so as not to inconvenience the law.'

'Your Excellency, I didn't come here to ask you to prolong his agony. I came seeking clemency.'

'And I have refused your request, Chébas.'

'Can we visit the prisoner?'

'You'll allow me to do so on my own,' the Maronite said, 'I know it's useless, I'm simply going to say goodbye.'

'We'll have to break down his door, his heart is sealed against outsiders: if we pre-announce our visit, he'll refuse to see us.'

'I'll respect the door to his cell as though it were the door to his house, Captain. I'll send word of my arrival and if the master of that cell refuses to see me, or excuses himself for being unable to see me, then I'll turn back.'

'You'll come and let me know how it all goes,' the general intervened. 'I'm curious to see such a show of pleasantries when standing before the gallows.'

'You'll receive my full report, General. It's highly unlikely Mr Chébas will visit us again so soon. He's a proud man who humiliated himself by begging you to spare Semereth's life: such an extraordinary gesture on his part that it should have met with success. Chébas is even prepared to kiss your hand to obtain a stay of execution, but he won't pay us a second visit merely to satisfy your curiosity.'

'Don't mind the captain, my dear Mr Chébas. He has some talent for the theatre, and structures everything he says into monologues, unexpected plot twists and miracles. The ceremony of Semereth Effendi's death is making his passions run high.'

'Your Excellency, once again, I implore you to pardon him,' the Maronite insisted, 'not out of love for theatrical miracles, but simply out of human decency.'

'Even *that* was rather theatrical. Wait a moment. Remain kneeling as you are. General, I too implore you to spare him: if you let him keep his head, I'll bring you another ten, hundred, or thousand heads to take its place, however many you want, I'll cut them off on the battlefield myself while the men are still gripping their swords.'

'*Mais que ma cruauté survive à ma colère? Que malgré la pitié dont je me sens saisir . . .*'

'There we have it, General. You already have the punch-line, so please go ahead and use it.'

'I'm afraid I must disappoint you, Captain: I'm not one of Racine's characters. Mr Chébas, I admire your noble intentions. Even though your posture is straight, I understand that you made your heart bend its knee to secure Semereth's pardon. I will accompany you to the main door, I want to satisfy Captain Martello's theatrical instincts and make a public show of my respect for you.'

III

Captain Martello stepped inside Semereth Effendi's cell. The light was casting Hajji Semereth's deep shadow onto the wall.

The captain dismissed the guard. He waited until he could no longer hear the guard's footsteps, then began:

'I've obtained a twenty-four-hour stay of your execution from General Delle Stelle. I'm offering you my help. Perhaps I'll be able to save you.'

A nod of Semereth's head made his gigantic shadow on the wall oscillate ominously.

'I've been told your attitude towards the military tribunal was hardly encouraging. I'd like it if you could adopt a different one with me. The treaty between the Italian government and the Sanussi Brotherhood will soon be ratified, and your sacrifice won't have been in vain. It seems strange to me that although you joined the rebels' ranks fairly late, you're now the only one of them to be so uncompromising.'

They lingered in silence for a few moments.

'Perhaps you recall my visit to your house three years ago? Now I'd like to try to save you.'

The prisoner stared at him as though he were facing the cell's bare wall, or a hole in the ground. Captain Martello was seized by wrath.

'I know your destiny, Semereth. Ever since I learned you were responsible for Zulfa and Ferdinando's deaths I've been motivated by a single desire: to avenge them. I searched for you everywhere, but with no luck. Once, we came close: you were the one who set the El-Hania market on fire, and this new charge alone would be enough to ensure your demise. But this matter concerns only the two of us, and the Italian government has no right to meddle: it would be cowardly to call upon the authorities to settle our private affair. Whether ungenerous or mocking, fate saw fit to deny us the chance to meet on the battlefield, and instead determined we meet eye to eye in a cramped prison cell. You're our prisoner. I'm offering you your freedom because I want to see your head impaled on my sword, and not rolling off the gallows and into the market square. I simply can't accept that fate has reserved a rebel's glorious death for you, and I want to punish you for the death of the beautiful Zulfa and that servant.'

He kept quiet while awaiting a reply. Was waiting a kind of invocation?

'I tried to save Ferdinando, I wanted to take him with us and send him back to his country. But he preferred to stay with your wife.'

Semereth's face didn't betray anything. It was useless for Captain Martello to provoke him.

'Ferdinando preferred to stay with his beloved rather than opt for freedom. You showed no mercy, and thus will be denied it yourself. I don't want to free you from this prison so as to save you, but rather so I can kill you myself. That sham of a military tribunal has offered you the chance to die a hero's death, thereby tarnishing the memory of those two youngsters by allowing their deaths to go unavenged. Should you refuse to duel with me you'll meet as infamous an end as that Venetian woman of yours.'

Captain Martello was claiming the sole right to kill Semereth, and this was a further example of his trying to insert himself into the narrative of the giant's life. Avenging the child bride and her lover wouldn't only placate their faint shadows, but would also quell his despair. He was even prepared to let Semereth escape and go with him; if betrayal was the price for that friendship, he was prepared to pay it. But their lives would have to intertwine.

'You're the one who failed to comply with the cease-fire agreement. But now you must swear that you were just following others. Blame someone else, put a spanner in the peace negotiations, put an end to all trust and hope. Once we're on a level playing field again, you and I will be free to confront one another.'

The captain continued to talk while vainly glancing at Semereth's distorted features. When he got up to head towards the door, Semereth followed him for a couple of paces, nodding his head once more in a parting gesture. Captain Martello thought Semereth's body already seemed inert, as if dangling in a void. However, the captain also felt as though he was being sucked into that void himself. They were performing their parts on a tilted ledge: Ferdinando, Zulfa and the Venetian woman had already preceded them into the abyss.

IV

Olghina crossed the square while the soldiers were still disassembling the gallows where that monster had been executed the previous day, and entered the covered market. Abdelkarim spotted her and dashed to the back of the warehouse to alert the master. Olghina was almost running as she entered.

'Forgive me Émile, I was alone in the house, and Semereth Effendi's ghost is roaming the city and frightening people.'

'Come in, come in.'

'It's the only thing people are talking about in Benghazi,' said Armand, who'd returned to the city after being forced to close the branch in Tocra due to a dip in trade.

'Will he be the last victim of the colonial conquest?

It's as though people actually want to celebrate the occasion in some way . . . '

'Don't mind Armand, Signora. He only looks on these events as mere setbacks.'

'I'm leaving: didn't you know that? Now that war has broken out, I'm going to Italy. If I enlist as a volunteer, I'll have the right to citizenship. Thus, I'll bid goodbye to the Middle East once and for all.'

'Goodbye, goodbye,' Émile parroted, clearly annoyed. 'Since your problems are now over, let's not rehash them – so shut your mouth. Were you really afraid? It was an evil act, and I'm also afraid, but not of Semereth's ghost, whose apparition would console me: no, I'm frightened of God's retribution.'

'Just what do the two of you find so extraordinary about that tow-haired monster? The past few years have seen so many victims interred and then quickly forgotten. Instead, Semereth is granted all this fanfare. Captain Martello says that my magnanimous brother even bent his knee in front of the general to implore his clemency.'

'I also heard that, which is why I came here, Armand. Semereth Effendi's ghost will respectfully leave this shop alone. Émile, did you see Semereth before he was executed?'

'I asked to see him, and he sent the jailer back with a note: *Tell him to forgive my mistakes, just as I have forgiven his*. It's the most drastic form of goodbye used in this country.'

'It's all over now, there's no need to frighten the lady.'

'Armand, one of your brother's finest traits is that one feels safe next to him'

'Indeed. My brother's like a church: he consoles and pontificates. But I'm a heretic.'

V

'Semereth Effendi refused to shake my hand, which I'd held out to save him,' the officer said, 'therefore I wanted to be present in the square. Was I trying to give him the opportunity to make some explanatory gesture? Or did I want to be numbered among the butchers? Even though I reached the final act of this affair, the part I played couldn't resolve its ambiguity. In any case, I still had the chance to look at his face and I didn't miss a single detail, I was only a few paces away.'

'But I couldn't read his expression: Semereth Effendi remained just as impassive standing on the gallows as though he'd been in his reception room when it was enlivened by the floral presence of Zulfa and Ferdinando. I uselessly tried to detect fear in his features, or hatred, or pious resignation. He said: *We return from whence we came*. Or maybe: *Devoted to God, to Him we return*. Every translation is a restless shadow.'

'How long had you known him, Mr Chébas? One of our informers tells us the Hajji's face was disfigured when a barrel of gunpowder exploded next to him. It seems he was once incredibly handsome. In other words, he was the beautiful prince that was transformed into a monster by a spell. We were merely the spectators who arrived late on the scene after the major events in his life had already occurred: he appears before our eyes from the valley of death, his face hidden behind a mask that doesn't fully conceal his rotting features. I sometimes suspect I'm more of an archaeologist than an army officer, and that I was in the grips of such folly that I dug a grave in order to make it speak! I even tried to explain this to the general: how everything in Semereth's life had already happened, and that we didn't mean anything to him. The general thinks there isn't much to learn from all this. He spoils everything by couching it in ironic terms, as though he was only amused by my part in all this, which was nevertheless minor, or as he put it, that of a "naïve spectator."'

'The monster's love for Zulfa, the lovely creature he'd captured, was both gloomy and tenderly desperate. He played the legal role of a husband next to the immaculate image that was as distant from him as a memory. I'll spare you the comparison between me and that monster. When I arrived here, I also desecrated the innocence of the natives, which our decrees did nothing to redress. This is the reason – in the way plans only intersect in the invisible realm of desire – why Semereth Effendi was forced, or perhaps resigned himself, to make so many concessions. Thanks to the disproportion between them, he was never able to consummate their marriage; and then another disproportion – perhaps a result of a banal disagreement – prevented him from saving Zulfa and Ferdinando. There's something pathetic about the giant, whose every loving act wound up bringing him closer to death.'

'For the sake of those two, he even went through the humiliation of going to talk to that senile uncle of his, and then deprived himself of the only link to the real world he still had, by allowing Ferdinando, who was already slipping out of his grasp, to run off with Zulfa. He wanted Zulfa to grow up so that they could consummate the marriage, and he simultaneously didn't want Ferdinando to grow up: the dead have unreal cravings. In other words, he wanted to bend time to his purposes so he could use it on people as he liked, like a watchmaker who whimsically pushes the hands forward on one clock, and then stops them on another.'

A few merchants tried to peer into the shop, but kept their distance on seeing Chébas talking to an Italian officer, as though the shop had become a theatre, a simultaneously public and intimate place that nobody was allowed to enter. The captain was speaking passionately, and seemed to want the spotlight to shine on him alone – or perhaps to run away from it entirely. They were dark days, afflicted by a collective anguish, and everyone went their own way in a hurry, especially in the evenings, when the shadows settled on the city, as though they wanted to reach their destination before everything vanished or fell apart: war confuses the reckoning of time.

'Seeing that body hang from the gallows, I asked myself: Semereth obeyed the call of his sacred inheritance, by paying it homage once more and dying while his countrymen protested the loss of a good Muslim – or was he instead playing the role of a warrior who was dying for his faith, like he once used to hide his heart's leanings behind his merchant's robes?'

'It seems I was the only one in the square who remembered his guilt over Ferdinando and Zulfa's death, since it doesn't really matter that others were involved and that they acted against his will: simply by drawing them into his circle, he condemned them to die. There was something cruel and possessive about that man, who exercised a strange pull on people – myself included, despite my age – and also made them suspicious. As if one lost one's way simply by giving in to him. Just like when a grown man spoils a child's game by insisting on taking part. In his case, what was at stake in the game were those tender youths; just like how a king is unable to let the regal mantle fall off his shoulders. After all, how could he possibly attain innocence, if he couldn't stop being omnipotent?'

'It's as if one of us tried to relive a past moment in our lives. Semereth had already lived out his lot, and yet kept living. That's why he was so pathetic, and it proved an inexhaustible source of ruin for everyone around him despite the cool courtesy he showed them.'

'Zulfa was of an age only fit for child's games. However, her role as wife had put her in Semereth's bed, where she couldn't fulfil his desire for carnal pleasure. Thus thwarted, the giant was unable to do anything but kill, there was no point in him even resisting it: when it tumbles, a boulder crushes everything in its path . . . My own, rather disconcerting, impression – call it cruel if you will – is that there's no such thing as destiny when we speak of modern men, or as we say, *civilised* men. Were all my efforts simply a way to discover my own identity, to pry from that man the secret of my destiny? General Delle Stelle would laugh at such thoughts: he understands only what our times allow him to understand – which isn't much.'

'The disproportion between the giant's body and Zulfa's indicated their lives were running on different tracks and fated never to cross: that doesn't mean neither belonged to this world, but that there wasn't a world big enough to accommodate both simultaneously. One can plan for everything – and in fact Semereth did conclude a marital contract with Zulfa – yet still be divorced from the event in question, just like a dead man has nothing to do with the funeral procession around his grave. Then again, would you believe me if I said that I relived that experience while visiting Semereth in his cell, having only stood a couple of yards from him, but we were separated by an immense river, which forbade any contact: our meeting was reduced to meaningless sounds. It felt like I was groping around in the dark, and falling.'

'Chébas, have you ever strolled through a cemetery? I wonder whether I also wanted to be drawn into that fatal ring in Semereth's house, or whether I just told myself a little story, like people do when they walk alone past rows of tombstones. I know you weren't present at his execution: your dignity forbade you from profaning your eyes with that heinous spectacle put on by the Expeditionary Force. If it had been up to me, I would have ordered you to watch. It's far too easy to remain ensconced in your shop like this, Mr Chébas, amongst cloths so fine they almost slip through your fingers, while other people's lives are offered up to death – who is a compulsive buyer, as sophisticated as any collector.'

The ledger had been left wide open on the desk just in front of Émile. The captain thought the multitude of numbers bizarrely laid out on the wide, squared pages looked like the pamphlets the local soothsayers kept on the sandy ground while sitting cross-legged in the tiny square to the east of the covered market's exit. Émile listened to the captain in silence. It was as though he were watching Captain Martello's suicide, or self-imposed execution, a futile mirror image of Semereth's public death. The captain constantly relived Semereth's tragic end, which was etched into him like a dream and played over and over in the bell jar of his mind. It was a ceremony, the final duel; but truth be told, he was simply lamenting that hero's death. In keeping with everything he was saying, Captain Martello's tone had changed, but it had nothing to do with Émile, since the two were not on intimate terms.

'The sun was scorching and the dust enveloped people

and objects in a single halo. But Semereth's golden words redeemed that miserable scene. He said: "We return from whence we came." The peace negotiations with the Sanussi Brotherhood, the relocation of military garrisons, the current war on the Austrian front, General Caneva's pompous ambitions on his arrival here, all that poverty, hunger, chaos, those men in rags, the soldiers . . . everything appeared to have been thrown upside down, far away, lost – along this road that begins with Him and which takes us back to Him. Standing on the gallows, Semereth almost looked like Jesus on the cross, or Moses holding the tablets of the law. It's the only way to ever get to know our world, to organise our perceptions and see it for what it is, and it changed the meaning of our lives, of the pain running through our bodies from head to toe. I nearly went down on my knees! Like John, I'd have pushed the heathens aside and taken him down from the cross. It was a brief but intense experience. Then I felt a kind of pleasure in watching that monster punished for the lovers' deaths. But because I could no longer question him, I too had been punished. As if I'd murdered a crucial witness by torturing him in order to make him talk.'

'Mr Chébas, you aren't answering my questions either. Perhaps you're playing the role of Semereth's comic sidekick in order to confuse me further? You know what? I think this execution was my equivalent of Semereth's barrel of gunpowder: it exploded and disfigured my heart. From this day on, maybe my life will be nothing but a series of past events, and I too will exit the scene on a downward slope towards death wearing my mask, this frivolous uniform of a colonial officer!'

'What do you say to that, Mr Chébas? Maybe even you, just like the general, can't understand. But one day you might find yourself a step away from your desire, and forbidden to move any further. My dear friend, promise me,' he said, standing up, 'that you'll come and confide in me: life sometimes grabs you by the throat, that's the real monster. I won't be able to save you, but I make you a solemn promise that I will—' he continued while both men stood at the shop's entrance, '—be a very attentive listener. In other words, your mirror.'

The officer was outwardly composed, having taken maniacally scrupulous care of his appearance even on that day: his confession seemed incapable of shaking even a single strand of hair loose on his head. But it was exactly this sort of precision and those impeccable standards that explained his attraction to Semereth, a man with a completely different stature and gait: the giant's silence was sucking that straight-edged man into his vortex.

The officer stiffened.

Looking elegant and unapproachable, he crossed the crowded market square.

Left on his own, Émile returned to his desk and bent his head over his ledgers.

Semereth's volition to keep falling behind, one step after the other, seemed to lie outside his control, which explained why he'd stayed so obstinately silent. Instead, that officer was being ruled by a crazed willpower: it wasn't only his destiny that had disappeared, even his laws had vanished, and that man was capable of everything. He was like the ghosts of men who, having been mown down by bullets, search for another body to inhabit; it was his destiny, as he himself had put it, to search for a tragic sense of peace, or at least a glorified fiction of it. How peculiar!

As for himself, Émile wanted to bring his soul the kind

of clarity he found in his ledgers: where everything was broken down into numbers, and understandable. Being ambitious, he wanted to satisfy his cravings for success in society, and not under the vain lights of some inner theatre. God be praised, he didn't belong to the army, a theatrical troupe that swept through that district making such a racket. No, instead he belonged to commerce, which is another form of arbitration. *When we accept that perpetual mutability guarantees the legitimacy of life, what sense is there in complaining about the damage to our sense of identity? Once we split into different selves, recombining them is nothing but an impossible dream. There,* he thought, standing up and moving the papers on his desk as though playing solitaire, *I have walked down a path, which included meeting Semereth on the boat that brought me here, and I reached its end when he was executed in the market square. Martello peered into his soul and cruelly watched him hang. He wanted to know if Semereth endorsed the rebels' manifesto: that dying in defence of one's faith was the most beautiful death a believer could hope to achieve. There were many of us at the funeral. We all know who the last executed rebel was, that this hanging would be the last of its kind, and that a new era would now begin, the last tremor that had brought the past full circle. Everyone breathed the fresh air of reconciliation. The atmosphere was festive.*

Semereth and I tried to treat one another respectfully. He wanted to protect me and I looked after his affairs for a while when he suddenly abandoned them. Solidarity is the true channel of communication between men. This wealthy merchant was my first customer, granted me one of his precious servants, and left me to manage his estate for two years; in other words, he abdicated in my favour, but never felt jealous or angry towards the man who took his place. So much so I feel I'm his heir. I still carry the note he sent me from prison, in which he invoked God to bless me, then forgave my mistakes and asked me to forgive his; I keep it in my breast pocket, close to my heart.

Semereth Effendi's death is the end of a journey. By taking his place, my education and training are over. Now, I need to satisfy Uncle Mikhail. Once the war's over, I'll return to Aleppo and get married. According to ancient traditions, returning home to choose one's bride is a pledge.

At that moment, Abdelkarim entered the shop. He looked at his master inquisitively and then fled; Semereth Effendi's death had shaken him to the core. Émile had observed him closely at the funeral as he stood looking shameful amidst all the grown-ups.

He chided him for being so late: where had he been? Why hadn't he finished the work he'd been assigned? Bales of cloth had been left half untied at the back of the warehouse. Émile used these reproaches to help the loyal lad, who badly needed a guiding hand at that difficult moment: when life falls off the bone like flesh, structure is the net that catches it.

CHAPTER 2

I

Captain Martello pondered his situation while sitting upright on his horse. Now that the colony's problems had been resolved, there was a pressing need to be quicker than everyone else and demobilise. He had looked for a gesture he could make that would stand out prominently in the eyes of others, but especially himself: he'd got engaged to an upper-class girl who was slender, blonde and the commander of the coast guard's daughter, as though wishing to signal, as they once used to say, that he'd made a fresh start. However, the marriage wasn't the first step of a new beginning, but more like a farewell. The captain found it difficult to picture himself a contented father and husband in a gloomy provincial garrison, awaiting the next promotion. Now that the Great War had caused an irreparable rift in Europe, it was certainly true that the colonial affair had assumed a secondary role: the dark cloud of conflict had completely absorbed that minor African episode, and nobody knew what the world would look like once it emerged from that storm.

The captain calmly led his troops through the country; it was unlikely the rebels would attempt an ambush. The atmosphere of defeat, which turns everything to rot, wasn't conducive to an act of aggression.

A Libyan non-commissioned officer rode alongside the captain. The boy had just returned from Sicily, where he'd been sent for a training course. The army wanted to clear those boys out of the colony: it was afraid of them. However, the army also tried to instruct and indoctrinate them in the hope they would rush to quell any new rebellion. Some even spoke of sending colonial regiments to the Austrian front. Captain Martello thought this was absurd, nothing but a fantasy cooked up in a wretched bureaucrat's office, and thus took no interest. The training course in Sicily had turned out badly, and the few remaining survivors had been sent back to Libya.

The young officer rode deftly; his wrist was steady, but the captain didn't fail to notice his frailty. Perhaps he was suffering, but Fathi seemed happy to talk and didn't appear bashful at all. He wasn't careful with his words – and this unusual trait, coupled with his aura of suffering, immediately endeared him to the captain. The monotony of the journey through those semi-deserted moors stoked the fire of his curiosity. Fathi painted a vivid portrait of life in Benghazi during the final months of the Ottoman Empire's rule, and swore he'd welcomed the arrival of the Italian Expeditionary Force as liberators. He'd chosen his side immediately, opting for the invaders, who'd then done nothing but prolong his wait. Poor and uneducated, Fathi had expected the opportunity to work and study which had been promised him. He said the Italians' biggest mistake had been to set foot in the hinterland, which no one had ever managed to bring under their control. Benghazi, on the other hand, was well equipped to welcome an Italian military administration – relationships had already been forged there, and the city already had a bureaucracy – but the interior was governed by traditions nobody could uproot. Even the Sanussi Brotherhood had asserted its authority by espousing tribal customs that pre-dated its existence, and in fact ended up making these customs even more unassailable. The Italian authorities would never manage to impose their own laws and do away with the customs that had held that society and its individuals in equilibrium. The Sanussis had been welcomed a century earlier as venerated Islamic teachers, whereas the aversion the Italians had encountered could be largely explained by the fact they were infidels. Fathi had quickly learned the newcomers' language, and found a job. He even knew how to read and write, and a soldier had taught him to play the accordion. Thus, he'd enthusiastically taken his steps down the path paved by the Expeditionary Force; even though it had come at the cost of a deep wound, the foreigners had poached the people away from their tyrant – perpetual stagnation. All of a sudden, both those who joined the rebels and those who believed the invaders' promises found themselves miraculously in a saddle, knights who held the reins of their destinies in their hands.

Captain Martello's ear was trained to detect flattery: when the natives spoke to him, they all said they'd welcomed the Expeditionary Force, that they were indebted to them for all the social progress they'd brought about, among other laudatory descriptions of the Italian adventure in Africa. But Fathi didn't flatter him, and had focused on plotting his own destiny during the mayhem of the past five years.

The humble manner in which he spoke gave his words the imprimatur of truth. Martello had rarely encountered such candour in that foreign, distant land before. He asked himself whether he'd been wrong to ascribe so much tension and meaning to people's words and gestures. Everything Captain Martello had been chasing up to that day, in other words a sincere exchange with the people of the place, now seemed easy and natural during that morning ride. He wondered whether the peace accords, which he didn't support because both parties harboured secret and fatal misgivings, might not be a step in the right direction. Meaning that demobilisation, which he'd hurriedly and ironically consented to, was turning out to be a fruitful avenue. For the first time, Martello believed he could continue living in that African land and enjoy a semi-legitimate position. He might even metamorphose into a colonist: his mind was flooded by pastoral scenes.

Perhaps Semereth Effendi's death had freed the country from a spell. Hostile to happiness and the rule of law, the man's mere presence had impeded the country from finding a peaceful solution to the conflict. Now that the country had been freed from that monster, it could finally live in peace.

Captain Martello knew how minor a role Semereth had played politically, and that he shouldn't confuse the limitless theatre of the country with the play being staged in his mind, which featured Semereth in the principal role. The resistance had organised itself long before Semereth joined it. In fact, the only reason he'd done so was due to a personal tragedy. But spells are hardly ever conspicuous, and whoever casts them is usually the last to fall under suspicion. Given to exaggeration because of his excessively confined nature, Semereth had channelled his fearless violence into action in tribute to his earlier life as a Turkish officer before he'd become a merchant in that forgotten province of the Ottoman Empire.

The captain turned his thoughts to the morning when he'd been locked up in his fort and watched as those rebel cavalry troops disappeared into the sandstorm after looting the market: an event that now belonged to the past, just like that legend from Herodotus, '*and having held counsel, they decided to mount an expedition against Notus, the south-wind . . .* ' He wanted to put his non-commissioned officer at ease, and so confided in him a little. He even told him that he'd got engaged, thus initiating him into a domestic intimacy, as though he would welcome him as a guest into his home as soon as the ride was over. He was determined to exert his influence over the boy and avail himself of his simplicity and candour: he was even willing to repay him in kind by being benevolent, maybe even caring, all to bury the differences between their stations, which the colonial context dictated, thus keeping them apart.

When they stopped in Tocra at the end of the first day, he took only the boy with him as he roamed the ruins of the ancient city of Teucheira, almost completely buried in the sand. He explained the little information that could be gleaned from those relics. The path they walked on, which stretched along the sea, was whipped by the winds.

It was as though they were following someone else's footprints; but the road was deserted.

Before sunset, he swam among the reefs inside the rocky enclosure around the fort. Fathi stayed ashore and watched him. He was scared of cold water. Martello stayed in the water for a long time, unable to let go of that happy day.

When he later stretched out on his cot, he feel asleep immediately: his tent protected him like a castle.

The following day, he didn't manage to speak to Fathi, as that leg of the journey was too short, and the terrain hostile and hard to ride through. They reached Tolmeta, the ancient Ptolemais, in the early hours of the afternoon. On the way he'd had the time to reflect on the previous day's conversation. His attention was focused on the secret symmetry between their experiences. He had once thought that his own voyage – from the motherland to the colony – would be irreversible, because the knowledge of a different social order was enough to show the inadequacy of the society he'd lived in, and now, as an officer of the Expeditionary Force, he believed the way it pretended to be more exemplary was sinful. In his turn, Fathi had thought of the Italian conquest and the escape of the Turks as irreversible, and had put much effort into carving out a niche for himself in this new world, learning the invaders' language to find employment, of course, but also so he could better understand this newly discovered world. Four years ago, the captain had purchased an ancient villa in Lombardy which he'd had painstakingly restored, but it had felt as though he had been building himself a tomb: just as with the ancient Egyptians, mustering all those traditions only proved useful for the journey to the afterlife.

At sunset, the captain took Fathi on a tour of the ruins of Ptolemais. Although the sight might have been better seen in the light of day, they were still imposing. Positioned underneath a fairly wide square were the vast cellars where the city's water was once stored in a series of labyrinthine tunnels that coalesced into an underground city. Fathi listened closely to his commanding officer's explanations. Martello didn't seem in a hurry, or keen to solicit the young man's confidences. Thus, by showing him the ruins, he prevented him from speaking.

Captain Martello evoked the empires and diverse influences that had dominated the country, conquests that belonged to the ancient past – the Egyptians, the Greeks, the Romans, the Vandals, the Byzantines – with the intent of forcing that young man to stay silent, in order to impress him so that, having overcome his diffidence, he could no longer speak freely. Martello told Fathi that they'd discovered an old fresco of Apollo surrounded by his muses and holding a zither in one of the main halls in his villa, concealed under a layer of whitewash. Apollo had founded Cyrene, which lay at the end of their journey. In another room a woman, most likely a metaphor for Venice, could be seen holding a crown aloft. He then told Fathi about Venice's eastern, Byzantine heritage. He always seemed to be wandering off and then suddenly reappearing before his interlocutor; it was a regal and almost reticent kind of dance. Every initiation ceremony is highly metaphorical: the invisible bursts onto the scene only to vanish again after being moved by unintelligible actions, which the gods use to threaten and seduce.

When the captain finished his history lesson, Fathi noted bitterly that he'd spent much of his time in Sicily looking for that Italy the captain was telling him about, but he hadn't seen the slightest trace of that splendour in the squalid little village where they'd been confined. The village hadn't looked anything like Rome, or Venice, or Byzantium – it was simply a village lost in the middle of a deserted interior, which looked a lot like the places they'd seen on their way to those ruins. Fathi said he knew those magnificent cities existed, but that once they'd crossed the sea, the Italian authorities had only shown them places that looked exactly like the ones they'd left behind, as if the only difference wasn't the distance between them, but this puzzling notion called progress. Their training course in Italy had had a single effect on them: disenchantment. They had simply been shown a facsimile of their old country, but populated by different people. As though his own country, which had been taken away from him, could never hope to change, and the future could only be a replica of the past. During their initial training the authorities had also tried to politically indoctrinate them. Then they'd forgotten all about them. Life in the camps had been lethargic, the days interminably long and purposeless. Only the shopkeepers took any interest in them: the soldiers' pay had swelled the parched rivulet of the village's commercial life. Many of Fathi's comrades had fallen ill, a few had died and been buried in someone else's country. Their only viaticum was the desperation of the renegades these new idols had refused to welcome.

Martello let him talk. He said he'd thought the whole project had been an arrogant fantasy from the start; that bureaucrats could only conjure sterile and reactionary dreams. He promised Fathi that a different Italy existed, and that he would take him there once the war in Europe was over. The prospect excited him. He forgot all the wrath and despondency Fathi's story had aroused in him. He said he hadn't meant to humiliate Fathi with stories of Italy's greatness and her perennially celebrated beauty; instead, he wanted to offer her up to him. He also told him that he didn't care about his military training or political indoctrination, that he didn't give a fig whether he would ever become a loyal subject. Getting drawn further and further by the fugue of images that flooded his mind, he said he simply wanted to welcome a friend, not a subject.

Fathi eyed him attentively. Irked, the captain asked him if he didn't believe him. The offence swept away the immense panorama he'd evoked, and at a stroke he once again felt like a colonial officer with a native recruit by his side.

But before he could say anything, Fathi began to cough, making an incredible racket. The idyllic scene of the voyage to Italy was juxtaposed with the inextricable gloominess of that chesty cough, whose rumbles shattered the silence of that isolated place. It was as though an abyss had opened up before them and a god were making a gesture or uttering a word. But it was a benevolent god.

That cavernous cough seemed even more horrible under that blue sky, which was unblemished by a single cloud, or the slightest tear.

It was nearly evening, and they walked back in silence.

In a tent a little removed from the military camp, a woman was busy weaving a carpet. An old man stood next to her, watching her work. Invited in by the old man, Martello and Fathi entered the tent. The woman didn't lift her gaze, and continued weaving. The loom was rudimentary. The weaver's slow hand would alternate between running the threads lengthwise, then crosswise, interlacing them through the loom. Fathi tossed a coin onto the carpet. Afterwards, once alone in his tent, the captain drafted a solemn letter to his fiancée by candlelight.

On the evening of the third day, they reached El-Hania, the little Eastern port where Émile Chébas's business had opened a branch two years earlier.

The captain inspected the market, where the merchants

recognised him and greeted him fawningly. He even paid a visit to Chébas's shop, and was astonished to see Abdelkarim there, whom he hadn't seen in a long time. Abdelkarim had grown a few inches and was now in charge of the branch. He came towards the captain, pleased to host him, but unable to conceal his awkwardness. Immediately amused, Captain Martello took in the entirety of the scene so as to spot any sign of benevolence, and Abdelkarim – who now looked so conventional thanks to the implacable passing of time – was cheered by his presence. Martello asked him if he remembered their first encounter in Benghazi, when he'd seen him with Ferdinando in Émile Chébas's warehouse. He asked after the Maronite and Abdelkarim told him the master was quite busy due to Armand's impending departure. Yes, Armand was going to Italy to fight the Austrians. From the way the conversation developed, the captain understood Émile was annoyed by his brother's decision, which seemed so removed from their actual concerns: after all, what did that colossal brawl have to do with them? The captain asked what had happened to that gloomy uncle of theirs, and Abdelkarim answered that Mikhail had gone back to Syria since his three daughters were now of marriageable age. At that moment, the captain heard something move. Unnerved, he shot to his feet and only then realised that Fathi was standing at the back of the shop next to a pile of multicoloured cloths. The boy's smile was impenetrable, reminding Martello of the expression on one of the statues the soldiers had unearthed after they'd stumbled on a stone foot sticking out of the ground, and which was now housed at the local military base. Abdelkarim said Fathi was his cousin and appeared surprised the captain knew his name.

Martello asked Fathi what he was doing there and why he was eavesdropping. There was a metallic hint to his voice, which made it seem as though the words were being uttered by his uniform. Fathi modestly replied that he'd greeted him on entering the shop, but that the captain had pretended not to notice. Enraged, Martello abruptly took a step towards him, saying he didn't need to pretend to do anything. The captain's sudden wrath made a big impression on Abdelkarim, who'd hitherto always seen him looking so courteous and composed, drinking one cup of tea after the other with his master. But instead of receiving a reply, Fathi's cough echoed through the shop, and the officer was struck by the sound, as if Jupiter had shaken the heavens with his thunderbolts to admonish his arrogance.

Abdelkarim invited Martello to have a cup of tea. His offer seemed a little reticent, as if he were playing a bigger role than he was used to. Martello accepted, but was surprised and disappointed when he saw Abdelkarim bring only a single cup. He knew it was a sign of deference, but still felt the bitter taste of estrangement in his mouth. There was an unbridgeable distance separating him even from Abdelkarim. Abdelkarim lingered a step away from the captain, while Fathi, having cheered up, stood like a pillar by the shop's entrance. Fathi was slightly shorter than average, slender, well-proportioned, pale-skinned, and he effused an aura of suffering, as though he were a statue surrounded by fog, and therefore barely perceptible.

Martello was amused by the scene, as though he were on stage at a theatre. He thought about General Delle Stelle: what would the general have said if he'd seen him sitting serenely in that exotic shop? The general loved opera, and was in fact fond of saying that a military career was the most 'melodramatic' option available to one in that mundane century.

Martello enjoyed being among all those cloths, so smooth and light that they slipped through one's fingers; he would stroke them with one hand, while holding his cup of mint tea with the other, which he sipped at. Jumbled memories of exquisite Viennese or Neapolitan Turquerie flashed through his mind, brittle figurines of shining porcelain which vanished and transformed into a mellifluous music that caressed his ears.

He would tell his fiancée about it all.

Who knew if that girl could even comprehend how reality sometimes becomes strangely complicated, that doors can open onto unknown places one ventures into without knowing anything about them, like in dreams, where different worlds are juxtaposed against one another? Or like in pentagrams, which the wise one has inscribed with mysterious hieroglyphs that an expert hand could decipher and transform into music in the ephemeral and seductive clarity that one can achieve when turning notes into sounds.

Martello stood up. He took his leave from his host with all due ceremony, thereby increasing Abdelkarim's confusion, as well as, so it seemed, his happiness.

The next morning, while they were climbing a ridge to reach the high plateau from whence they would continue to Cyrene, their journey's destination, their attention was drawn to a tomb. It looked like a tiny temple. The ruins of that distant, illustrious civilisation were the only language familiar to him in that impenetrable country. The ruins always emerged out of the sand alongside the coast, as if even the Greek colonists hadn't dared to venture into that boundless interior.

Martello had once tasked his soldiers with excavating one of those ruins and had been rewarded with a prize: a nearly intact mosaic decorated with subtle black arabesques on a bed of white. Martello could recite Catullus's verses from memory and as a practical joke General Delle Stelle had made him perform the most immodest ones in public. Both the front and back of the temple had been broken into. The officer stuck his head out of the opening, and as though he were peering through a telescope, he saw Fathi motionless on his horse. Martello was struck once more by how fragile he looked.

Having climbed back onto his saddle, he called Fathi over. They rode all the way to Massah without exchanging a word.

They stopped in the village for an hour, then continued to Beida. Along the way they saw Greek tombs dotted around the landscape like the footprints of a civilisation. They all bore a round hole made by thieves who had pierced the rock in order to stick their hands through it and into the tombs. Those acts of desecration made Martello feel uneasy. Feeling melancholy, he began to talk. He asked Fathi questions about the Sanussi Brotherhood, which had established its first *zawiyah* in Beida. He said he would gladly write a study on the Brotherhood, whose work he admired. Fathi had made the acquaintance of Sayyid Hilal al-Sanussi, the man who'd been put in charge of the Eastern regions and who'd abandoned the front the Sanussis had successfully held to set out on the road of betrayal. He said Sayyid Hilal was debauched, and incapable of leading the heroic life of the Brotherhood's members. He aspired to become the invaders' straw man, the sort of character other imperial powers were prone to protect. He'd sold out for nothing, and paid for it by shamefully tarnishing the Sanussi name. As for the invaders, they would exploit him for all he was worth and then, once he was useless, they would discard him and leave him to rot under house arrest.

Martello disagreed. This was the price every traitor paid: heaps of slander and conjecture that every onlooker claimed to have insights on. He asked Fathi more questions about the two Italian soldiers who'd been taken prisoner at the battle of Sidi al-Qarba and had recanted their faith and gone over to the other side.

Re-evoking betrayals on both sides, they entered Cyrene. The city had been looted by corsair archaeologists and its marvellous statues sold off to European museums, but they could nevertheless still gaze upon its impressive ruins. Much more could be seen poking out of the soft layer of grass. Captain Martello walked all the way to the amphitheatre's basin, which looked out onto the sea, and was flanked on its right by the hills of the necropolis rising like ramparts and studded with deep black windows into the realm of the underworld.

On Thursday evening, Captain Martello went for another walk through the ruins, going along the 'sacred way' that led from the fountain of Apollo to the Agora. He fantasised about rediscoveries, excavations, restorations and deciphering inscriptions. Walking slowly along that path was like taking part in a procession alongside invisible companions, releasing him from the boredom of the interminable hours spent sitting in school listening to a literature professor who tried to bring Greek and Latin grammar to life in a vaguely threatening manner. It was as though a door had been thrown open and Martello now stood face to face with the world whose sepulchral remains the professor had tried to impart on him. These lessons in Classics had turned out to be metaphorical disquisitions on eschatology; but now that he was in Africa, and standing amidst the solemn, sublime remains of an ancient civilisation, the captain had finally been granted a window into the afterlife.

To his great annoyance, he realised he'd forgotten all his Greek – it had been erased from his memory, the original hidden city. On the other hand, he'd managed to hang on to his Latin, as though the intimate landscape of his mind had decided which monuments to keep and which to eliminate, according to its whims. He silently recited beautiful Latin verses or the commemorations of illustrious authors. An identical ideal of beauty acted like a beam of light that linked disparate ages in history together until they appeared like different sections of a single fresco. He made plans to return there with his fiancée, and visions of German poets wandering through Roman ruins flooded his mind. He decided he would read Goethe's *Italian Journey*, then remembered Johann Joachim Winckelmann and the other great scholars of the Romantic rediscovery of the classical world.

Retracing his steps, he climbed up to the top of the amphitheatre, where one could enjoy an outstanding view: a kind of blue vortex that faded away in the distant mirage of the sea. The basin below filled with the tragic and alluring characters Martello's lonely walk had caused to leave the recesses of his memory, even though they spoke in unlikely and bombastic sentences that their enthusiastic translators had fed into their mouths, and which were widely available for sale in Italian markets. To his right, where the hills of the necropolis lay, a few ragged farmers, donkeys, goats and a few women in brightly coloured dresses – as well as the odd soldier – moved across the slopes. He recalled the little scenes of daily life that Renaissance painters would insert alongside the main subject, just like in Masaccio's *Crocifissione* and Botticelli's *Pallas and the Centaur*. One could put down roots in African lands through the classical culture that had blossomed in these places, this was the secret his walks had imparted to him. He had landed in Benghazi with the Expeditionary Force, and having followed Apollo's tracks, who had arrived there chasing a nymph, the captain had finally arrived in Cyrene: Apollo's presence turned history into a myth.

What did he care about Rome's greatness, whose remains were being flaunted by fanatical journalists and rambling generals to justify the colonial invasion? What use could he possibly have for those nationalist strategies? Those incredibly mellow ruins were more delicate than anything Claude Lorrain had ever painted, and that landscape, bathed in an inimitable light, which re-evoked the dainty, intoxicating rediscovery of the classics, had nothing to do with the remote uproar of triumphs. It recalled the first Christian writers who'd hailed from those shores: Tertullian, Augustine of Hippo and Synesius . . .

When he returned to the camp at sunset, he ran into Fathi.

Fathi said he'd seen him sitting on the bleachers. Martello asked him where he'd been.

Prostitutes plied their trade inside the tombs, which had been carved out of the rock and were often decorated with little columns, recalling the façades of temples, and business had picked up considerably amidst the ruins of that ancient city since the Italian soldiers had set up camp there. Captain Martello remembered that when he'd been standing atop the heights of the amphitheatre, he'd spotted women in colourful dresses walking along the necropolis.

Once it was time to move on, the regiment was put on a state of alert. They looked everywhere for Captain Martello, but in vain: he'd either fled, been kidnapped, or killed. He'd been seen in the vicinity of the amphitheatre in the afternoon, and then in the camp. The shadow of an officer had passed by a window frame, but nobody had left the camp after that hour. Serious doubts fell on Fathi, who'd been spotted talking to the officer, and repeated searches for Fathi also ended in failure. The prostitutes were driven from the tombs and interrogated. The soldiers rummaged around the tombs like thieves. It was getting late, and they returned empty-handed.

II

The fiancée wept over the loss of her handsome officer, his effortless elegance, how the fatuity of his words contrasted with the windows of his eyes, which opened onto a landscape where lights and shadows formed into patterns that were utterly incomprehensible to her, as they defied all the rules taught her by her education. General Delle Stelle had gone to offer his condolences, and after a tearful display, she formulated a few shy, awkward questions.

Her mother was present throughout the conversation.

'That man was a mystery,' the general said in a kindly tone. 'What was his life in Italy like before he arrived in the colony? It constitutes a preliminary chapter, perhaps an unnecessary one, in our attempt to understand the incident from his perspective. After all, we already know what our collective past was like: the education we received and the laws of our society. Martello felt he was disconnected from the "other," from our unruly colonial subjects, who would never welcome him as he wanted them to. Martello could never accept the solitude forced upon him by his role as a master, as a powerful man. One can't be a real character if one can't accept one's limitations!'

'But what estranged him from us? Encountering a world governed by different laws, the legitimacy of such a society, the irredeemable sin of our attempt to destroy it? It's as if he'd stumbled into an opera house for the first time in his life and was confronted with a reality that followed its own rules, and instead of sitting back and enjoying the show, he suffered an identity crisis, and could no longer draw any comfort from being a spectator. Any willed attempt to metamorphose oneself is both naïve and arrogant, and in the case of our dear captain, it ended in tragedy. Like a gambler who doubles his bets with each hand, he progressed from an indulgent feeling of curiosity to one of restlessness, and having thus fallen into a downward spiral of guilt, he wound up being crucified on the wall of despair. He believed in *change*, which demands a steep price: desertion, betrayal, honesty and self-criticism, a currency only valued in the environment he was running away from – *those people* have no idea what to do with our kindness and goodwill, or with our pity or honesty. Martello's sacrifice was as pointless to them as our sense of goodwill. They don't want to free themselves from us, they want to either make us run away or kill us: in their eyes, we can only ever be either guilty or foreigners, nothing else. Just look at that Semereth Effendi – he was indifferent to our presence there, refused to heed our summons, was indifferent to our respectful visits, or even our military tribunals, and eventually the gallows too. He never looked us in the eye. My dear girl, we'll never know what fate befell our brave captain: if he was kidnapped, or if he ran away, or is still alive. The secret sequel to this story proves too much for the spectator's impatience. This entire drama is missing an act. I wouldn't presume to write it myself, it would be a sacrilege, a counterfeit.'

Forgetting he was in the girl's presence and not chatting with one of his cohorts, the general let slip a smile, but then regained his composure.

'Martello's suicidal instinct was caused by his piety: he was incapable of giving his life any meaning, and lacked the willpower to find it, which flung open the doors of the occult. He was tormented by the quest to find the meaning to the sum of all these elements. This was the question that plagued him, and he found the other side alluring simply because it offered him the false promise of an answer – even though the other side, by which Martello was both charmed and repelled, confusing that backwater society with a terrestrial paradise, only offered a sure path to death. What good did it serve to keep obsessively poring over all those insignificant events, like when he visited Semereth Effendi in prison, and, as he himself put it, "wasn't greeted at all"? That monster was already on the other side of the river. Martello's desire to possess that child bride, the tears he shed over that young servant's death, the giant's robe which he wanted to wear after getting rid of his uniform, the bitter jealousy he felt when the Venetian woman preferred to remain in the giant's service, all this proves the vain hopes he entertained of reaching the other side, but all they did was bind him in chains.'

Martello's fiancée looked as though she had stumbled

blindfolded onto the scene. Moved to pity by how the general was pointlessly tormenting her daughter, the mother asked: 'General, do you think the captain loved my daughter? I believe that's what Anita asked you.'

The general protectively placed his hand on the girl's. Anita sobbed shyly.

'The walk Martello took through the necropolis which houses the women in colourful dresses,' the general continued, 'is a dead-end road he didn't hesitate to start on – I'm taking the liberty to mention this because it's public knowledge,' he added, turning to Anita's mother, as though to overrule any objection. 'It was inevitable he would make that step once he knew the peace negotiations were about to be concluded, thus dashing all his hopes. Had he finally found the irredeemable gesture he had long been searching for? Having linked his destiny to that giant, he followed his footprints. Semereth Effendi attacked the garrison in what was a suicide mission, and as Martello himself put it, all because he was "afraid of the light," meaning that the conclusion of the negotiations would undoubtedly have a peaceful outcome, and that everyone would therefore return to their mundane roles in their respective societies. Finding himself at the same critical juncture, Martello opted to head into a cave: who knows what tribunal was responsible for his execution? Finally, his resistance was overcome by a combination of misery and luxury, of human warmth and sepulchral dust. The harlot who called out to him from that tomb's abyss satisfied his passionate longing for an event that would forever mark his destiny, a phenomenon foretold by the Libyan non-commissioned officer who was Martello's guide from Benghazi to the ancient heart of that land. The captain's complicity in the colonial venture robbed all he'd been taught and believed in of any meaning. Are all of us bound to reach that insoluble conclusion once we firmly conclude our education is ultimately useless? What an exaggeration! To employ the same metaphor, it's as if a theatregoer convinced himself he had to spend the rest of his life under those lights!'

'An encounter with a society governed by different laws is an allegory for the encounter with an otherworldly reality, which inevitably leads to an immediate devaluation of one's original society and makes the newcomer anxious to prove himself worthy of the other society and flee into it in order to save himself. By entering that tomb, Captain Martello fulfilled his desire to imitate that monster who'd led an attack on our fortifications at the wrong time and refused to take up all those opportunities to escape, launching that assault under cover of night, when shadows snatch men away and make weapons completely useless, a final judgement that had been a long time coming. It's a duel: except that one's opponent is death, even if it does appear in the guise of a knight.'

The general interrupted his speech to pay Anita's mother a few compliments. He then stroked the girl's hair. Although she was very young, she was already a widow. Her hair was soft and silky, almost like a wig, and she looked just like one of those dolls that only make a sound when they're turned upside down. Anita broke into another sob. The general made a gesture, as though to pick her up again. He lingered motionless and perplexed.

'Instead of enlightening him, the events around him eventually destroyed him.' The general concluded, becoming suddenly impatient to leave, as though he were the last character left on stage. He stood, kissed the mother's hand, clasped Anita to his chest as though posing for a souvenir photograph, and left.

III

Saverio Delle Stelle thought the inquiry into Captain Martello's disappearance had been carried out very obtusely: so long as they continued in that manner, they would never follow the captain's tracks. He filed requests to receive the interrogators' reports and sought out different informers. The reports were full of fallacious testimonies and squalid, meaningless scrawlings. In the end he grew bored with them and sent them back.

He promised himself he'd take charge of the investigation as soon as an opportunity to go to Cyrene arrived. He was searching for the key to that officer's destiny. Martello's disappearance didn't shed any light on the meaning of what had happened, at least in so far as the investigators had been able to reconstruct it. His death, which couldn't be ascertained, could have meant either damnation or salvation. *What's certain is that once we cross over a secret, fatal line, there can be no coming back*, he concluded ironically, as though he had been giving a lecture.

But as his time was entirely occupied by following the progress of the peace negotiations, the general didn't manage to go to Cyrene as soon as he would have liked.

The memory of Martello drifted further and further from his mind.

The general thought about him again in October 1917. Sitting at his desk, behind his head stood the sumptuously framed proclamation General Caneva had delivered 'to the

people of Tripolitania, Cyrenaica and its adjacent provinces.'
Before the general's eyes lay a dispatch reporting the Italians'
defeat at Caporetto. He stood up and sat back down several
times, never managing to tear his gaze away from the
dispatch. He would be the one to give the Expeditionary
Force the news. Thanks to his penchant for the theatre,
Captain Martello would have been quite amused by the
sight of that proclamation on the wall still radiating its
illusory splendour while the general stood in the square
reading out the bitter communiqué informing his men that
the motherland had suffered a humiliating defeat.

By way of atonement, General Delle Stelle picked up
the dispatch and re-read it:

> *The absence of several divisions of the 2nd Army,*
> *which cowardly retreated without firing a single shot,*
> *or which ignominiously surrendered to the enemy,*
> *allowed the Austro-Hungarian forces*
> *to breach our left flanks on the Julian Alps.*
> *Our troops' valiant efforts were not enough*
> *to prevent the enemy from setting foot*
> *on our motherland's sacred soil.*
>
> *General Cadorna, 29 October 1917*

1920

THE MARRIAGE
OF OMAR

Die Linien des Lebens sind verschieden,
Wie Wege sind, und wie der Berge Grenzen.
Was hier wir sind, kann dort ein Gott ergänzen
Mit Harmonien und ewigen Lohn und Frieden.[3]

3 Untitled poem by Friedrich Hölderlin

I

'I'm tormented by the presence of these servants.'

'Those you call "servants," we who govern call "indigenous people," and their presence torments us too. But what should we do about it? Eliminate them? To live in this colony means we must accept their presence.'

'I can't understand why we must have them in our house,' Countess Rosina said.

'You want to exorcise their presence from these walls, turn the perimeter of the house into a magical barrier that guarantees our safety and keeps them at a distance,' the deputy governor retorted. 'Our conquest of this colony is based on the effect that the force of our faith, language, willpower and strength can have on their lives. We can't allow them to get distracted, there's even a Political Bureau that spends each day coming up with new ways to penetrate their thoughts. We want them to love us, but we don't want to renounce our ability to make them fear us. However, our measures have generated an equal but opposite reaction, which is what afflicts us. The indigenous peoples' presence is a shadow that pursues us and mimics our actions. Either we return to our ships, or we exterminate them and push them away to more distant borders. Or we could educate ourselves about them and try to make our presence here more acceptable to them. There are native servants in this house because the deputy governor wants to show their presence here doesn't bother him – on the contrary, it soothes him! Which is why I also welcome the city's notables into my house. Victor Emmanuel has granted the natives a Basic Charter guaranteeing their civil rights. But laws are useless unless they are put into practice. Khadija entering our room in the morning with a cup of coffee works on the same level as Parliament negotiating with a Cyrenaican tribal chief: a mutual recognition of each others' presence in these lands.'

General Caneva's Expeditionary Force invaded the Libyan coast towards the end of September 1911. Having vanquished the Turkish garrison, the Italians concluded a peace treaty with the Sublime Porte in Lausanne in October 1912. However, by 1921 the Italians still hadn't managed to break the back of the Libyan rebellion in Tripolitania and Cyrenaica. After numerous military vicissitudes, colonial power was still confined to urban centres, while sovereignty over the boundless, mostly deserted hinterland was still ambiguous, with power alternating from one side to the other according to how the struggle was going.

Both sides had been sorely tested and both sides were worn out, the conquistadors' problems exacerbated by the growing disorder in the motherland after the end of the Great War in 1918, when all desire for colonial expansion was silenced in Rome. The atmosphere of mass disillusion and exhaustion at the time created the conditions for an attempt at a compromise. They even decided to grant the Libyan people some satisfaction with the so-called 'treaty,' which granted the natives the right to elect representatives to a consultative assembly with tightly limited powers. It also established the equality of natives and citizens of the kingdom of Italy before the law, guaranteed the inviolability of one's home and property, and stipulated that the Italian Governor would have to submit all nomination for civil service posts before a council for approval.

By 1921, a parliament had finally been elected in Cyrenaica, the eastern province.

Since the army had failed to crush the patriotic resistance, the country had thus effectively been governed by a diarchy: on the one hand there was the colony's governor, who was the Italian King's representative in Libya and who resided in Benghazi, while on the other was Sidi Idris al-Sanussi, the Emir of Cyrenaica, who had his capital in dusty Ajdabiya, at the edge of the desert. Arms guaranteed the independence of the two powers.

Count Alonzo looked out of the window, as though searching for comfort as well as the affirmation of his plans.

He could see the entirety of the little colonial city, with its labyrinth of streets, its white terraces, and the odd garden. Beyond it lay the limitless desert plains, which were almost devoid of any vegetation or other signs of life. The house was surrounded by an ample loggia, and the windows that looked out onto it were always open, unless the sandy winds from the south happened to be blowing. Throughout most of the year, the sky wore the same expression: clear and uniform, just like the red earth, which was dusty and unvarying.

Then there was the blue oasis of the sea, choppy and luminous.

'Taking an active role in public life is your way of running away from family affections.'

'If I have to renounce all interests outside these walls whenever I come home, and become someone else, then I must confess it'll leave me wanting to spend as little time here as I possibly can. The Libyans are exhausted, they need tranquillity, but they're keeping their eyes peeled for an opportunity to pick up arms again. The peace achieved by the Basic Charter must make the resumption of hostilities impossible.'

'When the crisis in Rome is resolved, it'll undoubtedly dictate a definitive solution for the colony – the Basic Charter is nothing but a deferment. Your passion is disproportionate to the humble role you've been assigned,' the Countess replied.

The Countess hadn't been in the colony for long, and she displayed the melancholy of those forced to live in exile.

'Righteousness can turn the provisional agreement into a definitive one. Regardless, I'm unwilling to evaluate other options.'

'You'll ruin your career. But if this is the price we have to pay so that we can bring some serenity back to our marriage, then I'll accept it.'

There were no signs the pleasant North African autumn was drawing to a close. Just as when a sonata nears its denouement, picks up the plot and plays it out again in a pointless but delectable variation, the autumn was robbing the winter of part of its reign. Sometimes, the autumn even lasted as late as Christmas. Brief, torrential showers occasionally interrupted winter's agonising delay.

The window was like a frame designed to encase the Count's portrait. The whiteness of the walls and the blue of the sea filled the rest of the canvas. Rosina looked at the portrait as though she wanted to snatch it off the wall and run away. But where could she go?

'All travellers nurse the ambition to return to their native islands as strangers. Khadija matters more to my life than my Aunt Clotilde, and I'm more interested in colonial society's two components, national and indigenous, than the ups and downs of Lombard manufacturing, even if that's precisely where my fate lies, since Lombard industry might well determine how that ugly political game in Rome plays out.'

'So I'm wrong because I don't think of Khadija as my aunt?' Rosina exclaimed impatiently. 'These new kinships strike me as disloyal. Khadija is nothing but a servant and I don't like her. She cooks well. But she's so fat! She shakes the whole house when she walks.'

'First you say Khadija's only a servant, then you ascribe her magical powers. Fat and short as she is, with that majestic gait of hers, her ancient face still youthful and lucid, as well as her deep, placid eyes – which nevertheless flash with irrepressible force if angered – Khadija's the very portrait of her country.'

'That crow lords over us. My authority means nothing to her, she doesn't follow my orders.'

'If it makes you feel any better, sometimes she doesn't even obey mine. Your desire to dismiss her reminds me of those bureaucrats who want to push the Libyans further and further away so that we can finally dominate a country that doesn't even belong to us. Instead, even though we may seem like gods, we're only guests here. We must ensure our presence here is accepted and seen as the force for good that it is.'

'You see the conquest of Libya as our original sin, the root of all the evils that plague this city's inhabitants. The Basic Charter isn't just the recognition of these peoples' civil rights, it's become a prayer that you hope will cleanse the sin of our presence. I don't see why I should sit by your right, why don't we put Khadija in my place, starting tomorrow?'

It was as though Rosina wanted to wound her husband, so she could later rush to his aid, and thus have him all to herself.

'When speaking about me to other people, Khadija once said that His Excellency, may God forgive him, has never laid a hand on her. She called on God to forgive my sins, all for so little! She's as stern with God as she is with me, and her plea sounded more like an order. Only people with clean consciences speak like that.'

'When you left for Africa, I felt I was shut out from your thoughts and your heart. It either cost you a lot of effort to write to me, or you forgot about it altogether, and you spoke of things that didn't interest me in the slightest, in fact they annoyed me, because they widened the distance between us. I wanted to come here so I could be with you again. You welcomed me affectionately, but you were in a hurry. I'm finding it just as difficult to get you to accept my presence in this house as you're finding it to get the natives to accept your authority. But that I should be treated like this by my own husband?'

Count Alonzo stood to go and greet Doctor Amilcare.

'My husband accuses me of laziness,' the Countess said while Doctor Amilcare planted a kiss on her hand, 'he says I twist reality to excuse my lethargy and thus inflict the same on him, meaning, in other words, that I limit his world and ask him to adapt as soon as he enters the home.'

'Countess Rosina, anyone who speaks to your husband suffers the same accusations. He's very strict and impatient with his friends.'

'But not with our enemies. It seems they're the only ones worthy of special treatment.'

'The more arrogant and diffident they become, the more enthusiastic the Count grows in his mission,' Doctor Amilcare said, taking a seat on the sofa next to Rosina. 'Ever since the government granted the colony this Basic Charter, he hasn't wasted a moment in trying to win over the people of Benghazi. As for what we want, once the King signed that decree, all our wishes became irrelevant.'

'And how have the natives welcomed this Basic Charter? Alonzo's always vague on this issue.'

'The natives refuse to accept peace if it comes at the cost of our continued presence. His Majesty believed he could conquer them through a gesture of generosity. But the indigenous people know that we granted them this Basic Charter because we couldn't win the war. By entering this agreement we've conceded our partial defeat. The natives are even aware this is just a truce before hostilities inevitably break out again, at which point we will still aim to achieve their unconditional submission. Although both sides view this provisional agreement coolly and prag-matically, Count Alonzo, one of the most important officials here, has transformed an opportunistic edict into a binding law, and doesn't want anyone to voice any reservations: thus he accuses us of sloth and intolerance.'

The deputy governor's house, isolated from the city and its outskirts, was located on the strip of land between the sea and the *sabkhats*, the littoral lagoons, only a short distance from the old Turkish fort. Their conversation wasn't disturbed by any noise, as though the room on the first floor was separated from the reality around it by an unbridgeable gap – a reality that nevertheless refused to be bent to the will of the people speaking in it. The deputy governor listened out for any sounds: a donkey braying, children yelling, the cry of a horse-cart driver. The distance covered by a sound – or an object, or an animal, or a man – as it travels in one direction keeps shrinking if a traveller runs after it in the opposite direction.

'The political situation in Rome is such a complete mess,' Doctor Amilcare continued, having calmed down, 'that soon enough there'll only be room for criminals, martyrs and saints in government. Even the great King of Italy, as we melodramatically address him in our proclamations, might one day decide to replace Count Alonzo with a criminal: kindness, like violence, can sometimes be used excessively. In fact, the Count is the only new politician in this colony – in the coming days, more will come and occupy diametrically opposite ideas, but we are living in the era of excess: we are excessively virtuous, just as we are excessively cruel and dishonourable.'

In the afternoon, the doctor accompanied Count Alonzo and Countess Rosina on a long carriage ride outside the city. While the world, seduced by speed, was beginning to experiment with automobiles, the Count was in a carriage rolling through the limitless plain as he rediscovered the allure of travelling slowly along a path that was both pleasantly boring and familiar.

The plain was almost entirely deserted and the carriage raised a cloud of dust. Vegetation thrived inside humid hollows in the ground like giant basins, hidden from sight until one was only a few metres away, and the tops of the trees barely rose out of the surrounding plain. According to tradition, this was where the ancients believed one could find the Hesperides' fabulous gardens where golden apples grew, apples which Gaia gave to Hera as a wedding gift when she married Zeus. Further along was the great abyss, a cave traversed by an underground river, which was identified with the legendary Lethe, one of the five rivers of Hades.

'The indigenous chiefs of Tripoli,' the Count said to Doctor Amilcare, 'are in direct contact with left-wing forces in Italy and consider them their allies in their struggle against us. They even keep the Cyrenaican chiefs well informed. The natives' acceptance of the Basic Charter can thus be explained by the following motive: to gain time while Italy descends into chaos, or civil war, by which time we'll obviously need to abandon the colony. Or, if we don't leave, it will make it easier for them to boot us out. Therefore, as His Majesty's delegate, I'm willing to offer any concessions to avoid a complete withdrawal. What does the King really want? What can he do? How long will this last? And at what cost? Nevertheless, I won't hesitate in the slightest: we cannot vote for the worst simply out of fear. Let us put this Basic Charter into practice here, in fact let us consider it a choice: if everyone refuses the alternative, we'll be able to better defend democracy.'

Growing suddenly impatient, he added, 'I'd like to govern this colony, or at least contribute to its governance, in the same way that travellers used to visit countries two centuries ago – not to oppress people, but to get to know them.'

Rosina rose from the sofa and went to sit on the black stool next to the piano. She placed her hands on the keys, struck a chord, then her hands ran along the ivories, her fingers striking the keys in a thick, stormy hail. Omar, the young man who worked in the house, was astonished by that wild, painful sound and shifted his gaze from the garden. The windows of the great hall, those white rectangular frames cut into the enormous façade, had been thrown open, but nobody looked out of them and only sound spilled out in invisible waves. It was like a mysterious well one sees in a dream: indecipherable.

Khadija was sitting on a mat boiling some tea in a corner of the courtyard.

Her skin was swarthy, her face rotund, and her neck nearly non-existent. Her torso was barrel-shaped. She had short legs, which she kept tucked under her while sitting down. Her body was wrapped in a threadbare purple silk robe with silver stripes. She had gold bracelets on her wrist and a fish-shaped filigree pendant hanging from her neck. That gold was her nest egg, all the wealth she'd accumulated from her long days of hard work. A small ring set with a blue stone shone from her stubby hand. The blue stone and the fish shielded her from the evil eye.

There was a young woman next to her who was also ebony-skinned, long-legged and nimble – her daughter. She wasn't Khadija's flesh and blood, but was adopted.

Saber, Khadija's husband, lay stretched out on the mat. He was very old and only managed to walk with great difficulty, by dragging his feet. He was the doorman, but often fell asleep, and he'd keep the door slightly ajar, leaning his foot against it to prevent anyone entering. He was hard of hearing, and therefore ringing the doorbell was useless.

Many people were out of work in Benghazi, and everyone was astonished the old man had found a job – and in the deputy governor's house to boot. The ancient man's presence soothed the Count, who pictured Saber at his post as a protective measure. In the morning, the Count would linger in the atrium and enquire after Saber's health before leaving the house. Saber would thank the Lord and say he was in good health, and after having praised God once more, would invoke Him to bless the master: that was the viaticum with which the Count began his day.

Saber owned a donkey cart he and Khadija used to return to their village in the evenings.

The tea ceremony, which took so much time, exasperating the colonists – who confused efficiency with purity of heart, or organisational rigour with equilibrium – had never made the Count impatient. If Khadija ever saw the Count walk by, she would call him over and offer him some tea, which she'd pour into small, ribbed glasses. Omar sat next to her. He was roughly twenty-five years old, thin, of medium height, and light-skinned. The Count owned a cabriolet and Omar was his coachman. Driven by a single horse, the carriage was identical to the ones available for hire in Benghazi. It was open-topped, featured a seat broad enough for two travellers and lined in black leather, and a fold-away seat in front of it, as well as an additional seat for a servant next to the coachman. On Sundays, the Count would gladly take a carriage ride to the orchards of El-Fueihat. Omar had also been entrusted with making purchases at the local market every morning, where he'd go with a wicker basket in his hand and buy whatever the demanding cook needed. He would see to his errands in the city, sweep the courtyard and terrace, and wash the stairs.

The tea ceremony in the deputy governor's house wasn't usually held at that time, which was when the old couple would head home after the day's work, but Omar had detained them. This meant he was getting divorced. He didn't seem convinced about it, and when he spoke about his wife, his wrath concealed strong emotions. Khadija listened to him without looking at him or interrupting him. Impatience is a sign of ignorance: first he had to let the cat out of the bag.

Omar's mother-in-law lived in his home. She was a woman with a difficult and complicated past. Much was said about her, and some of it was mere conjecture, but nobody knew much for certain. Everyone saw a different version of her past, and as for her whole life, no one knew it intimately.

Such an interesting past meant many mysteries, and life with that woman was a contract with conditions that Omar was oblivious to. Being shrewd, Muna hadn't kept the gold Omar had given her to pay for her daughter's hand, but had instead sold it. What could she still want? She was a very demanding woman, always clamouring for their attention, and only described reality in a way that obliged them to see it through her eyes, blackmailing them with her past and pawning their future according to her whims. Muna's daughter was very beautiful, and very different from her mother: but there was no way to tear her away from that infernal woman, who dominated every aspect of her life.

Khadija lifted the blue tin teapot, and from a great distance, her arm all tensed, she poured the tea into the first glass without spilling a single drop on the floor. She tasted it, threw the rest on the floor, washed the little glass and put it back next to the others. She lifted her arm again and poured out three cups without making a single wrong move. She offered Saber the first, Omar the second, and kept the third for herself, beginning to sip it slowly.

Omar's face reflected the light of the moon, while the charcoal fire in the terracotta bowl burned brightly.

From the windows of the hall, where the Count, the Countess and Doctor Amilcare were talking, three squares of light fell on the floor. They looked like tarot cards, and Khadija, being an expert fortune-teller, was busy reading them.

Khadija had never really liked that woman with an overly interesting past. Muna hailed from the westernmost corner of Africa, even though she'd been born in Benghazi and hadn't ever spent much time away from that city. But her secrets meant as much as absences. The sum of those secrets was more important than her origins, which distorted the image.

Why hadn't Omar asked her advice when it came to choosing a wife? After all, she knew the complete ancestry of every girl in the city. Having too much of a past was a bad sign: honest people could always tell you their life story in a single breath. Who was the girl's real father? The man whose name she bore, and who'd been Muna's lawful husband, was dead. Perhaps he had only ever been a mask that concealed someone entirely different. Sobeida's beauty was a gilded cage: now Muna had Omar under her thumb.

Saber mumbled something. Young Aisha had fallen asleep. Perhaps even the old man was asleep, and had merely muttered something in his slumber. Omar now lived in the Count's house, in a little room at the far end of the courtyard. He occasionally spent the evening with his cousin Sharafeddin, who owned a shop in one of the alleyways that led away from the market.

A bachelor never gets up to any good, and Khadija was already thinking about Omar's second wedding. 'You'll get your son back by the time he's nine years old – you'll be free to educate him however you wish, as per our customs.'

Too much of a past indicated restlessness and confusion, and restlessness and confusion always led to the loss, or disavowal, of traditions, and whoever breaks with tradition is doomed to be lost. 'Keep him away from that woman, so people won't be able to say anything strange about him when he's older.'

Omar was in a gloomy mood. His divorce would free him from Muna: but he wouldn't only be leaving beautiful, unhappy Sobeida behind in that woman's infernal hands, he would also be leaving his son. He said he didn't have enough money to marry another woman.

'We'll help you,' Khadija replied, 'and then there's the master. You live in his house: he should take care of you.'

Omar made a gesture of refusal.

Employing a great deal of effort, Khadija rose to her feet. Omar helped old Saber stand up, and Aisha ran ahead. She'd woken up happy, and was laughing as she went. When they reached the door they crossed the street, Saber untied the donkey from the post, Khadija and Aisha climbed onto the cart, and they left in a cheerful mood. The women tucked their legs underneath them. For that old couple, the night was safe and bearable.

II

Sharafeddin had learned the craft of weaving in Tripoli, where it was a time-honoured tradition. Having brought his loom to Benghazi, he had opened a shop in one of the labyrinthine alleys around the covered market. It was demanding work: the weaver's hand threw the shuttle while his foot regulated the weft. One could hear the beating of the shuttle from afar, and Sharafeddin's shop was used as a reference point to indicate the street.

There were only a few artisans in Benghazi, which was mostly a centre of commerce for the immense surrounding region peopled by nomads and farmers; the city also served as the Italian army's general headquarters, and provided all the ancillary services it required. The colonial invasion had altered the social fabric: soldier's wages were highly sought after, regardless of which of the two flags one fought for. During the last years of the Great European War, a catastrophe that had immediately followed the entrenchment of the Expeditionary Force, the country had been ravaged by starvation and disease. Thus, Victor Emmanuel's lieutenant and Sidi Idris al-Sanussi, Libya's noble representative, had stretched out their hands in a gesture of reconciliation.

'All those people didn't fight and die in order to extract that little piece of scrap paper from the King of Italy, which he now offers us instead of the gallows.'

Sharafeddin and Omar sat on a straw mat, their backs propped against cushions. The room was narrow and low ceilinged, and the walls were rotting with damp. Their shoes were lined up along the edge of the mat. A photograph was hanging from one of the walls: it depicted a man wearing a red fez and sporting enormous black whiskers. The room, which was devoid of any items even remotely linked to the barbarian conquerors, was in keeping with the man who inhabited it, whose refusal of the Italian colonisation was steadfast and consistent. Sharafeddin was drinking *laghbi*, a fermented liquid distilled from palm leaves. He spoke calmly, only to suddenly be overcome by wrath. One of his eyes was opaque and hooded by a lid that was thicker than the other.

The Basic Charter the Italians had offered the Libyans, and which was to be considered a contract between the two communities, might have seemed like a reasonable compromise to those living in the deputy governor's house; but Omar only needed to visit his cousin's shop on the other side of Benghazi for the barrier that separated the two communities to once again prove inviolable.

In Tripoli, the Italian governor had summoned the Arab chiefs to the fort – which had once belonged to Charles V, then been passed to the Hospitaller Knights of St John of Jerusalem in 1530, subsequently become the seat of the independent Qaramanli dynasty in the eighteenth century, and finally become the official residence of the Sublime Porte's representative in the nineteenth century – so they could officially submit to him. The chiefs had arrived armed, on horseback, as though they'd decided to take the fort by force. In 1911 Italy had counted on the complicity of the great European powers, who'd avoided conflict in order to safeguard peace and the balance of power: the world war had broken that code of silence and the monopoly of strength. After all, hadn't the American president Woodrow Wilson spoken in favour of the emancipation of all peoples?

Sharafeddin was still drinking that dense, bitter distillation. He wiped his lips with the palm of his hand. That 'scrap of paper' was an act of capitulation, since the signatories weren't even obliged to honour it. 'People only abide by their own laws, not those of strangers. A day will come when you leave the deputy governor's house with the firm intention of destroying it, or escape from it after committing a murder. Everyone's got a role to play in life that befits their ancestry.' He went quiet. There was an impure conflict in Omar's heart: Sharafeddin and his room were fighting against the reality of the Count. 'There's no such thing as friendship unless one is among kinsmen, just like there's no pity for the defeated.'

Then Sharafeddin stretched out on the mat and fell into a deep slumber.

Omar watched him as he slept. Proof of the Count's sincerity lay in the confusion Omar felt in that wretched room: for the deputy governor of Cyrenaica and his coachman, the colonial experience was a journey, and Omar's confusion legitimised the Count's own confusion.

The presence of one in the life of the other was a landscape, as well as a journey.

III

Rosina sat in front of her piano every day. She would flip through white booklets with very wide pages and recite lyrics. The cook and the coachman couldn't understand a word of what she said.

Whenever she dusted the piano Khadija's arm was stiff, because she distrusted that gigantic, shiny black bird stuck in the middle of the hall. She'd once caught Omar making sounds by tapping on those black-and-white keys, at which point she'd sharply shut the lid and nearly broken his fingers. Even old Saber was curious about that instrument. He'd never seen the mistress play it, as he rarely went up to the first floor, since climbing the stairs tired him out. Besides, his hearing could barely register the sound, so all that dramatic singing would only reach him in muffled snippets while he was observing the crowds on the street, ensconced behind the door in the breezy atrium. But every time he heard the Countess suddenly yelling, he would shoot to his feet, frightened out of his wits.

'There aren't just five of us in the house now, but six,' Khadija said to the Count, without turning around. 'Either that or one of us has a doppelgänger.'

She was in the kitchen cooking meatballs on an open fire, a dish the Count was particularly fond of. She turned them over, one after the other, using a spatula with an elongated handle.

The music was the sixth presence. What did it mean? Everyone walks around with their own unique interpretation in their head. Now in the middle of the journey of her life, Khadija had been brought to bear with a warning. Now she would have to choose between different representations of a cryptic reality. Those who are blind see an encounter as a destination, while the intelligent see it as a crossroads. A spirit – music – was altering the direction in which the five characters were walking. Whoever had been walking along a riverbank suddenly found themselves on the opposite shore, whoever was walking in one direction found themselves going in the opposite; whoever was climbing down, would henceforth rise; and whoever was rising, would trip and fall. By denouncing the spirit, Khadija embodied it.

Magic is the means to ward off evil spirits and to travel through the dimension in which they operate. Khadija was defying invisible forces because she had the powers to beat them.

In the evening, Rosina accepted her friends' pressing invitations to dine out and consented to give a musical performance; but it was something different, a tender, consoling melody full of light. The spirit that had been spotted revealed itself in a misleading guise. Walking past Omar, Khadija barely nodded her chin.

When the Countess's nephew Second Lieutenant Antonino Venier, who was almost still a boy, arrived in the colony, the Count scrutinised Khadija's alert face: was

Antonino the sixth presence she had been referring to? But Khadija eyed him sternly, and suddenly turned hostile – she considered it a sacrilege to joke about the intuitions certain people are granted, since whoever gives a gift can always take it away.

Antonino was not the sixth person in the house, but the seventh. The sixth, a spirit which manifested itself in sound, remained invisible, that is assuming it wasn't a doppelgänger of one of the other characters. But who among them could have a doppelgänger? Would the metamorphosis of one character mean the metamorphosis of the others? Regardless of whether it was a sixth presence, or a doppelgänger, the spirit held the destinies of all five characters in its hand.

Venier had often heard stories about the colony, had read some books, and even met with veterans of the Expeditionary Force: men who told tales of heroism, of the implacable sun, of the boundless plains, of betrayals, and of a few acts of gallantry. Death sometimes made an appearance, but only in the consoling guise of heroism. He had chanced upon a book of photographs published by Treves on the war of 1911, the oval portraits of fallen soldiers arrayed across its pages like ornamental festoons. A closer look at those photographs revealed piles of murdered rebels lying on the floor, their clothes utterly wretched, as though they were rags hanging from their stick-like bones; as though they were nothing but hunting trophies. Venier was enchanted by the city of Benghazi, with its palm groves, whitewashed houses, and a sky that took up nearly the entirety of the boundless plain.

He was very emotional when he landed and came ashore, as though he'd entered a graceful little fable fenced off from the outside world by invisible borders. Antonino cheerfully embraced his aunt. His meeting with his uncle, the Count, was simple and affectionate. Shiny and black, the open-topped buggy aroused his astonishment, and he was the last to climb on, taking a seat opposite his aunt and uncle.

As soon as they reached the deputy governor's house, Saber came forward to meet him and mouthed incomprehensible words. Having left the driver's seat, Omar carried the suitcases.

Khadija's arrival into the hall left a strong impression on the new guest. Antonino was attracted by the gold jewellery she was wearing, which was splendid and unusual. His curiosity was piqued by her silk robe, with its silver and yellow stripes on a bed of blue, as well as by her large black bare feet, which were so majestically planted on the ground, by those short, stubby hands clasping his, by her fiery, delightful eyes, by the tunic she wore underneath her robe, with yellow flowers on a bed of red – large parts of which tufted out of her sleeves.

In her turn, Khadija looked at the officer in wonder: he was little more than a boy, rosy-skinned, with fragile, well-shaped hands, a svelte figure, a perfect tiny face, ruffled hair, pearly teeth. She was also drawn to his uniform, expertly tailored and hugging his waist like a clasp.

Khadija prepared a sumptuous lunch, threw open the windows, and advised Saber to leave the door open, since the whole city would undoubtedly turn out to welcome the boy who was dressed like an officer, and to congratulate the deputy governor. That swarthy, stocky woman looked as though she'd fallen in love with the second lieutenant, who was so nimble and light that he could barely fill his uniform. The Count, the Countess, and Omar and Saber had been shunted to the sidelines; the scene was now wholly occupied by Khadija and Antonino, a perfect couple.

When the guests left in the evening Antonino went downstairs, and the cook and the second lieutenant observed one another again and bid each other goodnight several times: the tender delays that occur when lovers part for the first time.

Antonino came down in good time the following morning, impatient to see Khadija again. The latter welcomed him with relief, and made him his breakfast downstairs while he stood next to her, although she always served the Count his meals in the dining room or the terrace. Antonino drank his milk, ate the slices of buttered toast with cherry jam Khadija had spread for him, then cracked open an egg and sucked out its yolk. He wiped his lips, put the napkin down on the table, but didn't move.

Khadija crossed the kitchen. She came back bearing a metal box that she opened before Antonino's awe-struck eyes and then reached into, drawing out a stale pastry and offering it to him. The box exuded a strong smell of rosemary.

Antonino was wearing a light robe over his pyjamas, and being so lightly dressed, appeared even more fragile and small; and yet he was considerably taller than her. He had carefully brushed his hair, which was fair and extremely fine. Khadija only managed to gesture, as though scared that this bird, whose feathers were so regal and fragile, might take fright and fly off.

Consecrated by the pastry produced from the metal box decorated with colourfully painted heroic scenes, Antonino and Khadija's friendship continued to develop over the following days. In fact, it already had its daily rituals, as though Antonino's beautiful aunt and black Africa were two hands that had stretched out a rope, leaving the young lieutenant to accomplish extravagant feats on it like an acrobat. Khadija tried to emulate him in the kitchen, ensuring she never served him the same dish twice, treasuring his compliments on her cooking in her heart, as though she were sliding coins into a piggy bank. She would serve him stuffed courgettes, eggplants, peppers, tomatoes and even potatoes, as well as wraps made of vine leaves or pumpkin. On Sunday she prepared an entire lamb stuffed with rice and almonds, even wrapping the beasts' legs – which hung immobile in the air over the silver plate – in tin foil, making it look bright and festive. Antonino was impressed by the sacrificial offering, but this didn't prevent him eating his fill. He would plunge his spoon into the carcass and happily extract its delicious stuffing. Couscous, the traditional dish, was always prepared in deliciously varied ways that constantly altered its taste. Antonino drank unfiltered Turkish coffee, punctuating his sips with long pauses, as though it were no big deal. A layer of black sludge would settle at the bottom of the cup, like a murky pond at the back of the garden. One only needed to slightly tilt the cup to see the sludge leave arcane hieroglyphs in its wake.

The Countess was very proud of her Meissen china set, with its dishes decorated in green arabesques on a bed of brilliant ivory, and she only allowed it to be used on special occasions. Khadija thought Antonino's presence constituted such an occasion. The young officer was enchanted by the way Khadija's black hands contrasted against the white cup. Antonino thought the scene before his eyes was the spitting image of the contorted ebony-skinned slaves depicted in those fabulous Venetian china pieces. Khadija's hands were as cool as the breeze one breathed in a grotto, and left him with a strange feeling that was simultaneously enticing and terrifying. He only needed to touch that hand to evoke a nocturnal world that was both sweet and melancholy, fleeting and impenetrable.

On the evening of the third day, the Countess grew apprehensive about the risks those precious cups with the slightly undulated edges were being exposed to, and she approached Khadija as she was pouring Antonino some coffee, saying:

'Come now, there's no need to use them every day, Antonino is not a stranger.'

Convulsed by a shudder, Khadija was silent for a moment, lost in her thoughts. Then, turning her torso to face her mistress, she angrily exclaimed: 'Which stranger's face could be dearer to our hearts than his?'

The steam curling out of the cup and into the air was growing thinner, and Antonino couldn't bring it to his lips. A veil of sadness fell over the room. Khadija stormed out grumbling to herself and even letting out some little moans.

Neither on that day, nor on any of the succeeding days, did Antonino manage to convince Khadija to decipher the arabesques at the bottom of his cup, since the expert fortune-teller refused to read this particular destiny.

Old Saber tried to pay the young officer the customary compliments, but Antonino was always in such a hurry that Saber eventually gave up. He watched him come and go at all hours. At first, he tried to stand up each time he saw him, out of respect, but always managed to do so too late. By the time Saber had stood up, the young man was already far away. In the end, he limited himself to moving his head, thus being able to see him disappear up the stairs or leave through the door. But Antonino went in and out of the house so often, irrespective of any schedule or devoid of any plausible explanation, that he wound up spending a great deal of time with the old doorman. Occasionally, Saber would hear his voice. He was a creature who belonged to a different species. Just like some birds are only ever seen with their wings spread in flight, Saber had always seen Antonino with his legs in motion. Did that little critter ever stop moving, and where did he sleep, and what did he look like when he rested? Once, Saber chanced upon Antonino while the latter, uncaring of his uniform, had stretched out on a bench in the courtyard and fallen asleep. Saber drew close to him. Antonino's chest was rising some-what hurriedly – perhaps he was dreaming? There was almost nothing inside that pretty uniform, little more than breath, the gulp of air he inhaled and exhaled. The old man marvelled once more at the variety of creation and praised the Lord, the Maker of everything that exists.

Omar was so silent and discreet for the first few days that Antonino almost didn't notice his presence. The swarthy Khadija had claimed all his attention. Antonino loved his beautiful aunt, held his uncle in timorous respect, and was so curious about Benghazi, and the people who belonged to this or that community, that he neglected Omar. But the latter was always ready to heed Antonino's orders, as though he were following him, and answered all his ques-tions frankly, so the young officer grew accustomed to Omar's presence. They ended up spending most of their time together, whether Antonino was in the house or out in town when Omar was off duty.

Omar was the shadow that followed Antonino, but he also silently guided him.

One day, when they were at the market, Omar and Antonino walked down a little alley and stepped inside Sharafeddin's shop. The latter was rather peeved at the sight of that couple, as he disliked them, and so he welcomed them rather awkwardly. He didn't even get up from his spot in front of the loom, and only reluctantly consented to give a demonstration of his work, at Omar's embarrassed insistence. Antonino couldn't hear Omar's explanations over all the noise the shuttle made as it swung to and fro, and was struck by the weaver's hostility. Antonino wasn't used to hostility, being more accustomed to indulgence and admiration wherever he went, as though he carried a talisman with him. Antonino was spellbound as he watched Sharafeddin.

Omar regretted that unfortunate outing. The two should never have met. Sharafeddin's mere presence had made Omar feel guilty about his relationship with the deputy governor's nephew. The rapport between the officer and the weaver — tense, silent, and violent in its unnatural awkwardness — didn't stop when the two left the shop, but was bound to carry on and would eventually come to light, regardless of whether it happened days or even years later. Although their paths — and the outcomes those paths would have — uncertain, mysterious forces were already working in the dark.

The following day Omar was in a bad mood, but Antonino had no recollection of his encounter with Sharafeddin. That evening, for the first time, he paid a visit to the loyal coachman in his room at the far end of the courtyard. That unexpected appearance confused Omar, so he detained the young officer and told him the story of his life. Antonino was incredibly curious to see the beautiful Sobeida. Omar didn't suspect that Antonino's attentions, or rather his obvious desire to identify with him, as though he wanted to replace him, were malign. Omar spoke innocently and Antonino wasn't in a hurry to interrupt that dream. The unfortunate incident helped cement their bond, and their conversation overcame the idea of insurmountable barriers. Sobeida was a mirror that lay between the husband who'd repudiated her and her would-be lover.

The next day, Antonino went for a carriage ride with the Countess. They asked to be driven to the market. The young officer was enchanted by the sight of a silver necklace, and so he bought it for his beautiful aunt. They were the sort of jewels typically worn by peasants: large hoop earrings, rings with enormous square red green or yellow stones, festive necklaces with thousands of pendants, delicate fans to be worn in one's hair, little cylindrical vials one could keep perfumes in, which were adorned with hand-shaped pendants. Antonino's games amused the Countess. They returned from their outing exhausted: the heat was unbearable and the market as stifling as a crowded theatre.

IV

The Count listened patiently to Professor Bergonzi and answered his questions unhurriedly, despite his surprise that this erudite young man apparently hadn't noticed that he'd stumbled onto a stage where a very different kind of play was being performed, one that differed greatly from those in Italian cities. This play featured different landscapes and characters, each with their own unique meaning, and answered to alien gods, thus praising different virtues and condemning different sins. Professor Bergonzi had arrived in Africa as though he'd shifted apartments from one floor of a building to another, where he brought the same familiar objects and where the same idols would be waiting for him. The colony had to become just another Italian province, and its different origins wouldn't be allowed to enrich or influence it, since the military conquest had made it into a legitimate part of Italy's heritage. Bergonzi never mentioned the Libyans, who didn't feature in his thoughts because they'd never appeared in the books he'd read, which was the only guarantee of reality besides the confusion of the present: his ignorance of the context in which he was operating was unshadowed by questions and doubts.

Books were not bridges extended across different dimensions of reality. Instead, they were bricks of an edifice surrounded by an impenetrable wall inside which he could bury himself.

Slumped down in a sofa, the Countess felt an all-consuming melancholy: why should they listen to everyone? An uninterrupted flow of people passed through the house every day, there was no choice, it was as if every citizen of Benghazi had the right to a moment of their attention. It was a regal waste of time, or a boring way to settle a debt. She would observe the intricate geometrical designs of the floor tiles coalescing into a sort of labyrinth, like the deputy governor's words, but unlike the Count's words, which had a false ring to them, the tiles were playful in their own way, thanks to their bright colours. The Countess looked at the bright patches of sky framed by the windows – devoid of all inscriptions, words or images, they were just homogeneously blue – and sought refuge in them.

Bergonzi wore spectacles on his nose, the distinguishing mark of the brotherhood of teachers. He would pour the irreproachable verses of Parini and the rotund odes of Carducci into the minds of the adolescents entrusted to his care, and emotionally recount the sacrifices the heroes of the Risorgimento had made to bring glory to the motherland. He planted the cult of the Latin era in their hearts, being very inflexible when it came to the purity of the language, and defending it against all contamination. He would attentively, or even impatiently, follow all the developments in modern literature, and was astounded by the Count's indifference. He had audacious opinions, would talk passionately about the problems posed by Ibsen's *A Doll's House*, and was enthusiastic about an Italian playwright called Luigi

Pirandello, whose last effort, *It's Nothing Serious,* he had seen in Rome. From what Bergonzi was saying, one could deduce that he believed adultery was the major problem faced by European civilisation: even if in a rather bookish way, he was well versed in its exquisite and infernal variations.

Bergonzi said he intended to establish a theatre company in Benghazi, since days in the colony were all the same, and made the spirit roil. He had chosen Leonid Andreyev's drama *Anfissa.*

He also outlined his idea for a mobile library, which would be open to civilians and soldiers alike, and asked for the deputy governor's support, or better yet his active complicity, so as to find the necessary funding. He would gladly select the books, as well as manage its day-to-day operations. 'Libraries are indispensable instruments,' he declared.

In addition, he told the Count of the municipality's plans for public gardens. His monologues seemed interminable, as though he were lecturing a class.

The wreath of verses the professor quoted, a litany that belonged to an incomprehensible rite, reawakened in Rosina the faded memories of her school days, like sinister shadows that moved around them in circles. The mobile library, the museum commanded by that secondary school principal, was a place she would never set foot in, since it was a graveyard-like place from which all life was banished. Neither did she entertain any illusions about the municipality's plans for public gardens: in that professor's hands, all would crumble to dust.

Why did they have to put up with him? Why had the mobile library taken hold of the house? Why couldn't they just kick him out? Why was the Count so patient? *What does he have to do with us?*

The questions lingered, restlessly hovering in mid air, accentuating the funereal character of the verbal ceremony.

Satisfied with the beautiful evening, the professor stood up at last, thanked his guests as though he were an actor peering out of the drawn curtains on the stage, and left. The Count paced up and down the main hall. *Leaving Italy behind was my destiny*, he thought, tense and surprised, as though a veil had suddenly fallen.

Rosina was playing a little ironic tune, almost a little carnivalesque, like a procession of ghosts. Omar woke up somewhat astonished; he'd never heard the Countess play the piano at that hour. The windows of the main hall were resplendent with light, but empty.

V

The deputy governor was irked by his nephew's presence, as though it further confused the reality he was trying to bring order to.

'Why were you so strict with the boy?' Rosina asked, 'You spoke to him so harshly on two occasions today at the club, and he was so crestfallen in the end that he stopped speaking.'

'He's been here for three weeks and he keeps butting in on all conversations, just to give his tuppence worth. He simplifies everything so unbearably. He's my nephew, he lives in my house, and I don't want anyone to think I share his reckless opinions.'

The tone he was using was not conciliatory.

'Omar, who is usually so shut off, has opened up to Antonino. Today, I saw the two of them sitting together on the mat for a couple of hours, talking and laughing nonstop. The encounter between the conqueror and the indigenous people, which opens the colonial drama, prescribes the eventual elimination of one of the two; in your imagination, the Basic Charter granted by the King will facilitate their reconciliation. But the harmony you've been so uselessly pursuing took place right there on that mat between Antonino and Omar.'

'Khadija spoke to me about Omar. Apparently he has divorced his wife, and since he lives under my roof, it's my duty to set him up in a new house.'

'We finally have a son! It's a pity we can't agree on who it is: you refuse to be a father to Antonino, while I refuse to be a mother to Omar . . . Khadija is always vigilant and keeps her eyes peeled: she spies on us.'

'Khadija is devoted to us, she's convinced that mysterious powers have taken a hold of us, and she's merely looking out for us, to protect us from them.'

'She doesn't like music.'

'You use music as a form of escapism.'

'After you've told me about all your problems as this colony's deputy governor, I open a musical score like a window and suddenly the stage turns into an infinite landscape. Music is a rallying cry. Your curiosity is reminiscent of the seventeenth century, it's inexhaustibly hungry for all that is different, and your tolerance belongs to that lucky century, but – beware! – don't adopt the same short-sighted view. When reason is the only instrument, one cannot go very far. It prevents us from seeing anything that isn't brightly illuminated – very little, all told! It prevents us from realising that we can't bring much order to anything! It makes us unable to believe in anything that can't be explained, which is very, very little indeed!'

Rosina illustrated what she meant with her hands; but instead of augmenting her speech, they made her appear as though she was on a different plane, as though her gestures were the graceful and ironic poses struck by porcelain dolls in shop windows. Instead of acting as a ferry, or a voyage, the conversation accentuated the distance between the Count and his wife, manipulating both time and space. It was as though they were each engrossed in reading a book which had the other as its main character.

'Forsaking reason is tantamount to making a deal with the devil. I find Antonino's sympathies for certain political tendencies insufferable.'

'Civilisation, the end goal of all the progress you preside over, is not a fixed, timeless paradigm, but is simply the expression of a powerful clique at a given moment in history. It's the rubble on which others will build another edifice once they've reconquered their freedom. There are no universal rules: the fury of nationalism finds its justification in this certainty, and strength is the only guarantee of survival. Antonino is cruel. Yesterday, I saw him squabbling with a man in the street while Omar looked on, white as a sheet, barely restraining his wrath. But by the evening, they were together again, slinging rocks at birds sheltering in the trees. There's something melancholy and altogether unhealthy about your mission, and the natives always notice that. The continuity of tradition, the identity of a nation, matter more than peace; neither is it possible to have peace if the continuity of these traditions is compromised. Your efforts to persuade these people it's in their best interests to stick with us, that we can teach them many useful things, that business will boom – meaning, in other words, that trading their freedom for economic, medical, and educational advantages is a good deal for them – is haunted by a wretched, demonic shadow: the surfeit of reason produces monsters.'

'We must be strong enough to go against the grain and ignore the consensus reached by others, to put up with the psychological burden of diversity, to go beyond limits others believed insurmountable. I'm not looking to play a specific role, but to bring together what was never meant to be separate – and reason is the bridge. When the Cyrenaican Assembly opens its doors, as the Basic Charter called for, you'll be seated in the place of honour – I'll keep you as a hostage. You'll see reality contradict everything you said. In fact,' he added while giving her a small bow, 'it will humiliate you.'

'I'll be happy so long as Antonino is there: that boy will avenge me.'

Later that day, Omar and Antonino paid a second visit to Sharafeddin's shop, where they were once again greeted with hostility: the offering of their presence had been refused.

They had sought out the company of Omar's cousin because of a story. Antonino was an agile, elegant rider, and despite his slender weight he guided the horse authoritatively. Omar had told him Sharafeddin was a renowned rider, which had sparked the young officer's envy. Far away, on the high plateaus, there was a serene valley where a marabout was buried amongst the ruins of a small Roman fort, and this was where the tribe's riders gathered every year, following the harvest. The women and children remained a hundred paces behind, having hung their veils from the branches to act as a screen so that they could uncover themselves. After midday they would send the riders camped in the olive groves vast copper trays heaped with tender meat and rice. Their eager horses, which were either black or a deep rusty red, not too dissimilar from the colour of the earth, were tied to the trees.

After lunch, the men would descend the hill and line up in two rows on the plain. The stirrups on the horses were ancient, and the saddles' blue velvet emblazoned with arabesques in silver filigree. A gold coin could be seen hanging from each horse's shiny head.

The riders entered the lane formed by the two rows of men at a wild gallop; once they'd reached the top of the hill, they would whip their steeds, invoking God. The men who formed the rows would accompany the rider with their yells, encouragements and curses. Someone would make a stinging comment, and those next to him would laugh.

The riders only entered the lane one at a time, ruling out any kind of competitive racing: it was a test of one's individual courage and skill. Sharafeddin shot through like an arrow, the hem of his robe fluttering in the wind like a flag.

At night, the men slept under the olive trees, in the dark valley.

Having heard this story, Antonino had asked Omar if they could visit Sharafeddin again. Only repetition runs on parallel tracks with peace: that was the Libyans' secret. No Basic Charter written by man could ever supplant the sacred law of Tradition. As such, Antonino wanted to challenge that renowned rider; both parties would bring their own law and square off. Sharafeddin didn't budge from his loom, concealing his wounded dignity, or oblivious to the role Omar's tale had offered him. But his nonchalance at the young officer's presence, which was only possible among equals, his calm, and that barely veiled hostility, were clear indicators and confirmed Omar's story. The man in disguise had rejected the challenge: the choice of weapon and locale would be up to him. It took Omar a great deal of effort to tear Antonino away from the weaver's shop.

But his memory was a benign demon, neither tormenting him nor holding him back: the young man walked with the lightness of a god. The sporadic way in which Antonino had taken an interest in Sharafeddin was similar to the attitude one adopts towards a book: once it's shut, it is nothing but an inert memory.

In the evening, Antonino went to look for Omar in his room at the far end of the courtyard, having left him in a gloomy mood earlier on. Antonino's unexpected appearance threw the servant into confusion. They talked for a long time. Later that evening, they left; meanwhile, in the lit salon on the first floor, the Count and Countess were engrossed in one of their interminable card games, where instead of faces the cards were decorated with concepts like conquest, sin, expiation, liberty, democracy, the Basic Charter, defeat . . .

The night was clear and calm. The path Antonino and Omar took was the same one they had taken in the morning: they crossed the big square and the covered market, then went down the long alley to the palm grove. The light had changed: the moon had taken over from the scorching sun, discreetly and conspiratorially, so they were now taking the path in the opposite direction.

The black prostitutes were twins, but they were dressed differently. The first wore the traditional red Libyan robe over a purple organdie tunic, her head covered by a veil with hems adorned in intricate designs of purple, yellow and pink; she also wore big silver bracelets and large hoop earrings. The second twin's robe was straw-coloured, with black stripes, and a white band around her waist; the tunic she wore underneath was blue, and her face was covered by a purple veil with whitish hems. A petrol lamp was hanging from a pole in the courtyard. On the ground there was a terracotta brazier filled with live coals. The first of the twins took Antonino's hand, while the second took Omar's. The young officer saw his friend and the second twin vanish into a room on the right. Antonino entered the room on the left: it was almost entirely dark, and Antonino could only detect the brightly coloured cloths and the gleaming silver jewellery. The bright lights were suspended like stars, and he could no longer make out the woman's silhouette. But he could clearly distinguish the contours of his own body – the fingers of his hands, his belly button, and – like in a mirror – his ears, eyes, and penis: cryptograms that nature had affixed to his ivory frame.

An initiation rite required either extraordinary, solemn or bizarre feats of patience, courage, strength or ingenuity. The trip to Africa was such a trial. *I haven't braved lions, nor crossed raging rivers or deserts, nor climbed impassable mountains; instead, I was welcomed into the deputy governor's palatial house.* But trials can come in deceptive guises. Instead of terrorising, deceiving, or plotting his downfall, Khadija – the black goddess, the nocturnal master of the house that belonged to the King's representative, his uncle – was actually protecting him. Antonino's trial merely consisted in alienating himself, and he had easily passed it. He hadn't been crushed by the heavy burden of guilt like his powerful and unhappy uncle; nor had he fled, like his beloved aunt, into music and games, into the infinitely small and the infinitely large. If the two communities were separated by a barrier guarded by two sets of gods – while the conquerors, who'd engineered the most monstrous cataclysm to have befallen those shores, adopted all the behaviours and stances known to them: cruelty, martyrdom, reason, prudence, violence, hypocrisy, piety – Antonino instead leapt over this barrier with the same ease and frequency with which he crossed the threshold of the house Saber watched over.

Antonino lacked both memory and a sense of mission, so he remained miraculously detached from the past and the future. If he passed his trial so easily, it was because he was fleeing from the power of the subterranean gods: time and memory, which bind everything together. Why had Sharafeddin refused his challenge that morning, or why had he postponed it? The threshold of that shop remained inviolable. Thus, even Antonino's happiness had limits, although he forgot they were there. If Sharafeddin had rejected his and Omar's approaches, here they were now, crossing the threshold that belonged to the prostitutes. He had seen many strange and marvellous things in Africa, but never any enigmas. The young officer wanted to test his courage and strength, and didn't shy away from conflict: but he wasn't restless, which is the fatal sign of alienation. The other shore, from which there might be no return, simply didn't exist for him: every step he took was leading him further away from it.

Meanwhile, having overcome his trial, Antonino was shut inside that room with the black silhouette, in a darkness barely pierced by a few faltering rays of light, busy accomplishing the rite. The women he'd had before this one didn't matter: they were either dreams or insignificant. That act of copulation put the seal on a new man.

Having stood up and dressed himself, Antonino watched as the woman re-acquired her silhouette, once again becoming the prostitute who had come up to him and with whom he'd gone into the little room – taking them back to the starting point.

When Antonino saw Omar again, it became immediately obvious that the same scene had played out on two different stages, like a mirror image. Consequently, even the twins must have been mirror images of the same woman; and their blackness had helped blend them in with the darkness of the place, which was punctuated by blurry colours and fragments of light.

Accompanied by Omar, Antonino went back into the street, feeling as though he had the power to communicate with every shape, object or sound.

The young men crossed the city without feeling either frightened or apprehensive, the airy excitement that followed them all the way home vanishing the moment they laid their heads on their pillows.

VI

Far from the city, on the mountains that dominated the Barca plateau, the two cousins stopped to rest. They had spent the past two days in tribal lands.

Sharafeddin moved nimbly among the boulders, his eyes wandering on the plain. Libya's boundlessness had always been a bulwark against invaders. With his baggy white pantaloons, Sharafeddin was wearing a greenish waistcoat with matching embroidery. Omar wore an identical waistcoat. Both sported the traditional red Libyan cap on their heads. Sharafeddin wore his at a cocky angle, while Omar's was pressed down to his eyebrows.

If at that exact moment, the first rifle shot boomed on the parched plain – Omar thought – *my choice will have been made for me.* One's loyalties were to one's kinsmen: tribal virtues were founded on this law. 'So long as I'm up here, I'm not scared by any general,' Sharafeddin said, clearly in high spirits. He seemed impatient for the war to start. He knew that even some Italian soldiers were impatient.

On his return to Benghazi, Omar found one of his nephews waiting for him at the door of the deputy governor's house. He was carrying Omar's son, who'd been bitten by a dog. Sobeida, Omar's repudiated wife, had left the city to visit some relatives, and her son had been playing with other children in an alley when a rabid dog had come hurtling towards him. The boy was feverish. Omar wrapped him in a blanket and took him to Doctor Amilcare.

The doctor welcomed Omar kindly, examined the child and disinfected his wounds. He told Omar to go to the municipality; they had to pick up the dog and keep it under observation. He gave him his visiting card to facilitate the process. The doctor then wrapped the boy up in the blanket again and handed him back to Omar. Omar clutched the boy tightly against his chest and looked at Doctor Amilcare with gratitude. Smiling, the doctor said, 'If he doesn't get worse, bring him again the day after tomorrow.'

'The mistress is asking after the boy,' Khadija said on entering Omar's room. 'Go and speak to her, I'll look after the child.'

Omar appeared in the hall, looking pallid. He was still wearing the green waistcoat he'd worn during his long journey with Sharafeddin and the red cap was still pressed down over his eyebrows. He remained standing while he narrated the incident.

Rosina went downstairs, drew close to the child and clasped him in her arms. Placated, the child became silent. Omar sat on the floor in a corner, while Khadija and the Countess fussed over the boy. Having been led there by Saber, the Count was very surprised to find everyone assembled in that little room at the far end of the courtyard. 'The Count!' Omar exclaimed. Omar declared he would not be sending his son back to his relatives: because the boy had been wounded as a result of Sobeida's negligence and her witch of a mother, the court would certainly award Omar custody.

That night the boy slept peacefully, but it was not such a tranquil night for the house's owners, or for the coachman. It seemed the dog bite had upset the equilibrium that had been established with such difficulty, and put uncontrollable forces into motion.

Rosina's eyes were wide open as she lay stretched out on her bed.

The following morning an usher appeared in the deputy governor's office to announce that a woman was insisting she needed to see him urgently. She was very agitated and had something important to tell him. What should he do?

'Show her in,' the Count said.

It was Muna, Omar's mother-in-law. She was wrapped in a coarse woollen robe that covered even her head, and holding open an aperture with her hands through which only a single eye appeared. She advanced as far as the deputy governor's desk, and thus shrouded, stood silently while waiting for the deputy governor to dismiss the usher. The Count hesitated until the usher understood there was no hope he could listen in on their conversation, and he left, shutting the door behind him in the blink of an eye.

Muna uncovered her face, which was still youthful, the heirloom of a bygone beauty, and observed the deputy governor closely. She was making complex calculations in her head, where evaluation and desires bolted around like arrows. There was something repulsive and yet irresistible about her gaze: it was demanding and conspiratorial. She was wearing very thin gold bracelets on her wrists and a blue tunic striped in gold.

'I am your son's mother-in-law,' she said.

The Count grew pale, different impulses cancelled each other out, and he didn't reply. He invited the woman to sit. Muna opened her woollen robe: her hair was ensconced in a blue veil with white stripes. She had a strong neck, but her skin was delicate. She indulged the Count, allowing him all the time he wanted to look at her. As she had long wanted to meet him, she was in no hurry. Even though she was staring straight ahead, she also threw him furtive glances, which were simultaneously shameful and questioning. Her gaze retreated and attacked, as though she were engaged in lovemaking. Experiencing a momentary impulse to rebuff her, the Count suddenly asked her what she wanted.

Muna began to cry. They were real tears, even if they fell fresh on her cheeks. She was holding a handkerchief and making gestures of desperation. She stood up, letting the woollen robe fall from her shoulders, and loosened slightly the vibrant robe held tightly to her waist by a red belt. Pushing her hips against the desk, she leaned forward and with wet, sharp eyes, asked His Excellency what he intended to do with her grandson, whom he was hiding in his house. She pressed her hand against the surface of the desk and her gold bracelets clattered against a thick ledger. But before the Count could reply, Muna had fallen back into her chair and started to cry again, this time keeping her handkerchief pressed tightly to her face. Here was the woman who'd shattered his son's peace. Omar had repudiated his wife because of that second-rate actress. The Count flirted with the idea of having her locked up in a cage under any old pretext, thus ridding the world of a monster! But they were thoughts that best belonged to a play; the Count seemed to have been infected by exaggeration. Consequently, he assumed an air of stern simplicity and . . . but his words came out altogether differently to how he'd planned. Although he'd wanted to reproach and threaten her, he instead spoke of Omar and the boy, and questioned her about Sobeida.

Muna dried her tears in a single swipe and told him all about her life. Everyone knew that Omar was very reserved and patient in the deputy governor's palace, where people took a liking to him. In his own house, however, Omar was often quick-tempered and irascible. He had become obsessed with separating Muna from her daughter. Sobeida was beautiful, but delicate and feeble. What would become of her without Muna's protection? Whenever Omar was gone, the house was incredibly peaceful! The boy played with his mother, while Sobeida would cook or receive visits from her relatives, and the hours rolled by pleasantly and unchangeably. But when Omar came home with a gloomy expression and slammed the door, one always had to expect a storm. He even made the boy anxious, often bringing him to tears.

'If he's so moody, it's means he's unhappy in that house – it's your fault.'

Muna looked at the deputy governor, satisfied. The Count's wrath was a mark of his commitment. She said she was well aware that Omar, that miscreant, had coached the deputy governor. 'I know you're biased against me. Antonino told me.'

The Count wrathfully slammed his hand down on the desk. 'You spoke to him?'

'Many times,' Muna cheerfully replied, 'Antonino is very kind and he even gave me some money.'

There he was again, the young officer: he was gifted with omnipresence! The Count's heart was afflicted by a bitter confusion. How could that witch have seen Antonino?

What did she want from him? What did he offer her? His nephew had set his sights on Sobeida. That was what gave Omar and Antonino's friendship its value, which Rosina had instead interpreted as a prime example of emotion and generosity, valuing it above the Count's more calculating approach. The Count felt deceived and marginalised.

'If Antonino wasn't away on duty, my grandson wouldn't have spent a single night in your house. Antonino would have brought him back to me, or opened a secret door to let me in: that young man isn't as calculating as you are. He trusts his heart.'

How Rosina reproached him for being so servile to reason! Had this woman put those words in his wife's mouth? The Count felt betrayed by everyone.

'What do you want from me?' he asked, aware the woman was observing him. 'The boy belongs to Omar, and he's free to do with him as he wishes. He said he'll refer the case to the religious courts so that he'll be granted custody of the boy. Omar lives in my house, and so long as he remains in my service, he'll be free to keep his son with him – whereas you're so simple-minded that you let a dog bite him.'

'My poor son!' Muna screamed, wringing her hands and shedding more tears. It took her a long time to calm down. She wasn't in a hurry to bring the meeting to an end. This time, she dried her eyes slowly, as though she were on her own.

His Excellency wished to wash his hands of the matter. He was bored by these little trifles. Although he could easily use his authority to restore peace to that family, he let them squabble like dogs. 'I will inform your devoted Omar, so he'll understand in what esteem His Excellency holds matters dear to his heart,' Muna ventured, 'you don't have any children, which is why you can't understand certain things.'

'If this is about seeing Omar reconcile with his wife, then I'll try to speak to him. But you know the price: you have to leave that house.'

'I've never been afraid of men!' Muna declared.

The Count smiled, and vague dimples formed on his cheeks, which Muna didn't overlook. He thought about that woman's past, a long trail of events which nobody had ever seen in their entirety. Muna repaid him with her own smile. His Excellency had caved in, and the smile he'd let slip was conspiratorial. 'If I were afraid of men, I wouldn't have come to speak to you. As for Omar, I'll see him in court. I won't let him have the boy: the law is on my side.'

The Count was a well-shaped man. While she'd been defying him, Muna had studied him closely. If at times he appeared uncertain, it was because he was scatterbrained and prone to sudden impulses, not because he had a weak character. A long time ago, Muna had made the acquaintance of another powerful man, and they both exuded the same aura: a certain steadfastness and weightiness. The kindness and arrogance of a powerful man were something altogether different from Omar's wrath and violence. Age had not dried him up or disfigured him – power seemed to go hand in hand with a healthy body. He had heavy hands and whenever they fell, they picked something up. Thus power became an antidote against death.

'You have a nice office,' she said, looking around.

The keys to the city – how long and how passionately the Count had looked for them! The Basic Charter, an instrument of reason, perhaps wasn't as useful as the emotions that had prompted it, the means which it utilised, and the objectives it proposed. He had wanted indigenous servants in his house, against Rosina's wishes, because he'd wanted to be in direct and prolonged contact with them and thus reap precious rewards. He had guessed that the keys to the city – the mythical *golden apples* – could only be found by forging close links with the locals: but these people were all walking on different roads. He had to trust that woman – she would be his guide.

He came to an abrupt halt. While outlining his public actions, hadn't he often mentioned that he was not interested in psychological experiments, nor was he trying to resolve any personal problems, or soothe a crisis of conscience and values – hadn't he always aimed to bring progress and peace to the country that had been entrusted to him, so its entire population could benefit from it?

While speaking to Muna, the Count had been thinking about Sobeida. His desire for 'pretty Sobeida' – a woman he'd never even seen, and of whom he'd only been given the vaguest description – shared the same root as his benevolence towards Omar. His individual journey seemed to want to supplant his public role. Muna, the witch, was ferrying him from one bank of the river to the other: but was she responsible for plotting his downfall, or was he bringing it upon himself? The private sphere that Muna was offering to guide him through was a diabolical path. A brief and illegitimate domestic happiness would be purchased at the cost of his sincerity and career. The high functionary seemed to be negotiating with someone who was offering him vague promises in order to secure his betrayal.

Time gnawed away at everything: how could he carefully plot his moves? Muna was offering him shortcuts that his logic was oblivious to, in fact, shortcuts his logic refused to accept. Taking them would compromise his dignity, but sometimes there were alliances one couldn't make without paying a high price.

'I haven't been able to convince you. Fine, Sobeida will try in my stead.'

It was as though she'd read his mind. She was offering him exactly what he so ardently wanted: to meet the beautiful Sobeida.

Local customs forbade any young woman from entering a man's office; but having broken through the traditional taboo, the action on the stage was about to grow lively. Merely by agreeing to see her in secret and welcoming her into his office, the Count was already offending the honour of the young man under his tutelage. It was an irreparable breach, and to cover it up, the Count would only be able to rely on Muna's discretion, her complicity. But that meant giving in to blackmail.

Embarrassed, the Count kept quiet, but wasn't sufficiently strong to reject the offer. That woman had distinguished the public man from the private one, a distinction Rosina had never managed to make. The encounter with Sobeida was an allegory of his deepest desire, the union of the two different parts of the city. It was a rite. He asked himself, exalted and afflicted, if his heart had reached the limit of lucidity, or confusion. The presence of that woman contaminated his thoughts: and now he was looking for shortcuts to infernal destinations.

'I want to see the boy,' Muna said.

Muna started acting as though the child were right in front of her, and laughed. Then she stood up. She threw her rough woollen robe to the ground and started wrapping it around herself while only hanging on to its hem.

'May God forgive you, father,' she said, her face once more veiled as she stood in front of him. The Count rose to his feet. His behaviour was somewhat gauche; as for Muna, who'd raised her hands back to her nose, leaving only a small aperture in her veil for a single eye, she stared him down.

She turned on her heels and took two paces towards the door. 'Sobeida will be luckier than me. She'll come to you tomorrow at this time. May God save you! As for those dogs you keep at your door, warn them that tomorrow a woman will come asking for you. They shouldn't dare to stop and question her. Those dogs!'

Suddenly pulling the door open, as though certain she'd find the usher trying to eavesdrop on their conversation, she vanished.

Alone in his office, the Count waited for Sobeida. That beautiful name, unique and sophisticated, had perhaps been suggested by Muna's powerful friend, the highly placed man who belonged to her past. Some events always repeat themselves, except with different actors. In fact, there were no new events, every role that we play once belonged to someone else. In the great theatre of the world, repertoires don't suffer additions and mechanisms are put into motion by oblivion and returns. The Count was playing a very old role, simply against different backdrops and involving other variables.

He had kept Antonino in Benghazi purely to indulge Rosina, but the young man was imprudent. When Muna had told the Count about her encounters with Antonino, the Count had mentioned to the city's commanding general that he would have no objections if Antonino were called up to the front in the east. He did so to protect his rival, whom he was trying, out of a spirit of generosity prompted by guilt, to supplant. But he was playing his role in a slightly different way, to affirm the status quo, not to change it: that was his justification. He was forty-four years old, and was as experienced and self-confident as a baritone. In order to nourish himself, a young man often creates much havoc. Age teaches us to nourish ourselves by leaving everything in the world – a tired, lazy monster – relatively untouched.

The wait was protracted and the Count wasn't able to take any interest in the papers lying on his desk, as though he couldn't even see them.

Once upon a time, young Nordic men would take up travelling to complete their education. Despite the fact they headed south and called it the *Grand Tour*, they were prudent enough not to cross the seas – and those who did go overseas weren't burdened by any guilt.

These days, anyone who travels to lands overseas must instead embrace their ancestors' sins and judge them in the way they deserve; but if one shies away from that loathsomeness, it will be difficult for the prestige of the education they received, which produced those sins in the first place, to remain intact.

Sometimes, everything around the Count would come to a standstill, leaving only his thoughts in motion, similarly to how dreams occur in silence at night.

Instead of tearing reality apart to satisfy the schemes dictated by his upbringing, the Count saw the reality before his eyes and realised that was where his individual path lay, and he defended it from the misrepresentations his education had created, and from confusing it with the collective path: *one can remain in lands overseas either by being one of the missionaries, who given the primitive nature of the local populations came to sell them a simplified world view, or by being like penitents seized with a crisis of conscience when confronted by a mysterious reality that contradicts the values around which we've ordered our lives . . .*

Waiting for Sobeida, in that large office where the warm winter sun seeped through the open windows, turned out to be useless. The Count knew a woman couldn't visit a man and show him her face and voice without her honour being tarnished. He had accepted Muna's promise to send the pretty Sobeida to beg for his help, as though he were just like his moody young nephew.

The Count smiled. *So long as we indulge our weakness for mythologising our sentimental mistakes, they never become obstacles.* Everything would turn out for the best: his loyalty to his wife and his devoted servant had remained intact. He couldn't claim any credit in the outcome.

'We don't deserve credit for everything that's a part of us,' he said out loud, in the empty room.

VII

Omar broke the news to the Countess: Antonino was back in the city and hiding at a friend's house. His Excellency had banished him so discreetly that Antonino's superiors hadn't understood it was a punishment. In fact, when Antonino asked to go on leave, they'd granted his request as a courtesy to the deputy governor, so the latter could see his nephew. The note Omar delivered read: 'My beloved aunt, I'll be coming to see you this very day to embrace you.'

Oblivious to this challenge to his authority, the Count was hurrying through the day's paperwork. He was at his most serene when it came to public functions, negotiating the problems posed by Italy's labyrinthine bureaucracy, making his decisions without undue delays.

He finished early and went out onto the balcony.

The sky was a perfect blue. A fishing boat was anchored in the port, where the dockers were idling peacefully. A group of porters waited outside the customs office for their names to be called. The balcony was empty, the streets deserted, and the city silent. *Leaving Italy was my destiny: but what did that even mean? I've been haunted by it ever since Bergonzi paid us a visit that evening.*

The sea breeze blew softly. Along the horizon, one could see the smoke plumes of the mail ship pull further away into the distance. *Unlike the sluggish colonists and their mental lethargy, my arrival on this desolate coast was the experience that shaped everything I think and feel, even my memory, the repository of all that I've been taught, a demon that guides our every step, which can either enlighten or blind us.* Whether in Rome or Benghazi, the Count was a link in the chain that connected ordinary citizens, or subjects, to the authorities. Perhaps he enjoyed a greater freedom of movement in Benghazi, since the distance from the motherland meant the central authorities had to allow him to make decisions they might have otherwise made for themselves. *And if I were to be recalled to Rome tomorrow, would I go back to being the bureaucrat I used to be, in perfect harmony with the nation's collective conscience, just like a drop of water is lost in an ocean? The Basic Charter is an attempt to crown our presence here by blessing it with popular consensus, which is why I made such a flag-waving cause out of it – in fact, it's more like a door through which our consciences will be able to flee: otherwise, we'll remain prisoners of our actions, regardless of whatever affirms our stubborn arrogance.*

While in Rome, I was convinced that the existing social order, which is safeguarded by power, was a contract all citizens had freely subscribed to. However, here in Benghazi I feel that authority and order are profanations and injustices: the contract is the attempt to crown the Italian presence with the blessing of legitimacy. Does everyone in Rome really acknowledge the legitimacy of authority and the validity of the social order as defended by the bureaucracy to which I belong? I could easily reply that the security of life in Rome, which I now long for, was a sign of blindness: one need only leave the upper-class milieu, which creates the order I know and which watches over it, to see that public acceptance of it is merely an illusion, while the law is nothing but a mask and an instrument of oppression. What else can explain the disorder on the streets of Italy other than that a section of the people does not recognise the legitimacy of the authorities and rejects the order that keeps it confined?

The previous day, the Count had had a heated argument with Rosina, who'd refused to accompany him to a public function after she'd already got ready to leave, like an actress who refuses to speak her lines after the curtain's gone up and her entrance on stage is imminent.

Like a pendulum, his mind oscillated between the private and the public, which at times looked like one and the same. Instead, he spoke to himself as though he were talking to a stranger, so as to identify with his past. *Is Rosina right to accuse me of oppressing these people, despite the appearance of generosity and justice, because I am forcing the reality I was entrusted with to flow in a riverbed that is fundamentally alien to it? How can I possibly expect to persuade these people to sign up to the Basic Charter if we are the only ones who had any hand in writing it, meaning it only addresses issues that concern us – or mirrors our preoccupations and interests, to which the other party are indifferent? Generosity cannot overcome our fundamental problem: is our presence here legitimate? What right do we have to interfere in their destinies? Did anyone ask us to bring order to their world? Landing on this African beach wasn't just about going from point A to point B, it was only a stepping-stone on the journey of knowledge: the immensity of the world contradicts and derides our vision of it – and transforms it.*

Occasionally, the Count felt that time stood still in Africa, where the hours went by slowly; but it wasn't a bad feeling, or a prelude to boredom. It seemed to him as though he were rediscovering the leisurely way of life shepherds used to lead, who roved in those lands from one place to the next, their souls as unblemished as the sky.

Every man receives an education, and although he may resist it a little or make some minor changes to it, he ultimately considers his education an infallible book, and writes his life in its pages. Well then, there comes a point when one's education cracks, and the order it expresses is revealed as false. This is the fatal hour of alienation: as though a ship drifted off on an adventurous journey in the nocturnal silence, floating down a river unknown to everyone except the ship itself. Instead of obeying orders and going through repetitive motions, man instead asks questions. The bureaucrat is conscious of the divinity he is duty-bound to serve, and wants to extend its empire to the furthest edges of the world; but he is also tormented by the doubt that this divinity is the devil itself. A rhythm with three tempos — sacrifice, escape and violence — multiplies and confuses its steps.

An acacia tree, its shiny green leaves like a saw's jagged teeth, appeared to contradict the aridity of the soil, while the silent breeze made the branches sway, as though they were floating on water. At the top of the tree, the orange blossoms looked like a flock of fleshless birds, as though made of straw.

Rosina was secretly waiting for her nephew, in her big silent house.

The Count was jealous of Antonino, of the ease with which his nephew had been welcomed by the indigenous society he was trying to command. He couldn't tolerate the boy being able to go back and forth effortlessly across the same river the Count had tried to build a bridge of paper over: *he doesn't understand that the bridge is only as long as everyone thinks it is, and that armies and bureaucratic machines cannot cross a paper bridge.*

The Viceroy of Libya couldn't tolerate that his wife preferred to dance on a platform as big as a giant chequer-board with her favourite nephew instead of staying by his side. Her absence disappointed his vision of reality – *and upset the scales. Unbeknownst to him, Alonzo's rival will remain hidden under his roof. I entrust myself to the exacting and useless rules of the game, which are completely opposed to goodwill, duty, responsibility, and self-awareness. Like music, games are a micro-cosm, pure escapism. The invisible and the artificial vie with one another to confine Alonzo's reality, whose limits constantly expand or contract in keeping with our psychological situation.*

'My dear Count,' Doctor Amilcare concluded, while the pair walked side by side in the dusty street, 'the alien-ation created by our education, meaning the detachment from one's fellow citizens that being in this alien society has caused, is diabolical: those who seek to divorce you from your past don't want to integrate you into their system. This is an enigma fit for a condemned enemy, and not something for a novice. These people are trying to confuse your beliefs – your loyalty to the King, and our people's charitable mission here – in order to take advantage of your sensibility; but they'll keep their door closed to you just like they do to us, they'll seek to profit from your restless-ness in order to throw us all out of the country as soon as they can, slamming their door in all our faces.

If their presence shatters your acceptance of the educa-tion you received, that's not to say our presence here compromises their traditions: on the contrary, perhaps it even reinforces them. Your generous efforts to at least partly understand and accept their civilisation doesn't interest them at all; in fact, they consider it a sign of weakness, or an anthropological exercise of the sort promoted by the government – a new instrument of oppression, in other words. An open dialogue with these people is possible only on one condition: as we are the stronger party, they should model themselves on us, meaning they should accept our teachings, and surrender their spiritual journey to whoever exercises temporal power over them. But in doing so, we don't honour the other culture at all, which is saddening: we'll simply end up wiping it out.'

Having reached his front door, Doctor Amilcare removed his hat and bowed ceremoniously, taking his leave.

The Count found the door to the first floor hall shut. Surprised, he knocked on it sharply. Rosina made her voice heard, and after a moment she opened the door.

'Why did you lock yourself in? You scared me.'

'So you were finally concerned about your wife, if only for a moment.'

'Yes, I was. But let's not exaggerate.'

Returning to his domestic milieu meant leaving certain rules behind and being subjected to different ones. Having cut his links with the outside world, he had suppressed his inner conflict so as to make room, in the sheltered drawing room, for frivolous and irresolvable contradictions.

A chair crashed to the floor in the adjacent room.

'What is that noise? Something fell down in the cupboard.'

'I didn't hear anything.'

'It's clear you must have many things on your mind.'

'About what?'

'Somebody's in there.'

'Who do you think it is?'[4]

'Oh, come now, enough of these riddles.'

---

4 Lines from *The Marriage of Figaro*, Act II; translation by André Naffis-Sahely.

The Count tried to open the door.

'Should I steady myself for a jealous outburst?' Rosina asked.

'Give me the key to this door.'

'I don't have it. But I want to know, is this an outburst of jealousy?'

'I want to break this door down, just for the sake of a little peace of mind – it's got nothing to do with jealousy.'

There was a crowbar in the basement, and they went to fetch it. He offered his wife his arm.

Rosina crossed the hall very slowly; every step she took was like a point scored.

The game, infinitesimally trivial, was an alternative to music. Vanity and the invisible were exhausting reality.

The paths the couple were walking didn't intersect. Each considered the other a traitor, or a prisoner, and made their individual mistakes seem like an exercise in freedom.

On leaving, Rosina took care to give the door behind her a little knock. In the way one does when a signal has been agreed on, the door opened and Antonino appeared on the scene, trembling all over. He ran to the windowsill, and jumped out.

He fell on the lawn, making a muffled thud, and ran towards the coachman's room at the far end of the courtyard.

'Omar!' he exclaimed, bursting into the room.

When the Count had knocked on the door, Antonino had sought refuge in the adjacent box room, but the fallen chair had reawakened the Count's suspicions. 'Go out onto the balcony and use the drainpipe to lower yourself onto the terrace, bolt yourself inside the box room before your uncle comes back – take my place, Omar!' Antonino exclaimed, and embraced him. Everything happened so quickly that Omar sped off to his post as though the game might end in unforeseen, risky ways, as if someone's destiny depended on it, as though being in that box room meant he was saving someone's life, and not keeping someone's secret.

'What a shameful scene!' the Countess exclaimed in an excessive outburst of wrath. The Count was holding a hammer in one hand and a crowbar in the other.

But as soon as he drew close to the box room door it was suddenly thrown open, as if by magic.

'Omar!' the Count yelled, stunned. A crevice had opened, letting reality drip down on the comedy's homogeneous fabric, altering it. The Count had opened his eyes during a scene he didn't like in the slightest, a scene that had gone wrong. His face was marked by astonishment, wrath, and bitter anxiety.

'Omar!' Rosina exclaimed, suddenly happy, if a little perplexed.

'What is it?' Omar asked, playing his role very poorly. In fact, it was his inability to give a convincing performance that fuelled the entire scene.

The Count and Countess felt the landscape of their security shrinking around them. Estrangement was tempting, and was in itself a form of seduction.

As Omar had taken Antonino's place, Rosina's heart – which was torn in two –could no longer understand the rivalry between the Count and the man locked in the box room. The two knights were no longer fighting over her, but for mastery of the world, which they interpreted in vastly different ways. The young god, who was only a boy, had vanished, and been replaced by a monster. In reality,

Omar and Antonino nursed versions of the other within themselves, and could summon them at will. Pandora's box had been tampered with, and its mechanism became destiny.

'*Je le tuerai! Je le tuerai.*' '*Tuez-le donc, ce méchant page!*'[5]

The Countess was pointing at Omar.

Omar felt ashamed, since whoever gambles is inevitably outsmarted. What overwhelming confusion he'd felt when Antonino had embraced him and ordered him to occupy his place, so that he could be caught in flagrante delicto coming out of the box room in the presence of the deputy governor and the Countess. The seemingly unbridgeable distance between Omar and Countess Rosina appeared to have shortened at the moment when Omar's identity and that of Rosina's beloved nephew became one and the same; as for the deputy governor – that big, omnipotent fool – he'd edged close to the real secret, and had become as intolerable as a rival.

'I can't understand what made you pull a practical joke like that today,' the Count said, as soon as the servant was dismissed. 'What will Omar think of seeing us play such silly games?'

'I can't besmirch your honour,' Rosina bitterly replied, 'but I want to at least besmirch your dignity. The practical joke made complete fools of us.'

Rightly or wrongly, being excluded from the Count's life was pushing Rosina to add and subtract with eyes wide shut; a mechanism like the spring in a wooden chest would have worked magically.

The door opened noisily and Khadija appeared.

'Who jumped out of the window and into the garden?'

5 Lines from Beaumarchais' *Le mariage de Figaro*, Act II, Scene XVII.

Khadija's sombre features contrasted against Omar's introverted, limpid face.

'I heard a thud and a shadow flew past the wall. But when I reached the window, there was nobody on the lawn. Who trampled those flowers?'

'I did,' Omar replied, his chin buried in his chest.

Every time it was Omar's turn to play this game, he would contradict himself and bend out of shape, fading away. The tension between his masters was dying down and a thread – thin but strong – bound them together at an invisible point. The game had stopped being a perfectly illuminated goldfish bowl in which all possibilities could be seen: it had become a journey, like music.

Destroying the conventions and habits of the world leads to a breakdown . . . the Count ruminated. *Knowledge brings a stranger closer and pushes the ordinary away, making it once more incomprehensible, and the absence of meaning degenerates into oblivion, an oblivion from which an altered sense of the ordinary may one day be recovered, if it can be recovered at all. Knowledge and madness, knowledge and destruction: a catastrophe is nothing if not intolerable knowledge.*

Khadija glared at Omar.

'And what is this?' she asked, opening an identity card she'd found in the flowerbed. Antonino's tender features smiled at the three characters in the little photograph.

Khadija mumbled something and then, clasping the portrait of her favourite master to her bosom, she left.

That night the Countess appeared in the courtyard. She wanted to speak to Antonino. She crossed the yard and approached the door of the room where Omar was sleeping. Antonino was hiding inside. She gently opened the door.

The room was lit by the moon. Omar was stretched

out on a rudimentary wooden bed. He was alone and fast asleep.

The previous scene was being played out again, except inversely. Once again, Antonino's presence in a small room had been replaced by Omar's, but this time, Omar was the one who was confused, while last time, it had been Count Alonzo.

Omar's hands were resting on his chest; his legs were together, while his feet opened up into a fan, like pastoral pipes. This was how Byzantine painters depicted their subjects: in rigid symmetry, exactly in the way late Gothic sculptors modelled their saints. Just like those warriors gripping their swords tightly in their hands while lying in their funereal mausoleums.

The Count instead slept in a rather disorderly way. A river divided the two images: one belonged to a world where order still reigned, the other to a world that was falling apart. For the first time, Rosina understood· the fascination Alonzo felt for that archaic society, with its fixed rules. *Alonzo almost never features in the fable . . . he's always on the sidelines. But it's precisely his inability to be like the others that makes him who he is in the first place! He considers the reality of the others as nostalgia, a voyage – however impossible it is – back to the past.*

She'd often watched the Count while he slept, as though trying to speak to him in a nocturnal scene. But how different Omar was! How noble that servant's features were! The secret of that image was the order that framed it.

The Basic Charter: now, she too would create a Basic Charter of her own, so as to overcome the distance that separated her from that man.

Rosina's fear that the Count would notice her absence

pulled her out of her reverie. She carefully closed the door and crossed the courtyard. She saw her shadow, projected by the light of the moon, stir on the ground. She quickened her pace and went back inside the house.

VIII

The Count laid his book down on the floor. The month of fasting had begun, and the streets emptied around sunset – even most Italians hardly left their houses. Occasionally, the Count liked to go out for a stroll precisely at that time, enchanted by the silence of the city. He toured Benghazi like a museum: the stillness made every object precious and rare.

The books he'd read on Africa, even the ones that had seemed promising, had disappointed him: they were full of impressions only fit for those who lived far away. The uniformity of the images they offered was caused by omissions intolerable to anyone like Count Alonzo, who compared these books to the reality before his eyes. They proved poor guides to the conflict he'd committed himself to waging: by crossing the sea, those books had been exposed to a light that altered them, and had rotted away. *They're like spoilt fruit,* he thought, *and anyone who eats them will also expire.*

He stood up. He wouldn't find the sought-after keys to that country in those books, and it was pointless to read or even leaf through so many. They were more like sounds than words, or maybe more like objects.

He approached the window. The courtyard was deserted:

the servants had left the house an hour before the breaking of the fast. *Moderation doesn't mean imposing limits on oneself – one must walk lightly and gracefully down the path of experience and knowledge. The motto of Renaissance humanism was 'Festina Lente'. Its splendour intact, it had crossed the seas.* While reading so many dishonest books was humiliating, his contact with Libya's indigenous people was growing more cheerful, even if it caused his outlook to grow more sombre than he'd previously imagined: the conversations led to deeper depths, the sacred place to which all rivers led. *The strength to endure all that's obscure, to not maim reality simply in order to console ourselves – that's what makes destiny into a journey! The more time passes here – and the more we follow this liberal course with the Basic Charter, which we treat as though it were some magic talisman – the more we complicate the situation, rejecting all our efforts. We have granted the natives this Basic Charter because of our inability to pacify the country by means of arms; nevertheless, we've painted it as a grand gesture, as though granting these inferior people the right to open the book of civilisation. When I try to gain the natives' acceptance, I should employ the same efforts as when I try to impose these 'Basic Charters' on them. In fact, the Basic Charter was a passport designed to make them accept us. What nourishes the desire for acceptance? Am I repudiating the society I come from? Or perhaps I'm worried that my beloved civilisation is reaching the hour of its inexorable decline, and by bonding with the 'barbarians', I'm trying to guarantee my survival?* This monologue was the direct result of solitude, an irrepressible weed which grew in that savage, forsaken place. *My political zeal conceals a secret desire: my high-ranking position is only a refuge, a mask. I offered these people a Basic Charter, and identified with that mission in order to hide my eagerness for them to share my heart and my bed.*

The landscape outside the window was static, like the backdrop to a non-existent play. The sky was blue, just like it always was. The province of Cyrenaica lacked adequate aquifers, even if the few rain showers that occurred were extremely violent, like an outburst of heavenly wrath: the city had been conquered and it had submitted, and it thus returned to its former swamp-like state.

Anyone who's angered by their desires is afraid, and won't go far in their journey; having reached a crossroads, and instead of proceeding cautiously, they'll shut their eyes or run away, torn between hope and desperation, between ardour and dread. Desire has conjured a vision before my eyes, and I shoo it away, slowly but earnestly. Renunciation is not tantamount to weakness: I'm the deputy governor, the city's eyes are on me, and secrets aren't allowed. I'm not angry with myself, nor do I deny the force of the vision. But I won't grant that desire the freedom to run roughshod over my duties.

Is Omar loyal to me? And yet this precious servant is a 'native', meaning therefore a potential enemy. On the other hand, I represent a more generous political power; we granted them the Basic Charter. My own job is that of a humble servant; but if the efforts of the Basic Charter's supporters and those aiming for reconciliation fail, the country will be split in two, and Omar will become my enemy. He will be a native who defends his land, his sacred homeland, grieved by the violence of strangers.

We all follow our own paths. Likewise, the wooden boats we set out in to come here will go in directions determined by elements that for the most part elude us: like in a dream, the beach we landed on isn't the one we embarked for. All of us, including kind, loyal Omar, will see our feelings change according to how the negotiations between the two warring parties progress. Our bond grows in the narrow patch of shadow created by the Basic Charter. If this should disappear, we'll be forced to part ways.

An antithesis always implies an attachment. In this house, Omar and I represent the two warring parties: what binds us together? If Rosina dislikes the servants so much, it's because she senses this attachment. At least part of this attachment is patently obvious: the servants are natives, who belong to an oppressed group, whereas I belong – albeit with reservations – to the oppressors. Oppression is an injustice, and injustice is the fatal link that binds us.

They interpreted the civilisation we gave them as a 'gift' as oppression. The Libyans will refuse the Basic Charter we granted them – all in order to show these barbarians how they would be better off as citizens, even if only second-class citizens – and they'll tear it up along with the Italian flag. To be a foreigner is a magical condition: this land will never belong to me, no matter how many cannons and rifles I bring here; weapons will only protect me, and I don't know how long that will last. Alas, you can't put down roots with cannons. Regardless of what that witch Muna says, Omar isn't my son: he's my rival. Not my heir, but he who will triumph from my defeat. If I were his father, I'd belong to his past: but how can you change someone's ancestors? That is the only miracle that's never happened, and whatever binds us pales in comparison to that conflict! Omar is my prisoner, and no real bond can exist between us, except through oppression. He doesn't want to be adopted by me, since he thinks this would mean forsaking all his ancestors, the most abominable murder conceivable.

The Count picked up the book he'd laid on the floor. Deemed an expert on African affairs by the ministry, the author had long hoped for the conquest of Libya to happen – an innocent, even generous act of bravado – as well as its colonisation. Having entered the stage as an actor in the third or fourth act of this tragedy, the deputy governor of Cyrenaica envied that writer who'd appeared in the serene atmosphere of the prologue, oblivious to how events would unfold.

His passion, like all deep sentiments, was devoid of pedantry. Even though he despised these books, which had been used for ends that differed greatly from the reasons they'd been written, he collected them because they distracted him. Plagued by exhaustion, he wound up identifying with the innocent traveller: he just needed to picture the 'savages' as peaceful apparitions. The stern mantle of the King's representative fell from his shoulders. The barbarian conqueror, the aggressor, took on the garb of the honoured guest. Once reality's implacable sun faded away, the little theatres of lies became playful and plausible, in fact legitimate.

At that moment, his responsibilities and burdens as deputy governor seemed very easy to bear. The tragic stage of life had been reduced to the size of a little theatre. Sleep surprised him during the performance.

IX

Rosina was standing next to the piano, which looked like an enormous black book. The window in front of her was wide open.

These were the last days of the year, and night fell quickly, a tidal wave that submerged everything. Rosina loved that cheerful hour: a secret and constant flux of thoughts guided her through the shadows.

Alonzo's reality is the web of conflicts in the society we live in: he's not interested by the power struggle in Rome, but rather in a formula that might resolve the colony's contradictions.

Nevertheless, these legitimate efforts were linked to something obscure and indefinable. The resolution of conflict in the colony seemed like the finishing line at the end of a different life. Her life companion appeared to be absent because he was treading an altogether different path.

Alonzo annoys the collaborators. What annoys them most about him is the infinite patience with which he observes indigenous society, and how he constantly demystifies all the conventions of colonial ideology. His thoughts are like clear water that surges out of a distant spring and does not mix with the stagnant swamp.

*The native is a living shadow, while our fellow Italians are like
a scrubby field they no longer wish to harvest.*

*The anxiety prompted by his quest is not caused by the
conflicts he's trying to unravel: its origins lie elsewhere, or at most
have a tangential link to those conflicts. Alonzo is fond of saying
he's not aiming to psychologically analyse anyone's soul, or to
resolve an inner conflict. He has lost his fundamental bond, the
vision of the world within which he's been educated, and alienated
from the world he comes from, he's looking for a new connection,
a new spiritual wholeness: the natives' gestures, even their most
insignificant, hypnotise him as fragments of a totality, a circle where
all the points are joined by a single line. Is this what we call the*
Mal d'Afrique?

*Alonzo's refusal to change course and turn around shows that
he's hiding behind his public persona's deceptive appearance. The*
Mal d'Afrique *is the pain caused by alienation, the fatal wound
of a spiritual organ.*

*'You use music as a form of escapism!' he thundered. Music
offers a glimpse into a different reality and acts as a bridge to it:
if Alonzo speaks with such wrath it's because he's trying to avert
suspicions from himself.*

*If I lose myself on these ivory keys, the sound of the native
flutes has led Alonzo's soul down secret paths, far away from all
that's familiar. He's not only grown distant from me, he's grown
distant from himself; his destiny is in the hands of a cryptic
doppelgänger. It's as if the conqueror and the native had become
bewitched by each other's presence: the native threatens the stability
of the conqueror's world, and this threat causes murders, regrets
and deliriums. As for the conqueror, the native transforms from an
object of optimism to the source and living embodiment of the
conqueror's anguish.*

Does death mask itself as a native? A bloodcurdling discovery that isn't limited to the field of battle, when the wounded officer sees the enemy on horseback hurtling towards him, it can even occur in a tidy office in a well-defended barracks, or in the palaces of government, during the midst of a sumptuous public ceremony or luncheon.

Music lies in the opposite direction to Alonzo's destination. But even these opposites are linked. Alonzo in his office and me at the piano are either travelling or praying. They're both transitory ways of being.

He accuses me of escaping into music, but flight is the opposite of a quest, although they too are interconnected.

Even for me, leaving Italy was like crossing a border that divides two very different experiences. Why this rift? Alonzo doesn't love me like he once used to. I'm no longer the Rosina who once made his heart ache. Je suis la pauvre Comtesse Almaviva, a sad woman he no longer loves. Je l'ai trop aimé! Je l'ai lassé de mes tendresses et fatigué de mon amour.[6] Both his wife and the concept of marriage itself belong to, or indeed symbolise, the very society he is rejecting. The interest he takes in his public life is only an alternative to bourgeois life. What he sees in me, as his wife, and in this consecrated union that binds us, is a diabolical pact whereby he has traded his soul for a dull sense of peace. But if Alonzo is fleeing from the law, he is also looking for it. The law is the reconstructed circle. Any other shape is inharmonious. This is the root of the deputy governor's haste: he needs to reach an accord before the two parties resume fighting.

The essence of any religious phenomenon is the division of the universe into two orders that mutually exclude one another. The encounter with a completely alien civilisation works similarly: knowledge always leads to discord.

6 Lines from Beaumarchais' Le mariage de Figaro, Act II, Scene I.

At the sound of the first rifle shots, Alonzo's journey will come to an end, and he'll be the first victim: he won't be found dead on a battlefield, but will be forced back into the very museum that going to Africa allowed him to escape.

What will I be able to offer him? The sound of my music will torment him − it's like offering a man petrified by a spell a thousand roads to walk down.

What was the Countess doing alone in that hall, already submerged in darkness? Khadija soundlessly climbed the stairs and saw the door was ajar. She observed Rosina standing still in the middle of the room, next to the piano's curving recess. Who was with that woman?

In Alonzo's case the fear of the other civilisation, which poisons the conqueror's mind, became the end goal of his quest. The two civilisations − the one we represent, which left a splendid mark on history, and that of the barbarians, which history ignores − can if not integrate, then at least come together, like a married couple. Nevertheless, the terror of the intersection inevitably leads one down the fatal steps to that intersection anyway. The fear of breaking the law makes one break the law. This breach is designed to lead to the restoration of a pre-existing unity, but every diabolical dream has the rhythmic ebb of a return.

What is chaos? A horrible past, a monster controlled by the social order in which we were educated − or the last barren, uncultivated land where order hasn't yet installed itself? The longed-for God . . . At times, something breaks and turns upside down in the conqueror, who is the deadly embodiment of order. Like in Alonzo's case . . . Whoever considers their civilisation a dogma becomes a traveller; whoever destroys, becomes he who seeks. The new opportunities chaos creates turns he who sows into he who reaps.

Lifting the fall board, Rosina sat in front of the keys.

She leafed through the books whose wide pages had made the cook so suspicious. Under Rosina's small, frail hands, the demons imprisoned in those occult books transformed into sounds – their natural state, the way in which they manifested themselves and accomplished their deeds.

Khadija slammed the door. 'What shall I make for dinner?'

Sound versus sound: the innocuous demons lingered on the large book's thick, black lines.

If one wanted to divine the Countess's nature, one had to approach her circumspectly. The invisible, whether auspicious or not, never reveals itself except reluctantly.

Khadija grabbed hold of the Countess's hand and examined it: there was nothing extraordinary about that little perfectly proportioned hand. It contained an invisible sound. Khadija brought it up to her ear.

'All right, tonight I'll cook a traditional Libyan soup,' she said.

X

A perfume was altering the equilibrium of the house, and Rosina searched in vain for its source. It had entered all the rooms, descended to the courtyard, and spied on the people who lived in the house: now it had grown more intense, and wandered around autonomously, alternatively running away from her and heading towards her.

One Sunday afternoon the house had been prepared to welcome guests. They had not been selected according to the Count's sympathies, but by the necessity of bringing all the spokes of society's wheel together. The attention Rosina had put into the preparation of the canapés and the sweets unburdened her of the need to tend to the guests; she welcomed them indifferently.

The perfume was the unexpected guest, and it was the first to arrive.

Their paths crossed in rooms that were still devoid of people. But it would suddenly slip out of her grasp, and if Rosina tried to chase it, she soon lost its tracks. The invisible guest was hot on the heels of someone else, and it was impossible to tell whether this second character was visible.

Khadija looked serene but inscrutable. One could observe

her features until one's eyes grew exhausted, but never find a thing: she buried her secrets in her face as though it were a patch of earth.

The afternoon was consecrated to Italian opera. To attentive ears, melodrama offers a reading of reality – linking together elements previously believed to be irrevocably divided, unscrupulously utilising polarity as a plot device – and could, if properly understood, be a constant repudiation of hackneyed patterns.

Rosina crossed the hall and sat down in front of the piano. She was alone. The *épouse délaissé*'s imprudent hand opened the fall board. The invisible guest revealed itself.

The cook had sprinkled the keyboard with a burnt incense, as a ceremony against the evil eye, the lord of all evil spirits. Magic is the means whereby one can travel in the reality where these spirits operate. It was customary to draw seven circles with the incense on the head of people who'd been possessed by these malign spirits, before eventually burning it. Either Khadija had done this to the Countess in secret, or she had sprinkled it on the keyboard because that's where she thought those spirits manifested themselves.

The perfume was the spirit under Khadija's control. Whom did sound obey? Was it the sixth guest in the house, or was it the doppelgänger of one of the other five characters? It was a plane of reality that ran parallel to the visible world, thus doubling reality, a path superimposed on the path one walked in public. Sound is a bridge. Travelling through sound waves, the impossible – the armour of the unpredictable – would become possible, and fear led back to its positive roots: love. Fleeing is the opposite of falling, but he who falls has already reached his destination, and the precipice is nothing but an illusory distance, vanishing before he who braves his trial.

Khadija was on the tracks of the spirit of sound, challenging it for the right to bind and unbind souls. The row of black-and-white keys was the pillow on which the Countess laid her head, where the spirit weaved lofty and frightening intrigues. The burnt perfume had to wake her up. Transformed into a perfume, the heavyset Khadija kept watch over the house.

Following the reception Rosina went to bed. Doctor Amilcare arrived immediately to prescribe her some medicine, scrawling it down in that horrible handwriting of his, although he didn't seem very concerned. Khadija also came to fawn over the Countess, convinced that her illness was a manifestation of the malign spirit's death throes.

The next day, Rosina refused to see anyone at all. She spent the entire day alone, in silence.

On the third day, Omar appeared at her door. He said that Antonino was in the city, and would be arriving at any moment. The Countess cheered up at the news and later received her favourite nephew warmly. He was on duty, and would have to leave the following day. He didn't say what sort of mission he was on, and spent the rest of the day sitting on the Countess's bed, telling her one fantastic tale after the other.

Rosina now appeared relaxed and amused, then melancholically lay back on her pillows. A number of times Omar caught the phrase: 'Oh, silence, silence . . . '

Antonino's departure threw her into discomfort, as though something had got stuck.

The Count was busy meeting one of the city's native notables, and wouldn't return soon. When even Khadija and Saber left, Omar remembered his mistress's lament: 'Oh, silence . . . '

He appeared at her door with a flute in hand: two little straws next to each other, punctuated by holes at almost regular intervals. At the top were two hollow horns, which opened out into a fan. Rosina was sitting on her bed, her head leant against the headboard. She watched him rest his back against the doorpost, lift his flute, and bring it to his lips.

It was an indecipherable monotonous tune. Omar was employing much effort, his cheeks fully inflated and his eyes growing small.

Those servants the Count treated with such respect in his house, heedless of the mockery this caused him among other Italians, seemed to be taking her husband away from her. But the secret lay elsewhere: it was carrying both of them away.

The Count was annoyed to see Antonino and Omar together, envying their bond's youthful ease. So much ease made a mockery of reason, of his persevering and meticulous efforts to find common ground with the natives.

In the meanwhile, other bonds were being forged, eluding his observation. If Omar had appeared at her door with a flute in hand, Antonino had been in the room before him. Even in theatre, actors swap roles with one another. Similarly, Antonino and Omar replaced one another interchangeably; they looked like identical knockers fixed to the same door, but painted in different colours.

XI

MOHAMED AL-MAHESHI, MAYOR OF BENGHAZI

In the name of the Municipal Council, I hope His Highness will allow me to express our gratitude for His recent visit, and further allow me, at this most solemn hour, to voice the feelings of devotion, gratitude, and intense joy that reverberate in my countrymen's chests for the high honour that His Majesty The King has bestowed on the whole of Cyrenaica, and in particular the city of Benghazi, by sending us His representative to witness the inaugural session of the Cyrenaican assembly. Today, our city greets His Majesty in the form of a noble son of the undefeated House of Savoy, and the worthiest representative of the mighty King of Italy. Our city sees your visit as a new challenge to rise to, and a solid guarantee of those rights that the King of Italy granted to the people of these lands, as well as the accomplishment and fulfilment of the new Basic Charter. The grafting of Eastern civilisation with that of the West will find fertile Cyrenaica the most apt of soils in which to fecundate the bonds of Italian and Libyan brotherhood, which will be an example to the rest of the world. This chapter of history will be a new pearl in Victor Emmanuel III's crown, and the memory of His Majesty's visit to Benghazi will remain impressed in the hearts of all Cyrenaicans, who will pass this story on to future generations, to the everlasting glory of the House of Savoy, whose resolute reign is erected on the foundations of justice and liberty.

FERDINAND OF SAVOY, PRINCE OF URBINO

Your noble words are synonymous with the chivalrous virtues of these Arab peoples, whose ancient civilisation we are well acquainted with. When you speak of Cyrenaica as a fertile terrain for the grafting of our two civilisations, the East and the West, you hit on exactly why these lands, which are tightly bound geographically to the Orient, and which stretch out towards the shores of Europe, will act as a gigantic bridge, uniting the fruitful currents of knowledge and commerce. Destiny has brought them together, and in the name of His Majesty, I as his representative, and a supporter of the liberal institutions that His Majesty has bestowed upon you in Benghazi, where the most different elements of its varied population are already working together, recognise in your Municipal Council the first signs and example of what is already a reality today, and will continue to be so tomorrow.

The inauguration of the Cyrenaican Assembly the following day was a splendid cacophony of sounds: trumpets, applause and countless words.

The banquet held at the Roma Club was attended by three hundred guests.

'Our mission,' a high functionary of the Political Office told the guest seated next to him, who had come to the colony as part of His Highness's entourage, 'is to bring certain institutions in this society to a point of crisis by employing either persuasion, example, or force: the others will crumble accordingly. Growing increasingly insecure, the indigenous people will progressively absorb all the qualities of European civilisation, or at least become harm-less, even if still harbouring vain ambitions of violence. Having been forced out of his centuries-old lair, we've offered the native the splendid edifice of civilisation: he'll be the one to decide whether he wants to walk towards this light, or be left to rot. Indigenous society will be unable to survive our presence as an organic whole: every day that passes sees us removing a stone from its foundations.'

'But we've no need to destroy this civilisation, as though we were punishing them,' the gentleman who belonged to the Prince of Urbino's entourage said, growing animated, this being his first time in Africa.

The high functionary smiled: all the new arrivals talked like this.

'Our presence here,' he continued, holding forth peda-gogically, 'stirs the opposite reaction in the indigenous people: they will sanctify every aspect of their culture, refuse our help, our physicians, and their fanatics will even refuse the bread we offer them. Religious faith will become the national ethos. Thus, either we forsake continuing our pres-ence here, or we must consider all aspects of indigenous culture a citadel of the enemy – precisely because it has been *sanctified* – and apply ourselves to dismantling them, one after the other. Strategy is as important when it comes to spirituality as it is on the battlefield. Believe me, it will not take much for the rest to crumble.'

XII

The Count was looking down. Having learned that Muna had knocked at the door of the house to pay Khadija a visit, he leaned against the windowsill and was watching the atrium from his box. Passion is a stranger to pedantry: attentive and diligent in his public life, Count Alonzo would be incapable of smiling if he saw a woman's secretive steps cross his field of vision instead of a group of warriors.

Muna and Khadija's meeting followed the strictest adherence to ceremony. They came towards one another, shook each other's right hand, brought it to their lips, and each planted three kisses on the back of the other's hand. Khadija then repeated obsequious words of welcome and Muna replied in an equally grandiose manner: it was a meeting of queens.

From his box, the Count breathed a sigh of relief. He'd had the impression Muna had darted a secret, hurried glance at him, like an actress making a subtle gesture on seeing a friend amidst the thousands of people in the audience. He wanted to rush down to the scene, but dejectedly remembered the highest of duties he was expected to shoulder.

The playwright's shrewdness played a dirty trick on

him. Why had the women disappeared after the customary pleasantries, leaving the atrium empty? Everything had to be kept a secret, it was a pact that had been forged between two forces of darkness.

The Count sighed. He would wait until dinner time to learn any news. Muna took her grandson with her when she left: he was a rosy doll with sparkling eyes, dressed in an oversized tunic that kept tripping him up, with a hand always held out in front of him.

The Count appeared in the kitchen. While Antonino would noisily burst in and immediately demand the answer to whatever he wanted to know, the Count instead prudently entered it as though he were stepping inside a salon, propped on the crutches of pleasantries and small talk.

Khadija invited him to sit. She didn't appear surprised in the slightest, as though she'd foreseen consigning an hour to their meeting. Omar was also present, and he remained standing.

Khadija offered her master some tea. Tradition demanded that a guest should be received in silence, in fact that one should offer it so as to put the guest at ease; long pauses were a sign of respect, not of embarrassment. The guest is sometimes left alone, since the room that honours his presence belongs entirely to him.

Khadija had turned her back to the master and was replacing the cups in the cupboard on the other side of the kitchen. The Count's impatience gave way to a melancholy tranquillity: he drank his tea slowly and reflected, without coming to any conclusions, on the secret of that different reckoning of time.

Sobeida would go back to Omar. As sharia law proscribed, they would celebrate their second wedding, since their divorce had already been granted. Muna had made many promises.

'I don't believe any of it. That woman is lying. I did it for the good of Omar's son,' Khadija declared, her eyes blazing. Omar's face was pale, and his brow split by a thick furrow. Khadija crossed her arms and remained pensive. Then she approached the table, and picked up the cup.

'Life is a struggle, my father!' she said, returning sombrely to her chores. The Count had been dismissed.

XIII

Omar was going back to Sobeida's house, so he gathered up his few belongings. Everything had been restored to its natural order, like in the last act of a play. Only the final feast was left: the second wedding. However, tradition forbade any displays of excess. Two people were present at the signing ceremony in the presence of the judge: Sharafeddin stood in for Omar, while Saber – designated by Muna in a conciliatory measure to her old rival – represented Sobeida. The betrothed and the women were not in attendance.

For the traditional 'night of the groom's entrance into the bridal chamber,' Sharafeddin invited his cousin to dinner, as well as two young men who worked in his shop. The modest atmosphere was shattered by Antonino's festive arrival. The young officer had obtained a transfer to Benghazi, and was happy to have arrived in time for Omar's wedding. Antonino had also been invited to the weaver's house.

The feast had been prepared in the room behind the shop, which opened out into a courtyard. There was a straw mat on the floor, and some cushions, as well as a green bench, crudely inlaid in metal and glass. On the wall was a sumptuous example of silver filigree calligraphy praising

God, and in front of it that photograph depicting the man with his stiff black moustache.

The two young assistants were very intimidated by the presence of the guest. Sharafeddin had drunk a lot already, and he offered them some *laghbi*, a cloudy alcoholic drink distilled from palm leaves. Omar brought a bottle of beer, but Antonino refused it: he wanted the exotic drink instead.

The groom was happy to be returning to Sobeida, as though he'd never wanted to separate from her, but had been forced to. He offered Antonino a cushion, and they stretched out on the mat. Antonino didn't seem to care much about the state of his uniform. They'd removed their shoes. Omar ordered the assistants to start playing the tambourine again.

Since this was a renewal of vows after a divorce, music and dancing would be a defiance of custom. But Antonino's presence at the dinner had prompted Omar to bring with him the traditional popular instruments, loud whimsical guests that could keep the guest of honour entertained. Sharafeddin put two glasses at a small distance from one another, and then accompanied the tambourine by beating a flat knife against the glasses. Antonino grimaced each time he brought the fermented palm wine Sharafeddin offered him to his lips, but insisted on drinking it regardless. It seemed that the alcoholic beverage was having a strong effect on him, triggering his metamorphosis.

A great calm reigned in Sharafeddin's eye, which lay semi-concealed under his drooping eyelid: Antonino continued to look at him, as though that eye were a hole beyond which one could see a panorama, or perhaps an olive-shaped chalice filled with a bright and mysterious water. Having learned that her favourite master was going to that so-called feast, Khadija had prepared a pot of minced meat in red sauce, as well as marinating pieces of lamb in oil and black pepper so the men could grill them.

Sharafeddin dominated the room. He sat cross-legged on the floor, facing the fire and placing pieces of lamb on it at regular intervals. Antonino was stretched out in front of him, and the glare of the fire endowed his body with a vibrant luminosity. Omar sat apart from the others, distracted by thoughts of Sobeida, the beloved wife he had repudiated and then remarried.

Like animals in a wood, the young assistants continued with their concerto, oblivious to what had transpired between the three men. Occasionally, Sharafeddin would sing along: a gloomy rumble that unsettled the musicians and visibly fascinated the young officer in uniform stretched out in front of him on the floor, his head propped up by his pale hand.

When Omar stood up to announce that the time had come for him to leave, Antonino suddenly remembered the feast was in celebration of Omar's second wedding. He cheerfully sprang to his feet, seemingly reluctant to let his servant friend go, and promised to wait for his return, saying that he would have given anything to be married to the beautiful Sobeida, among a thousand other festive and melancholy things.

Tradition dictated the groom not spend the entire wedding night with the bride, but leave her after they'd consummated the marriage to rejoin his friends and celebrate until dawn, while the bride was entrusted to the cares and attentions of her female relatives. But this only applied to one's first wedding, when the woman in question was a virgin. By saying he would await Omar's return, Antonino had mixed the customs up, but Omar didn't want to disillusion him, so he promised to return.

Sharafeddin's farewell, on the other hand, was terse.

Antonino's words had moved and saddened Omar. A vague feeling was keeping his soul in limbo – as though something more important than his wedding were about to happen.

Having reached the top of the alley he lingered for a moment, preoccupied, but then he heard the flute and tambourine again, and feeling suddenly relieved, with his mind wholly focused on the beautiful Sobeida, he ran through one alley after the other, as though dancing through them, until he once more stood at the door to his house. He pushed it open.

A few old women welcomed him, ululating; this was yet another infraction of custom, since that vivid traditional trilling was only used for the first wedding. It was as though Muna had wanted to assert her daughter's value by preparing such a loud reception.

He pushed open the bedroom door, and there was Sobeida. Pale, her eyes circled in Kohl, she was wearing the long thin silk robe of their first wedding night, blue with silver stripes, the organdie emblazoned with flowers, a white cotton belt, and heavy slippers that made her feet look even smaller than they were. She was not wearing the gold jewellery he'd given her, and Muna had treacherously sold. But this was not the time for investigations and recriminations – those pale arms were no less beautiful for being naked. On her finger was a silver ring mounted with a flat rhombus that almost covered the two adjacent fingers. Two engraved cylinders of silver were clasped around her ankles, an addition prompted by the second wedding. She had a small mouth and a chin-tattoo of three drops arranged in a triangle.

On seeing Sobeida in the room where he'd left her, the separation now seemed to be a necessity, or a trick of geography, and not a repudiation sanctified by the law. Mountains, rivers, fields and deserts had kept them apart. However, as they joyfully reunited, it was as though their parting had been bitter. They could hear the old women chattering in the adjacent room, as well as Muna's imperious voice: the voices wafted in like the natural sounds of rain, or wind, devoid of any psychological link. So long as they remained alone in the room, they would be safe.

The second wedding's lawful façade was irrelevant, and they slept together with an old couple's intimacy. Only their hearts were tense and confused. The long separation they'd endured weighed on them as though they'd just come out of prison.

Mindful that he'd promised Antonino he would see him again at Sharafeddin's house, Omar imposed a new separation on his wife. This time, his absence would only last a single day, in fact only a few hours, a contrived rerun of the old drama they had lived through, which would exorcise the memory of that first, bitter separation. But Omar was restless.

From the first moment he and Antonino had set foot in Sharafeddin's shop, Omar had been struck by his cousin's aversion to the young officer.

The usually taciturn Sharafeddin only became devilishly loquacious when he wanted to convince people there was no way to resolve the conflict peacefully — and that soon the two warring parties would take up arms again and meet in battle, sweeping the Basic Charter into the dust. To Sharafeddin, the sight of Omar and Antonino together was a picture right out of the Basic Charter, meaning Sharafeddin found it both abhorrent and laughable.

Whenever Antonino arrived anywhere he quickly gained entry, as though nothing were off-limits to him. The way he sped past the door where old Saber slept appeared to be an ironic illustration of this particular talent of his: when the frightened Saber opened his eyes, Antonino had already vanished. Instead, the door to Sharafeddin's shop seemed to be impenetrable, as though it were guarded by a dragon.

Omar crossed the neighbourhood again, running through one alley after the other, until he reached the street where the shop was situated. It was late at night by then, and the street was quiet: neither tambourines nor flutes could be heard.

When the Countess played the piano, Khadija's face lost its hearty glow, and she would appear barefoot at the threshold and look compassionately at the beautiful Countess. The morning creature for whom she braved the Count's severity, Rosina's favourite nephew, Antonino – whom Saber had been astonished to chance upon while the officer dozed on a bench in the garden, and who was still so youthful despite his military uniform – would never change, Khadija had confided in Omar: maturity and old age would not be a part of Antonino's destiny.

Omar pushed the door to the shop open and stepped inside. In the semi-darkness, the loom that took up almost the entire room looked like an infernal machine enshrouded by impenetrable shadows. He pushed the little door that led into the back room. The assistants had vanished, but Sharafeddin had his back against the wall, his head bent slightly, his eyes half open. Antonino was sprawled face down on the floor.

Omar knelt down and rolled him over. He was drunk. Omar argued bitterly with his cousin. He was afraid to leave the shop with the officer in that state. The only people out at night on the streets of Benghazi were patrols of suspicious soldiers.

Once he'd chased Sharafeddin away, he repositioned his

friend more comfortably, covered him with a blanket, and fell asleep by his side.

Omar woke Antonino at dawn and tried to make him look respectable, but Antonino pushed him away and left. Omar ran after him, but kept at a distance. The streets were deserted.

Facing out onto the little streets of the old city were modest-looking secret houses, their only distinctive feature an ample door with engraved door knockers. They were whitewashed, with a grey band at the base of the walls where the humidity had rotted the plaster.

The pink two-storey houses, on the other hand, displayed an array of doors and windows on the ground floor and little balconies on the first floor, one right next to the other. They were inhabited by members of the city's ethnic minorities, who lived according to different customs. All their windows were kept shut.

The city was very inhospitable in the freezing dawn. The young officer crossed it, shivering: it was like walking on the mysterious, iridescent floor of the sea.

At ten in the morning the Count returned home looking very pale, his hands all tense, as if he'd been crumpling up endless sheets of paper: Antonino had fallen from his horse and cracked his skull on a rock, his curly haired head seemingly drawn to it like a magnet. His regiment had been on manoeuvres at Ayn Zayana, to the east of the city, where the lone spring on that boundless plain had formed a lake almost parallel to the sea. The lake was surrounded by dunes, with tufts of green palm tree foliage sticking out of the snow-white sand.

Next to the spring, the dunes gave way to large slabs of rock. Spooked by the booming sound of a trumpet breaking the silence in that desolate place, Antonino's horse had tripped on one of the slabs, throwing the young officer from his saddle into the hard ground's embrace.

When the Count announced the news, the loyal Omar shielded himself and retreated a few steps. He saw a horse rider hurtling towards Antonino and unseating him: it was Sharafeddin. Omar's cousin was the closed door past which Antonino couldn't go. Wherever else he went, Antonino would easily find his way in, but Sharafeddin was the human embodiment of his limits. That silent, desolate lake was one of Sharafeddin's favourite places: the guardian of the lake had risen up out of the water to kill the intruder while he was surrounded by his fellow soldiers.

What was his loyalty worth? Omar remembered that he'd been the one to take Antonino to see Sharafeddin in that shop in the old city, dominated by that deafening hand-loom. Sharafeddin had given them a hostile reception. The shop was narrow, and there had barely been enough room for them. The duel had taken place on the boundless plain, on the lake's untouched shores.

Omar went to hide in the room at the far end of the courtyard. Who would believe that such a banal fall could have caused a mortal wound? Only he had seen who else was present at the scene: the trumpet had merely been Sharafeddin's ruse to escape being detected by Antonino's fellow soldiers. Right from the beginning, Khadija had kept an eye out for characters who manifested themselves only in the form of sound. The tragedy had reached its conclusion on a barren plain devoid of words and sights.

XIV

Ten days later, once all hope was lost, Antonino was transferred from the hospital to the deputy governor's house on a stretcher. His head was bandaged, a kind of white disguise that framed his small face in a military pose. Now that the great door of death barred his path, the peculiar discrepancy between his childlike face and the role of a warrior and lover that life that thrust upon him seemed to be the culmination of his pathetic destiny.

Sitting on the edge of the brass bed inside the brightly lit guest room in his house, while the sea breeze filled the ample muslin curtains with air, swelling them like sails, the Count felt as though he were the accused appearing before the court.

What sins had Antonino committed? Perhaps that of believing he could pass through every door, that he could disregard all the rules? Or was that agony nothing but a journey, the visible form of a metamorphosis whose outcome was always unpredictable?

But perhaps instead of a court with incomprehensible laws no amount of pity would have placated, there was the personal and secret envy of a god from whom Antonino had cajoled the secret of how to walk anywhere without leaving any tracks. The Count asked himself whether he hadn't also envied his nephew and whether he hadn't actually put that weapon in the hand of that god. Perhaps it had been due to the difficulties his plan presented, as well as the uncertainty of where his own path was headed, but it was a vain torment, which added to his already considerable discomfort.

Antonino slipped in and out of consciousness for hours at a time. Whenever he came to, if his beloved aunt was in the room she would hysterically suffer through his agony, either defying the irrevocable, or trying to make it insignificant. She wasn't preparing his soul for the unknown, but was defending herself from it – embodying the laughable, ironic refusal of moderation when faced with the blackmail of the immeasurable.

That frivolous, vain attempt was a pantomime played out before the solemn gate of death, not with a view directed at the afterlife, but instead with a gaze fixed on what was about to be left behind – a tender, heartrending goodbye.

When Antonino was alone with the Count he no longer concealed the horror of that inexorable path, and the discrepancy between his childlike face and the solemn majesty of those pearly gates could no longer be reconciled. Shock and fear hadn't aged that boy's face by a single day.

'I'm so scared of dying in such a distant place!' he said, clasping the Count's hand.

XV

On hearing Khadija mercilessly pounding their bedroom door with the palm of her hand, Count Alonzo and Countess Rosina understood that death had solemnly entered their home. The Count switched the lights on, but hesitated. Then he laid his hand on Rosina's shoulder and drew her close to him. He got out of bed, and slid his feet into his slippers. He had to open the door for Khadija, but he would never allow her to enter the room where they shared a bed.

When he opened the door, Khadija stepped inside. She took the Count's hand in hers and kissed it. 'What is good lives inside you,' she said. She crossed the room. She was barefoot. Rosina was sitting up, her hands folded in her lap. Khadija put her hand on the Countess's head, tilted it, and kissed her white forehead. 'Praise to He who remains alone.'

The Count was confused by a few incomprehensible gestures, as though his body had lost its centre of gravity. He drew near to his wife, and murmured a phrase into her ear that nobody heard. 'Let her cry to her heart's content,' Khadija said, putting a stop to his useless efforts.

She slid her mistress's feet into her slippers.

When Rosina stood up, Khadija headed for the door, leading the procession out of the room. The Count and Countess followed her along the corridor and down the stairs. The Count was hypnotised by Khadija's feet: she moved in the shadows of the door that so terrified the young officer without either hurrying or being afraid, as though she'd known all along when and how that precious life would end. The Count thought back to Antonino's first days in the colony and the cook's indulgence towards that boy in his military uniform – but the expert soothsayer had refused to divine the boy's fate by examining the black sludge at the bottom of his coffee cup. The wrathful shadow that crossed her swarthy face wasn't moodiness, it was experience.

As soon as they entered Antonino's room, Omar rushed towards them. He had stretched his friend's arms out along his sides, in the way believers should be prepared for meeting God. 'He wished you well with what strength he had left in him,' he said, clasping the Count's hand firmly. Then he clasped Rosina's hand. 'We will grieve *together*,' he said.

The Count took a few steps towards Antonino's slender white body lying on its deathbed. He grazed his fingers against Antonino's cold hand. Rosina seemed both drawn and repelled. Eventually she went to the Count's side, knelt before the bed, and buried her face in her hands.

Old Saber appeared on the threshold. He'd heard footsteps and strange noises. His skin had become very pale, as always happened when he was troubled. He could barely stand on his feet, and his knees were tired. He made a gesture as though trying to catch everyone's attention. Rosina still had her face buried in her hands. But she found the silence behind her unsettling, and she stood up. Saber walked a couple of steps closer to the bed. How fragile that old man was, and how faraway he seemed. 'Praise be to God,' he said, 'since nobody survives after Him.'

Rosina saw before her the little gold theatre on whose boards they had so pompously played their roles up until that moment, and the illusory candles of 'civilisation' that had shined a light on their every move. In that hour's solemn darkness, the only candles they could use to guide their way were the traditional phrases of the indigenous people, the sound of their voices the only light.

Alonzo wasn't the one who was in danger in that distant land, as in fact she had been saying ever since he had left Italy for Cyrenaica, always seeing him far away from her, and from himself, as though he'd lost himself in that passionate journey. Or perhaps death had missed its intended target and struck an innocent instead? Destiny first plays with words, then throws the designated victim onto the scene; and destiny alone chooses the victim, out of whimsy. An angered god had hidden a rock in his hand, which Antonino's head had smashed against after he was unseated from his horse. That land could only belong to a single people.

But the time for analysis and conjecture had come to an end: they were nothing but vain and useless wreaths lain against the ashen faces of the dead . . .

The top part of Antonino's head was wrapped in bandages, but the lower part was white and transparent, like the asphodel flowers that jutted out of the fields of the acropolis in Tolmeta. Once, when he'd been on his way back from the ancient city, Antonino had left an asphodel on top of the shiny black piano. Rosina thought she could hear the notes of Chopin's posthumous waltzes. Antonino's face looked like those waltzes: it was tender, and tragic.

Omar asked if he could wash his friend's body. He

didn't know anything about these foreigners' customs, but a guest had to be buried with the same considerations that applied to one's brothers. And since prayer – an act of appearing before God – cannot be performed without the necessary ritual ablutions, no body could be buried without being washed, so it could properly present itself before God.

The Count remained silent, lost in his thoughts. He didn't trouble Rosina with any questions or affectionate caresses. Coolness of manners is a virtue. There would be no such discretion the following day when their fellow Italians learned the news. Rosina thought with horror about those empty phrases she would be forced to hear a thousand times:

'*Please accept my condolences.*'

'*He was so young.*'

'*To be killed by falling off one's horse!*'

'*What grief it caused me.*'

'*You can count on me.*'

. . . and so on and so forth.

She felt so tired that she wanted to go back to bed. The Count followed her. Once she'd reached the door, she was startled. Something had got stuck yet again, and could move neither forwards nor backwards. Her robe was loose, revealing her well-shaped breasts. The prominence of her bosom made her look like a soprano. Old Saber walked ahead of her, leading the way with little dragging steps.

Rosina leaned her hand against the Count's arm. For the first time since she had arrived in Benghazi she was grateful to have those servants in her house. Thus reconciled, they followed the old man up the stairs and down the corridor, until they reached their bedroom door.

Epilogue

BENITO MUSSOLINI, PRIME MINISTER

I have the honour of announcing to Parliament that His Majesty the King, in his decree dated October 31st, has accepted the resignations of the Right Honourable Luigi Facta from the office of President of the Council of Ministers, and of his colleagues, the Ministers and Under Secretaries of State, and has asked me to form a new government.

Gentlemen!

For many years, in fact for too many years, Parliament saw fit to create and resolve crises in Government through more or less tortuous and underhand tactics, so much so that a crisis came to be regarded as a regular scramble for portfolios and the ministry, as caricatured in the comic papers. Now, for the second time in the brief space of seven years, the Italian people, or rather the best part of it, have overthrown the government and formed an entirely new one, which lies wholly outside the current system and refuses any appointments offered to it. The seven years of which I speak lie between May 1915 and October 1922. I shall leave to the gloomy partisans of super-Constitutionalism the task of discoursing, more or less plaintively, about all this. I maintain that revolution has its rights; and, I may add, so that everyone may know, that I am here to defend and give the greatest value to the revolution of the 'black shirts.'

I could have carried our victory much further, and I refused to do so. I imposed limits on my actions and told myself that the truest wisdom is one which survives even after victory. With three hundred thousand fully armed young men who are ready for anything and zealously prompt to obey any command I give them, I could have punished everyone who slandered the Fascists and threw mud at them. I could have made a bivouac of this grey hall; I could have shut up Parliament and formed a government composed exclusively of Fascists . . .

'Bivouac Speech', November 16th 1922[7]

The Count, who was the managing director of a textile company where his father-in-law was the major shareholder, was walking along the Via Santa Margherita in Milan on a clear evening in September 1931. He had attended a dinner at the house of some friends, a discreet pretext under which fellow anti-Fascist liberals could meet and discuss politics. Implacable dogs were defending economic interests: the cult of liberty was blooming in those elegant catacombs. The Count had listened closely to noblemen, scholars, and passionate discussions.

Two days earlier, after a celebrated trial had taken place in the rooms that once housed the dissolved

7 Translation by André Naffis-Sahely.

Cyrenaican assembly, the legendary leader of the twenty-year Libyan resistance to the Italian occupation Sidi Omar al-Mukhtar had been hanged at the age of seventy-four. The execution had been carried out in Solluk, a wretched little village to the south of Benghazi. The man had the same name as the young man who'd lived in the Count's house when he was in Africa.

The Count was astonished that his anti-Fascist friends hadn't mentioned that murder during their noble, scholarly, and passionate discussions.

1927

THE NOCTURNAL
VISITOR

The night is an intermission. Standing upright on the threshold, Sheikh Hassan scanned the empty room. The candle was making the shadows dance and flicker across the walls. In the right-hand corner was a wooden chest filled with books. To read is to travel. He mulled over the secret his wife had maliciously decided to confide in him. The night had subjugated him: the reptile that had entered his house now lingered there, spellbound. Sheikh Hassan held the candle aloft, then lowered it. It made him happy to distance himself from others. He moved the candle to and fro as though performing an exorcism. To leave the world behind, then enter it again through the portal opened by books. Those mountains and that splendid valley were dearer to him than any other place on earth. After nightfall, they fitted into the hollow of the hand. His eyes embraced the tiny valley illuminated by the blinding sun; the candle's wan glow revealed a world without borders, which had been magically preserved in a few books.

From the little window in his room Sheikh Hassan was able to keep contemplating that deserted place by the light of the moon, which gave the valley the calm clarity of a sheet of paper. Sheikh Hassan took to his days with a lord's calm condescension: a tension that was at times fiery, and at others intolerable, but always exaggerated, fleeting, useless. *Nothing left except books.*

He would have to choose sides in the predicament his wife had revealed. History tells us of dazzling individuals who inspire in readers a confused admiration and a gratitude that is occasionally intertwined with fear and horror. But that particular incident was devoid of merriment: a judge, which was the role he'd been allotted, was merely a conduit for the application of the law.

Sheikh Hassan sat on his mat. He opened the wooden chest and pulled out a tome. The day is a bizarre dream when irrelevant images preoccupy our attentions and force us to take an active part in events, sometimes proving painful. Whenever one's eyes open on a book, it makes those confused images vanish, and reality comes back under the jurisdiction of the mind.

Harun al-Rashid, the Caliph of Baghdad and undisputed master of the colourful kingdoms of fables, had a sister he was tenderly devoted to whose name was Abbassa. Jafar, his vizier, was the other being who was close to his heart. Our desires have deep roots: Harun bound his sister and friend in matrimony, but forbade them to consummate it. Having fallen in love, Abbassa broke the rule by copulating with her lawful consort. The story goes that Jafar was drunk at the time.

What had prompted Sheikh Hassan to seek this grim vignette in the pages of Ibn Khaldun's *Muqaddimah*? Ibn Khaldun used the tale as an example of historical improbability. Abbassa's adventure wasn't in keeping with her religious faith, or her social origins and rank. The princess was the daughter of Muhammad ibn Mansur al-Mahdi, son of

Abu Ja'far al-Mansur, son of Muhammad al-Sayyad. Rectitude of faith and a strict adherence to customs were in her heritage. She had no knowledge of the lush pastures of sin! Jafar was a freed slave. How could Abbassa possibly marry a slave's son? How could Harun al-Rashid, the Leader of the Faithful, allow it, or indeed order his favourite sister to marry a man of such inferior rank? Who could possibly hope to come between those siblings?

A historian is both a moralist and an apologist. The hero, who is an example, cannot be discouraged by accounts of his weaknesses and mistakes. Ibn Khaldun vents his wrath whenever he encounters asinine storytellers who unhesitatingly depicted Harun al-Rashid as a drunk. A young thug wanders the streets of the capital, making the fateful decision to visit unknown houses, where he squanders both himself and his wealth on love intrigues: was this really the Leader of the Faithful? Ibn Khaldun restores the immaculate purity of he who leads by example to his hero. But what exactly was he defending? The towering figure in the popular imagination – which was excessive and disrespectful – or an unrealistic portrayal of the purity, steadfastness and coherence of a man descended from the noblest lineage who was destined for the highest office? Abbassa may well have loved that vizier, if the latter, as history tells us, was the favourite of her brother, the Caliph. The princess's favour was by no means less precious than the King's. Both these blessings rained down on the same head, thus their two weaknesses justified themselves reciprocally. By betraying her brother, Abbassa reaffirmed his decision. By coming together, the Caliph's darlings had excluded him – and Harun al-Rashid hated it as though he'd been imprisoned!

'*And then historians must beware of another risk: that of*

ignoring the changes in the conditions and customs of nations and races owed to the passing of time . . . their customs and beliefs do not retain their usual shape, but always metamorphose with the passing of time and change from one state to another.'[8]

'God will inherit the world and everything it houses,' Sheikh Hassan said out loud. He'd seen very little of the world outside that Cyrenaican valley where he'd been born and still lived. But what an education he'd had, even in that remote place! On the hilltops one could still see the ruins of Roman fortifications, and children from the area could still find coins bearing the effigies of lords who had been dead for centuries. A marabout – an object of veneration for the tribe led by the Sheikh – could be seen resting between the stones of an old fort. What the *Muqaddimah* demonstrated in its endless flow, the valley could show just as well in a single image: various civilisations had come and gone, leaving only a few dramatic ruins behind. Ibn Khaldun writes that historians must compare the present and the past, and analyse the similarities and differences between them. Similar cycles repeat themselves, as though impulses, like human beings, followed a trajectory that adhered to set rules. Thus whoever follows this river will be captivated by its course, musing over its variations while ceasing to desire a destination: in the end, the journey becomes an intellectual exercise.

Hassan had studied at the Sanussi university in Jaghbub, the most celebrated institution in North Africa after Cairo's al-Azhar. He'd been a restless youth. Employing both severity and compassion, a venerated teacher had taken him under his wing: the university was strictly orthodox, and Hassan's restlessness had easily led him into the fatal arms of dissident

8 All translations of Ibn Khaldun by André Naffis-Sahely.

factions. Heresy is a diabolical dream. The young Hassan displayed a natural curiosity nevertheless well disposed to obedience. He was vivacious, but conciliatory, as well as strong, if not overly eager for clashes and disagreements. His master's severity proved an unbreakable dam; after all, the teacher had spent his entire life in sincere and serene adhesion to orthodoxy. The university's celebrated library, which housed eight thousand volumes, opened up infinite paths: the restrictions placed on Hassan only closed off a few of them, the most impractical.

For the following twenty years, Sheikh Hassan's life had been devoid of any remarkable incidents. After his studies in Jaghbub, he returned to his fields and led a tranquil existence. Occasionally an emissary from Jaghbub – or somewhere further away – would come bearing a book, his only link to the wider world.

'History,' Ibn Khaldun wrote, '*is a science: it deals with the principles of politics, the nature of things, and the differences between nations, places and historical epochs, ways of life, customs, sects and schools.*' The ruins of the great ancient monuments, numerous examples of which could be seen even in Cyrenaica, were testament to that diversity as it unfolded over the course of time – a simultaneously fertile and corrupting force.

Sheikh Hassan travelled little in his life, and usually only from one mountain village to another. He saw the ruins of Cyrene, the celebrated ancient city, as well as Benghazi, the city on the coast which few loved, and where he'd found himself a wife. But he read every adventurer's account he could get his hands on. His curiosity knew no bounds. He was obsessed by the encounter with the other, which paved the way to knowledge.

Who were those conquerors who'd washed ashore on

his lands in October 1911? What had led them there? Which laws did they obey? What were they looking for? He abhorred those people who sowed death and violence wherever they went, but their presence was a frame of reference. Sheikh Hassan had never seen one of them up close: he hadn't been to Benghazi since the city had fallen into their hands, but he was hungry for any news about them, asking anyone who crossed his path many insistent questions in order to discover details others considered insignificant.

Subject to set rules, man's life is made insecure by the multiplicity of options before him. '*Man*,' Ibn Khaldun declared, '*is a creature of habit.*' In other words, he's subject to contingent forces. Thus, how else could one find any release if not by reading, which was a metaphor for travel and the intellectual knowledge forged by diversity? Without this crucial element, historical contingencies could be mistaken for necessity and metaphysical order. But where diversity is observed so closely that it affirms its legitimacy, what remains of the truth behind the rules that were followed? Doesn't this diminish laws by codifying them into habit? If people don't hang on to their conventions over time, it's equally true that those very conventions have multiple natures. If change is tolerated purely because it would be impossible not to do so, this means that everything different or foreign is also legitimate. Travellers' accounts challenge the placid certainties that are the foundations of habit and the homogeneous fabric of the societies to which we belong; by being a testament to multiplicity, they reconcile themselves into a metaphor for how relative laws really are.

The encounter with the other, a man shaped by a different past. Every man's head lies under the same sky. Is war the only possible encounter? And yet travellers and philosophers have crossed foreign lands without swords in their hands, gripping instead the soft reins of a peaceful beast. They hadn't destroyed, but merely observed – and their booty wasn't gold or silver, but words. The other inspired a passionate nostalgia and deep-seated curiosity in these men. How did they bear their own foreignness? What force – what blindness – kept them going? Standing motionless in his room, Sheikh Hassan followed those interminable peregrinations in his books. He wasn't tormented by duplicity, the protector of laws and travellers. However, it was certainly true that his passion for reading had given rise to rumours in the village that he was guilty of witchcraft. But these were fables that only the poor believed. To read was to open a window onto the world. Bent over his books by a candle that fought against the blindness of the night, Sheikh Hassan could see cities and their inhabitants, empires rising up and then crumbling, as well as tragic individuals who burst onto the scene only to perish in miserable ways. Ibn Khaldun tells us that certain peculiar people believe that Iram of the Pillars is *invisible except to soothsayers and magicians.*' A reader is both a magician and a soothsayer. While the poor people living in tents or shanties in the valley slept, Sheikh Hassan was locked in his room like a wizard, conjuring up images of richer cities than Iram of the Pillars, of fabulous civilisations governed by bizarre laws, and of individuals who'd made the world hold its breath, if only for an hour.

A soothsayer, a magician . . .

Being ironic, Sheikh Hassan smiled at these accusations. Ibn Khaldun writes: '*If prophets are inspired by God's mercy, which is intrinsically divine, soothsayers' souls can employ diabolical powers to commune with the invisible world.*' Is reading a diabolical power? Lost in a land where reading was the privilege of few, Sheikh Hassan never stopped pondering its meaning. Suddenly, a multitude of roads appears, and man is subtracted from the homogeneous environment where he's lived and been educated, and is presented with the infinite roads others throughout history have walked. Literature is a transaction with the outsider, or he who obeys different rules. Were these outsiders really demons? Whom did they obey? Does every traveller's identity split in two?

Sheikh Hassan's nature was conciliatory, and when cornered, he didn't slip into solitary dialogues with the invisible to avoid being a hypocrite. Even irony – the ability to intentionally de-dramatise a question – is hypocritical. He would often say that the cheerful reports travellers sent from infidel lands were among the gems of Arabic literature and science; he was guided by a sense of innocent curiosity, and curiosity is a benign familiar. Reading, like dreaming, is a vision of remote and absurdly interwoven things. One need only invoke God's hallowed name to banish such confused images.

If individuals inevitably drift back to the superfluous – Hassan hadn't limited his education to the essential, or rather to knowledge of the sacred book, but had read many others besides – the superfluous can sometimes spill into the diabolical. The promise of Salvation is a great doctrine, but impassioned research is an enchanted voyage at the mercy of unknown powers. Ibn Khaldun wrote: '*The secret of Bedouin society lies in its simplicity and its moderation and reserve.*' Did literature violate these virtues? Ibn Khaldun tells us everything '*decays, crushed by the superfluous.*'

'*When sophistication reaches its apex, it enslaves us to our desires. Suffering from a surfeit of beauty, the human soul is blinded by a multiplicity of colours that obscures its vision of this world, or the next.*'

Magic is the attempt to recover worlds shunned by

civilisation. Is literature a form of magic? Nature transformed into the divine. What does that mean? Doesn't that imply a return to polytheism? Apostasy?

'What do you need all those books for?' a stern and proudly illiterate uncle once asked him after peering disdainfully into the chest where Sheikh Hassan kept his tomes.

He edged the candle closer and turned the page. Anyone who reads is looking for a non-existent page where he can stop. The superfluous rejects any sense of measure, and therefore grows unabated, independently of the person's willpower. The nocturnal abandon of the valley below made everything in sight seem both near and distant, both passionately desirable and useless. The nomad who gets lost in the city renounces all his blood ties, loses himself in that crowd and vanishes: to read is to isolate oneself, rejecting all ties so as to plunge into the simple, peaceful knowledge of our ancestors. It is an all-devouring impulse to learn that knows no limits: one page only leads to another. For its loyal inhabitants, the valley is their homeland, a self-sufficient miniature of the world. The yearning for knowledge defies the limits wrought over time immemorial by one's forefathers: a rejection of the image of the world they preserved. Is one's well-being confined by one's horizons?

The accusations of sorcery weren't only false, they were also laughable, and Sheikh Hassan didn't hesitate to refer to them ironically when in public. But where was that yearning for knowledge leading him? Ibn Khaldun writes: ' . . . *a man's intelligence and competence tell us that he thinks too much, just like stupidity is an excess of apathy. As far as human faculties are concerned, any extremes are to be avoided, and one must strike the right balance. And this can only happen through generosity – which is preferable to prodigality – or through courage, instead of temerity or cowardice. And this applies to all other human qualities. Thus, people who are too intelligent are suspected of possessing a democratic soul. These people are then often called demons, or suspected of being possessed. God creates what He wills.'*

'God creates what He wills,' Sheikh Hassan obediently repeated, shutting the book. And he added: 'God gives the kingship to whom He will.'

Ibn Khaldun says that '*serving a master is not a natural way of earning one's living.'* Anyone who goes to town these days goes to serve a master. The inhabitants of Benghazi weren't indigenous to the area: they had fled from the island of Crete, or immigrated from Misrata or Djerba, or were descended from Turkish officials or Janissaries. They had simply adapted to the virtues of whichever new master ruled the city while focusing on their individual journeys to wealth, power, or mere survival.

The Italian Expeditionary Force had believed conquering Benghazi would mean they would control the rest of the country, but Benghazi meant nothing to the tribes, who merely saw it as a useful convenience, or a deadly bridge. The city had always been ruled by foreigners: by Tripoli during the time of the Qaramanli family, by Istanbul, and now by Rome. General Caneva's Expeditionary Force had replaced the Turkish garrison, but after many years and much bloodshed, most of the mountainous areas and distant oases had retained their freedom. The patterns that Ibn Khaldun thought history followed – the foundation of a city, its flowering, and its subsequent decay – didn't apply to the natives of Cyrenaica, but to the colonists, regardless of whether they were ancient Greeks or newly-arrived Italians. As per the Italian government's instructions Benghazi, the capital, was being redesigned and expanded. There would inevitably come a day when the conquerors would reverse that process: the architects of its flowering would become the architects of its decay and decadence.

Going to Benghazi made Sheikh Hassan feel as though he'd just woken up: an intolerable restriction after a full night of reading, dreams, and rest. Whenever he was in the city, Sheikh Hassan longed for the countryside's limitless expanse.

Families in Benghazi wouldn't willingly marry their daughters into families from the countryside because they respected different customs and were very reluctant to embrace the 'civilisation' that made people in the city feel so proud. To them, civilisation meant the imitation of whoever ruled the city. Sheikh Hassan had much respect for his forefathers' customs and displayed a great intellectual curiosity for anything that was different, but he loathed imitation, which was the antithesis of reading. He had married a woman from the city who'd been promised to him ever since she'd been a girl: an exception made for the good of the family's prestige.

Sheikh Hassan didn't love his wife, who was finicky and always prepared to make unfavourable comparisons between the sophisticated urbanites and the ill-bred mountain people: but in those parts a man's authority was unconditional, and his wife's chatter came and went like a mosquito's monotone buzz. Ibn Khaldun praised the Bedouin way of life because it safeguarded them from the '*mediocrity of the cities.*'

Zazia hated Hassan's books. Since she was illiterate, she had no idea what they contained. Those jinns isolated her husband from the rest of the world. She would vent her wrath on the people who lived in the house and constantly asserted her rights. Nobody paid her much attention because these were simply an unhappy woman's vain, venomous wailings, and only the master's wrath was omnipotent.

Zazia had given Hassan a son who was tough, scornful and ignorant.

Sheikh Hassan was always shadowed by Anwar, a servant who could either no longer remember why he'd arrived or else kept his reasons secret. That man didn't belong to anyone. Sheikh Hassan had taken him on out of compassion, curious about that peculiar creature. Sheikh Hassan had given the man two wives. The first had abandoned him and gone to live in the city, while the second lived in Sheikh Hassan's house with her son Rafiq and Ghazala Anwar's daughter from his first marriage.

The way that Anwar turned reality on its head when he interpreted it revealed the many defects, strange possibilities and senses of identity inherent in that reality; he had a genius for dissecting habits, and he was a precious lantern that lit the path through the deceptive uniformity of everyday life.

The abominable sin recalls the beginning of time, the dawn of humanity, or heralds its end, the twilight of the fatal night. Once time comes to a grinding halt brother and sister, a union that history turned into a taboo, will come together again: the divine and the natural, two worlds that were intertwined for centuries, will break asunder.

Ghazala had accused her brother Rafiq of trying to molest her. Divine law sacrifices anyone who contradicts it. The tangle of feelings and desires, which is proof of nature's monstrous fecundity, can't often be clearly resolved. A young man who lived in his house had dared to break the laws Sheikh Hassan had sworn to uphold, or perhaps he had done so out of sheer ignorance. Who was guilty then? O fate what curse was keeping Rafiq from the path of knowledge? In the deepest depths of night Sheikh Hassan, the judge who was suspected of sorcery and satanic spells, turned into a botanist as he observed that proud young heart as though it were a colourful and powerfully fragrant flower. The mistake was illuminating something morbid and incomprehensible as though it were a beacon lost in the limitless plain. Was anything more important than the law? What was Rafiq hiding? A lifelong devotee of the other, the uncontaminated, and civilisations governed by different rules, and a steadfast friend of the tempters who revealed the infinitely distant reaches of time and space, Sheikh Hassan now found himself with an abominable monster under his roof, whom he'd nurtured and indulged, and who would now test the limits of his curiosity, or else make him regret that curiosity entirely.

Sheikh Hassan didn't care much for the dawn – he found it very difficult to wake up because it was such an instant abatement of the nocturnal world. The morning would force on him the boring company of his family instead of the enigmatic travelling companions he enjoyed at night. He would leave his bed reluctantly and get annoyed if he heard anyone speak. He was particularly restless that morning. The man who loved to read felt that the unpleasant moment when one is forced to do what others expect of him was fast approaching. A judge is enslaved to the public will, as expressed by the law.

The door suddenly swung open and Rafiq appeared. He didn't linger on the threshold but instead threw himself at the Sheikh's feet. Sheikh Hassan pulled him up by his hair and gazed into his eyes – which he'd shut, out of shame – and those sealed, trembling lips. When the boy stood up, Sheikh Hassan pushed him away; nimble as an insect, Rafiq quickly headed towards the door and disappeared.

As for Zazia – who looked on those peasants as primitive

and ignorant, and thus undoubtedly guilty – her wrath was powerless: Rafiq had fled, secreted away by his mother, Dhahab, who insisted her son hadn't been the nocturnal visitor, but someone who looked exactly like him.

She had seen him on numerous occasions, and he could only be spotted at night.

The young man had definitely escaped to Benghazi. Who would catch up with him? The truce was over now, and the two sides, the Italian government and the patriots of the Sanussi Brotherhood, had taken up arms again. The Italian government was now headed by Benito Mussolini.

Rafiq entered the city through the eastern gate. The emotional impact it had on him was overwhelming, and the guards looked at him suspiciously. He was searched and interrogated, but they let him through.

It was the first time he'd seen Benghazi. He was tired and hungry. It would be difficult for the master to lay his hands on him, as they were now separated by the front line where the war was being waged. Maybe Sheikh Hassan's son Nagi would show up instead. Then there were the family's relatives who worked in the city, who would soon learn of the news and be hot on his heels. Feeling vulnerable, he decided to run away again, as soon as he could, and go much farther away.

The poor young man was innocent. His mother's revelations had shocked him. If he wasn't Anwar's son, then who was his real father? Why had she waited so long to disclose this secret, why hadn't she mentioned his real father's name, who did he belong to, what new obligations did he have, and which obligations no longer applied?

He had seen his stepsister Ghazala in the fields. She knew something. But it felt as though someone were watching them.

That night he'd been unable to catch a wink of sleep. Ghazala slept in a room set aside from the others, along with Sheikh Hassan's mother. Rafiq had slipped into the room and managed to prevent Ghazala from screaming and thereby alerting the others to his presence. But having snuck into her room in order to talk to her, words had failed him. But who was this girl he was clasping in his arms? If he wasn't Anwar's son, then Ghazala wasn't his stepsister. There was no holy barrier between them. His desire to have Ghazala rested on the foundations of his mother's revelations. After all, how could he possibly desire her if she was his sister? Beneath the obvious order of things, he perceived the existence of another order. Who had led him to that place? What was he doing? The poor young man asked himself one pointless question after another. And he didn't even notice the scratch his sister had left on his cheek.

Rafiq had never seen so many people or so many houses. This mayhem was both frightening and consoling, because he was fleeing his persecutors, but felt an insurmountable sense of insecurity at being so far away from his family.

He saw an uninterrupted stream of faces and images without feeling either pleased or satiated. None of these images could be linked together, or made any sense. One image chased another away, before he'd even understood what it meant. On seeing a new face, it would immediately be replaced by another, and the first one would be consigned to oblivion. In the evening he felt so exhausted that he wanted to be found by his persecutors, seeking death as a way of restoring the old order of things. There was no room for his youth – neither in his home, nor in that city. To be condemned for a simple slip appeared to be his destiny. Where could he run to? A man belongs with his blood relatives; and if the latter decided he should die, then it would be better to perish than to abandon his native soil and be torn away from them.

The following morning Rafiq presented himself at a barracks where the new masters of the city were hiring men for various jobs that needed doing. Helping those people wasn't an act of revenge against his kinsmen: he was merely fulfilling his destiny. Besides, all that work, which was very tiring and entirely different from the work he'd done in the mountains, helped to distract him. He evaded questions because he didn't want anyone to discover his origins, but it was always the same faces, the same place, and his life once more acquired a sense of continuity – and continuity is already an order in its own right. The second day proved even smoother, and so forth. He was either adapting or waiting.

Sometimes, Rafiq was so prudent he even went to the lengths of hiding his face, afraid his executioner would chance upon him. At others, he would smugly walk the streets as though he were untouchable. One day, on entering a little shop in the covered market, he thought he could see himself as though he were looking into a mirror, and behind the sales desk he saw his own face – although the body's movements didn't correspond to his own. Feverishly, he turned on his heels and slipped away. His mother had denied that the nocturnal visitor was her son, but insisted that he was simply an abominable nightmare crazy Anwar's daughter had conjured. When others testified that they'd heard footsteps, she told them firmly that it hadn't been Rafiq, but a young man she'd seen several times who was Rafiq's perfect lookalike.

On seeing that young man in the shop, Rafiq realised that his mother had been telling the truth. He became more prudent. His desire to keep living returned to him, because he now knew he would be able to return home one day. The young man behind the sales desk was a pledge that his mother had secretly offered him, after mouthing mysterious words. Rafiq bought a new shirt with that week's wage, paid the barber a visit and washed meticulously. Once his appearance was more reassuring, he took up a position outside the little shop until he saw the owner leave. Then he presented himself before his doppelgänger.

The young clerk was rather shy, and he eyed Rafiq circumspectly as though he were a devilish apparition, trying to conceal his confusion. Reassured by the presence of this brother he could hand over to his persecutors in his stead, Rafiq on the other hand adopted a calm, almost authoritarian disposition. He was the master of his own spitting image – who was slowly beginning to conquer the stupor and insecurity his doppelgänger's presence had caused. He calmed down, albeit warily. Rafiq had won. He didn't leave the shop until he'd become fast friends with the youth, whose name was Saad.

However, a secret fear kept Rafiq away from the house where Saad lived with his mother. If the conversation ever veered towards their respective origins, both men were overcome by an unconquerable diffidence. Rafiq was afraid Saad would discover the ignominious accusation that weighed on him. Saad didn't know his father either, and he in turn thought this was shameful. Nevertheless, the deep-seated insecurity they both concealed actually strengthened their friendship, and when strangers saw them together and referred to them as brothers the two young men kept their mouths shut, as though they had struck a conspiratorial understanding.

Rafiq gradually convinced his friend to leave Benghazi with him. He promised him an unspoilt peaceful way of life in the mountains, and that the journey would symbolise their allegiance to the patriots fighting against the invaders who had come to steal their land. Saad let himself be swept along in these discussions, and only saw the solidarity that existed between him and the man people thought was his brother. Saad began to find life in that little shop and that hateful master of his unbearable. Rafiq converted Saad's fear of his mother into a desire for independence and adventure. Two months later the two men walked side by side through the eastern gate and went to the mountains.

The journey was very long. Rafiq had grown shrewd during the few months he'd spent in Benghazi, and knew how to surmount any difficulty. He wasn't in any hurry to reach their fated destination, and neither was Saad, for that matter, as he experienced a constant excitement at vaga-bonding around with his brother. They passed through the village of Tolmeta, where colossal stones indicated a glorious past. Rafiq said his master possessed a boundless knowledge of science. Just like merchants spent their lives in their shops, his patient master spent countless hours in his room with a book in his hands.

Ever since they'd left the city Rafiq had been growing more sincere. He spoke of his ancestral lands and the people who lived there. He mentioned his sister's name for the first time and, on seeing Saad's surprise, Rafiq promised he would see him married to Ghazala. This was what he'd decided. Saad listened to everything and accepted it unques-tioningly. The promise of marriage overcame all of his apprehension, and made abandoning his mother and city a necessary and legitimate step on his road to adulthood.

Rafiq was hungry for any new signs of loyalty on the part of his 'brother,' and constantly put his dedication to the test. The game was going to his head. Saad didn't spare any effort, and finally said passionately that he would brave death itself in order to save his friend. They were on a remote beach, beyond the promontory of Tolmeta. Saad's oath left Rafiq in a pensive mood. A shadow fell over his face. He was silent. Saad vainly tried to snap him out of it, but Rafiq appeared to have run away and got lost somewhere. Saad was suddenly gripped by a new fear, and was unable to hide it. As soon as Rafiq realised what was going on he came to, and reassured his friend with silky words.

In the meantime, the youths had changed direction and were heading away from the coast. After their long journey, it seemed Rafiq had become impatient to reach his ancestral lands. Saad didn't suspect anything, and put his fate in the other's hands.

Having reached the uplands of Barca, Rafiq grew wary. He told Saad that the uplands were divided between the conquerors and the patriots, and that they needed to be careful. Saad was a little taller than Rafiq, and more nimble. His skin was fairer. He displayed the mannerisms of a man who'd grown up in the city's confines, and not someone who'd been born in the mountains. Rafiq was more stocky and solemn than Saad. Two models of the same person. Before leaving Benghazi, Rafiq had asked Saad to wear the same clothes as him, even down to in the same colours, in an effort to emphasise their similarity, and Saad was happy to comply. Thus, he aped his friend's mannerisms, gait, voice, and even his accent, which was so different from his own. It was as though Rafiq wanted an exact replica of himself, and Saad diligently obliged.

Having crossed the uplands of Barca, they began to climb up once again. By now, Rafiq was no longer paying Saad much attention, and he kept looking around without growing distracted. Once they'd reached the summit of a hill, Rafiq pointed out the valley below, and his house, through the stones of an old fort: this was his homeland.

Rafiq told Saad he'd have to obey his every command, and Saad swore that he would. He was reassured by the sight of Rafiq's house. Rafiq spoke once more about Ghazala, albeit confusedly. He ordered his friend to hide. At the first shadows, he would descend into the valley alone to speak to his elderly mother.

Saad obeyed, but couldn't help jutting his head out from the boulders. Rafiq proceeded cautiously and soon disappeared, camouflaged by the night. He returned a few hours later. Frightened, Saad welcomed his friend with relief. Rafiq swore they would never part again.

Rafiq said that he'd spoken to his mother. Sheikh Hassan was suspicious of people from the city. They would walk down together unseen, but the guest would have to enter secretly into an empty room and stay there. Rafiq would then go and meet the master. As soon as Rafiq secured the Sheikh's consent, Saad would be free to leave his hiding place. They would pretend Saad came from Barca. The plan left Saad feeling a little melancholy, but he didn't know where else he could go, and thus he handed himself over to Rafiq, who cheered his friend up by saying that his new wife was waiting for him. Even though all these precautions were necessary, Saad was sure to be warmly welcomed. Saad only wanted to be consoled. When they got up, he played his part without even thinking about it.

A dog barked in the night and then suddenly appeared

beside them, but Rafiq shut it up. They nevertheless remained motionless for a moment before resuming their journey. Rafiq stopped in front of a cluster of trees, holding the dog by the scruff of its neck. The house could be clearly distinguished, thanks to the arrival of moonlight. Rafiq pointed out the wall Saad needed to climb and the window through which he could slip into the empty room. Saad was so eager to put all the mysteries to an end that he agreed to everything. Rafiq promised he would quickly join him. As soon as Saad climbed through the window, Rafiq would incite the dog, make his presence known, and enter the house.

Saad left. He climbed the wall and disappeared into the house. A few minutes later a scream was heard, the dog began to bark, and Rafiq let him loose. Then there was a gunshot.

Thus, order was restored and justice done. Dhahab showed everyone the body of the man who looked like her son and had once more tried to enter the room where Ghazala slept with the Sheikh's old mother. Sobbing, Ghazala said she recognised him, that this was the same devil who'd tried to molest her the first time, and that she'd unjustly accused her brother. Rafiq was innocent.

The men carried the demon's body away.

When peace was restored to the house later that night, the Sheikh's old mother rolled out the prayer mat. Sheikh Hassan walked past her and asked her to remember him in her prayers. She replied that she always did so. 'What more do you want?' she said. Sheikh Hassan's feet were already on the threshold. He was so tall that he had to stoop in order to pass through the door. He turned and replied, 'Pray that my fall be bearable.'

Rafiq returned home a few days later. He threw himself

at Sheikh Hassan's feet and asked for his forgiveness, and because he was innocent, he was granted it.

The triumph of justice allowed life in Sheikh Hassan's house to resume its serene quotidian flow in its lawful riverbed.

Ghazala was married off the following spring. Zazia said it was their duty to invite Fatima, who was the bride's mother, to the wedding. As the laws of hospitality demanded it, Sheikh Hassan consented, despite the obvious unhappiness that it caused Anwar's second wife, who was the bride's stepmother. The wedding was therefore postponed to give a messenger enough time to go to the city and invite that silent woman, who'd never been seen after the divorce had been granted. Fatima hadn't set eyes on her daughter since the girl was nine years old.

Fatima worked in the house of an Italian government functionary.

She listened to the messenger and replied that she would come after a few days, but that the wedding would need to happen quickly, and that there could be no further delays since her job in the city would be waiting for her. Exceedingly thin, she spoke in a hurry, as though engaged in swordplay. The Italian functionary often laughed with friends who came to visit, because the stern woman who opened the door didn't allow anyone to enter without the master's permission, and didn't hesitate to throw anyone out if they dared cross the threshold. Fatima often hummed interminably long lullabies from the mountains. She didn't display the slightest curiosity for her new masters' lives, nor did she ever confide in them. She didn't try to learn their language and never touched anything that wasn't offered to her, finding pride in her frugality. She indulged the master's children, but didn't hesitate to scold or beat them if they made too many mistakes, such as going out into the street. She thought of them as pets that only needed to be fed and confined so they wouldn't run away.

Three days later Fatima reached Sheikh Hassan's house. She greeted everyone in the same manner, regardless of whether they were strangers, masters or servants. She even kept the same reserve when hugging Ghazala.

Ghazala left the house where she'd grown up on the back of a camel, in a sumptuous ceremony that crowned the bride's departure from her family's home. Many accompanied her procession, including a man who'd been accused of a terrible murder, Rafiq. The groom's family had sent a few relatives to escort the bride to her new abode. Ghazala was seated on a high-backed multicoloured throne. The morning was bathed in a gleaming light and the sky was an unblemished blue. Drenched by recent rains, the soil promised a happy bounty come harvest time. The camel proceeded along the plain, followed by people on foot and magnificently attired horsemen.

Atop his steed, Rafiq rode ahead of the procession in silence. Separating from Ghazala was proving almost unbearable. Saad's face flashed right before his eyes. Saad's sacrifice had seemed necessary so long as Ghazala had lived in Sheikh Hassan's house, since it was the only way Rafiq could have ever returned home. If not, the accusation of impiety would have led him to exile himself further and further away. He had sacrificed his loyal friend, the young man who had lovingly tried to emphasise their similarities so that he could appear in an honoured role before his stepsister.

For a few fleeting months, Saad had been his beloved brother.

Who could possibly claim to be Ghazala's groom if not

Saad, to whom she'd been promised during their long journey through the mountains? What woeful destiny was forcing Rafiq to accompany his stepsister to the man and strangers she had been given away to, separating her not only from Rafiq, but also from the other one, Rafiq's spitting image, who people believed was his brother? Saad would have clasped her to his chest without feeling any guilt.

Restlessly galloping back and forth, as though trying to draw the bride's attention for one last time, Rafiq pondered the horror of the separation: his stepsister had been given away to a stranger. She had been torn from her brother to be given to a stranger.

Rafiq galloped further ahead and came to a halt on top of a hill. From that vantage point, he could see the simultaneously sumptuous and funereal procession that was accompanying his stepsister to that strange new house, which appeared as distant as the house of the dead.

Before heading back to Benghazi, Fatima entered the room where Sheikh Hassan was busy reading. She said she'd heard of the accusations that her daughter Ghazala had levelled against Anwar and Dhahab's son, Rafiq. The runaway had arrived in the city where he'd met Saad, a young man who bore a perfect resemblance to him. Having won his confidence, Rafiq had dragged him to the mountains to meet his death. Saad was innocent.

Sheikh Hassan had buried the incident in silence. Once the stranger had been killed, nobody had dared mention him to the Sheikh any more. What did that old woman want? And why had she waited so long to say anything? Rafiq was guilty and the stranger was innocent. Thus, Rafiq was doubly guilty: of having lusted after his stepsister, and of having led an innocent man to his death.

Fatima waited. She was not intimidated by the Sheikh's authority. Sheikh Hassan suspected she was harbouring other horrible secrets. She was a forthright woman, incapable of lying. *But what proof can this woman possibly have?* he asked himself in a jolt of soothing scepticism. 'What proof do you have?' he asked her, loudly.

'Saad was my son,' she said.

Something stirred deep in the master's heart. No memory can remain buried for ever.

'Your son?' he asked, not because he doubted her sincerity, but to gain a little time.

'He worked at the market, with a goldsmith. When Saad fled the city, people told me he'd been with a young man who resembled him, but was a little shorter. On entering this house, I saw Rafiq and ran up to him. Even I was fooled and thought he was my son. Rafiq looked at me, scared out of his wits. Nobody knew I had another son, and so I kept quiet. Rafiq was the young man people in the city had told me about. But how could I suspect he was my son's murderer? People said they always went every-where together, and that they looked so identical everyone thought they were brothers.'

It was like the tragic story of Harun al-Rashid, his beloved sister and his closest friend, Jafar the vizier: where the union of two people is sacrilegious, a third wheel is often added, a prelude to further sins.

Fatima waited in silence until the master could see clearly through the heart of the matter, as well as his own heart. Even Sheikh Hassan was a patient man, since reading engenders patience. But everything had already been explained and there were no further questions to ask. He had no choice but to summon Rafiq and confront him with these accusations; if what Fatima said was true, he would lure him into a trap and kill him without anyone ever discovering the real reason. The execution had to look like an accident. Or it could look like a vendetta carried out for sins unknown to anyone in the Sheikh's house. Only once Rafiq had been executed would the whole regrettable matter finally be brought to an end. The house had been tainted by the nocturnal visitor, and it needed to be purified. Justice demanded that the guilty party be properly punished, and not that an innocent person be sacrificed.

Sheikh Hassan's thoughts turned back to the young man he'd seen at the head of the procession a few days earlier as it led his stepsister to the strangers' house. He experienced an overpowering horror at the thought of dipping his hand into that young, restless blood. That blasphemer, that traitor, he didn't deserve anything but death. But why had he deserved it? Who had led his heart astray?

Sheikh Hassan stood up. He was very tall, and his chest leaned forward to the point that he always seemed on the verge of snapping in two. He slid his feet into his slippers. Finally, he put down the book he'd been holding.

'You won't say anything to anyone,' he said, 'It's my duty to see that justice is served.' Fatima wrapped her veil around her face and took the few steps that separated her from the door. 'Of course it's up to you,' she said, 'Saad was your son.'

Neither Fatima, who'd kept the secret of the son she'd had with the Sheikh during one of his forgotten visits to the city, after she'd divorced Anwar, nor Sheikh Hassan, a man who always waited impatiently for the night so he could shoo everyone away and seek refuge in his room by candlelight, wanted people to witness their conversation.

However, Sheikh Hassan's finicky wife Zazia, a city woman who detested peasants and their culture, heard everything.

Just as she had once brought Ghazala's accusations against her impious brother to Sheikh Hassan's reluctant ears, thereby earning Dhahab's wrath, Zazia now urged her friend Dhahab to be on her guard: Saad was Sheikh Hassan's son. This no longer had anything to do with saving a stupid servant's honour, it was about avenging her son's death: 'Rafiq won't escape this time.'

On leaving Sheikh Hassan's room, Fatima picked up her bundle, lightened by the absence of the gifts she'd brought for the bride, bid her relatives goodbye, and set off on her journey, accompanied by an old man: she would spend the night at Barca, where she'd part ways with her chaperone. She even hurriedly bid Rafiq goodbye, pushed into her path by Dhahab. Zazia and Dhahab accompanied her for a stretch of the road, with ceremonial perseverance.

Fleeing Zazia's malign vigilance, Dhahab entered Sheikh Hassan's room. Zazia was busy keeping an eye on Rafiq, who idled about in a field to keep his distance.

Dhahab spoke prudently. Sheikh Hassan wasn't even listening. Those hags who came in and out of his room tracked the mud of life onto his floor. What did that woman want? The mother of his son's assassin! Sheikh Hassan heaved a heavy sigh.

Dhahab used the opportunity to say that life is a burden, but that God was there to help them. That God was merciful. Sheikh Hassan suddenly rose. He swelled to gigantic proportions, frightening Dhahab. 'Don't do anything you might bitterly regret tomorrow,' she said as though trying to cast a spell, 'Fatima told you that the young man who was killed in this house was your son. May God forgive that young man, and the rest of us, too.'

Dhahab's tiny body drew closer to Sheikh Hassan. 'Because Rafiq,' she continued, 'is also your son: he wasn't an early product of my marriage to Anwar, but a fruit of your loins. I consented to marrying a crazy servant to hide the fruit of my love with his master. I was the one who told Rafiq that he wasn't that fool's son. Rafiq is our son, just like Ghazala is Anwar and Fatima's daughter: they're not related, and while Rafiq's desire was sinful, it wasn't unholy. Justice turned him first into a fugitive and then into a murderer. There was no way out: he would either have had to live far away from his homeland until his persecutors caught up with him, or he could have tried to trick them in one way or another. Keep the secret. That young man can't bear another accusation.'

Nagi's sudden arrival was warmly and enthusiastically greeted by his mother, Zazia. The young man had gone off to fight against the invaders, and had joined the little bands of rebel patriots that operated outside the major population centres where Italian authority reigned supreme. Scornful and tough as he was, nobody could deceive him. Even if Rafiq tried to flee, Nagi would eventually catch up with him. Nobody was stronger or faster than him.

Zazia took Nagi aside and told him what had happened during his absence, explaining that Saad, the young man who'd been killed, had been his brother.

During the initial hours after Nagi's arrival, Sheikh Hassan told him nothing and Dhahab did nothing either.

Thanks to Nagi's arrival, Sheikh Hassan finally realised that Rafiq had nowhere to run. Would he execute his own son? Would he delegate the task to Nagi, his legitimate son?

Being sure of himself, even Nagi didn't seem to be in much of a hurry.

Nobody would say anything in that house without it being overheard. This time, fate decreed that Anwar eavesdropped on the conversation between his wife and the master. What did it all amount to? Which resentments did they stoke? Who could they possible benefit?

Anwar fled the house and caught up with Rafiq, who was loitering in a field so as to keep his distance. He very excitedly informed Rafiq that he was Sheikh Hassan's son, and that he had killed his own brother. Then, as though afraid he would be caught in Rafiq's company, he returned to the house and spent all his time in the courtyard, in plain sight.

Even Nagi was waiting. His father was to be the first to speak. Zazia and Dhahab kept their eyes focused on the men.

Rafiq didn't doubt the crazy man's story. Saad was his brother, as testified to by their perfect resemblance. Hadn't they been called brothers in Benghazi? And hadn't Dhahab told him that Anwar wasn't his father? His father was the master, Sheikh Hassan. Rafiq had found his father after killing his own brother. He'd saved himself from accusations of impiety by committing an even unholier crime: fratricide. It was certainly true he'd sought out Ghazala knowing that she wasn't his sister, and that he'd killed Saad not knowing he was his brother. But what did it matter now? Why keep living? What horrendous accusations would they use to persecute him now? Why should he taint the Sheikh's hands with his blood? Why hand himself over to Nagi, who although also his brother, would willingly – and lawfully – murder him? There was simply no room for his youth anywhere: not in his own home, nor anywhere else.

Rafiq reached the hill fort from where he'd observed, only days earlier, Ghazala's procession, the bride ensconced on a high throne atop a camel on her way to that distant house. The strangers' house! Rafiq wasn't heading towards the house of the dead, he was running away from it.

He hurled himself from the fort's highest wall and landed on the rocky hillside. His death brought the sad affair to a close. '*God does as He wishes.*'

Epilogue

In the summer of 1927, after bloody clashes dispersed the bands of rebel patriots still hampering the Italians' advances sixteen years after the aggressors had first landed, the tricolour finally flew from the serene valley where Sheikh Hassan had his house. The Sheikh had fled the previous night. His family and servants had found refuge in a nomad encampment. Nagi had been killed.

Once again, Sheikh Hassan avoided gazing upon the faces of the men who'd come to pillage his land. Their presence was symbolised by a column of smoke rising from the remnants of his house. His incredible voyages into the farthest regions of the world had led to that defeat, meaning what the Sheikh had implicitly abandoned had been taken away from him and burned to cinders. The Italian soldier, one of the innumerable characters evoked by his reading, had triumphed in the Sheikh's own home. It hadn't happened in one of those godforsaken cities where lapses of reason occurred, but in his own beloved, unlucky country. Alongside a few other fugitives, the Sheikh headed for Kufra. His other books had perished in the fire, but the Sheikh still carried the holy book with him, which he'd committed to memory at a young age.

When even that oasis became indefensible, the Sheikh abandoned Kufra, and headed east, accompanied by other travellers. Among them was a certain X, who was much loved by the Brotherhood's *ikhwan* and who'd also wound up in Kufra after his father had turned himself over to the Italian government, after extracting a promise that they wouldn't exile him from Cyrenaica, but who had instead been banished to the island of Ustica. X's illustrious family had placed all its hopes in him, and he possessed a sense of irony, was unfailingly gracious, was tolerant towards others and demanding with himself; and just like his illustrious ancestor, he had a high awareness of his mission.

The travellers' road is neither happy nor lucky, as is their arrival in foreign lands. No arrival is ever as exciting as the return. This was the hope that the exiles carried with them.

Translator's Note

I made a fairly daring choice while translating these first volumes of *The Confines of the Shadow*, but months after putting the finishing touches on the manuscript, I remain satisfied with my decision. Spina had filled the spaces between the chapters of the first instalment, *The Young Maronite*, with quotes from various books, newspapers and government decrees. His motivation for doing so was rather obvious: as mentioned in my introduction, he was writing to an Italian public which barely remembered the tricolour had once flown from Libyan shores, and he had therefore set himself the task of resurrecting that episode from the oblivion into which it had shamefully been cast. Unfortunately, I don't think this stylistic technique proved very successful: it heavily impeded the flow of his exquisite prose, and broke up his fable-like narrative, needlessly confusing the reader along the way. So I decided to cut these quotes out. Spina lived during a time when public libraries didn't exist in Libya, and when books and newspapers were hard to come by. Almost anyone reading this epic today will be able to conduct further research online. Furthermore, Spina himself didn't think much of this technique, which was why he never used it again in the subsequent instalments of *The Confines of the Shadow* (aside from citing a few lines by Ibn Khaldun in *The Nocturnal Visitor*, which is also included in this volume). Anyone interested in the history of the time would be better served by reading the several historiographies that have been published in the century since these events transpired. There is, however, a tome I would like to single out for attention: Francis McCullagh's *Italy's War for a Desert, Being Some Experiences of a War-Correspondent with the Italians in Tripoli* (London: Herbert and Daniel, 1912). This is by far the most cited book in *The Young Maronite*, and for good reason; it was perhaps the only contemporary account untainted by the usual pro-colonial jingoism that saturated most Western newspapermen at the time. In an article penned in 1913, McCullagh predicted that the war correspondent was marked for extinction, and that he would soon be replaced by a new breed of armchair journalists, who would talk about the war from the hardships of the front while ensconced in the comfortable safety of conference rooms and hotels. Anyone who watches the news today knows this to be true.

Glossary

p.000 *Mal d'Afrique*: 'Africa Ache' or 'Africa bug.'

p.000 *Effendi*: Turkish honorific whose English equivalent is 'Sir.'

p.000 *Majlis*: reception room for male visitors.

p.000 *Sanussi Brotherhood*: political-religious order founded in Libya and Sudan in the early nineteenth century. King Idris I of Libya, who reigned from 1951 until Muammar Qaddafi's coup in 1969, was the founder's grandson.

p.000 *Jinn*: 'spirits' possessed of free will which can be neutral, malign or benevolent.

p.000 *Turquerie*: art produced in Europe from the sixteenth to the eighteenth century mimicing Turkish culture, which was highly fashionable at the time.

p.000 *Il balen del suo sorriso*: 'The light of her smile,' an aria from Verdi's *Don Carlos*.

p.000 *Mais quoi! . . .* : So what! Life is cheap in these parts!

p.000 *Quirinale*: once the principal palace of Italian kings in Rome and now the official residence of the Italian president.

p.000 *Salesian monks*: Catholic order founded in the late nineteenth century.

p.000 *The Betrothed*: *I promessi sposi* (1827) by Alessandro Manzoni (1785– 1873), arguably the first Italian historical novel.

p.000 *The geometrical locus . . .*: from Hugo von Hofmannsthal's *Andreas* (Pushkin, 2013).

p.000 *Mais que ma cruauté . . .* : 'But that my cruelty should survive my anger, despite my soul being seized by pity' (from Racine's *Andromaque*).

p.000 *Zawiyah*: either a monastic complex or a shrine-like tomb.

p.000 *Sidi al-Qarba*: also known as 'Yawm al-juma'ah'.

p.000 *What is that noise? . . .* : Lines spoken by Count Almaviva and Countess Rosina Almaviva; from Act II, Scene X of *The Marriage of Figaro*.

p.000 *Je le tuerai! . . .* : 'I'm going to kill him! I'm going to kill him. Go and kill that wicked servant!' Line spoken by Suzanne in Act II, Scene XVII of *The Marriage of Figaro*.

p.000 *Festina Lente*: Latin motto meaning 'make haste slowly.'

p.000 *Je l'ai trop aimé! . . .* : 'I loved him too much! My tenderness tired him out and my love exhausted him,' Lines from Act II, Scene XIX of *The Marriage of Figaro*.

p.000 *épouse délaissé*: 'neglected wife'.

p.000 *Muqaddimah*: 'Introduction,' an outline of Ibn Khaldun's (1332–1406) theories on history.

p.000 *Iram of the Pillars*: lost city in Southern Arabia that is mentioned in the Qur'an and whose story bears some similarity to that of Atlantis.

p.000 *God gives the kingship to whom He will*: Qur'an, Sura 2.247 (trans AJ Arberry)

p.000 *Janissaries*: Elite soldiers usually recruited from

Christian families that served the Ottoman Empire for centuries.

p.000 *khwan*: religious militia composed of nomadic desert tribesmen.

p.000 *Marabout*: Qur'anic teacher, or wandering holy man.